The Welles-Turner Memorial Library

2407 Main Street
Glastonbury CT 06033

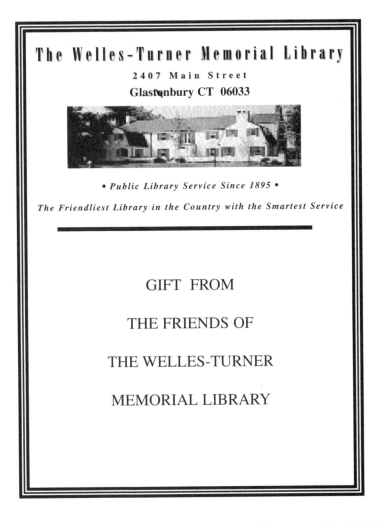

• *Public Library Service Since 1895* •

The Friendliest Library in the Country with the Smartest Service

GIFT FROM

THE FRIENDS OF

THE WELLES-TURNER

MEMORIAL LIBRARY

Going Overboard

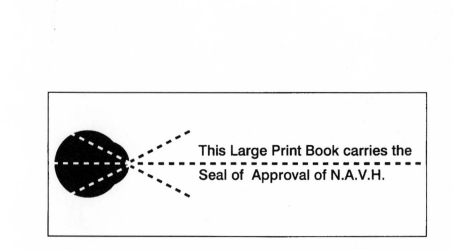

This Large Print Book carries the
Seal of Approval of N.A.V.H.

Going Overboard

Christina Skye

Thorndike Press • **Waterville, Maine**

Published in 2001 by arrangement with Dell Publishing, an imprint of the Bantam Dell Publishing Group, a division of Random House, Inc.

Thorndike Press Large Print Americana Series.

The tree indicium is a trademark of Thorndike Press.

The text of this Large Print edition is unabridged. Other aspects of the book may vary from the original edition.

Set in 16 pt. Plantin by Al Chase.

Printed in the United States on permanent paper.

Library of Congress Cataloging-in-Publication Data
Skye, Christina.
    Going overboard / Christina Skye.
        p.   cm.
    ISBN 0-7862-3591-8 (lg. print : hc : alk. paper)
    1. United States. Navy. SEALs — Fiction.   2. Women photographers — Fiction.   3. Caribbean Area — Fiction.
    4. Large type books.   I. Title.
    PS3569.K94 G65 2001
    813'.54—dc21   2001041515

With Warmest Thanks

to Earl Martin for his technical expertise, tactical details and great sense of humor;

to Keith Swezey, a true miracle worker, for the crash course in fades, dissolves, pink gel filters and general lingo ("we'll super in the logo over the cruise ship");

to Sherry Pace for insights into shipboard protocol and security procedure;

to Kathy Marks for firsthand knowledge of the miracles of ultrasound.

Chapter 1

Carolina Sullivan needed a man's body desperately.

She scanned the humming cruise ship, working a knot in her neck. "What about the muscular guy by the stairs?"

Her design assistant squinted into the streaming Caribbean sunlight, oblivious to the glories of St. Thomas rising in the distance. "Too pretty. He bloody well knows it, too."

"You're probably right." The wind ruffled Carly's short red hair as she studied the man in question. Neither the flawless sky nor the shimmering expanse of tropical ocean helped her relax. "What about the young Van Damme type lounging by the deck chairs?"

"Definitely YBG."

Young blond god.

Carly knew the code perfectly by now:

DDT: Drop dead thighs
CTDF: Chest to die for
HAA: Heart attack abs

"I saw him in *GQ* last month." Carly sighed. "We need someone completely fresh."

"So you keep telling me." Carly's assistant rolled her eyes. "In the last three hours we've covered every deck on this misbegotten boat."

"Ship," Carly corrected her absently.

"Whatever. If we don't find a man here, we're sunk." A former model with impeccable taste, Daphne Brandon was also Carly's dearest friend, and she had happily agreed to pinch-hit for Carly's regular assistant, who was enjoying her honeymoon in Tahiti. In the past five years Carly and Daphne had become deeply involved in their own pursuits, forced to maintain their friendship via cell phone and E-mail, and it had been a happy coincidence that Carly's assistant had gotten married just when Daphne had some free time. In the early days of her career, Carly had honed her photographic skills with the help of Daphne's practical experience on the other side of the camera, and being teamed up again now was a dream come true. If it weren't for Carly's current problem, the assignment would have been sheer pleasure.

Instead of absolute agony.

Daphne stared at the crowded deck. "When I agreed to stand in for your regular assistant, I had no idea you'd have me checking out half-naked male bodies."

"Is that a complaint?"

Daphne grinned. "Not a chance." She scanned a circle of young athletic types engaged in a noisy game of volleyball. "What about one of them? There's not an inch of flab in sight."

Carly wrinkled her nose. "No, something's missing. We need someone special, someone who projects complete control. At the same time he has to emanate brooding power, ready to explode under the right conditions."

"Yum yum," Daphne murmured.

A ball hurtled past and dropped into the pool, splattering Carly's legs. "Great. There go my snakeskin sandals. I'm glad they're only fakes."

Daphne didn't answer. She pointed across the deck to a tall, beautifully muscled man climbing the ladder from the pool. Water skimmed down his rigid abs and dotted his powerful shoulders. Every movement he made was smooth, every inch of his body a testament to controlled power.

Carly felt a little punch of heat in her stomach.

This was the one, she thought, mesmerized by those lean, rippling muscles.

"Ground control to lunar lander."

Carly didn't answer. She was too busy imagining that lean body silhouetted against the warm golden glow of the sunset. She gave a soundless whistle when he tossed a towel over one shoulder, resulting in another display of rock-hard muscles.

"Definitely HAA," Daphne whispered. "I'd say he's your man."

After her years as a model, Daphne wasn't easily impressed, but this man could inspire awe in the most jaded female heart. His abs were beyond stellar. In fact, his whole body was just shy of illegal.

Carly dragged a hand through her hair. Experience had taught her that sheer looks weren't enough for a successful photo campaign. "I suppose he might work."

"Might?" Daphne whispered. "If you don't take him, I will. Be still, my beating glands."

"Heart," Carly corrected fondly. "And you're married, remember?"

"Engaged. And just barely."

"The last I heard, your wedding dress was being designed in Paris."

"All of which might change any second." Daphne gave a long sigh. "Just kidding. My misspent youth is behind me, I'm glad to say." She stared at Carly impatiently. "What are you waiting for?"

"He's got the body, there's no doubt about that." Carly nodded slowly. "He's got the walk, too. Quiet, with utter focus." Carly raised her digital camera, framed a test shot, and captured her subject drying his extraordinary shoulders. The image in her viewer made her pulse spike. The man photographed even better than he looked, which was saying something.

She rested her camera on her arm, frowning. "What do you think he does for a living?"

"A man who looks like that doesn't have to do anything but stand there."

"Be serious, Daphne. My whole project is at stake here. I need a completely fresh look for this set of commercials. The cruise people made that crystal clear before we left Miami."

Daphne clicked her tongue. "Too bad the original model they sent you didn't pan out."

Carly snorted at the thought of the well-coiffed California actor who had been booked for the commercials. Unfortunately, his body had turned out to be less than impressive, and Carly found out that his portfolio photos had been retouched with a blowtorch. She'd immediately launched her search for a temporary stand-in, all too aware that the close-up shooting had to start immediately if she was to meet the tight deadline. Until now she'd had no luck.

She fingered her camera, studying the man across the deck. "He doesn't look like your usual cruise type. He looks too focused, not like someone who's here for idle pleasure."

"With a body like that, the pleasure would be anything but idle." Daphne sighed. "The guy has to work out big-time. I'd say he owns a chain of upscale fitness clubs. Something sleek, all teakwood and mirrors. Hot, hot music."

"If he's that successful, he won't be interested. He would hardly need the money."

"Then forget money and appeal to his ego. Gush over his amazing body." Daphne gave another appreciative glance. "It's certainly worth gushing over."

"I don't gush," Carly said irritably, snapping two more quick shots that turned out even better than the first. Did the man ever take a *bad* picture? "I especially don't gush over men."

"No, you never did that," her friend said thoughtfully. "I was always the one going overboard, gaga over some poet or bullfighter. It took me a few years, but at least I worked it out of my system in time to find my wonderful David." Daphne smiled wickedly. "Looks as if it's your turn. That man is the answer to all your dreams. You'd be a fool to let him go."

She was right. Carly knew she had to bag this prospect. Every photographic instinct was on red alert, screaming that he would bring her elegant, atmospheric theme to life.

Now all she had to do was drop the bait and reel him in.

Unaware that he was being tracked, the prospect in question stretched slowly, ignoring the noisy volleyball game at the far end of the pool as he slid back easily into the water.

"An Olympic swimmer," Daphne mused. "Or maybe he tests jet skis for a living." She watched him cut through the water with silent, powerful strokes. "Better get moving. Otherwise, you'll lose him."

Carly fought down a wave of anxiety, then squared her shoulders, smoothed her silk blouse, and reminded herself that this wasn't personal. It was strictly business. Emotions had no place in the equation.

So why was her throat so dry?

She grappled with her nerves as the man swam closer. Business, she told herself, bending down to make herself heard above the volleyball game. "Excuse me."

His head angled up. His eyes were a deep gold framed by surprisingly long lashes. One brow arched in a face of arresting angles and shadows. Carly saw experience, cynicism, and humor in his expression. It was a fascinating combination, especially to a photographer.

"Ma'am?" He stood up slowly, water beading over his shoulders.

Carly cleared her throat. "I'm sorry to interrupt your swim. I — I wanted to ask a question."

He smiled. "Just one?" There was a trace of a drawl in his voice.

Carly wondered if he was from Texas or somewhere farther west. Wyoming, maybe. Not that it mattered. His body was all she needed. "Actually, it's more of an offer. You could say it's a business offer." She gathered her courage and rushed on. "I'd pay you, of course. I realize it would be an interruption of your holiday, but if you're good, you could make five hundred dollars for an easy hour's work."

His eyes went a shade darker. "Sorry. I don't have any free time."

Carly ignored the frown edging down his forehead. She couldn't lose him now. "Then I could go higher."

His biceps rippled as he crossed his arms.

"You could, could you?" He shook his head slowly. "Do you do this often?"

"Only when it's absolutely necessary." She tried not to be irritated or nervous. She needed him too much to bail out now. "Sometimes I can't find the right man any other way."

He laughed darkly. "I see you're honest. Most women wouldn't be. But I'm not interested."

Desperate, Carly bent closer as she saw success sliding out of reach. "Why not? It would only be for a few hours." Behind her back she crossed her fingers. If he was as good as she thought, she'd try to persuade him to give her two full days, but she wasn't going to tell him that yet.

"Just call me old-fashioned." His eyes narrowed. "You see, I like to do the asking."

She barely heard him, already visualizing those sculpted shoulders against a sunlit deck. "In that case let's say seven hundred fifty an hour," she said breathlessly.

Pride and anger snapped across that controlled face. "Still not interested," he said curtly. "I don't bed down for money."

Carly blinked. "Bed?"

"Or any other flat surface where you expect a man to perform."

She swallowed hard, her face burning.

15

"Now wait a minute, you've got this all wrong."

"Nobody else available? Well, the day's still young." He leaned against the pool ladder and studied her trim body, from silk blouse to delicate sandals. "Especially for a woman like you." His lips curled. "Even without throwing in the money."

A red-hot haze of fury drove Carly's mission from her mind. "You think I want sex? With you?"

One dark brow rose. "Don't you?"

"You conceited ape. I wouldn't consider sleeping with you — not for a cool million."

"Got a redhead's temper, do you? I guess that shade didn't come from a bottle." His gaze brushed her slender thighs and came to rest just above the hem of her short, drifty skirt. "Might be interesting to find out."

A fresh wave of fury struck as she realized where he was staring — and why. Someone needed to take this Neolithic throwback down a notch or two. "I'd rather get naked and dance with a cactus," Carly snarled.

He smiled as if he was enjoying the image.

The smile only made her angrier. "Let's get something straight, tough guy." Carly stood up stiffly, clutching at her silk scarf and the remains of her dignity. She should have known the man was too gorgeous to be

16

true. The last thing she needed on her photo shoot was a walking case of male hormones and unbridled ego. She smiled tightly. "I'll use tiny, little words, so your tiny, little brain can take them all in. I don't want to have sex with you. Not now or ever."

"Just as well. At seven hundred fifty an hour," he said thoughtfully, "you must expect a real workout."

For a moment Carly was speechless. A shadow moved at the corner of the pool, but she paid no attention. "Open your ears and try to understand. You're the *last* man on earth I'd consider having sex with."

She was shouting but she didn't care. Dimly she heard water splash. Someone called out across the deck.

The man in the pool rose, reaching out a hand.

"Forget it, Don Juan."

She turned her head and saw a volleyball hurtling straight at her. As if in slow motion, water sloshed up over the side of the pool as her infuriating Adonis jumped high. In one smooth movement he swung sideways, opened his hand, and captured the runaway ball in midair.

Only inches from her face.

Chapter 2

It was a real shame he didn't have time to accept her offer, McKay thought as he savored the view of wet, clinging silk.

Damned nice breasts, he noted, as the redhead glared at the ball locked in his hand, then down at the blouse dripping onto her shoes.

McKay wasn't a man who followed the vagaries of women's fashion, but he recognized quality when he saw it. The flirty silk blouse and matching scarf had probably cost her a bundle in some fancy boutique. He had a feeling her strappy sandals weren't cheap either, and now they were probably beyond repair.

Definitely a high-priced package, he decided. Teaching her a lesson might have held a certain appeal under any other circumstances. The lady was clearly spoiling for a fight, and McKay enjoyed a good argument with a woman who knew her own mind.

He palmed the ball and tossed it casually to a deck chair with a withering glance at the collegiate type who had thrown it dangerously off course. "Sorry about your shoes, ma'am."

The redhead shoved wet hair from her face, oblivious to her clinging blouse.

McKay was far from oblivious.

No bra, he noted. And the lady was firm in all the right places. He took another look, surprised to feel a jolt of pure lust. The woman wasn't even close to his type. She was too pricey and too polished.

Still, a man could look.

He swung one hand out, brushing her shoulder as her scarf drifted past him in the water. In one easy motion he snagged the bright square before it could float away. "Looks like you're losing your clothes, ma'am."

She snatched the wet silk with trembling fingers, her cheeks burning. McKay found himself enjoying that too, before he pulled himself out of the water.

He forced himself not to smile as he swept his towel off a deck chair and held it out. "Looks like you could use a towel."

A vein throbbed at her throat. "I'd chew plutonium first."

Furious and no mistake. Definitely a natural redhead. He shrugged calmly. "Suit yourself."

"Oh, I plan to."

"Carly, are you okay?" A slender blonde in orange capri pants pushed between them, looking worried. "I thought that ball was going to deck you," she said breathlessly. "It's a good thing your friend has such amazing reflexes."

"He's no friend of mine." The woman named Carly flung McKay's towel right back at him. "I might have caught it myself if Mr. Mesozoic here had given me half a chance," she huffed.

"No way. That ball would have nailed you." The woman in the capris stared from one to the other. "Am I missing the subtext here?"

"None that matters," McKay drawled as he draped his towel over one shoulder. "Happy hunting, ma'am."

"Pig."

"Morning, ladies." McKay gave a two-finger salute, then headed off through the crowded pool area.

A perfect start to a perfect morning, he thought irritably. The pool was too small for a serious workout and the recreation deck was a battle zone. In the last twenty-four hours he'd been propositioned at least ten times by women in search of intimate companionship.

Not one of them had been as blatant as the redhead.

McKay laughed grimly. Given her fury,

he figured he'd seen the last of her, which was just as well. This cruise was no pleasure trip for him. On the other hand, since he was a healthy, red-blooded male, he couldn't help replaying the moment water had splashed high, soaking her silk skirt and blouse.

McKay scratched his jaw. To give the woman credit, she hadn't expected to be doused, caught in a blouse that captured every detail, right down to her dark, pouty nipples.

He shook his head in disgust. *Hell, McKay, forget about the woman's breasts.*

As he approached his stateroom, awareness prickled along his neck. Without any change in stride, he detoured down a side corridor, all his senses alert.

Two women in expensive warm-up suits passed, deep in conversation. McKay caught the words *alimony* and *hidden assets* before they rounded the corner.

A door closed behind him. He dropped his towel and halted casually, surveying the empty corridor before and behind him as he scooped it up. None of the doors opened.

Get a grip, he thought in disgust. No one knew he was here except Navy chain of command and his one onboard contact. The chance of someone having him under surveillance was nil. There was no reason for him to be jumpy.

He glanced at his watch and realized he was going to be late if he didn't get the lead out and stop daydreaming about stacked redheads with an attitude problem.

Silence met him when he opened the door to his stateroom a few minutes later.

"Izzy, are you here?" McKay scanned the quiet room, reining in his impatience. He had been flying blind for twenty hours since he'd been pulled from the water, airlifted out of his current SEAL training mission in the Pacific, and been given cryptic orders to board this cruise liner. All McKay knew so far was that he was to present himself as a wealthy civilian enjoying a much-needed vacation. The details of his assignment were secret, to be imparted on board, courtesy of a freelancer he'd worked with before.

A week in the Caribbean aboard the love boat.

All in all, it should have been a plum assignment.

Except that he'd only left port that morning and already he was stir crazy. He was a SEAL, highly trained and fiercely motivated. He was here to work and he damned well wanted to get down to it.

The punch caught just under his lower

rib. Spinning fast, he landed a hard jab in immediate retaliation.

He sighed in irritation when he saw his attacker's white uniform, mahogany skin, and Cheshire cat grin. "Nice uniform, Izzy," McKay growled.

Ishmael Harris Teague, Izzy to his friends, was smart, cocky, and well on his way to making a fortune in the private sector. An electronics genius, he had a wicked sense of humor along with a reputation for enjoying his work. "Room steward, Mr. McKay." His smile widened. "Bringing your lunch, as ordered."

"Like hell you are." McKay looked him over. Izzy was clearly in top shape, and that would make their assignment easier.

Whatever the damned assignment was.

Suspected terrorist assault on the cruise ship?

Smuggling operation?

High-profile assassination?

"Don't try coming up behind me again. In another few seconds you would have been dog food."

"Dream on." Izzy pointed to his loaded food cart. "What do you think of my cover?"

McKay had to agree that it was top-notch. A worker in uniform was invisible to a casual observer. "Get your papers set up.

I'm going to change."

When McKay emerged, Izzy glanced at his white polo shirt and linen jacket. "Snappy clothes for a brown-water Navy SEAL."

McKay shrugged. "Cover, same as yours. What have you got for me? No one would tell me anything except that the mission has top priority."

Izzy slid a leather case from beneath the table skirt, unzipped it carefully, and removed the contents. From experience, McKay knew that his contact was not only a genius with every sort of electronic gadget but a thorough professional. Not even a stray piece of lint got past him. As a DEA agent, Izzy had worked in hot zones in a dozen countries and had never lost his cool. His irreverence had annoyed his superiors, but McKay knew the cocky attitude helped to keep things light. Now, as a freelance security agent, he still had that same cocky humor.

Izzy pulled a stack of grainy satellite photographs from the case. "Meet Nigel Brandon, the governor-general of Santa Marina. Our man's an Oxford graduate with honors in medieval history. He spent four years with a merchant banking firm in London, then two more in Asia overseeing start-up energy companies."

McKay stared at the urbane face in the top photo. "Hardly your usual Caribbean functionary."

"It's in the family. Impeccable bloodlines. The Brandons have been running Santa Marina for generations." Izzy shrugged. "But now the governor has trouble in paradise."

"What's the emergency? Santa Marina is a perfect example of modernization in action. They've got a solid economy, a stable political system, and a satisfied population — not to mention thousands of well-heeled vacationers who hit their perfect beaches every year."

"Maybe not so perfect." Izzy held out a thick envelope. "These are your official orders, direct from D.C. In the last six months Brandon has been receiving death threats. They also target his family, including a woman whom he adopted ten years ago. Since she's legally still a U.S. citizen and usually off island working in the States, he contacted an old friend in the State Department and called in a few favors. He wants this kept low profile, but he wants her safe."

"Personal protection?" McKay bit back a curse. "I was hauled out of an important training mission, outfitted with designer clothes, and raced across the country to become a high-society baby-sitter?" He scanned his written orders in disgust and found them exactly as Izzy had outlined. McKay had heard about his getting assignments like this. The favors were usually discreet, but very much a fact of life in the military, where politics greased the wheels that kept appropriations flowing.

And orders were orders, even if they stank.

McKay snorted and tossed Brandon's photo back onto the cart. "I can tell from your face that there's more."

"What Brandon wants, he gets. The man's got solid-gold contacts. His country has been key to maintaining stability in the Caribbean. Ours is not to question why."

"But why a SEAL?" McKay snapped. "Why didn't they just pull in some spit-and-polish type from Georgetown or one of the Caribbean embassies?"

"Because Brandon is picky. He wants the best of the best, someone who can keep the woman safe, no matter what. He wants skill and substance, not polished charm."

"Hell."

"I agree, but a job is a job. The high-tech boys at Langley figure we don't need to know any other details until they have more intel on who's behind the threats. Meanwhile, our orders are to protect the woman in question. Brandon has his own people protecting the rest of his family and staff."

McKay scowled out the window at the islands strung against the shimmering blue water. "Let me get this straight. The State Department and Langley pulled me out of a training mission and drafted you from the private sector so we could be baby-sitters?" He shook his head. "Brandon's friend in State must be a regular top gun."

"As high as they get," Izzy said cheerfully. "Our mission, whether we choose to accept it or not," he quipped, "is to provide round-the-clock protection for one Carolina Sullivan. She's very close to Brandon's daughter, who is safely tucked away in the family compound on Santa Marina."

McKay rubbed at the back of his neck in frustration. "Why doesn't State just put her into protective custody on the mainland until everything blows over?"

"Too overt," Izzy said. "Brandon asked that this be handled quietly, without any discernible break in routine that might alert the bad guys. He's sensitive about a bunch of spooks running around his country, too, so your only job is one-on-one protection."

McKay heard the tension in his voice. "But what?"

"My guess is that something else is going on, and it's bigger than a few personal threats. If this blows up into a political situation, the State Department will be glad to have a man in place inside."

McKay had already figured out that much. It was the only way the assignment made sense. "Tell me about the woman. What do I need to know besides the fact that she's tight with the governor and his daughter?"

"She's some sort of wunderkind shooting a series of commercials for the cruise line. She's got the creative talent to go way beyond commercials, I'm told." Izzy shuffled through his stack of photographs and tugged one from the bottom of the pile. "I'd say she's one hot redhead."

"Redhead?" McKay felt a sinking sensation as he glanced at the photo. "With the temper to match," he muttered.

"You two have already met? Fast work, McKay. When and how?"

"This morning. If you could call it a meeting. She made me a proposition she assumed I couldn't refuse, then turned huffy when I did just that. After things got rowdy near the pool, I saved her from being

28

beaned with a volleyball. In return, she bit my head off. End of story."

" 'Fraid not," Izzy said. "You have to get close and stay close. Since you've met, you're halfway there."

"Are you telling me my duties involve personal services to Ms. Sullivan?" McKay demanded.

"I'm telling you to make nice. Improvise. Find out what it takes to get close, then do it."

Not in this or any other lifetime, McKay thought. Improvising was way down on his list of favorite things. He liked his work neat and clean, scripted by the book whenever possible. In missions filled with dangerous variables, going by the book was the only way to stay sane.

And stay alive.

"So what's the unofficial part of the assignment? We're not only here because of Brandon's request."

Izzy nodded. "We're to keep our eyes and ears open. If we find anything that doesn't add up, we're to report it immediately."

"Without knowing what we're looking for?"

"That's all I have so far. Brandon's ticklish about revealing too much. Meanwhile, I understand the redhead has been looking for someone to fill in for her current model."

"How do you know that?"

"Because she's been prowling every inch of the ship for hard bodies. Apparently no one has panned out yet."

"I did," McKay said, torn between embarrassment and annoyance as another puzzle piece slid into place. She hadn't wanted a bed partner but a model. He might have been flattered if he weren't so damned furious at the direction the assignment was headed.

"Pass Go and collect two hundred dollars, my friend. This will put you exactly where you need to be. There won't be any funny business. From what I hear, she's a workaholic with no time for games."

"Probably sleeps with a Palm Pilot." McKay made a sound of disgust. "How did she get hooked up with the Brandons?"

"She and Brandon's daughter were close at school, and they got closer after Carly's parents died. Brandon went through the process of legal adoption, and Carly still spends time in Santa Marina whenever she has a break in her schedule."

McKay thought of his summers shoveling manure in Wyoming and baby-sitting tourists with too much money and too little sense. Apparently Carolina Sullivan was used to the easy life. "Spoiled rich girl, if you ask me."

"Spoiled or not, she's your current assignment. Tell her you'll help in any way she needs. It's the easiest way to stay close to her right now."

"What if my face ends up plastered over prime time TV?" McKay scowled. "To say nothing of my near-naked body. That's not the kind of publicity the Navy enjoys."

"Go with the flow, McKay. I'll check in with Washington about any security concerns with the photography. And look at it this way: If you ever get tired of working for Uncle Sam, you might have a whole new career going for you in daytime drama."

"The thought thrills the hell out of me." McKay glared as Izzy's laptop beeped. "What now?"

"Priority message from D.C." Frowning, Izzy studied the message on his screen. "Looks like a glitch. Brandon's daughter left Santa Marina while Daddy wasn't looking. She's on board, too." He held out a photo from his case.

McKay scanned the image of a leggy blonde in a thong bikini barely larger than her designer sunglasses. "Nice . . . er, smile."

"You can say that again. Word is, she's getting married soon to the son of an old French banking family. They're planning a huge wedding on the island. Now she's slipped Daddy's leash and left a note saying she has to go help her friend."

McKay looked at the photo more closely and stifled a curse as he recognized the woman in the capri pants with Carly Sullivan near the pool. Resigned, he pinched the bridge of his nose. "Swell. I met her, too."

"She's filling in as Carly Sullivan's assistant on the shoot. Brandon is fit to be tied." Izzy packed the photos and equipment back into his bag. "The good news is that Brandon is circulating the story that she's at home with a nasty flu bug so the bad guys will think she's still at the estate."

"Color me happy," McKay said sarcastically.

"Don't worry, Daphne Brandon's not your priority. We concentrate on protecting Carly. Brandon has already begun to make new arrangements for his daughter's protection." He stowed the packed bag carefully beneath the food cart and flipped down the tablecloth. "Don't knock it, my friend. Some of us get assigned as room stewards and have to do menial work."

McKay snorted. "Better than being propositioned a dozen times in twenty-four hours. Men used to wonder what women wanted, and now we know. Sex and lots of it. They're not afraid to name the time and place." He gave a rueful laugh. "How did I miss the sexual revolution?"

"You were busy saving the world for peace, honor, and the American way." Izzy dug in his bag and produced an aluminum box. "I'm told you weren't issued any ordnance." He lifted out a 9 mm pistol. "This is for close encounters of the hostile kind, and here's the shoulder harness. There are walkie-talkies and extra ammo on your bed. Keep them handy just in case there really are hostiles aboard. Brandon doesn't seem like the type to be spooked easily."

McKay summarized his opinion of Brandon and his mission in one short, pithy phrase.

Izzy laughed. "Gotta go. See you on TV, McKay."

McKay made a noncommittal sound as he cracked open the door to check activity in the hall. Out of habit, he stepped back behind the door as a steward appeared in the corridor with a package of laundry. When the coast was clear, McKay gave Izzy a two-finger wave, then stood back to let him wheel the food cart outside.

"Watch your six o'clock," Izzy muttered, closing the door.

"Count on it."

Out in the Caribbean, the sleek yacht rocked quietly at anchor. Three men sat unsmiling while sea birds wheeled above them in the sunlight.

"It is a most unusual thing," the biggest of the men said, his sad eyes gleaming. "You see this?" He pushed aside a Baccarat crystal glass as if it were cheap plastic and fingered a stack of bills. "What you see here is paper, nothing more. But men live and die beneath the weight of a single sheet. They howl, they grovel, they kill, all for this."

As Nikolai Vronski studied the green and black lines in wonder, the handpicked men around him said nothing. Their silence was loud in the large boat that rocked in sunlight so far from the bitter cold of Mother Russia. Nor did the men speak when Vronski lit a match and touched the flame to the crisp U.S. hundred-dollar bill in his hand.

President Franklin's face blurred in a fine wisp of smoke. The Russian bent closer, as if catching warmth from the small fire, though the day was hot and the sky cloudless.

"Paper," he repeated, dropping the flaming sheet into a metal box already littered with the ashes of a dozen other U.S. bills. "Only paper."

It was more money than Nikolai Vronski had once imagined could exist in the whole world. One bill alone could have kept his tiny Russian village alive for years, children, old men, stoic women, and howling dogs.

There had been no money then. There had been no shoes, no flour for pierogi. No music and no joy, only pain and hopelessness without end. All because of paper like this.

On a bitingly cold night while the hungry dogs howled, he had lost his father. And on the same kind of night of cold and desperation, he had lost his only son.

Fate? He considered the question long and well. As a Russian, he knew the face of fate like an old, frightening enemy.

Or was it simply the power of this thing called paper, which immortalized dead men and condemned others to early, anonymous death?

The bill fell away into ashes and Vronski lit another, silent in his expensive deck chair while his men watched impassively and the sea churned beneath them.

Chapter 3

No way out.

Desperately, Carly checked the row of fresh photographs hung by clothespins along the wall of her shipboard office.

Beside her, Daphne stalked from photo to photo. "The snake should have told you he couldn't do the swimsuit shots, not with *that* stomach. Now you can't use him, but you still have to pay him."

Carly pulled down a photo and sighed. "His agent was better than ours." She crumpled the print and tossed it into the garbage can. "It's too late to hire another model — the swimsuit scene has to be shot tomorrow while we're in port." Carly sank onto the desk. "Who's in the file? Wasn't there a surfer I interviewed for a coffee commercial two years ago?"

Daphne shook her head. "He moved to Costa Rica, started a new religion, and hasn't been heard of since."

"You're kidding."

"Cross my heart."

Carly raked her hair back from her face. "I give up. What else could possibly go wrong?" Right on cue, the phone rang on her desk.

Daphne glanced at Carly and answered in her calmest voice. One brow rose as she handed the phone to Carly. "Your boss," she whispered.

Mel Kirk was the youngest woman ever to become creative director at a major New York ad agency. It was no coincidence that her staff called her Captain Kirk behind her back. She had a string of successful commercials behind her, and she wasn't afraid to throw her weight around.

Carly had a feeling that weight was about to be thrown her way. "Mel, great to hear from you. Any developments?"

"The client is delighted with our slogan. 'We've got your dream' is exactly what he wants. The problem is, he wants preliminary shots right away. I know you've had a problem with the model we signed in California — but I can't put the client off much longer. Have you had any luck with a replacement, at least for the body shots?"

"I think so. I found someone who photographs amazingly well."

"Then go get him. I'll double the figure I quoted you this morning, just so we can get something on film. You've got until tomorrow, Carly." She sighed. "Otherwise we're going to lose the account."

Carly stared at the line of drying prints

and mentally substituted a different body. One with washboard abs and sculptured shoulders.

The Adonis from the pool was her only answer.

"Carly, are you still there? This marine connection is terrible."

"Right here, Mel. Don't worry, you'll have digital film by three tomorrow, which will give you time to download and color correct before your late-afternoon meeting."

"I sincerely hope so, Carly. You were my first choice for this project, and I'm counting on you to make it work. Meanwhile, I'll be sure we strike Griff Kelly off our list."

Carly scowled as she thought of the out-of-shape model and his current girlfriend, who billed herself as his voice coach. "I'm on it, Mel. We'll finish the lighting layouts and test shots this morning. At least we can count on the weather down here." Carly saw a saltshaker on a tray and dumped a healthy amount over her shoulder. So who was superstitious? "Turquoise water and clear skies ever since we left port in Miami."

"I'm glad you're on top of things. Just give me something exciting to buy us another day or two. Whatever you do, don't skimp on the body shots. The client's wife has him convinced that fitness will be a big draw in the commercial for both male and female viewers."

Don't skimp on the body shots.

Carly felt the first stab of a headache. "No problem. We'll give you body shots from here to Sunday. Talk to you tomorrow, as soon as I've finished the digitals."

Carly put down the telephone, caught between paralysis and hysteria. "Sometimes I wish I'd gone into something sensible like shark photography or quark research."

"No, you don't." Daphne gripped her arm. "You're the best and you know it. If anyone can pull this off, you can." She tossed Carly a map of the ship, with one cabin circled in red. "I've done some checking. Your Adonis's name is McKay."

Carly worked her lip between her teeth. "I don't think the money matters to him. There has to be some other way."

"Think nice thoughts. Flutter your eyelashes and apologize for the misunderstanding at the pool this morning. Tell him how thankful you are that he was there to save you from a broken nose."

Carly rolled her shoulders, feeling the headache build. "I think I'm going to be sick."

Daphne pushed her toward the door. "You can be sick later. Right now you've got serious groveling to do. His cabin is portside, Crystal Deck."

"Traitor." Carly rubbed her forehead. "I might even be coming down with pneumonia."

"Get going."

Carly tilted her head and fluttered her eyelashes. "What big biceps you have, Mr. McKay. What amazing thighs." Her voice was low and throaty. "It's all my fault that I didn't explain sooner. Silly me. Honestly, I can't imagine why you thought I wanted you for sex." More fluttering of eyelashes.

"Atta girl. He'll be eating out of your hands."

Carly felt the headache stab deeper. She reminded herself that she was a professional with seven years of experience. She could plot, charm, and micro-manage with the best of them. When a job hung in the balance, she could leap tall buildings in a single bound, and right now the clock was ticking. After rehearsing her wide-eyed-ingenue role until her eyelids hurt, she left to confront her target.

She was halfway down the corridor when her former model's angry shout stopped her cold. "Stop avoiding me, Sullivan."

40

Carly tried to hide her impatience. "I've been very busy, Griff. As you must know."

He yanked his designer polo shirt up over his tanned but unimpressive chest. "See this?"

Carly stared at dozens of red welts. "You're allergic to something?"

"Clams. That's why I kept checking to be sure last night's stew was strictly vegetarian." He jerked his shirt back down. "Someone in the kitchen lied to me."

"I'm sorry to hear it." Carly resisted an urge to scream. "But I'm really busy right now and —"

The actor smiled coldly as he slid an arm around his girlfriend. "Not that it matters to me, after you hatcheted me for the body shots."

"Griff, it's nothing personal," Carly began.

"Everything's personal, and you'd better remember that. But the problem's yours now, Sullivan." He scratched absently at his chest. "Good luck finding a replacement out here at sea."

"I think I already have," Carly murmured.

"No one who's half as good as Griff." Aimee Joy, the newest girlfriend and supposed voice coach, ran a hand protectively along his cheek. She was dressed in black today, Carly noted. The color matched her lipstick. Nice look, if you were into vampires. "I've made him an appointment with the ship's doctor," she snapped at Carly. "I'm taking Griff there right now. Whatever he needs, he'll get. And I'll put it all on your account."

"I'm sure you will." Carly smiled sweetly and turned to find Daphne beside her.

"I see Medusa is wearing all black today. It suits her." Daphne watched Griff and his girlfriend disappear around the corridor. "Good riddance to both of them. Meanwhile, I figured you could use some good news. The computers are all set and the system is purring. Lucky for you I used the same system back in Santa Marina. Now all you need is digital feed, and you'll be in business."

Carly blew out a breath. "Wish me luck. I'm off to charm Adonis."

Daphne straightened Carly's blouse, then nodded. "You look good. Go bag him."

"You bet I will," Carly said weakly as she straightened her shoulders and headed to the Crystal Deck.

By the time she reached McKay's room, she felt marginally better. She gave her hair a quick swipe and smoothed her skirt, about to knock when the door opened. The biggest man she'd ever seen came out carrying a stack of folded towels.

He gave her a measuring look, his rugged dark features sliding into a grin. "Room steward, ma'am. You looking for Mr. McKay?"

Carly nodded, feeling dwarfed. Where had all these big men come from? Room steward or not, the man reminded her of McKay — watchful, quiet, and very controlled. "Yes, I am. Is he busy?"

"I'm sure he'll make time for you." He slid the towels to his other arm and moved past, holding open the door for her to enter. "He's just shaving, but maybe you want to wait."

No, she didn't want to wait, but she had no choice. Every minute counted, and every minute she wasn't on deck shooting made her sick with dread. Carly nodded coolly. "I'll wait."

"I'll tell him you're here." Smiling faintly, the steward knocked at the closed door to the bathroom, then opened it. After a few words, he turned. "He'll be right out. Make yourself at home."

After he'd left, Carly surveyed the floor-to-ceiling windows and the calm, azure sea dotted by trade-wind clouds. Apparently

Mr. McKay could afford the luxury of a suite with a private veranda, which meant he wouldn't need the small change she could offer him. That meant she had to think of some overwhelming inducement.

The water was still running behind her, and she fought an inclination to bolt. Failure was not an option.

She prowled the sunny stateroom, toying with a pair of mirrored sunglasses and high-tech binoculars. The bed was made, the pillows neat. No dirty clothes in sight. The man was organized as well as spectacularly photogenic.

Determined to make the best impression, Carly shrugged her shoulders to release a knot of tension. "Okay, here goes." She forced a bright smile. "I want to apologize for this morning, Mr. McKay. My outburst was unfortunate." She practiced batting her lashes. "Actually, it was unforgivable, considering that you protected me from a possible broken nose. It's hardly your fault that I've been under a little stress lately.

"Who am I kidding?" Carly sighed, tunneling her fingers through her hair. "If I don't get someone for this shoot, I'll be sunk. We're talking raw desperation here." She closed her eyes. "Oh, why am I even bothering? The jerk probably won't listen to me."

Hearing a sound, she lurched away from the window. Her right arm was snagged seconds before it collided with a freshly shaved male jaw.

Steam billowed from the bathroom as McKay stared at her. "It's me. The jerk," he added dryly. "The room steward said you wanted to talk to me."

Carly flushed. "That's right, I did. I do." She cleared her throat, unable to pull her eyes from the damp chest above a pair of low and very well broken-in jeans. Where had the man gotten that lean, amazing body? She visited a health club when she had time, but none of the men looked like *this*.

It had been months since she'd enjoyed an evening of laughter and lazy intimacy with a man. Maybe deprivation was doing weird things to her perception. "Look, about this morning —"

"No problem. Just forget it."

Carly raised a hand, pleased to see it wasn't trembling. "I need to apologize. No, I *want* to apologize."

"So I heard." One brow spiked. "Especially the part about unfortunate and unforgivable. By the way, I liked the jerk part best, because it sounded honest. Now tell me about the raw panic." Water slid down his chest, settling in the soft hair above the opened button at the waist of his jeans.

Heaven have mercy.

His chest was even more remarkable up close. So was the rest of him.

Calm, Carly thought. *Bat your eyes and play to his ego.* She managed a sickly smile. "You heard all that?"

"Every word."

"I'm sorry we got off on the wrong foot. I completely misread the situation at the pool this morning, and I want to apologize for that."

"Apology accepted."

Carly held out a hand. "Carolina Sullivan. It's a pleasure to meet you, Mr. McKay."

"Make that Ford."

Carly wanted badly to wipe her damp palms, but resisted as he took her fingers in a firm handshake that had her nerves jolting. She managed a cool smile, then pulled free. "I'm here shooting a series of TV spots for the cruise line. That's what I wanted to discuss this morning."

He rocked back, shoving his hands into his pockets and making the jeans strain even tighter. "Are you any good?"

"I'm extremely good at my job."

He nodded. "So you're some kind of

wunderkind," he said with a dry smile. "Why the raw panic?"

"Going right for the jugular, aren't you?"

Something crossed his face. "It's the best way."

When Carly looked him square in the eyes, she was struck by the intelligence there. The man was more than a mass of well-toned muscle. There was power and cool reason behind his gray eyes. Odd that she hadn't noticed before.

She realized her fingers were still hot where he had touched her. Frowning, she slid her hands up and down her arms.

His focus never wavered. "You haven't explained the panic yet."

Carly sighed. "The panic is professional. I've got a killer deadline and no model."

He shrugged one powerful shoulder in a way that had her yearning for her camera. "What's the problem? The ship's full of men."

"Not one that looks like you. And there's that quiet, controlled way you move, as if you owned the place." She realized it was time for the naked truth and no more fluttering eyelashes. "You'll burn up the camera."

Something between pain and irritation crossed his face. "Being photographed is right at the bottom of my wish list." He held up a hand as she started to speak. "And you're dead wrong about my acting skills."

"It's my job not to be wrong," Carly said firmly. "I flunked geometry in high school, and I occasionally botch my checkbook balance, but not reading people. That's my job. You'd be good, Mr. McKay. Very good."

He made an exasperated sound and Carly found it fascinating to see such a powerful man look befuddled. "You don't have to worry about privacy," she assured him. "We'll be shooting in a stateroom, and I guarantee it won't be a zoo scene."

"Why me? I thought you people hired professionals for work like that."

"Sometimes their shoulders are wrong or their proportion to the other actors is off, and then we fill in with a body double. It happens far more often than you might think."

"And you're asking me to do that? Be some kind of body double?"

Carly fidgeted under the force of his cool gaze. "I'm desperate. Our current actor just won't do, the clock is ticking, and I'm sunk without a replacement." She reconsidered her rehearsed flattery, but the words wouldn't come. Even if they had, she was certain this man would see right through them. "I'm prepared to grovel here, if that's what it takes."

Humor touched his eyes. "Groveling can be interesting, but in this case it won't be necessary."

Despite the finality in his voice, Carly made one last stab. "Please give it some thought. I'd be completely in your debt."

"I'm afraid not."

"Your choice." She turned away to hide her disappointment, one hand pressed to her burning stomach as failure flashed ugly before her. She didn't want to consider the results of losing an account this important.

"You're pale." His eyes narrowed. "When was the last time you ate?"

"I don't know." Even as Carly considered, hunger sent a stabbing reminder. Two cups of black coffee at dawn, hunched over a pile of disappointing photographs. A small carton of yogurt before she'd gone in search of Daphne. "What does it matter?" Her hand worked up and down over her stomach.

"If you don't eat, you can't think. Take this." He held out a plate of cream puffs stuffed with fresh strawberries.

"You're good at giving orders, aren't you?"

"When it's necessary. These were delivered less than an hour ago. You look like you could use one."

The sun was behind him now, haloing his impossibly chiseled shoulders. Carly imagined him in a tuxedo, reclining against the deck railing. Or in a swimsuit, his taut body gleaming with oil that she would smooth on herself.

When she didn't move, he shoved a rich pastry into her hand. "Eat, blast it."

Surprised by his concern, she balanced the pastry and licked off a strawberry as it started to totter, then sighed in pleasure as her tongue closed delicately around a scoop of whipped cream. It took her a moment to realize he was staring at her. "I'd prefer if you didn't watch me right now. This cream puff and I are having a spiritual encounter here." She licked a piece of strawberry off her palm, frowning at his continued scrutiny. "What?"

"Hell if I know." Sunlight poured through the windows as McKay watched her finish the pastry, then lap a final bit of white froth from her lips. She wasn't beautiful in any conventional sense. She wasn't even close to being his type. Her mouth was too wide, her hair too short. She was too edgy and too stubborn.

But there was something ruthlessly inter-esting about watching her dive into that cream puff, ignoring everything else around her. She probably made obsession an art form. McKay wondered what she'd look like without that frown knifing down her forehead.

Not that she was on his agenda for any personal involvement. He was a man who could stand his ground, even if a woman's perfume distracted him and her restless body goaded him to find out what it would take to make her relax.

He took a sharp step back. Damn, this was official. There couldn't be even a second of anything personal between them.

Especially when she wanted to capture him on camera like a champion steer.

He was all set to tell her that her idea was impossible when something in her eyes cut him off.

Regret.

Entreaty.

Stubborn pride.

He saw exactly how much it had cost her to ask.

"I'll think about it," he said gruffly, feeling like a fool. Hating the fact that he would use her to accomplish his mission, even if he would instruct any man under his

51

command to do exactly the same in a similar situation.

"You will?" She looked stunned.

"It's not a yes," he warned.

"But it's not a no. Thanks again for the food."

As she turned, he flanked her with silent steps and cut around her to the door. "You might still find someone else."

"No. When you see the best, you want it. And that's not because I'm desperate, but because it's true." Her voice was level.

Damn, she almost had *him* convinced. "You're pushing."

"I never said I wouldn't." She smiled and closed the door softly behind her, leaving McKay to rub his neck in irritation.

Modeling, he thought in disgust. *No way.* It was absolutely out.

The phone chimed from the nearby table. "What?" he barked, certain who was at the other end.

He heard Izzy's dry chuckle. "You told her no, didn't you?"

"Damn right I did."

"Get ready to tell her yes. I just heard from Washington, and you are good to go, McKay. Whatever she wants, whenever she wants, however she wants. Consider it an order."

Chapter 4

"Call Armando downstairs. Tell him we won't be needing the forty-six-long tuxedo for Mr. McKay after all. I've given him two hours, and he hasn't returned my call." Carly shoved files into a mound with unsteady hands, fighting her disappointment. "As soon as I finish here, I'm going to call Mel. She needs to know this deadline is impossible."

Daphne looked unconvinced. "Maybe you should wait. Your Adonis might give in eventually."

"Not in time to matter." Carly couldn't hold back a sigh. "And he's the one, Daphne. His biceps made the photographer in me weep."

"What did they do to the woman in you?"

"The woman in me was smart enough to shut up and let the professional get on with her job."

"If you ask me, that's a huge waste. Work isn't the only thing in life."

But Carly didn't hear, darting into the kitchen for a roll of film from the refrigerator. She ignored the knock at the door and Daphne's quick footsteps. She was too busy tossing out old photos and having a nervous breakdown.

"Carly." Daphne took her arm and gently pulled her around in a circle.

Ford McKay stood in the doorway. One look at his black jeans and form-fitting black T-shirt made Carly's legs shaky.

The sane part of her mind admitted he had every right to refuse her and get on with his vacation. The photographer in her wanted to scream at the unthinkable waste of raw material.

He slid his hands into his hip pockets, making his jeans even tighter. Carly framed him mentally, imagining him on a windy beach with the sun setting behind him. The shot would be a killer. It might even make her career.

If only.

She forced herself to stay calm, hiking one hip over her worktable and raising a brow. "I hope you're not here for more groveling."

Daphne stared at Carly. "You actually groveled?"

"Close enough," Carly muttered. "But I won't do it again. If that's what you came for, you're out of luck, Mr. McKay."

"No, I came to give you an answer." He scanned the room, taking in its controlled disorder and expensive digital film equipment. "Looks as if you're well supplied. That's a nice computer setup."

"We're in great shape with equipment. What's on your mind?"

"I have some questions." He prowled the room, glancing at lighting equipment and an array of cameras. "How long is the commitment — *if* I say yes?"

"Two days, tops." She could possibly squeeze things into two days, Carly thought. Maybe.

He lifted a camera, checked out the small monitor. "Nice toys you have."

"They're not toys," she said coolly.

"You're right." He put down the camera. "What would I have to do?"

"Don't worry, no nude shots," Daphne called throatily.

McKay turned, his face shuttered.

"Hey, just a joke." Daphne gave a slow sigh. "Too bad for the women of the world."

"My friend has a strange sense of humor. Please ignore her," Carly said, shooting a dark glance at Daphne. "And to answer your question, you'd be wearing a tuxedo in one shot and casual clothes in the other. The first shoot would be aboard ship today; the second would take place tomorrow in Barbados."

He seemed to digest the information stoically. "Is someone meeting you there?"

"We'll have a local support team, but my crew is aboard. They'll handle everything but transportation."

McKay tapped his fingers on a board filled with clippings of Caribbean beaches. "Sounds reasonable. Only one day in Barbados?"

Hope glimmered. Was he giving in after all? "One day should be enough."

"One day aboard ship, one day in Barbados." He studied the framed photographs on Carly's desk. "What then?"

"Maybe a half day of touch-ups, if necessary. If not, you'd be done."

"I see. Then you leave the ship after the filming is done?"

"No, we'll stay on for filler shots and some sound work, then return to Miami." Carly gave in to her impatience. "Is this relevant?"

He made a noncommittal sound and lifted a black-and-white photo of a small boat hurtling over angry rapids at the base of towering canyon walls. "Nice shot. Looks like it was taken from a boat. Damned hard picture to get." He looked across at Carly. "Your work?"

Cold brushed her as it always did when

the memories came. She took the picture from his hands, studied it for a moment, then replaced it gently on the table. "My mother's," she said stiffly.

"She's good. Shooting in that part of the Grand Canyon takes guts as well as skill."

"You've been there?"

"A time or two. Using a camera was the last thing on my mind."

"She wasn't afraid of much." *Except missing the next shot,* Carly added silently. Maybe that was why she hadn't been able to stay home for more than a month at a time, why they had kept moving, state to state and country to country until —

"I saw a photo with that same energy in *Life* about twenty years ago, a dramatic shot of sharks near the Great Barrier Reef."

Carly blinked, pulled from her bitter reverie. "Hers. She liked dangerous things." Carly saw the photo in her mind, just as she had watched it take form in the developing bath in her mother's darkroom years before. The violence and the danger in it had left her uneasy even then.

"You must have had some amazing times."

Carly ignored the question in his voice, refusing to look back where so much pain lingered. "Have you made up your mind? I

57

think I've told you all there is to tell."

McKay leaned against the wall and watched her.

No, she hadn't come close to telling him everything. Emotion simmered in the hard set of her jaw and the flash of her eyes. His questions about the photos had pushed a button all right. He'd run that particular stretch of white water only two years before as part of a special training mission. Even fully equipped with protective gear, a man felt his stomach knot when the monster power of the river took hold, tossing boats into the air like toothpicks. How much more dangerous had it been twenty years ago, riding a flimsy wooden frame with a camera gripped desperately in hope of the perfect angle and the perfect light?

McKay couldn't even imagine.

Pain had swept Carly's eyes when she'd taken the photo from him, and her hands had trembled. He made a mental note to find out why.

But first he had to swallow his distaste and get on with his mission, for which Uncle Sam was going to owe him big time. "Okay," he said slowly.

"I beg your pardon?"

"I'll help you with your body shots or whatever you call them."

She looked stunned. "You will?"

"When I give my word, it holds."

Even if it was unrelenting torture.

Her eyes narrowed. "What changed your mind?"

"Maybe I'm in the mood to be a nice guy." He shrugged. "I figured it was a small thing to drive the panic out of your eyes. And I liked your honesty." His lips curved. "For a jerk, I have my moments."

Carly's face filled with heat. "I apologized for that."

"So you did. Very nicely, too. So when do we start?"

"There are contracts to sign. I don't suppose you have an agent?"

"No agent."

"In that case, we'll go with a standard contract, with all the usual rights and waivers."

"Whatever."

McKay looked up as Daphne slapped a sheet of paper and a pen onto the table in front of him. "Just sign on the dotted line." He raised a brow as Daphne swept the contract away before the ink began to dry.

"Can you start right now?" Carly gave him a gleaming smile. "I did tell you that I'm desperate."

Yes, she had. She proved it now, pacing

with edgy energy, then tugging props out of drawers and checking her cameras.

"Why not?" McKay said. If she gave him half a chance, he'd find a dozen reasons why he couldn't start at all.

"Don't sound so excited. I promise to bring you back alive. Take it from me, you're going to sizzle. You have a killer body."

He didn't give a damn how he looked on film as long as it kept him close enough to see that she was safe for the next week. "Thanks. Even if I don't believe it."

"You'd better believe it. That wasn't flattery. It was a statement of fact from a professional." She turned away, scooping up a light meter. "Will you phone the crew, Daphne? Tell them we'll be setting up for the sunset shoot. And don't forget the ice bucket for the champagne."

"Already done. I made the calls from the bedroom while you two were bickering. The tux is already on its way to the set," she called.

"Perfect." Carly gripped her new star's arm and rushed him to the door. "Let's go make history."

"I say the shea butter for the swimsuit scene."

"And I say the baby oil." As she spoke, Carly drizzled some oil on her palm. "Would you mind raising your arm?"

McKay complied reluctantly, wondering if the whole world had gone mad or only he had.

For an hour he'd been poked, probed, and tested with meters. Now six people were huddled in a circle arguing about what kind of oil to use on his shoulders while a woman did something to his hair with a big comb.

McKay had been in dangerous situations before. He had bellied through leeches and fetid mud beneath a blazing sun and waited motionless for a sniper's lethal fire. Not once had he felt as trapped and frustrated as this.

"You see?" Carly ran oil-sleek fingers over his skin. "We want a subtle glow, not a major corona effect. We're creating dreams here." She turned to a lanky man with spiked hair. "How's the light, Hank?"

The man jammed a light meter against McKay's cheek and nodded. "Perfect, boss."

"So, where's my dream woman?" McKay hoped he wouldn't be paired with some high-fashion prima donna.

"There is no woman," Carly said briskly.

"That's part of the theme. We focus on you and your reactions. That way women viewers will project themselves into the scene, reinforcing brand loyalty."

"What about male viewers?"

"Not nearly as important. Most cruises are purchased by women or for women, so that's our target market." Carly studied the horizon. "In twenty minutes the sun should be positioned just right. Let's get into place, people. I want more orchids on that chair, and someone please mist the champagne bucket so it has the right condensation. Hank, check those gel filters, too. Drinks are on me when we finish."

She was good at this, McKay decided. She had an eye for every detail without being overbearing, and somehow she motivated her staff to equal enthusiasm. The result was a team effort, efficient and very smooth.

Maybe their worlds weren't so far apart after all. A training mission had to run the same way, as a team effort.

"The tux is here," Daphne called out. "I hung it in the bedroom."

"Finally," Carly said with relief. "I need you to hurry getting changed, Mr. McKay. If you need some help —"

"Ford," he reminded her. "And I think I

can manage to dress myself."

"Just remember, no shoes, no socks. Tie undone. You've come outside to relax before a big social evening on board."

"Yes ma'am." He resisted the urge to salute. How was he supposed to look relaxed with all those people hovering around him with cameras and lights?

Carly frowned at him. "Your hair is awfully short."

"So sue me," he said irritably. Someone shoved another light meter against his neck. "Aren't they about done?"

"Details count. You don't have a problem with a woman giving orders, do you?"

His voice fell. "I take orders from the person who's best equipped to give them — man, woman, Martian or gorilla. For now, you're it."

"Fine. I guess I'm a little touchy on that subject."

"You've probably got your reasons." McKay imagined she had encountered all kinds of male egos in her work. No doubt some baboon had stepped on her toes after she'd given him a perfectly reasonable order. Maybe he'd caught her in a deserted corner and decided to find out how that trim body felt beneath all that silk.

He scowled at the thought. "And if I ever

get my hands on the man who gave you those reasons, you might want to leave the room."

"I'm not sure whether to be grateful or insulted."

"Neither," he grumbled. "Let's just get this job done." He turned away, tugging off his shirt as he headed for the bedroom to change.

Carly refused to be nervous. He was just another body and this was just another job. There was no reason for anxiety. She frowned down at the third battery she'd dropped in the last five minutes.

Daphne watched Carly reach for her cappuccino as they stood on the veranda. "You want to watch the caffeine consumption. That stuff is pure rocket fuel."

"Who's jittery? I'm solid as a rock." Carly stuck out her hand and watched it lurch. "That's just ship movement." She raked back her windblown hair, scanning the horizon. The sun was perfect, a ball of liquid gold glowing behind red clouds. The props were ready, and her crew was focused and in place.

So where was he? If he didn't hurry, they'd miss the light.

She turned toward the cabin and stopped

dead, facing six feet two inches of hard, dangerous male in a tuxedo that fit like a masterpiece. The silk skimmed his broad shoulders and rode smoothly at his lean waist. As she had instructed, his feet were bare, his cuffs were rolled up, and his formal black tie lay open over his unbuttoned shirt.

He was all control on the surface, but an edge of violence simmered beneath, and the contrast was striking. Carly swung up her camera and ran a few frames, unable to take her eyes from the monitor.

He claimed the screen. The man was a study in disciplined power, right off the alpha chart.

God help the women of the free world when this picture hit the airwaves.

"Catch me," Daphne whispered. "I'm going to faint."

"Don't even think about it. I need you sane and focused so I can finish this scene in time to save my job."

"Forget sane. Does the man look half as amazing as I think he does?"

"Absolutely," Carly murmured. "He also looks annoyed as heck and ready to back out any second. Hank," she called. "Let's get those colored filters fine-tuned and the champagne misted."

With the last details covered, Carly

turned and took a deep breath. "You look —"

"Phenomenal," Daphne said.

Carly ignored her. "I'm glad the tux fits so well. If you'll stand beside this line taped on the deck, you'll be in position for the cameras." She guided McKay into place, ignoring a sudden stab of tension. She wasn't going to be silly about this. He was just a job, after all.

"Let's get started." She raised her camera, checked the lens, and cleared her throat, realizing something was wrong.

"The camera is upside down," Daphne said helpfully.

"Of course it is. I was checking the battery," Carly lied.

Pre-shoot nerves, nothing more.

She moved one of the teak deck chairs, pulled the champagne bucket closer, then arranged two crystal flutes on the glass table next to a spray of Indonesian orchids.

Satisfied, she stood back, watching McKay — watching sunlight turn his face into an arresting clash of light and shadow. It was a pity that his features would not appear in the final scene, since they were still committed to use Griff Kelly for the head shots. The transposition work would take place after the filming.

Carly scanned the main cameras, painfully aware of how little time they had until the sun went down. "Hank, how's the setup?"

"Okay over here, Carly. Ready to roll."

"Excellent." She looked at McKay, his expression cool and arrogant, impatience in every hard line of his body. *He really hates doing this,* she thought.

On impulse, she decided not to tell him the cameras were rolling, afraid he would tense up. "Hank, you are cued." Her cameraman nodded. He knew her well enough to guess what she was doing.

She saw the red light appear, indicating that the film was running. "Let's run through this once for practice, please. Look toward the sun, Ford. One elbow on the deck rail. Yes, that's perfect."

"You mean I have to do something?"

Carly almost laughed at the wariness in his voice. "No bungee jumping or skydiving, I promise you." She turned him slightly, adjusting his silhouette against the sunset. Then she moved back out of camera range. "Now lift the silver picture beside the orchid."

He muttered something as he picked up the photograph.

"That's it. Now pour a glass of champagne, then turn toward the rail and raise the glass. It's your toast to a dream that's finally coming true."

The man was enthralling. He didn't seem to give a damn if ten people or a thousand were watching. Every movement was casual, yet hinted at absolute control and cool intelligence. Carly knew that every woman who saw him would yearn to be the one who could pierce that tough male shell.

"Hank," she murmured, "are you getting all this on your end?"

"Oh yeah," the cameraman whispered.

"Okay, Ford. You're doing fine. Now we hear the door opening." On her cue, one of the camera techs re-created the creak of hinges. "Slow footsteps. Very expensive heels. Daphne? You all set?"

"Ready, Carly."

"Stay just off camera until I tell you." She nodded as Daphne straightened a bracelet that could have fed a Third World country for a week. "Lift your hand, Daphne. Let us see the bracelet." Carly framed carefully, catching the gleam of diamonds against McKay's black satin collar. "Now we hear the opening strains of Vivaldi. Softly, then swirling louder."

The lush melody of violins and brass swept the deck. The sound would actually be dubbed in later, but Carly liked to use music to key up the atmosphere for her actors.

And right now the atmosphere couldn't have been better. It was almost too perfect, in fact. Something had to go wrong.

Carly fought off a wave of anxiety, angling in on the diamonds gleaming like white fire against the sunset. "Turn around, Ford. Very slowly. Very controlled. Daphne, keep your hand right at his shoulder. Follow him as he turns without breaking contact."

Mentally, Carly raced through every detail of the scene. The focus was tight, the mood perfect, and she had never done anything better. But she knew that most of the credit belonged to her new model. The man was lethal — all tough eyes and tough body, claiming the camera just as she'd predicted.

"Daphne, move in slightly and raise your hand to his jaw. Tender, okay? As if you have all the time in the world."

Carly's pulse hammered as she watched Daphne's hand move into place. She gripped her camera, almost afraid to breathe. "Hold it. Draw it out, that's right. Done," she called. Suddenly giddy, she collapsed against the deck railing. "Daphne, get that bracelet back into its case and call security before I have a heart attack. Ford, you're a killer. Hank, you and the crew take a break. Champagne all around." Her legs were unsteady and she was still clutching her camera. Somehow she couldn't let the scene go.

"Why do we need a break?" McKay asked tensely. "Aren't we going to shoot the real scene?" When a wave of laughter spilled from the crew, he crossed his arms over his chest. "Well?" he demanded.

"I'm delighted to say that we have just completed a flawless scene in one take. Congratulations," she said breathlessly. "You were brilliant."

For the space of a breath, anger flared in his eyes. Carly watched in fascination as he blocked his reaction before anyone else noticed.

So the camera hadn't lied. This was definitely a man who valued being in control. No emotion got through unless he wanted it to.

Aware that soothing of the waters was due for her deception, Carly filled a glass with champagne and held it out to him. "Sorry. I thought it would help if we jumped right in."

"Very smooth. It's been a while since anyone conned me that well."

"And that bothers you."

"Damned right." He tugged off the tuxedo jacket, frowning when she put her hand on his arm.

"I was only trying to make this easier for you."

"I know." The anger in his eyes receded slightly. "Otherwise you'd be looking for another actor right now." He took the champagne glass and drank slowly. "Apology accepted, on one condition." He turned the glass, studying her over the rim. "You. Me. Dinner, tonight."

Chapter 5

"Dinner?" Her wariness was instant. "Why?"

"Because you have to eat. Since we're going to work together, it will help if I get to know you."

"Reasonable, I suppose," she said finally. "But I have to check film, then pack up cameras for tomorrow."

"Your staff can handle that. They won't miss you for a few hours." McKay finished his glass of rich, fruity Roederer Blanc de Blanc. "Time's up. Yes or no?"

Carly studied her crew, busy picking up props. "I can't stay long."

"Agreed. I'll meet you here in ten minutes." He slanted her a look that skimmed from head to toe. "Wear something comfortable."

Carly watched him stride off, aware of the curious glances of the crew. She heard a chuckle and flushed. "What's so funny?"

"Hey, going to dinner with him is fine by me," her head cameraman said. "We'll finish up here."

"The bracelet's gone back to the vault under guard." Daphne took her arm. "I'll make sure all the cameras are back in the office before I lock up."

"But —"

"Go," Daphne said impatiently. "Just because you're busy doesn't mean you can't have a little private time. It's true, getting to know him will help your work."

"It sounds even thinner coming from you than it did from him," Carly said flatly.

"Then why did you say yes?"

She shrugged. "Curiosity. Or maybe because I can't turn down a challenge."

Daphne studied Carly in thoughtful silence. "Wear the linen sundress with a single strand of pearls."

Carly flushed. "I will not dress up. This isn't a date."

"You still want to look your best." Daphne tapped her cheek. "Definitely the red linen." She shooed Carly toward the door. "Your cabin is across the hall, remember? Along with the life you keep forgetting to live."

"This is ridiculous."

"Go. The man just saved your job. The least you can do is thank him."

Thanking him was one thing, Carly thought. Suffering was another.

"We can't be eating here." She stared at the wall of windows overlooking the ocean.

"Not in the health club."

"I told you comfortable." McKay studied her dress as he opened the door. "Not that I dislike your choice, but pearls may be a little overdressed for the treadmill."

"So sue me," Carly grumbled, stealing his line. "I try to avoid places like this."

"Too busy, right? You figure you get enough exercise working out with your camera. Or maybe bench-pressing your Palm Pilot."

"How did you know I have a Palm Pilot?"

"Call it a lucky guess."

"How do you know so much about me after less than a day?"

"Must be a gift I have."

She tried not to fume as they were greeted warmly by a stunning woman in yellow spandex.

"Why is no one else around?"

"Being famous has its perks."

"You're famous?" Carly whispered.

"No, you are. Martina was delighted to open the club as part of your research." He ran a finger over her pearls, one brow raised. "Nothing reduces stress like exercise."

Carly realized that Martina was waiting patiently, a towel and a red spandex leotard in her hand.

The outfit should have sent her running

for the nearest exit. Spandex meant a serious workout, while the faded sweat suit McKay produced from the bag over his arm implied a man who showed no mercy on himself or others.

Carly didn't have time for any of it.

She was ready to turn tail when McKay took her arm firmly. "Not scared of a little sweat, are you?"

"No way." Goaded, she took the exercise suit and sputtered a thank you.

"Good. You can change in there." He pointed past a ficus tree. "I'll warm up your treadmill."

"How kind of you." Carly tried not to fume as she wriggled into the spandex, feeling like an absolute fool. Irritably, she tugged at the high-cut leg openings. What had made her think the man had any romantic intentions?

On the plus side, rather than outline every imperfection, the spandex smoothed and complimented, making her body look more toned than it was, and the tights that went with the leotard were surprisingly comfortable.

McKay's gaze lingered longer than necessary as she strolled across the empty exercise area. He had changed, too, and his sweats looked like they had suffered major abuse in the name of peak conditioning.

"You're serious about this, aren't you?" Carly resisted an impulse to tug at the form-fitting spandex.

"Absolutely. Your water's over there. Use it frequently. Hydration is the number-one rule."

"Do you own a health club?" Carly asked suspiciously. "Daphne swore you did."

He seemed to fight a smile. "No, but I spend a lot of time working out. Lie down," he ordered.

"I beg your pardon?"

"I'm not going to jump you, Sullivan. You need to warm up before we start."

"Oh." Mortified, Carly sank to one knee beside him. "I guess that doesn't mean hot chocolate with marshmallows?" she said wistfully.

McKay didn't crack a smile as he took her through leg lifts and stretches, then steered her toward a sleek steel treadmill. "Five minutes, no incline, just to get your heart rate up. We'll start you at a walk."

"What's this 'we' stuff? I'm the one doing the work."

"You'll be getting the benefits, too."

"You're really into all this exercise stuff, aren't you?"

"Your body is your finest tool."

"Funny, I always considered it my weakest link."

But five minutes passed before Carly knew it. At the end of ten, she felt comfortably flushed, more energized than she had in weeks. "Okay, I'm pumped. Where do I sign up for kickboxing?"

"First things first, Champ." McKay steered her to a machine with a padded seat. "Stomach crunches next. Hold, exhale, and tuck. Form counts."

Carly stared at him. "Don't tell me you're some kind of personal trainer."

"Stop procrastinating."

She slid gingerly onto the seat, embraced the metal bar, and tucked as ordered.

"Good. Only forty-nine more to go."

"Wait a minute," she snapped.

"Just a joke. Keep your back to the seat. No sliding forward or you'll end up with pulled muscles."

Carly huffed her way to ten and sat back with a gasp. "Since this was your idea, tell me what we've learned about each other, beyond the fact that you have an unhealthy liking for pain, especially when it's someone else's."

He held out a bottle of water and waited until she drank. "I've learned that you can stay the course." He handed her a towel for her face. "That you like a good challenge. Stubborn to the bone."

Carly hid a smile. The man had her pegged. "Is that a fact? What else?"

He braced an arm against the weight machine. "You've learned that I have your best interests at heart and that I'm probably not going to jump you."

There was absolutely no reason for her to be disappointed. "How do I know that?"

"Because if I'd planned to jump you, the sight of you in that sexy spandex would have clinched the deal."

Carly felt a little light-headed. "I'm not sexy. I'm —"

McKay skimmed her cheek. "Sexy as hell, Sullivan. Case closed."

He was suddenly too close, too calm. She felt a surge of relief when he gripped a horizontal bar and slid into effortless pull-ups. Carly lost count after fifty and simply indulged in the pleasure of watching the play and recoil of his muscles. "Are you in the military?"

"What makes you think that?" His voice didn't change as his body rose and fell, utterly controlled.

"Something about the way you stand, the way you move. There's a sense you give off." She frowned, searching for the right word. "As if you're . . . ready."

"It's something I pride myself on." He dropped from the bar and tugged off his sweatshirt.

Sweat glistened on his chest. Carly stared, aching for a camera.

"Ready for the bench press?"

"Probably not."

"Here, slide in. I'll keep the weight low. This will help your camera work by building upper-body strength. Go for ten."

"Sure, why not? All I can do is break both arms." Despite an initial awkwardness, she was surprised to feel a pleasant heat in her arms as the bar rose and fell smoothly. "What do you do when you're not giving fitness lessons?" she asked between lifts.

"I keep busy."

"Busy, as in investment banking? Car dealerships? Real estate?"

"I move around a lot." He reached over and caught the bar. "No more. You don't want sore muscles while you're juggling lenses." He laughed at Carly's expression of utter horror. "Don't worry, it's not going to happen." He tossed her the water bottle.

"Are you in the travel industry, McKay?"

"Not exactly."

"Then what, exactly?"

He flicked his towel lazily. "Recently I've

been developing deep-water rebreather technology."

"As in scuba diving?"

"Close enough."

She considered the answer. "So you're some kind of scientist or engineer or something."

"Or something."

"Are you with a giant corporation or are you in independent R&D?"

His lips curved. "Our corporation's pretty big. Our team is damned good at what they do."

"Why do I get the impression that there's a whole lot you're not telling me?"

"I have no idea. Now back to the treadmill before you cool down."

Before she realized it, Carly was on the machine beside him, easing into a comfortable trot while red lights raced over the elaborate panel. "I know some of these lights show speed and distance. What do the others mean?"

"If you can read them, it means you're still alive. That's always a positive sign."

Carly huffed on. "You're pretty good at this stuff. If you ever want to become a personal trainer, you could probably make a fortune."

"I'll keep that in mind," he said dryly. "So

how did you get started behind the camera? Did your mother show you the ropes?"

Carly ignored the sudden tension at her chest. "Now and again. Mostly I learned by watching."

"You're good at that." His stride lengthened. "Your mother must be very proud of you."

Carly missed a step, then fought her way back into stride. "She's dead. I lost both my parents when I was fifteen." Aware of his gaze, she concentrated on the flickering lights.

"I'm sorry." His pace was effortless and unflagging. "You've got some amazing photographs. You must have wonderful memories to go with them."

The red lights blurred for a moment. Carly punched the power button, slamming the machine to a halt. "She left me memories," she said, breathing hard. "Lots of memories."

She grabbed her towel and stepped down, hating the pull at her chest. Hating the swirl of bitter thoughts. "I've had enough."

"Stay."

"I can't." To her fury, her voice was ragged.

Without warning, she found herself pinned against a vertical bar. "Talk to me," he ordered. "Don't turn away and go inside yourself."

"I don't want to talk." She swung out one arm wildly, fighting to break his grip. "Let me alone, McKay. Who asked you to —"

She fought back painful memories, furious to feel the bite of tears. Her pulse was hammering and her legs were shaky. "I don't want to talk about it. Not now, not ever."

His hands settled gently at her face. "Why?"

"Because my past is no one's business."

"I pushed. My fault."

She stiffened as his knuckle skimmed her cheek. "I think we should go shower and change."

"In a minute." There was something hungry in his eyes, something that tore at her breath.

"You said you weren't going to jump me," she blurted.

"Plans change. I like how you sweat, Sullivan."

"Who's sweating?"

"Both of us, last time I checked."

Her gaze fell to his lips. She wanted to run, but not as much as she wanted to feel that hard mouth locked on hers. She closed her eyes as he traced her jaw. His fingers tightened, and she felt his tension as he lowered his mouth to hers.

Flustered, she tried to pull away, shocked by the smooth slide of contact.

He eased a hand into her hair. "No more questions."

Why did her pulse falter? Why did she let him take her mouth again and want him to take more?

"Bad idea." She pulled away, struggling for calm. "Let's forget this happened." She raked her fingers through her hair. "It's late and —"

He covered her mouth with one finger. "Stop running away from me. Stop fighting and let me see who you are."

"What I am is sweaty, tired, and a mess."

He shook his head slowly. "Brave, scrappy, generous. And you don't even see it."

He swung around sharply as a key turned in the lock. The door was opened by a man in a white uniform, and Carly recognized the room steward she had met that afternoon.

"I have your dinner, sir." He waved one hand over a cart laden with covered dishes. "Grilled shimp with fresh salsa and roasted asparagus. Where shall I serve you?"

"The table by the window should do

fine," McKay said dryly. "You're right on time."

The steward's expression was bland. "Service is our highest priority, Mr. McKay." He slid the dishes into place, then laid out linens and silver. "Will there be anything else? Things are a little busy on the floor tonight."

McKay seemed to stiffen. "Busy how?"

"Ms. Sullivan's crew was celebrating today's shoot. There have been quite a few beverage orders." He sent a measuring glance at Carly.

"Exactly how many beverage orders?" she asked uneasily.

"Six bottles of champagne. Your crew seems to enjoy German beer, too."

Carly sighed. "I'd better go."

"No need to rush." The steward scratched his jaw lightly. "Your assistant told them that if they wanted more champagne they would have to foot the bill themselves. She seems to have them in line. Before I left, she was dispensing imported coffee and reminding them they have an early call tomorrow."

Carly had to smile at the idea of Daphne as den mother, but she knew from experience that Daphne made exacting work more fun than it had any right to be. She could charm the smile off a barracuda.

"Daphne can handle the troops. I promised you dinner." McKay filled a plate for Carly, a rainbow of mixed salad greens. Next came shrimp salsa and asparagus. He lifted another lid. "I didn't order this sweet potato soufflé."

"It looked excellent, so I added it to your cart, along with the chocolate eclairs. Enjoy." The steward whistled softly as he headed to the door.

McKay studied the steward's back in exasperated amusement.

"He's got great taste." Carly took a bite of the soufflé and sighed. "In fact, everything looks delicious. I suppose Daphne can take care of things for a little longer." She paused over a wedge of avocado. "By the way, do you want to have a look at today's film?" She laughed at the wave of horror that crossed his face.

"You couldn't pay me enough."

She rested a hand on his arm. "That makes your help especially kind, considering how uncomfortable you are at being photographed."

"I'm discovering that it's hard to say no to you." He filled his plate and sat back, the Caribbean a restless shimmer of indigo behind him. "Are you seeing anyone?"

This was the last question Carly had expected. She coughed and grabbed her wine. By the time her throat was clear, she could answer calmly. "No one in particular." She tilted her head. "What about you?"

He studied a piece of escarole. "There have been one or two women."

"Past tense?"

He looked up, unblinking. "Getting personal, Sullivan?"

"Shouldn't I? You started the twenty questions, so I figure I'm entitled to ask a few of my own."

"Fair enough." He looked out at the sea. "It was bad timing. Bad choices." He swirled his wine. "Relationships require time, care, and patience, and my work keeps me on the move."

He'd surprised her with a thoughtful answer and a hint of regret in his voice. "Tough luck."

"If I'd wanted something more, I'd have found a way." He snagged a slice of mushroom untouched on her plate. "What's your excuse?"

"The usual. No prospects when I had the time, and no time when I had the prospects. Having a demanding career is a wonderful method of birth control," she said dryly. "Not that I've given any thought to children. Or marriage or anything else."

"Some people find the time."

"So I hear." Carly began stacking plates neatly on the table. "Right now my time is up. I have film and props to organize."

"What about the eclairs?"

"Tempting, but I'll pass. I've got to get back." She pointed at the lacy green leaves on McKay's plate. "Don't you know that real men don't eat frisee?"

"So that's what it's called." He took her silverware. "I'll do that. Sit down and enjoy your wine." He finished stacking the silver, then rolled the cart back to the door. When he turned, Carly was right behind him.

"You give fitness lessons and you clean up, too?" She put one hand over her heart. "I just might have to marry you, McKay." She flushed. "Maybe I should have skipped that last glass of wine. It's going right to my head."

He lifted the glass from her fingers. "Maybe it isn't the wine."

"Oh no, I'm not falling into that one."

McKay bent slowly, intrigued by the light in her eyes. "We all fall sometime, champ." If she'd been his type, he might have been in danger of falling himself. Since she wasn't anywhere close, he simply enjoyed the sight of her face flushed with color.

Amused, he brushed her lips, savoring the gentle contact. Then he had a strange compulsion to try it again.

She raised her hand to his chest.

He caught it, bringing her palm to his lips and smiling at her faint tremor. The woman had no clue how responsive she was.

Slowly her hands climbed to his chest, and she gave a dreamy sort of sigh. Heat rocked McKay as she moved closer, exploring his mouth.

Suddenly there was no gentleness in what he felt, no logic and no clarity. He wanted that slim, ladylike body quivering beneath him, lost in the same sensual haze that he was fighting. He wanted it absolutely and without question.

Damned odd, considering that she wasn't his type at all.

When he eased away, she sighed, seeking him with her pliant body. It took far more control than he expected not to pull her back into his arms and feast.

"Carly," he murmured, enchanted by her warm oblivion. "Back to earth, champ." He whispered the words against her hair simply so he could smell her perfume and feel the soft slide of her body.

There was a definite glow in her cheeks as she stared blankly into space. After a moment, she looked down at his hands circling her wrists, then drew a jerky breath. "I'm going to pretend none of this happened," she muttered. "It had to be the wine."

"Put it down to curiosity." He slid a damp strand of hair off her forehead.

Her brow spiked. "Is curiosity what's going on here?"

For McKay, what was going on was focused lust. Because he wanted badly to haul her close and kiss her again, he took a stiff step backward. "Close enough. We'd better shower, then go."

"My shower can wait. I need to get back and check on my crew while they're still rational." She glared down at her exercise attire. "Besides, it could take me an hour to wiggle out of this spandex thing."

"I'd be more than happy to help you."

"I'll just bet."

Smiling faintly, McKay guided her to the door. As he flipped off the light, a clatter echoed through the corridor outside.

Cursing, he pushed Carly behind him, shielding her with his body and locking a hand over her mouth.

Chapter 6

Footsteps shuffled up to the door.

McKay pressed Carly flat against the wall.

There was a low click in the darkness, and the door opened slowly. He gave Carly's arm a warning squeeze as a long object emerged.

He slammed one shoulder low, caught the object and twisted it free, then pinned the man who'd been holding it to the floor. "Get the lights," he ordered.

In the sudden glare of the overhead fluorescents, McKay saw a man wearing a gray uniform with the logo of the cruise line. He was white-haired, probably seventy, and clearly terrified.

The object he'd been carrying was a mop.

Water flowed from an overturned bucket near the door, and McKay realized that had been the source of the sound from the hall. He helped the old man to his feet, then dusted off his shoulders. "Sorry," he said briskly.

The man edged sideways. "Tonight's my cleanup duty here. It's on the schedule. Call and check," he said anxiously.

McKay straightened the bucket and

dropped the mop inside. "No need. I'm sure you're right." But he intended to have Izzy check the story just the same. "The fault was mine. Anything I can do to help?"

The man pulled his bucket across the room, shaking his head. "Just a simple mistake."

The moment McKay had escorted Carly out into the corridor, she spun tensely.

"You didn't learn that move in any health club." Her face was pale. "What's going on?"

"He took me by surprise, that's all."

"Don't brush me off. I have eyes. Who are you?" She swallowed. "*What* are you?"

He'd been expecting this. A woman of her intelligence was bound to notice his vigilance sooner or later and demand an explanation. His only surprise was how much he disliked lying to her. "I've worked in some unsettled places. When I hear a loud noise, I drop first and ask questions later."

"But you didn't drop," she pointed out tightly. "First you shoved me behind you, then wrestled that man to the floor, all in total darkness. It appears to be something you do a lot." She crossed her arms. "I'd like an explanation."

"Nothing to explain. He took me by surprise and I reacted too fast." He said nothing more as he guided her to the glittering art-deco elevator.

"That's pure rubbish." Carly pursed her lips as the elevator doors closed. "Lucky for you I'm too tired to argue. But I'll find out, I warn you."

As soon as they reached her floor, she stalked out of the elevator, the mood of easy friendship shattered.

At her stateroom music drifted through the closed door, nearly drowned by laughter. Carly found her key and opened the door, amazed to see her head cameraman dancing a reckless hula in a red plastic skirt.

Hank smiled guiltily. "Just getting in the mood for tomorrow. You two have a nice date?"

"It wasn't a date," Carly said firmly. "It was a business meeting."

"Tell it to the IRS," someone called out. The Hawaiian music stopped as Daphne appeared with a tray of fruit and cheese.

"One more for the road, everybody." Her eyes widened as she looked from Carly to McKay. "So you're back. How was your date?"

"It wasn't a date," Hank said, grinning. If he noticed Carly's flush, he was too polite to mention it. Instead, he glanced at his watch.

"Okay, people, party's over. We've got a five a.m. departure for Barbados and I want you revved and ready to roll. Let's call it a night."

The crew members drifted to the door, and McKay followed them, giving Carly a last, appraising look. "You sweat well, Sullivan."

"Compliments will get you nowhere." She rested one finger on his chest and tapped lightly. "And my promise stands. You were lying and I'm going to dig the truth out of you."

Not without a topflight security clearance, she wouldn't. "Happy hunting. Be sure to tell me if you dig up anything really incriminating."

Daphne waited four seconds, then pounced. "So spill. How does he kiss?"

Carly tried to look affronted. "Are you suggesting I can't spend an hour in a man's company without locking lips?"

"Not with that man, you couldn't. Where did you go?"

Carly stacked dirty coffee cups and carried them to the kitchenette. "The health club. His idea of fun is going one-on-one with a treadmill."

"He's certainly not your usual type."

Carly's amusement faded. "Type?"

"Don't tell me you've forgotten your penchant for practical men. Last year it was the tax lawyer. His idea of romance was outlining a three-year plan to overhaul your stock portfolio."

"He seemed charming and attentive. I still can't understand it."

Daphne coughed loudly. Carly suspected it was to hide a snicker.

"He wanted to get his hands on your assets, if you ask me." Daphne waved a finger. "What you need is a man who won't let you order him around. Someone who will make you sizzle while he gets under your skin."

"Sounds like a nasty rash."

"Don't be flippant. It's time you learned to let go."

"What it is," Carly said with a glance at her watch, "is time for me to check today's footage, then get some sleep. You too. Early call, remember?"

Daphne gave an expressive shrug. "When I was working in Paris, I'd be on location in full makeup by four, with a ten-hour day in front of me."

Carly rolled her eyes. "Such terrible torture having to wear exquisite designer gowns and have your hair and face done by the best talent in the business." Carly frowned as Daphne tucked some papers under her arm. "No last-minute faxes from New York, I hope. If Mel's switching plans, I'm going to have a serious meltdown."

"No, these are for me. Father again."

Carly put down the orange she had been peeling. "Uncle Nigel? Nothing's wrong on Santa Marina, I hope?"

"Not with him. It's me he's driving crazy," Daphne said dryly. "For the last month he's been monitoring every move I make, keeping track of where I'm due and calling if I'm even ten minutes off. When I ask what's wrong, he turns stone faced and says it's perfectly natural for a father to worry about his daughter's safety."

Carly squeezed Daphne's arm. "You're getting married soon. Sounds to me like he's suffering from separation anxiety. Having someone worry about you isn't such a bad thing."

Daphne sniffed. "He won't let up. I even think he has me followed," she said angrily. "That's partly why I jumped at the chance to pinch-hit on your shoot. I actually had to leave him a note and sneak off the island to get here."

"Not many places safer than a cruise ship," Carly said cheerfully. "Unless it's the

Titanic. He should be thrilled that you're here."

"Hardly. He keeps blitzing me with messages and asks me to check in with his office three times a day." Daphne sent Carly a warning look. "Don't think you're safe, either. Now he's demanding every detail of tomorrow's shoot on Barbados."

Carly strode toward the phone. "I'll call him. There's no reason for him to worry."

"No, don't. He'll demand that you put me on and then we'll argue."

"But you can't let him worry this way."

"He knows I'm here and safe. That will have to do. I'll phone him from Barbados tomorrow, I promise." Daphne studied the equipment humming on the long table. "Let's see today's film. I want to find out if my imagination is as good as the real thing."

"He does have an amazing body," Carly murmured, remembering how McKay looked on the treadmill, holding an effortless stride. "But let's see what the camera says."

Across the room, Daphne powered up the camcorder plugged into a high-resolution screen. "These are the test shots you made this morning at the pool." She watched McKay climb out of the water in full, chiseled glory. "Is the man buff or what?"

"He burns up the screen, just the way I knew he would." Carly scanned the rest of the crowd. "Everyone else seems to disappear. Okay, move forward." She sat mutely, savoring the sight of McKay cutting through the pool while the volleyball game raged off to the side. "This is where they started to get rowdy." Abruptly she sat forward. "Wait. Pause and go back."

She watched the crowd morph backward, then repeat their movements. "There," she said, pointing to a man in a deck chair.

"The skinny guy with the bad hairpiece?" Daphne leaned closer to the screen. "That orange Hawaiian shirt really has to go."

"He seems to pop up everywhere I am. He was watching us before, on the opposite side of the deck. Now he's there in the corner, looking right at me. I'm beginning to feel stalked."

"The man is just a tourist soaking up some sun. Since we happen to be astoundingly beautiful women, of course he's watching us, too."

Carly sank into a chair beside Daphne. "I guess you're right. He's gone in this next pan. I must be suffering from post-treadmill trauma."

"The shots from this afternoon are next." Daphne crossed her legs, smiling smugly. "I have a feeling they'll be phenomenal."

Ten minutes later, Carly sank back in her chair, feeling her heart slam.

The footage was unforgettable. McKay in a tuxedo against the dying sun. McKay holding up a glass of champagne to an unseen companion, cool triumph in his eyes. The man was a glory to behold.

"He's incredible." Daphne's eyes crinkled. "Hank says he's never seen anything close in fifteen years of shooting."

"I've got a feeling that we're about to make history," Carly whispered. But for some reason, the thought left her uneasy.

Nikolai Vronski hated the Americans. Of course, he hated most Russians, too. Humanity in general was tedious, incompetent, and self-indulgent, and Vronski prided himself on being none of those things.

He swept past the lone man sweating in the yacht's converted stateroom. With an impatient glance he scanned the long steel worktables. "What developments?"

The aged Japanese artist turned beneath the bank of bright halogen lights. His hands were scarred from decades of pounding and shredding fibers to make the highest quality Japanese brush paper. "It is slow work, as I have explained before."

There was little sense of movement below deck. The boat was perfectly stabilized to protect the expensive equipment that filled the shelves and long tables.

"I did not ask if the work was slow or fast." Vronski's keen gaze ranged over the gleaming metal trays. "I want results. What have you to show me?"

The Japanese man bowed, shaking his head. "It is still too soon." He was sweating heavily.

One blow from the Russian's fist sent him staggering to the floor.

Despite the pain, he was wise enough to stay absolutely quiet while Vronski stormed out.

Chapter 7

Waves lapped at the white sand beach, while palm trees rustled soothingly. The scene could have been lifted right off a postcard, McKay thought.

Too bad it wasn't a real vacation so he could enjoy it.

Beside him, Daphne sighed. "Give me a box of Godiva chocolates, an Andrea Bocelli CD, and I'll be in paradise." She drew in a hearty breath of sea air and jumped down onto the sand. "Barbados is spectacular, isn't it?"

He vaulted down beside her. "Definitely beats crawling though the mud in an Alabama swamp."

"Are you from Alabama?"

His mouth quirked. "I don't believe I said that."

"Secretive, aren't you? Not that it matters. You're rescuing Carly and her shoot. That's all I care about."

"I still don't see how she's going to get the film from here to New York in time to help."

Daphne slid her huge bag over one shoulder. "The wonderful world of modern electronics. She sent a digital proof file late yesterday from the ship. A second proof went off by express courier when we docked today. Now, if you could only get her to relax. With the pace she's keeping, she'll end up in a padded cell."

"What makes you think she'd listen to me?"

Daphne stared at Carly, who was sorting lights and camera equipment in the back of a battered Jeep. "Something tells me you can be very persuasive when you want to be. You've already managed to get her to exercise — something she's studiously avoided for months."

McKay tried to hide a grin. "Is this called matchmaking, by any chance?"

"Perish the thought. She'd have my head. I'm just planting a friendly, good-natured suggestion." Daphne's eyes narrowed. "And if she asks, this conversation never happened."

"I'll keep it in mind." McKay shook his head as Carly's assistant trotted away. Today Daphne was wearing skintight blue jeans, a white T-shirt, and diamond earrings, a bizarre combination that somehow worked on her. But her suggestion was pointless. No one could force Carly Sullivan to relax when she was in her professional mode.

And she certainly was today. She'd been sorting, guiding, and worrying since the crew had assembled at dawn. She was on her third list and her fourth cup of coffee and the actual shoot hadn't even begun.

McKay knew the feeling. It came to him every time a transport plane carried him to a jump zone for a mission. The trick was to tap the nervous energy and use it before it had time to eat a hole in your stomach.

Something told him Carly hadn't yet mastered that particular skill.

They'd work on it, he decided.

Meanwhile, she had him decked out in cargo shorts and a splashy Hawaiian shirt. The only way he could look more like a tourist would be if she loaded him down with a set of cameras. He scowled as she waved excitedly from the Jeep, where she was talking with a man in a dark suit.

Suddenly, as he crossed the beach, McKay felt a dead certainty that they were being watched.

The watched sensation crawled along his neck, one of a dozen survival instincts honed over long years of covert missions under deadly conditions. He forced his body to relax as he turned casually, his eyes flicking around him. By the road, two women in straw hats walked a dog. A man was selling fruit from a wooden cart close to the base of the cliffs. Nothing seemed out of place. Casually, he scanned the cliffs, picking up no sign of movement, then continued across the beach.

Carly gave him a measuring glance. "This is Mr. Charles from the tourist board. He helped to coordinate today's shoot. This is Mr. McKay, our primary actor." As the two men shook hands, she turned to the beach, looking worried.

McKay followed her gaze. "Something wrong?"

"The beach was supposed to be closed today. I don't like having to shoot around visitors."

"Only a few are here," the tourist official protested. "And the man who was to put up the signs had a puncture on his way from Bridgetown. I am making some calls, but it is difficult to close the beach now." He trotted off to his car, cell phone in hand.

"I hate surprises." Carly drew a long breath, then brightened. "You look wonderful. You'll start a rage for flowered shirts."

"My secret ambition in life." McKay tried not to fidget as she opened one more button at his collar and smoothed the bright cotton lapels.

"I don't know how you do it, but even in these clothes you look dangerous."

McKay ignored the question in her voice as he pulled the heavy equipment bag out of her hands and slung it over his shoulder. "After you."

She pointed up the beach, where spray shimmered over a single rugged boulder. "That's where we're shooting."

The two women with the dog strolled past and smiled. The beach vendor cut up mangoes. Just another quiet day in paradise.

Except McKay knew that every paradise had its dark side. He was glad that Izzy had wrangled a free day and was somewhere nearby, silent and invisible backup, which was the best kind.

"The lighting looks just about perfect." As Carly spoke, something flashed on the hillside behind her, once and then again.

McKay kept his face impassive as he tracked a blur of red up through the trees. To buy time, he caught Carly's hand while he studied the slope behind her.

"What are you doing?"

"Making you slow down," he lied smoothly. "If you keep charging around in this heat, you'll crash before the shoot is done."

She tilted her head. "You know a lot

about heat and the tropics, do you?"

"Enough."

McKay was a patient man when circumstances required it. He fingered the silver pendant at her neck, tracing the whimsical curve of stars suspended by tiny silver chains. "Nice work."

Color touched her cheeks. "Too expensive, but I couldn't resist. The artist is M. E. Kincade."

"Never heard of him." He twirled the stars slowly, noting that there was no more movement from the trees.

"Her. She's an American jeweler based in Scotland. Now maybe you'll tell me why you're pretending to be so interested in my necklace when we both know you couldn't care less about mixed metals."

"To slow you down." He gave her a cool smile. "And to give myself the pleasure of touching you."

"Forget the charm, McKay. I saw you watching the trees behind me."

She was more observant than he'd realized. He lifted her pendant, tracing the delicate bits of silver. "Maybe I wanted to wish on these stars of yours."

Her eyes were frankly skeptical. "You're hiding something, and I don't like it." She pulled away, tugging primly at her shirt.

"Can we get to work?"

Behind her a dusty bus lumbered around a curve and came to a shuddering halt. Seconds later waves of noisy schoolchildren flooded onto the beach.

Carly gasped. "Can you believe this? Everything was arranged. This beach was supposed to be closed today."

"Looks like someone forgot to tell the kids," he said dryly.

"I can't possibly shoot here now." Carly stared at the darting children, a hand pressed against her stomach.

McKay watched her fingers flatten. "Steady. We'll work something out. Let's go corner your friend from the tourist bureau and check out options."

Her face was pale in spite of the heat. "I need a minute. Just a minute." She closed her eyes and dragged in a breath.

McKay rested his hand on hers where it lay against her stomach. "How long has it been hurting?"

"About five minutes. Since the school buses arrived."

"No," he said patiently. "I meant how long ago did your stomach problems begin?"

Her eyes snapped open. "What do you mean? What makes you think —"

"You're sheet-white." He caught her wrist and shook his head. "Your pulse isn't the steadiest. All in all, I'd say you're steering yourself toward an ulcer."

Carly's face closed down tight. "I appreciate your concern, but you're wrong." She pulled away and started up the beach. "And I don't have time to discuss it."

More children thronged the sand as McKay charged after her, scanning for possible threats. By the time he caught up, Carly was arguing with the official from the tourist board while Daphne tried to cut in.

"Just listen to me," she said sharply. When silence descended, she nodded briskly. "That's better. I know an incredible spot up the northeast coast, complete with cliffs and a waterfall. I'll have to make some calls, but I think I can arrange for us to use it for a few hours. The owner is an old friend of my father's."

"How far away?" Carly demanded. "We don't have any extra time in the schedule."

"About thirty minutes should do it. Why don't we go to the inn up the road while I contact the owner?"

"I'll take anything, so long as it's quiet." Carly moved restlessly from foot to foot. "The waterfall sounds good. We could work that into a dramatic background pan. Let's try it."

McKay watched her stride toward the crew gathered around their battered Jeep. Like Daphne, he was beginning to wonder how long she could keep up this pace.

"Carly, wait."

She just kept walking, head down, deep in thought as she fingered the camera hanging around her neck. McKay cursed as he saw one of the school buses shudder into reverse and lumber over a row of old tire tracks filled with water from a recent storm.

But Carly didn't see.

He shouted again, sprinting forward and jerking her back with inches to spare as water and sand flew up from the big tires, drenching her face and shirt. Only her quick reflex in cradling her camera saved it.

"Wake up, dammit. You almost walked into that bus."

She hugged her camera protectively. "I saw it."

"Sure you did." McKay took her arm firmly. "Come on. I'll walk you to the Jeep."

Carly glared at him. "I don't need a keeper."

"Don't you?" He kept his voice low, audible only to her. "You don't eat and you don't slow down. You push yourself to the very edge. I'd say a keeper is exactly what you need." Concern had him itching to pull her close and shake her.

Color swirled into her face. She started to speak, then closed her eyes. "I do push myself." There was desperation in her eyes when they opened. "A job like this doesn't come often, and if I fumble now, I may never get another chance. I need you, McKay. You're magic on film. I've never seen anything like it." She managed a partial smile. "So don't tell me you're backing out, or I'll have to shoot you."

"I'm not backing out," he said tightly. "But when we get to the inn, you're going to eat something. And you're coming with me in the Jeep when we drive to this waterfall of Daphne's. No one else, understand? While I drive, you're going to rest. Not fidget, not plan, not worry or issue orders."

Her first response was an angry protest. Then she closed her eyes and sighed. "Okay. Sure, whatever."

He motioned to one of the crew, who gunned the Jeep toward them over the sand.

"Did you find it?" she asked softly.

"Find what?"

"Whatever you were looking for up on the cliffs. I watch people, McKay. I see things. It's my job, remember?"

He kept his face expressionless, annoyed that once again she had noticed too much. It seemed her inattention was only for herself. "You must have sand in your eyes."

The Jeep careened to a noisy halt. McKay helped Carly climb in, then turned, weight centered, hands freed for action. He scanned the cliffs and the narrow road below. Dogs barked and children shouted, but no one appeared to be interested in Carly and her crew. Nothing at all seemed out of place.

So why had the stab of warning returned, keener than ever?

Carly was pacing the upper bedroom at the inn even before Daphne began to dial. "How do we know the owner will agree? And if he does, will the location be good enough?"

"Trust me, you'll love it." Daphne motioned sharply. "It's ringing."

Carly tapped her fingers on a rattan table. "Why doesn't he answer? Maybe he's —"

Daphne straightened. "This is Daphne Brandon calling for Marcel. Is he available?"

Carly's tapping grew louder.

"I see. Could you have him ring me back when he finishes his meeting? It's quite important." She rattled off the number at the inn, then hung up. "He should be finished in ten minutes." She frowned at Carly. "Stop fidgeting."

"If I don't fidget, I'll scream." Carly glanced at her watch, fixing the time for the return call. "Maybe I should try to find someplace else while we wait. Or maybe I should —"

Daphne pointed toward a deep chair by the window. "Sit. Marcel will come through. He's one of my father's oldest friends."

"We've barely got eight hours of daylight left. When is he going to call?"

There was a knock at the door, and Daphne strode across to open it before Carly could move. "Perfect," she said, inspecting the tray carried by a young man in a bright cotton shirt. After she'd paid him and closed the door, she handed a plate to Carly. "Fruit. Soup. Tea sandwiches and conch fritters. Eat."

"But I'm not —"

Daphne fixed her with a iron stare. "Eat every scrap or I won't answer the phone when Marcel rings. You'll be on your own."

Carly snorted. "You and McKay should pair up. He pulled the same blackmail routine on me outside."

"I'm liking the man more every second." Daphne looked at her soberly. "Do you think I don't notice how you work yourself to a lather, then forget to eat? Do you think you're hiding how you clutch at your stomach and wince."

"I don't know what you're talking about."

"Like hell. This is Daphne you're talking to, remember? I know all your tricks, and I've tried to keep quiet while you charge around at a killing pace, but you're frightening me. We've both lost people close to us." She took a harsh breath. "I couldn't bear to lose you. I couldn't."

Carly's anger died in her throat as Daphne stormed to the window. For ten years they had been more than friends, more than sisters. Carly cursed herself for not seeing beneath Daphne's flippant cover to the concern beneath. "Round one to you. Now tell me what *else* is bothering you."

"For starters, Father. When he isn't tracking me obsessively, he's sequestered with his top advisers. Something is going on, I know it, but when I ask, he brushes all my questions aside." Daphne gave a dry laugh. "Then there's my amazing invisible fiancé."

Carly stiffened. "When I saw David last winter he looked fine."

"Oh, he's thriving. I just can't get him to thrive on my side of the ocean. He's in Switzerland or Paris three weeks out of four, and even when he's with me in Santa Marina, he's juggling some currency deal or other. I'd like to plan our wedding, but we can't find a date because his schedule is always changing. It's starting to be tiresome."

More than tiresome, Carly thought. Any man who couldn't clear his appointment book for his own wedding probably didn't want to get married.

"And in the middle of all this chaos," Daphne stormed on, "here I am, determined to be careful and practical. To be *solid,* for once, and I'm terrified I'll fall flat on my face. I'm warning you, if something happens to you, I'm going to fly to Madagascar, check into a hotel, and have a mental breakdown." She turned, her face streaked with tears. "Go on, laugh."

Carly fought a wave of self-recrimination. "You should have told me what was happening. I'd have come immediately."

"I don't want you worrying. I just can't bear to see you driving yourself, always restless, always pushing to be perfect. Just like —"

Daphne stopped, looking shaken.

"Just like my mother." Carly finished the

113

sentence quietly. Nothing could take the sting from the words or the dark memories that followed. "She was always chasing the next sunset in Crete or tiger hunt in India. She wasn't ever satisfied and she couldn't ever stay." She laughed bitterly. "No matter how much I needed her to."

Daphne's face was pale. "I didn't mean to hurt you."

"Why should it hurt? It's the simple truth: blood always runs true."

"You're not like her. You *care*. It shows in every piece of film you take. It's not an abstraction or a game for you, not the way it was for her."

Carly shook her head. "I wish I could be certain of that. I'm hungry for the pictures, too. When I'm riding that flow of colors, I forget everything else. That makes me just as bad as she was because I hurt the ones I love, too."

Daphne sat beside her, on the arm of the chair. "We all hurt the people we love. Sometime it's for good reason, sometimes for bad. I think it's called the human condition." She gave a laugh that wasn't quite steady. "The very fact that this is worrying you, eating at you, means you can't be like her."

The phone rang, startling them both.

"And this conversation is nowhere near being over. Understood?"

As Carly nodded, Daphne swept up the receiver. Instantly all her calm and polish were there again, firmly in place, her hurts and anxieties pushed deep.

Carly watched in amused admiration as she charmed and cajoled her father's old friend. No one could say no to Daphne for long.

"I'm so happy. I'm only sorry you won't be able to drop by while we're there. It's been too long, Marcel."

Daphne was nodding, giving a dramatic thumbs-up, as she hung up. "All set. Marcel's always a dear. They're just clearing a fallen tree from a recent storm, but they'll be done in an hour." She frowned at Carly's half-eaten lunch. "Finish that or I'm going to get nasty."

Carly wolfed down a sandwich, then jammed a banana in her pocket. "Now can we go?"

Daphne sighed in exasperation. "Aren't you forgetting something?"

"No, my camera's right here. I've got extra batteries in the Jeep."

"You've also got sand all over your shirt and dirt crusted on your legs."

"Oh, that." Carly looked down and

shrugged. "It can wait."

"You're selling dreams and capturing beauty, yet you can't take five minutes to pull your own image together?"

Carly frowned, scrubbing at her leg. "See, it's gone already. Almost. Partly." She caught her breath as a clean shirt flew at her, disgorged from Daphne's huge leather bag, a mainstay of her modeling days. Even now it was always full of scarves, makeup, and jewelry.

"Go change. The blue linen will set off your eyes. You've got three minutes, then I'm sending the cavalry in after you." Daphne's lips curved. "Or maybe I'll just send McKay. Something tells me he's better than any cavalry."

Chapter 8

McKay scowled at his watch. How much time could two women spend making calls, brushing their hair, and changing clothes — or whatever they were doing?

He glanced over at the inn's small bar. Noisy and full of tourists, he noted sourly. Despite his careful scrutiny, he had seen no one move toward the rear corridor that led to the stairs. Carly was safe, along with her friend. But there was no room for error, and that meant not taking chances, especially when his instinct warned of trouble.

When the third passing tourist bumped him in the elbow, McKay carried his untouched drink out to the veranda, choosing a seat that allowed him an unobstructed view of the rear stairway.

He hadn't seen Izzy, but he knew he was nearby. He was also certain that Brandon had a handpicked crew watching Daphne. He wished he knew their faces.

"Busy place today."

McKay frowned at a stocky man leaning against the porch rail. "Appears that way."

"You new on the island?"

"I heard this was the best place for a quiet

117

drink." Four more tourists in floral shirts moved past him, jostling his arm as they headed for the bar.

"Your information was wrong. The Grey Parrot is always crowded."

McKay sat back, measuring the speaker. Mid- to late forties, all solid muscle. There was a holstered weapon beneath the right arm of his loose print shirt. "What about you?"

"I come here whenever I can. No one makes a royal punch better than this." He raised his drink, which looked untouched.

McKay's gaze snapped to the garden as a second man appeared. He too wore a loose shirt, probably to conceal a weapon.

McKay slid his glass onto a nearby table, prepared for action.

The stranger's smile was casual, but his eyes were cold. "Are you McKay?"

"I could be."

The man moved closer. "I think you're the officer we were told to expect, the one sent to protect Miss Sullivan."

McKay kept his face expressionless. "Who is 'we'?"

"Santa Marina police." The man held out a hand. "Malcolm St. John, acting director, at your service."

McKay didn't shake. "You have a badge

to match that gun you're carrying?"

He handed over a stamped photo ID, and McKay examined it carefully, then tossed it back. "Everything appears in order." He sat back and steepled his fingers. "How's the fishing off Paradise Cove this time of year?"

"Not many tuna left. You'd be better off farther east."

McKay nodded. The code words had been passed and answered. Both men relaxed, but only fractionally.

"I'm McKay. If anyone asks, I'm here strictly as an actor."

"Of course. An actor." The officer ran his tongue over his teeth. "Any problems so far?"

"All quiet. What about your end?"

"The governor has received several more threats directed at his family, and we're still narrowing the possibilities. Any thoughts on that?"

McKay scanned the quiet staircase. "Until this thing is over, you and the governor would be wise to be suspicious of everyone — all his business partners, all his political colleagues, and all his enemies."

"That covers a lot of territory." St. John tapped his fingers softly on the wooden rail. "The governor of Santa Marina is an important man, and big men make big enemies.

Mr. Brandon accepts that. But when they threaten his daughter and others close to him, he draws the line. He's worried that Miss Daphne makes too easy a target with the public life she leads, even though an assassin would have to get past me first," he said grimly.

"Has he ever received threats like this before?"

"Never." The officer checked the backyard and then the side. "We're watching the local gangs as well as some new crime groups from Jamaica. We're also looking into an influx of Russian expatriates. Until we have answers, Mr. Brandon wants his family protected around the clock."

McKay's eyes narrowed. "You've got someone watching Daphne aboard the cruise ship, I take it."

"Already arranged."

McKay nodded, his gaze returning to the back stairway. "Have the two women known each other long?" He had read the official file, but he wanted to hear St. John's spin on things.

The inspector chuckled. "Seems like forever. In and out of trouble, the two of them, every summer. Especially after Carly lost her parents off Tortola."

"When was that?" McKay hadn't seen details in the official report, which had focused on Brandon and his family.

"She was fourteen or fifteen, as I recall. She came back white-faced and quiet, with no more laughter and no more smiles. But Miss Daphne soon put the fire back into her. Those two got into every kind of trouble, jumping out of trees and hiking up to the cliffs alone. It was a different world then." He shrugged. "No one would have harmed a hair on their heads."

"And now?"

"Now there's no such thing as an island paradise, McKay. I figure that's why we're here." He crossed his arms. "How do I know you're any good?"

"It's my job to be good."

St. John seemed unimpressed. "You'd better be. Otherwise, you'll answer to me. Any special plans?"

"Stay close and stay alert." *And count everyone as an enemy. Even you.*

A door opened upstairs. The steps creaked.

Malcolm St. John moved swiftly, vaulting the rail and jumping down into the garden. "You didn't see me here. Miss Daphne will be full of fire if she finds her father has anyone following her, and that will make my job harder."

"No problem. I've been sitting here alone

enjoying my drink."

St. John nodded, then trotted around to the side of the garden, disappearing before Carly and Daphne reached the bottom step.

McKay pushed to his feet, about to ask what had taken the two so long, when he caught sight of Carly's blue linen shirt, the red sarong draped snugly around her hips, and the crimson hibiscus tucked behind her ear.

He could have sworn the veranda dipped sharply. She had gone inside with sand streaking her shirt and mud on her legs. Now she emerged casually elegant, sporting some kind of distracting floral perfume.

Clearly, Daphne had been at work.

"Everything's set. We need to be at the site in an hour." Carly started to walk past, but McKay snagged her wrist and spun her in a slow circle.

"What happened to the mud?"

Carly's lips twitched as he finished his slow, thorough appraisal. "Image repair, courtesy of the fashion police over here."

"That's me," Daphne said sweetly. "She looks wonderful, doesn't she?"

McKay flicked the tiny diamonds at Carly's ears. "Maybe you should try out the other side of the camera."

"Yeah, right." Carly looked down at her

watch to hide her blush. "We're running behind schedule. Are Hank and the crew ready to roll?"

"Awaiting your command." McKay saluted, a lazy, two-fingered gesture that left Daphne chuckling and Carly red faced as she headed to the parking lot.

"You handled her just right. Cool and calm to her nerves and energy." Daphne's voice fell. "But if you hurt her, I might have to do something unpleasant. Clawing out both your eyes comes to mind."

McKay's gaze stayed on Carly. "Remind me to be sure you're on my team."

"It's always a good idea. I may look like a lightweight, but I'm not. For an intelligent woman, Carly can be incredibly blind. I won't see her hurt."

There was nothing to add.

Since McKay had the same goal, he was smart enough not to try.

Orchids and ferns trailed down granite cliffs. The air was perfumed by exotic flowers, just as Daphne had promised.

A waterfall spilled from the mountaintop, then vanished in the trees, only to reappear far below in a smooth curtain plunging to a quiet glade.

"You really picked it this time," Carly

said to Daphne. "This is a real slice of paradise. I apologize for doubting you."

"Apology accepted. Now go work your magic."

Carly brushed the flower behind her ear and it dropped to the mossy ground. "I guess I'm just not a flower person."

Daphne shook her head, then turned back to study McKay. "Something black and tight would be lovely on him."

"Blue," Carly countered. "And his suit's not going to be suggestive."

"Darling, on that man, full body armor would be suggestive. Don't forget to oil his chest while you're at it," Daphne called sweetly. "The sunlight needs to catch every muscle."

"I'll do the directing here," Carly muttered. "And I was already planning on the oil."

"Good. In that case you'll need this." She tossed Carly a pink bottle, then gave a silent whistle as McKay appeared looking long and lean in a blue swimsuit. "He doesn't look happy."

Gripping the bottle of oil, Carly hurried toward the waterfall, ready to counter any and all of McKay's protests about his suit, which fit him admirably. Even the white towel around his neck looked sexy.

"I believe the crew is all set to shoot," she

said, pleased that her voice was crisp and professional. "Did Hank go over the scene with you?"

"A dozen times. I walk out of the pool, cross those rocks, then move to the waterfall. It's not exactly astrophysics."

"One more thing." Carly dropped the pink bottle into his palm. "Oil up."

McKay slid off the towel and slapped a line of oil over his chest. "How's that?"

"Oh, Ford, let me know if you need any help," Daphne called.

"Same here," a prop woman echoed.

Grinning, he stroked oil slowly down one arm, aware that Carly was watching every movement. "I've got a technical question here, chief. How much of this am I supposed to use?"

"That looks adequate."

"Maybe you need to help me out." He tossed the bottle back to Carly. "Just to be sure I get the details right."

Gritting her teeth, Carly tapped out some oil and pressed it against the center of his chest. "That should do it."

"Feels like you missed a spot." Because it annoyed her, McKay took her hand and slid it across his chest. If she was irritated enough, he figured, she couldn't obsess about the shoot.

"That's it," she snapped. "You can let go of my hand."

McKay scanned the cliffs, relieved to see Izzy on a path high up in the trees with a camera case over his shoulder. There was more than camera equipment inside it.

"Guess you're right." He turned, satisfied with his appraisal, which had also revealed St. John in a Jeep parked beyond the road. "Why don't we get started."

Somewhere a bird cried, shooting through the foliage.

McKay froze, staring up the hillside, then bit off a curse as he reached for the canvas bag at his feet.

"What's wrong?" Carly demanded.

He gestured to Daphne, who jumped down from a nearby rock. "Get down," he growled. "Both of you. Now."

"I don't understand," Carly said. "Why —"

He lunged toward the edge of the pool. As he shoved Carly and Daphne down onto the cool moss, noise exploded around them.

Chapter 9

Bullets screamed from everywhere at once, snapping branches and ringing off the rocks.

McKay opened the canvas bag and pulled out a gun. A swimsuit wouldn't conceal his Browning automatic, at least not the suit Carly had given him.

A bullet slammed past his head and he rolled into a crouch, his Browning level along his leg. "Are you two hurt?"

"No," Carly rasped, huddled beside her friend. Her eyes widened at the sight of the Browning.

"Keep down, both of you." Crawling toward the edge of the pool, he peered around the waterfall.

Someone shouted. Hank was huddled over a tripod, his headset clutched to his chest. The prop woman was frozen behind a rock.

Despite their danger, McKay knew his duty lay here, protecting Carly and Daphne. Izzy couldn't break his cover and would be doing what he could in the background. St. John had to be aware of the attack by now and would be moving in with his men. Meanwhile, McKay had to buy the police officer some time.

He crawled toward a pile of props and equipment, searching until he found what he needed.

Sandbags.

Electrical tape.

Heavy steel wire.

A fair start for a SEAL trained to improvise.

Bullets cracked off the rocks, splintering nearby branches. McKay looked back at Carly and Daphne and realized they were still exposed to the sniper fire coming from the trees just south of the road. He crossed toward them in a low crouch and pointed up the cliff. "Climb beneath that overhang, both of you. Stay low."

"But who —"

"Do it," he ordered, already uncoiling the wire and pulling it over the ground. He tethered the first line near the base of the falls, wound around two boulders at ankle height. No one could pass through the water without crossing the wire. He tugged the second wire into place close to the women's hiding place, positioning it five feet high, stretched between two trees.

The first line would trip an attacker. With any luck the second would do some serious damage as the body was catapulted forward into a fall.

His first task done, McKay grabbed the heavy tape and wrapped the smaller sandbag in position at his chest. It didn't come close to tactical Kevlar, but the packed sand would afford some protection against a bullet. He had to stay alive to keep the women alive. To do that, he had to even the odds.

He crouched near the ground and listened to the gunfire, picking out the distinctive burst of an automatic weapon. By counting bursts, he calculated that close to twenty rounds had been fired. The sudden silence meant an empty magazine, which would give him a short break between cycles so he could move if he had to.

"Is my crew safe?" Carly rasped behind him.

"No casualties when I looked." Not that he'd had time for details. Damn, where were St. John and his backup?

Water jetted, then suddenly sprayed backward. A man slammed through the waterfall, hit the first row of wire, and went down hard before he could get off a shot.

McKay knocked him out with a slashing stab from the side of his hand, making certain he was removed from action.

Carly stared at him, her face colorless.

A burst of machine-gun fire exploded off

the cliff, raining chips of granite as another man broke through the waterfall. McKay tackled him hard.

Across the bank, Carly watched the men grappling. Their images seemed blurred, like old film flickering on a bad screen.

Only it wasn't film.

The danger was terrifying and real. Either the attack was a random robbery or these men were after Daphne. The daughter of the governor of Santa Marina would be worth a fortune to the right people, Carly knew, and even as a girl, Daphne had been coached in security procedures by her father's staff.

The man on the ground coughed, struggling to sit up. McKay was busy grappling with the second attacker as the first surged to his feet, looking for his fallen weapon. Blind instinct sent Carly plunging down the rocky slope to get the gun first.

"Carly, stop," Daphne hissed.

"Stay back," she snapped. Stumbling, the attacker made for the weapon glinting in the sunlight. He smiled as he lunged forward, not far from the rock where Daphne was hidden. The smile fled as Daphne hurled a champagne bottle at his face, and Carly swung up a metal pipe from the prop pile, toppling him to his knees.

Daphne closed in and hit him on the head with a sandbag to finish the job, while Carly gripped the pipe protectively, ready to help if necessary.

Something whined through the waterfall behind her, sending up a spray of glittering silver. The world seemed to tip, pain exploding through her side.

Her knees buckled. Around her, water flashed like smoke, and her vision blurred. She tried to ask if her crew was safe, but the words came out jumbled. She looked for McKay, desperate when she couldn't find him.

"Daphne?" The word was a mere breath of sound, swallowed by the savage burning at her side as she fell.

"Carly, can you hear me?"

McKay clamped a towel over Carly's side. Beneath the welling blood, he saw the ragged path a bullet had torn through her skin.

He cursed when she didn't answer. The sight of blood spreading over Carly's blue shirt had stunned him. Then his training kicked in and he scrambled to stabilize her, controlling the blood loss.

Daphne knelt beside him, her face white but determined as she fought down panic.

In the distance came the sound of frightened questions. Otherwise all was quiet.

"How bad is it?" Daphne whispered.

"She hit her head when she fell. She probably has serious blood loss combined with a head injury," he said grimly as Carly began to twist in his arms.

He managed to hold her still as he heard the distant two-note whine of sirens. "About damned time," he said savagely. Even as he spoke, Inspector St. John seemed to melt out of the trees, flanked by three armed men. They had cuffed two attackers between them, and McKay was glad to see that being gentle wasn't high on St. John's list of priorities.

"Are any of you hit?" The officer rounded the waterfall, and his gaze swept down, hardening as it settled on Carly.

"She took a bullet. Possible trauma to the head when she fell."

"We've got an ambulance en route."

"Damn it, en route isn't good enough." McKay snapped. Despite his steady pressure at her side, she was losing blood fast.

Daphne looked up with an audible intake of breath. "Inspector St. John, what are you doing here?" Her face lost its last hint of color. "Did my father send you?" She swallowed, pushing out the words. "You think this was meant for me?"

"No way to know, Miss Daphne," the police officer said gently. "Not until we question these men."

McKay saw her shudder, just once, before she clamped down on her fear. "Do something for Carly. My God, if she doesn't —" She was blinking hard.

"She will," McKay vowed. "I'll see she gets through this." He was already replaying the attack, searching for clues to motive and source, cursing the fact that Carly hadn't stayed where she was supposed to stay.

But the blame was his. He should have been faster. He should be the one lying hurt, not Carly. Pain was part of his job description, right next to danger, no private life, and risk of life and limb. Carly was a civilian, and his job was to keep her safe.

He'd failed, and because of that Carly was wearing the blood right now.

McKay couldn't shake the cold weight of that knowledge as he looked down at her strained face. He barely noticed when Daphne touched his hand. The siren wail was very close now, but time seemed to stretch out, measured in eternities before three men in white jackets scrambled up the rocks carrying medical kits and oxygen equipment. Inspector St. John pulled him away from Carly as the medics went to work.

Nikolai Vronski chose a peach and studied it carefully. "Report."

"The work is being done at this moment."

"The details were made clear?"

"All of it arranged by phone, as you required." His subordinate, a former champion weight lifter with buzz-cut blond hair, put a cellular phone on Vronski's granite coffee table. "They will phone me when the work is finished."

Work. As if they were writing a report or building a dam. At another time Vronski might have found it amusing.

He slit a wedge of skin gently from the peach. "And the payment was accepted?"

His subordinate permitted himself a slight smile. "With no problems. I thought it wise to haggle about the price at the last."

Vronski stared at the tender, peeled peach. "So they wouldn't think we gave too much, too easily. Very thoughtful, Sergei." He fingered the neat piles of hundred-dollar bills stacked near his right hand, more money than he could once have imagined. It was pleasant to riffle through the bills, watching the ugly face of the American president gleam in the tropical sunlight. But something continued to bother him. "It might have gone badly today."

"The threats had to be carried out. You had no choice."

Something moved in the depths of Vronski's eyes. Regret, or perhaps simply weariness. "A man always has a choice. You forget that at your peril, Sergei."

"Of course, sir." The athlete nodded, silent and respectful.

"That is all. Go below and check on Yoshida."

In the quiet that followed, Vronski's hands closed on the neat pile of bills. He raised his face to the sunlight and closed his eyes. "So it begins," he whispered.

She tried to make sense of the voices. She needed to tell McKay that something was on fire, maybe her side, but the sound wouldn't come.

Someone kept shaking her, the movement like metal teeth dragged across her burning skin. She asked if Daphne was safe, if her crew was unharmed. She asked again and again.

No one seemed to hear.

Chapter 10

Blackness blurred into gray. Weight pressed down on Carly's chest.

Can't breathe.

Light burned into her eyes. An eternity came and went, followed by silence that faded, rising into muffled sounds. Someone was talking, touching her forehead. McKay . . .

No.

Disappointment fell with crushing force. Where was he? Where were Daphne and the crew?

She blinked as a woman in a white coat held a light before her eyes, every movement making Carly's head ache. She wanted to tell her to stop, but the woman's voice was too gentle. Her espresso-colored skin was smooth when she took Carly's pulse.

"Daphne?" Carly winced at the effort to speak, her throat painfully dry. "Where's Daphne?"

The woman put down her light and laughed. "She's pacing right outside your door. You two appear to be quite a team."

"A regular Laurel and Hardy." Carly's fingers tensed. "She's not hurt, is she?"

"She's as healthy as anyone can be with three gallons of coffee racing through her system. How do you feel?"

Carly rubbed her forehead and felt the outline of a bandage. "Like I got shot out of a cannon." She tried to move and gasped at the immediate burst of pain. "I feel as if I lost an argument with a cement truck."

"You're in spectacular shape, considering that you've been shot. You also took a nasty bang on the head when you fell."

Carly stopped trying to move, the effort too painful. Even thinking hurt. "Who are you?"

"Dr. Harris." She released Carly's wrist and slid her stethoscope neatly into her jacket pocket. "We've stitched you up and given you something for infection and pain. You've lost a fair amount of blood, so Mr. McKay contributed a pint to help you out. Ms. Brandon was ready to slit her own wrist to help, but your types don't match. She was furious, in that well-bred way of hers. A good friend, I'd say."

Carly smiled at that. "The best."

"Mr. McKay is outside with Ms. Brandon right now. He doesn't drink coffee, he just scowls. He's frightening my staff to death."

"Was he hurt?" Carly was almost afraid to ask.

"Completely unscathed. I think it angers him that he couldn't take a bullet for you. Interesting man." Her eyebrow rose. "Macho, but interesting. He said a lot of things when he carried you in. Most of them do not bear repeating."

"He carried me in?"

"He also maintained pressure on your side, cutting down on blood loss until the medics arrived, probably saving your life. All in all, he seems like a good man to know." The doctor's eyes crinkled when she smiled. "I'd better send in your friends, so you can stop worrying. Only for a few minutes, however."

Carly felt a sudden stab of nerves. "I need to brush my hair, and this hospital gown is —"

"Don't worry, he's not going to see anything but your smile. You will smile, won't you?" The diminutive physician grinned wickedly from the doorway. "In my experience, good spirits make good medicine."

Daphne came in first, looking pale and edgy and trying to hide it. "It's about time you woke up. You always did know how to sneak out of a tight spot and leave me holding the bag. Or in this case the champagne bottle."

"At least you had good aim. What happened? Who were they?"

Daphne smoothed Carly's pillow. "Too soon to tell. The police are questioning them now."

"How are Hank and the crew?"

"A few bruises, and the grip was cut on the leg. Otherwise they're all fine. They're downstairs arguing about who gets to see you first."

Carly took Daphne's hand. "What about you?"

"Only a bump on my arm, but I was terrified." Her voice broke. "Don't ever do that again."

"Do what?"

"Try to protect me, dammit. I know what you were doing."

"You think this had something to do with you and Uncle Nigel?"

"I don't know what to think. I told you how he's been acting. Right now I'm angry and I'm scared. If anything had happened to you —"

Carly squeezed her hand. "Let's not play what if." She fought back a yawn.

Dimly she heard footsteps, then the door closing. Sleep was working through the edges of her mind now that she knew the others were safe.

But safe from what?

The question drifted as sleep closed in.

Carly awoke to shadows moving on the wall.

McKay was sprawled in a chair beside her bed, his sleeping face lined with strain. Beneath his unbuttoned jacket, she saw the edge of a leather holster.

She closed her eyes, memories slamming through her. McKay crouched and pulled a gun from his bag, moving with no hesitation, as if violence was familiar to him.

Who *was* he?

She turned her head on the pillow. He sat up instantly, one hand snaking beneath his jacket.

To reach his gun, as if by reflex.

His face was hard and watchful, relaxing only after he had checked the room. "Welcome back."

She raised one hand, tracing his cheek. "You're cut."

"Dr. Harris tells me I'll survive." His jaw was a tight line that betrayed no emotion. "Other people might not have been so lucky. Dammit, why didn't you do what I told you?"

"I'm not used to taking orders. I'm not used to gunfire and armed attackers, either."

"You should have listened to me. Next time —" He shook his head.

"Next time what?"

"Just a figure of speech."

Carly knew she should follow up, but she was too tired to argue. Instead she reached out, taking his hand in hers. "Thanks for the blood."

"It seemed the thing to do at the time since you were bleeding all over everything and scaring the staff."

"I hate it when that happens."

Emotions roiled across his face, then control won out, as it always did. "You had us worried."

"I was a little worried myself."

She watched him pull his chair toward the bed and angle it slightly, so that he faced the door. So that he could see anyone approaching before they saw him.

"What happened today?" Something was very wrong here, and he knew things he should be telling her.

"Yesterday, you mean."

She blinked. "I've slept that long?"

He nodded, cradling her fingers in his palms. "Your wound is clean and healing nicely. Dr. Harris says you can leave tomorrow if you promise to take things easy."

"You didn't answer my question."

Carly's throat was dry and she was afraid of the questions pounding in her head. "Who were those people?"

"Preliminary reports say they were local gangs involved in a turf dispute. We happened to get in the way."

Carly pulled her hand from his, reviewing her blurred memories of the encounter. "Why would local gangs pick a remote location on private land for a confrontation?"

"Who knows? If they were smart, they wouldn't be criminals."

"The first man seemed to be looking for something. Or for someone."

"I doubt you were thinking too clearly at that point."

"But you were," Carly whispered, chilled by the memory of how cool he had been, how lethally he had responded. "You were prepared. You had a gun in your bag. You've been in situations like that before. Just like at the fitness center on the ship."

"Forget about me."

Carly felt pain sliding into anger. "Don't change the subject, McKay. I don't buy this talk about a turf war."

"Then ask the police, not me." He ran the back of his hand gently over her cheek. "Better yet, lie back and practice relaxing. Those stitches must hurt like hell."

"They would if I weren't shot full of woo-woo medicine." She studied her hand, which seemed to be connected to her body at an unusually great distance. "Definitely woo-woo."

"Daphne told me to get her when you woke."

"Why? I just talked with her."

"Yesterday."

Carly lay back with a sigh. Everything was becoming hazy. She moved her right arm slowly and winced. "When can I start shooting again?"

"When the doctor says and not before." There was a snap to McKay's voice that hadn't been there before.

"I can't lounge around here in bed. I've got film to shoot and my crew —"

"Your crew has some time off while you recuperate, courtesy of your boss. Hank tells me your preliminary film received a round of applause when it was shown in New York. There's even talk of a bigger budget." He studied her face. "Congratulations."

Carly forced herself to focus on the good news and stop obsessing about Daphne's safety. She was hardly an expert on criminals and their behavior, so the turf-war story could be right on target. With that thought firmly in mind, she shoved at the covers. "It's a start."

"Of what, a beach house in Malibu and a rambling estate in the south of France?"

"No, professional recognition and economic independence. I don't want to make commercial footage for television forever."

"What then?"

"None of your business." Her secret goals were too fragile to share with anyone. She tried to sit up, only to find McKay gripping her shoulders to hold her still. "I need my clothes. Then I need to get up."

"The doctor gave strict orders. You're off your feet until tomorrow, Sullivan."

"Let me up," Carly snapped, furious to be so weak. Desperate for answers that he wouldn't give. Ignoring her pain, she shoved away his hands. "I know how far I can push myself."

"Too far. Just the way you always do," he said grimly. "How's your stomach, by the way? No doubt you forgot to mention that to Dr. Harris."

Carly jerked on her robe. "I'll manage my own health, thank you." If and when her stomach got worse, she'd seek a medical opinion, but not before. In any case, it was hardly his concern.

He moved in front of her as she started to

stand up. "Stop fighting. I'll leave you in peace if you promise to stay in bed."

Carly looked away. "Agreed."

"I'll hold you to that." McKay moved tensely to the door, and Carly saw two long welts at his neck and a bandage across his wrist.

Her breath came hard and sharp. "You didn't tell me you were hurt anywhere else."

"Because it's not important." With a shrug, he shoved open the door, letting it swing wide behind him.

Chapter 11

"You don't look like someone who's resting," Daphne said icily as she entered Carly's room. "What were you two fighting about?"

"Same old same old," Carly said wearily. "The man couldn't give an honest answer under deep hypnosis and Pentothol."

"He was honest with me. Your problem is you can't stop obsessing. First work, now McKay." Daphne planted her hands on her hips. "I know you perfectly. You're demanding to get back to work."

"Your point?"

"Are you a complete idiot bent on self-destruction?"

"One out of two isn't bad." Carly closed her eyes and rubbed her forehead. "Please stop. This is not a first-class moment for me, and I'm busy trying to be stoical." She smiled faintly. "While I obsess."

Daphne shook her head impatiently. "Someone has to hiss at you. You've been hurt. The only thing on your mind right now should be rest and recovery."

"Aren't you curious about why the man carries a gun?"

146

"Maybe he has a military background or some involvement with law enforcement." Daphne made a minor adjustment to Carly's pillows. "Did you ask him?"

"He kept changing the subject."

"Maybe you should stop looking for problems."

"I'm good at finding problems, bad at relaxing."

"Don't I know it. In the interest of keeping you quiet, I've already asked Father for a background check on McKay. He told me not to worry. That should make you feel better."

"It doesn't." Carly stared at her linked fingers, trying to smile. "There's some good news. I hear we were given an extension with the filming."

"Five blissful days, and I expect you to rest for every one of them." Daphne studied Carly thoughtfully. "Let me guess the real problem here." Her brow rose. "The problem isn't with him, but you. You're worried that you're not in control anymore. In short, you're terrified things might be getting personal."

"Not a chance," Carly snapped. "No way is this turning personal. He's just a face on my monitor." She pulled the covers over her head. "And if I could actually believe that, everything would be rosy."

Daphne wrestled the covers away. "Welcome to the real world — messy, confusing, and chaotic."

"Messy and confusing is what I expect every day in my work. My life is supposed to be different. That stays clean, simple, and uncomplicated."

"Not anymore."

Carly stared at her friend. "When did you become so sane and sensible? In school, you were the one who fell in and out of love with nauseating predictability. It was hunk of the week with you."

"And you were the one who bolted in the opposite direction at the first hint of a real relationship."

"This is *not* a real relationship. It's not even a semi-relationship."

"Of course it isn't."

Carly pulled the sheet back over her head. "I hate it when you agree with me. Why don't you go torture some other postsurgical patient and leave me in peace?" Her hand shot out, gripping Daphne's. "I didn't mean that. I'm edgy today."

"No, you're scared," Daphne said perceptively. "It hurts to suddenly get reacquainted with your hormones. And your heart."

"Don't bring my heart into this. Hormones, yes. But no heart involvement is taking place anywhere soon." Carly sat up and crossed her arms. "I owe him for saving my life, but the owing stops here. Everyone knows that mixing business and pleasure is a mistake."

"Bogart and Bacall did it beautifully. So did Tracy and Hepburn."

"I refuse to talk about this anymore."

"Then let's talk about me." Daphne toyed with the cuff of her linen jacket. "I think . . . I need your help."

Carly couldn't keep the surprise from her face. "You never ask for anything."

"I am now." Daphne pulled a box out of her leather bag and set it on the bed. "The Tradewind Foundation is finally ready for real publicity, and this tape is the beginning. We have three clinics established now but my goal is twenty, and as soon as the cruise is over I'm tracking major sponsors." Daphne turned the boxed videotape restlessly. "This tape is the first of a series focusing on island children at risk. We're ready to send out ten thousand copies to businesses and foundations around the world, and I was hoping you could put in a word with the cruise line. We could use their sponsorship."

The public saw Daphne as a jet-setting

clothes horse, but Carly knew the real woman beneath the gloss. Daphne was as staunch a fighter as her father, and she was determined to see that the children of Santa Marina had access to the best medicine available. For two years she had worked tirelessly to make that private dream come true. Now it seemed she was ready to take her dream public.

"Get me ten copies and I'll shoot them off to the right people." Carly frowned as Daphne turned to pace restlessly. "Wasn't David helping you with that?"

"David has been wonderful. He funded this first video, then steered me to possible sponsors last year. I only wish we had had more time together." Daphne twisted her engagement ring. "I want a real home, a real marriage, but we can't even agree on a wedding date. Maybe we'll get married via camcorder over the Internet."

"I doubt the wedding night would be very satisfying. What else is bothering you?"

Daphne took a deep breath. "I just got the news this morning." Her voice trembled. "I'm pregnant."

"Pregnant?" Carly sat back, stunned. "As in Lamaze classes and transition breathing?"

"The whole amazing, miraculous thing. I'll probably be terrible at motherhood. I'll be thrown out of prenatal classes and throw up at the worst times." She touched her stomach wistfully. "But I want this baby desperately. I want a family with David, even if neither of us has any idea what's normal. David has no family at all, and I lost my mother so young that she's only a blurry memory." She sank onto the bed next to Carly. "Maybe you could film the delivery. On second thought, no. If I have to scream for an epidural, I'd rather not have my hysteria immortalized on digital film."

"You'll do exactly what's right." Carly squeezed her hand. "How's David taking the news?"

"David? I refuse to convey the most exciting news of my life over the hiss of a transatlantic phone connection. It will have to wait until he returns in two weeks."

There was a light rap on the door. "Daphne, may I come in?" Nigel Brandon's voice sounded tight with worry.

"He's been outside talking with his security chief from Santa Marina," Daphne whispered. "I don't want him to know about this, not until I've spoken to David."

Carly drew her finger across her lips.

Daphne nodded gratefully. "Come in," she called.

Nigel Brandon was the height of elegance

in a gray tropical suit and an Hermès tie. "Still getting into trouble, I see." He gripped Carly's hands tightly as he searched her face. "How are you feeling?"

"Nearly human again. It's lovely of you to come."

"Lovely?" For a moment anger flashed in his eyes. "I should have prevented what happened. You should never have been hurt."

"It's not your fault. We're not even on your home territory here. Bad luck put us in Barbados at the wrong place and the wrong time."

"Bad luck. I suppose you could call it that." A muscle worked at his jaw. "Is your room adequate? Is there anyone you need to contact?"

"Only my crew. After that I need to get back to work."

"Your crew is booked into a resort hotel in Bridgetown near the beach. They refused to return to the cruise ship without you." He gave her a stern, fatherly look. "Set aside any thought of work for the moment. That bullet missed any deep tissue, but you can't disturb those sutures." He put his hand on Daphne's shoulder. "Meanwhile, we have a little surprise for you."

He opened the door and ushered in a uniformed attendant carrying a huge arrangement of orchids and four large foil-wrapped boxes.

"The flowers are from me, the chocolate from Daphne. In addition, we hope you will fly back to Santa Marina with us when you leave the hospital. I've missed having noise and turmoil at the estate, and you two always make me feel young again."

Carly grinned. "Or very irritated."

Brandon raised one brow, every inch the distinguished and powerful public official. But the warmth in his eyes enfolded Carly, just as it had the first summer she'd spent with Daphne in the islands. "Not in the slightest. Will you come?"

"I wish I could, Uncle Nigel." Carly sighed. "But I can't possibly leave this project in the middle."

"I told him you'd say that." Daphne sent her father a smug look, waving a set of keys. "Uncle Patrick's estate is only thirty minutes away, and everything's arranged with the staff. You'll love Paradise Cay."

"But I —"

"There'll just be you and McKay, along with half a dozen of my uncle's staff."

"Why McKay?" Carly asked suspiciously.

"Because you'll try to overwork. If McKay's there, he'll keep you in line." Daphne smiled innocently. "I phoned your boss in New York and she agrees with me."

"You did *what?*" Carly closed her eyes. Daphne and her father never thought twice about meddling when they were convinced they were right — and they generally were.

"Mel was wonderful. Your footage has created a real stir. Thanks to you, the CEO of the cruise line wants to triple their ads."

Carly couldn't seem to breathe. "Triple?"

"That's what Mel said. While the lawyers thrash out a new contract, you are hereby instructed to take R and R on Barbados, then pick up the cruise ship on its return to Miami. Mel wants you to think about some new ideas, of course, but nothing concrete until the lawyers are finished. In short, you have nothing to do but rest for a few days."

"Triple," Carly repeated breathlessly, sinking back against her pillows. "That means we could add a water sequence, maybe some snorkeling. Even scenes of night-life aboard the ship."

"You could shoot the snorkeling scene right at Paradise Cay. There's a gorgeous beach that's completely private."

"Enough talk about work." Nigel gripped Carly's hand tightly, almost con-vulsively. "Rest, that's an order. Now I need to go talk with Mr. McKay."

Carly stiffened. "Why?"

"I want his description of what happened."

"Daphne and I can tell you that. Why do you need his version?"

"The more information we have, the sooner we'll find the people who did this. I want them all behind bars for what they did," Brandon said savagely. "But that's my worry, not yours."

Carly sighed. As usual, they had pegged her just right. It would be a relief to leave the hospital, and the privacy at Paradise Cay would give her a chance to take some sample shots of McKay. Maybe something with mist and water in the free-form rock spa.

The thought left an odd hitch in her chest.

"Go on," Daphne said to her father. "I know you have appointments this afternoon. I'll take care of Carly." She swung her leather bag over her shoulder. "But first I'm going for coffee."

"Shouldn't you skip the coffee now?" Carly caught Daphne's warning look. "I mean — you've had five cups already."

Brandon studied his daughter with concern. "You are looking edgy, my dear. Maybe you should see a doctor while you're here."

"Don't start nagging or I'll ask why *you* were up pacing half the night."

Brandon frowned. "Bloody paperwork, nothing more."

"You'd tell me if there was something wrong." Daphne's voice grew tight. "You would, wouldn't you? No secrets?"

"Absolutely." Brandon cleared his throat. "You, my dear, are to do nothing," he said sternly to Carly. "I'll have my spies checking just to be certain. All I can say is I'm sorry. I'd give anything if all this had never happened." His hands fisted, then opened slowly as he bent to give her a hug. "Now rest."

Daphne shook her head as the door closed behind him. "There's something wrong, I know it. He's quarreled with his staff, which he never does. Lately he broods, staring at the ocean and saying nothing. If I can't work the truth out of him, I'll tackle Inspector St. John. Remember when he caught us trying to run away to St. Thomas one summer?" Daphne smiled at the memory. "He pointed to his car, drove us home, and never said a word to anyone. We were in misery for weeks, certain he would blow the whistle on us, but he never did. It seems like yesterday, doesn't it?"

There was no answer.

Carly was sound sleep.

Daphne straightened the covers, but her eyes, as she watched Carly sleep, were dark with worry.

Chapter 12

The governor-general of Santa Marina looked like a man trying hard to convince the world and himself that his problems were small ones, though the lines of strain around his eyes argued otherwise.

"First of all, Mr. McKay, I want to thank you for saving the lives of two people I love greatly."

McKay rubbed his jaw, wishing he had taken the time to shave before their meeting. "No thanks necessary, sir. The ladies managed very well on their own. Your daughter took down one man with a champagne bottle, and Carly finished him off with a rusty pipe."

The two men were sitting in a secluded courtyard at the rear of the hospital. Sunlight filtered through fronds of lush bamboo ringing a pool filled with goldfish.

The surroundings should have been restful, but Brandon looked anything but calm as he measured McKay. "I won't fault you for what happened at the waterfall. None of us saw it coming. But I can't say I like it." He took an angry breath. "You've been fully briefed?"

McKay nodded. "You've been receiving threats from an undetermined source. I'm to provide Carly Sullivan with round-the-clock protection until the situation is resolved."

Brandon's eyes were probing. "The cruise-line documents list you as a rancher from Wyoming off for some sun and fun in the Caribbean. I pulled strings to get someone here, and I want to be sure you're the best. Are you one of those Delta Force men?"

McKay said nothing.

Brandon steepled his fingers. "Navy SEAL?"

"I'm the man who'll do the job, sir."

"And that's all I need to know? When Carly came close to being killed and is lying in a hospital bed?" The governor tossed a piece of gravel from hand to hand, his expression savage. "Understand this: My life doesn't matter, but my daughter's does, as does Carly's. I want assurance that if another attack occurs, you won't bungle things. One man isn't enough."

McKay clamped down hard on his anger. "I have all the support I need, sir. If circumstances warrant more manpower, it will be available." He weighed his next words carefully. "Meanwhile, you might want to ask why St. John and his people didn't notice the presence of one sniper and two associates until the attack was already in progress."

Brandon waved his hand impatiently. "A mistake, certainly, but St. John has explained that. There was a school bus caught in the middle of the road and his men had to push it out of harm's way. He offered his resignation for the mistake. I turned him down."

McKay rubbed his jaw. "Check on the driver and the bus company," he suggested. "And consider putting a new protection team on your daughter. When their faces aren't known, men work more efficiently."

"Good point. But what about Carly?"

"I'll be keeping her close. No one will get to her again."

Brandon stared at him in stony silence. At the other end of the pool a goldfish burst to the surface, rocking the overhanging bamboo. "I want whoever did this caught and locked behind bars." His tone implied that he wanted even worse done to them, but was managing to control the instinct. "I want them soon, McKay."

"Perfectly understandable. Who are your most likely candidates?"

"Our criminals have never attacked political targets before, but we're not ruling them out. We're also checking newcomers from Jamaica who've been scouting territory in Santa Marina."

"Anyone else?"

Brandon frowned at a pair of carp gliding in the shadowed depths. "Do you know a man named Nikolai Vronski?"

"A Russian?"

Brandon picked up a piece of bread from the bench and tossed it into the water. "Part Russian, part Gypsy, part Kirghiz. He used to be highly placed in the government. Later he moved abroad to pursue lucrative joint ventures in Albania and Southeast Asia. Six months ago he contacted me about a possible business venture. We were supposed to have our first meeting this week, but Vronski pulled out suddenly, and I haven't heard from him since."

"You think there's a connection?" McKay hid his impatience. If Vronski had become a key suspect, McKay should have been informed immediately.

"So far he checks out, and the capital investment he's proposed for Santa Marina would be a considerable boon to modernizing our port facilities. On the face of things the project looks perfectly solid. In spite of that, I believe I'll dig deeper."

Waves rippled against the stones at their feet as Brandon tossed out another piece of bread. "I pulled strings to get you here, McKay. I won't apologize for that. Carly needs my protection now, just as she did after her parents were lost." His mouth curved slightly. "I still remember her first visit to Santa Marina and all the trouble she and Daphne brewed between them." Still smiling, he reached into his pocket. "Here are the keys to my Triumph. It pulls slightly to the right on the curves."

"I'm not planning on driving anywhere."

"Yes, you are. My brother has an estate here on Barbados, though he's often in Europe these days. I've arranged for you to take Carly there while she recovers. I hope you'll consider Paradise Cay as your own."

"I don't think that's a good idea."

"Odd, Carly seemed to think the same thing."

He was being maneuvered, McKay knew, and he didn't like it one damned bit. "I'll have to check with Washington."

"No need. Everything's been cleared. Strings, remember? I didn't become governor-general without knowing when to cash in old debts."

"I'll check, just the same."

"As you wish. Meanwhile, Daphne and I

are staying in a secure location in Bridgetown. I'll speak to St. John about a new protection team for my daughter. Now I'd better go rescue Carly from Daphne before exhaustion sets in."

"You should be proud of Daphne. She doesn't scare easily. She's also got great aim with a champagne bottle."

"I am extremely proud of her." Overhead the tall trunks of bamboo creaked in the wind. "Of both of them. I'll leave Carly in your hands. God help you if you let anyone hurt her again." And then he was gone, the bamboo fronds waving delicately behind him.

"Things are heating up." Izzy's voice was tinny but otherwise clear through the secure cell phone he had provided McKay before they had left the ship.

"Damned right. What story are you using to explain your unexpected absence from the ship?"

Izzy gave a racking cough. "Some kind of terrible bronchitis. I'm really laid low. I'll probably be sick for a week."

"Just in time to join the cruise ship on its return swing," McKay said dryly.

"No doubt of it. In fact, my illness is entirely at your disposal, chief." Izzy's voice tightened. "How's Carly?"

"Healthy enough to be arguing again. Brandon arranged for us to stay at his brother's estate here on Barbados while she recovers. We leave tomorrow."

"Fast work."

"The man knows how to pull strings with the best of them." McKay paced the deserted corridor, his voice low. "Brandon mentioned a Russian interested in port development in Santa Marina. Nikolai Vronski — what else do we have on him?"

"He's been involved in dozens of speculative joint ventures in Southeast Asia. He's successful, but not well liked. Seems he wants things done only one way."

"His," McKay concluded dryly. "Still, it's not a crime to be arrogant and egotistical. What about the driver of the bus that stalled so conveniently?"

"I tapped into the local police computers, and according to their investigation, he was not a resident of Barbados, just a fill-in driver for the day. The police checked his address and found it was an abandoned warehouse. Here's the interesting thing: One of the other drivers noticed he had a wallet full of crisp U.S. hundreds."

McKay watched the door to Carly's room. "Nice money for driving a bus. I'd enjoy a chat with our friend."

"Don't hold your breath. The Barbados police haven't found him yet. He could be in Miami or Munich by now. He had enough juice to get just about anywhere."

"Keep at it, Izzy."

"Russian tanks couldn't keep me away. If the situation starts heading south, I know a secondary location on the island. The house belongs to an old friend from my Thailand days, someone you can trust without question. Keep it in mind."

"I will. It's always nice to have a Plan B. Meanwhile, I want notice of anything unusual in the hospital or on the grounds."

"I'm on it. Brandon gave me a contact in security who's keeping me briefed."

"Right now I don't trust anyone. We rely on firsthand information only, understood?"

"That's a roger. Anything else?"

The conversation with Daphne's father continued to nag at McKay. "See what you can dig up on the Russian, Vronski. Brandon seemed worried, as if he wanted the deal to be solid but he had his doubts."

"Too good to be true, maybe?"

"Something like that. Dig deep." McKay fingered the welts at his neck. "Let's find out why Comrade Vronski isn't winning any popularity contests around the world."

"Will do. Expect a call at 1800 hours. Meanwhile, keep your powder dry."

"That and everything else," McKay muttered.

Chapter 13

Twenty-four hours crept past. Carly watched the ceiling and stared at her unpolished fingernails.

By the time Dr. Harris gave approval for her to leave, she was fully dressed and ready to go out of her mind.

"Is the equipment squared away?" she asked Hank, who had come to see her off.

"All done, boss. The sum total of damage to the equipment was one camera and one tripod."

"Thank heavens for that."

"Yeah, pretty strange. All those valuable electronics, and those creeps didn't steal a thing."

"I doubt they're big in the brains department, Hank. That explains why they're bushwhacking tourists rather than running legitimate businesses in Bridgetown."

"I still think it's odd." Hank took the bag Carly was fussing with, zipped it expertly, and stowed it at the foot of the bed. "So what's next?"

"I'll phone you from Paradise Cay over the weekend after I work through a few ideas."

"Don't rush on my account." The cameraman stretched lazily. "I plan to be hard at work sampling rum punches by the pool for the next twenty-four hours. You should forget about work for a few days, too. Concentrate on getting well." He beamed at her. "Maybe have a fling — avoiding those stitches, of course. I can imagine a dozen ways to spend the time off. Not one of them involves a light meter." His brow rose. "Unless it's used very creatively."

"I'm going to rest and then I'm going to work," Carly said firmly. "Romance isn't anywhere in the picture."

"Whatever you say." Hank glanced at his watch. "Almost noon."

Carly stared at him suspiciously. "Expecting someone?"

"McKay. He told me to —"

The door opened, and McKay strode in as if he owned the hospital, looking tall, lean, and dangerous in black jeans and a black jacket. He scanned the room, saw Carly reach for her bag, and picked it up without a word.

"I can carry my own things, thank you."

"We can argue feminist theory some other time."

Carly swallowed her protest. Her side was hurting and she wanted to leave before she was tempted to sink back onto the bed. "I have to say goodbye to Daphne and Uncle Nigel."

"No need. They're going to meet us at Paradise Cay."

"Time to hit the road, boss." Hank rolled a wheelchair over from the door. Balloons decorated the back, and a huge floppy bear sat on the seat. "All yours."

"I can walk," Carly said stiffly.

"Relax and enjoy it." McKay pushed her gently into the chair, then set the bear on her lap. "You two look good together." He moved behind the chair and nodded at Hank. "I'll handle the hard case from here."

"Sure." The veteran cameraman studied McKay in silence, then nodded. "Take care of her. If anyone can, it's you. I'm on call if you need me."

To Carly's amazement, he gave a crisp salute, turned sharply, and marched from the room. She thought he muttered "semper fi" as the door closed.

"What did Hank mean?"

They were threading through heavy Bridgetown traffic. McKay was savoring the hair-trigger responsiveness of Nigel Brandon's vintage Triumph and trying not to notice Carly staring at him. "You mean the salute?" He swept neatly past a smoke-belching truck. "It was a mistake. He took me for a Marine."

"Because of the semper fi thing." Carly tilted her head "Are you?"

"I am not, nor have I ever been, a member of the illustrious United States Marine Corps," McKay said dryly.

"There must have been some reason he said that."

"Maybe it was his idea of a joke."

"No way," Carly said thoughtfully. "Hank was a Marine. He considers it some sacred brotherhood thing. He'd never joke about it."

McKay shrugged. "Beats me."

Carly studied him some more, and he felt the force of her deliberation. "I still can't believe Uncle Nigel let you drive his Triumph. This car is his pride and joy. He never lets anyone near it, even Daphne." Carly frowned as they shot past a stalled bus, then maneuvered deftly around an old man on a bicycle. "I suppose he was right to let you drive. Your reflexes are amazing." She stiffened as McKay cut past a delivery van with inches to spare. "Where did you learn that?"

"Here and there."

She made an irritated sound. "Sure.

Right. Why do I even bother to ask, when I know you won't tell me a thing?"

"There's nothing to tell."

Ahead, offices and apartment buildings gave way to bright shingle houses with flower-covered steps.

McKay looked across at her, smiling faintly. "Tell me about you instead."

Carly sniffed. "I'm not falling for that trick again. *You,* this time. Answers, McKay."

"I'm boring. You're not." The road forked, and he feathered past a mud-spattered silver Audi. "You're an adopted member of one of the most important families in the Caribbean, but you choose your own path and work until you drop. That interests me."

"Because you enjoy masochism?"

"No," he said frankly. "Because I enjoy you." The road snaked uphill, curving past quiet beaches. "Tell me about the Brandons. It can't have been all pleasure being relocated to paradise."

Carly sighed. "I came to the island at a bad time. Daphne and her father took me in and treated me as if I were family, with no questions asked." She looked down, watching waves race onto the beach. "A few months later I became a legal part of their family, and I can never repay them for giving me a place to belong at a time when I desperately needed one."

"I doubt they consider it a debt to be repaid." McKay glanced back as the Audi pulled off the road and stopped under a tree. "Obviously you and Daphne have stayed close."

"Stop steering the conversation. We were supposed to focus on you. I warned you I would ferret out every detail of your murky, misspent youth."

"Murky?"

"Definitely. Come on, McKay. Let's have it."

He stared at the twisting road. "My first fifteen years were spent in Wyoming. After that I left to see the world. I signed on to a freighter and worked my way through every time zone and back again. Nothing murky about it."

"A good experience?"

"Absolutely. I grew up on that freighter."

"Didn't your parents want to keep you close to home?"

"They were smart enough to let me go. I was pretty wild back then." He grinned, re-membering fast cars, faster women. "A dusty little mountain town couldn't hold me."

"So what do you do now?"

"I've still got some land in Wyoming. And I've got my nautical-design work." It wasn't too huge a lie. Equipment research and modification happened to be one of his specialties.

McKay slowed for a curve and saw the Audi reappear in his rearview mirror. He bit back a curse, feeling little hairs rise along the back of his neck. "How about something to drink?"

He didn't wait for her answer, turning off at a roadside stand stacked high with coconuts, mangoes, and a dozen kinds of exotic fruit.

"You keep watching the mirror."

"That makes me a good driver."

Carly sat very still. "That makes you someone who's worried."

McKay swung out of the car, one eye on the road. The Audi was nowhere to be seen as he ordered two lime-mango coolers from an old woman with leathery skin and a high-voltage smile. He carried Carly her drink and finished his while standing where he could see the road in both directions.

"Is he there?"

"Who?"

"The silver Audi who's been following us since the last fork in the road," Carly said tensely. "I'm a photographer. I see things, remember?"

"Must be a coincidence."

"You saw him, too. I think that's why you turned off."

McKay slid into the driver's seat and revved the motor to a smooth purr, then headed uphill. The Audi was nowhere in sight when he passed the wooden sign with a painted seabird, which Brandon had told him marked the turn for Paradise Cay.

"Almost there." Towering trees closed in around them, filtering the sun to a rich green haze. "Brandon said the house is about a mile ahead. Have you visited before?"

Carly shook her head. "I've heard it has a location to die for, with ocean views in three directions."

All McKay cared about was whether it was well protected in four directions.

They climbed through cool green shadows that offered only brief glimpses of the ocean below. At the top of the hill, he glanced back through the trees toward the main road.

He caught a flash of silver as the Audi slowed, crawling past the turnoff behind them.

Carly turned in her seat. "So much for coincidence. What do they want?"

"I have no idea, but it probably has nothing to do with us. This is a small island and that was a public road."

"Nice try, McKay. Did you get the license number?"

After a moment he nodded.

"We'd better tell Uncle Nigel. Maybe it's one of his people."

Or maybe not, McKay thought.

Chapter 14

A public road, hell. They had definitely been followed. At least McKay hadn't persisted in his lame story once she'd confronted him directly. For an insulting routine like that, she might have had to kick him.

Not an easy job with sixteen stitches.

Carly stared at the road behind them and tried to understand why this was happening. Every answer brought her back to Daphne and her father, a powerful public official who happened to be honest — and because of that honesty, a man with an army of enemies.

Her side hurt as they bumped over the gravel. Judging by McKay's grip on the wheel, he was trying to make the ride easy on her. *Two points to the rancher from Wyoming,* she thought, biting down on a wave of pain. Except she was pretty sure he wasn't currently a rancher or anything close. If Hank thought he was a Marine, he couldn't be far off.

Then why the slick lies?

Carly was still grappling for answers when the road curved sharply and the house burst upon them, its pink stucco walls ringed by bougainvillea, hibiscus, and graceful jacaranda trees in full purple flower. Against that explosion of color, ferns crept along curved steps and lined the shaded porches that overlooked the crashing surf of the north coast.

McKay slowed the Triumph and stopped precisely at the edge of the steps.

Not exactly on a dime, but close enough.

"Haven't I seen this house on *Lifestyles of the Rich and Decadent*?" he asked dryly. "Why did Patrick Brandon locate here, instead of Santa Marina?"

"He said Santa Marina was too small for both brothers. He's involved in tourism, fishing, and construction here, and when Barbados became a free nation in 1966, he prospered right along with them. Now he's a pivotal part of the new government." Carly watched sunlight gild the sweeping balconies. "He works harder than a dozen men and he leaves nothing to chance. He's been very good to his brother, and he's helping Daphne keep her foundation afloat."

"It sounds like she'll make a difference with the Tradewind Foundation. A lot of women in her position wouldn't make the effort."

"With Daphne, what you see isn't always

what you get. She can curse like a stevedore and drink like a Dane, but when she commits to something it's complete, without limits."

"A good friend to have." McKay reached across the gearshift and unsnapped Carly's seat belt, then rounded the car to open the door. "Take it easy."

"I believe I can manage to get out without fainting dead away." Despite her bravado, it was getting harder to ignore the stabbing pain in her side, and she was glad to take McKay's arm as they climbed the steps. At the top, they were met by a tall man with mahogany skin, a pristine white jacket, and a spectacularly broken nose in an otherwise aristocratic face.

Carly summoned a smile. "Archer, you haven't aged a day since I last saw you at Santa Marina."

"Tell that to my stiff back. But first come here and give me a good, long hug."

Carly did just that. "Watch the right side," she murmured. "It's still a little touchy."

Archer released her carefully. "There won't be any problems here," he said. "I'll be taking care of things during your stay at Paradise Cay." He glanced at McKay, his eyes narrowed. "I believe it's time you introduced me to your friend."

Carly flushed. "Sorry. This is Ford McKay, who's involved with the commercial I'm shooting. Ford, meet Archer, who has been with the Brandons since time began. Possibly before, for all I know."

The men scrutinized each other, shaking hands in utter silence. Carly looked from one to the other. "Am I missing something?" Long seconds passed before Archer cleared his throat and released McKay's hand from a hard grip.

"I'm glad you settled that," Carly said. "Whatever it was you settled."

Impassive, Archer took Carly's small satchel and pushed open the front door. As he did, a flashbulb snapped and Carly stepped into the foyer to a chorus of cheers. Her crew gathered around her in a ragged line, waving balloons, party hats, and tropical drinks with little paper umbrellas while Nigel Brandon enjoyed the scene from a wing chair. Daphne stood at his side, looking very pleased with herself.

"You put them up to this," Carly said, glaring at Daphne.

"No. I did." The crowd parted to reveal a tall woman with razor-cut red hair. Tiffany earrings were a sleek counterpoint to her black silk pantsuit.

"Mel?" Carly stared at her boss in shock. "What are you doing in Barbados?"

"Making sure my wunderkind and crew are safe. You look pale. Sixteen stitches, was it?"

"They won't stop me from finishing the project," Carly insisted.

"Good. Now I want to see our new model." She pursed her carefully tinted lips and studied McKay. "Hank didn't exaggerate. I believe we're going to make advertising history, my friends." She held out her hand. "A pleasure, Mr. McKay. I owe you for protecting Carly and preventing the destruction of our equipment. I don't like being in debt, so tell me how I can repay you. Within reason, of course."

"I guess the vacation in Bali is out."

Mel gave a throaty chuckle. "Afraid so. Of course, if our client responds to Carly's finished footage the way I expect him to, our budget will go through the roof."

He pretended to deliberate. "How about half a million in small, unmarked bills?"

Mel patted his cheek. "I like a dreamer."

"In that case, I'll settle for Carly having some time off — no faxes, phone calls, or E-mails."

Mel Kirk brushed a hand across her perfectly cut hair. "Our client is concerned about delays. He doesn't want the competition coming up with a similar campaign in time to air this fall." Her mouth hardened. "I should be able to iron out any problems when I get back to New York. Carly has as long as she needs, the same for the crew." She studied one glossy nail. "I'll need you all to be on that cruise ship when it returns to Miami, but we can discuss the details later. Right now I want Carly working only on one thing: getting well. Meanwhile, don't any of you get hauled in drunk and disorderly or you'll be completely on your own. You don't call me Captain Kirk behind my back for nothing." When the laughter had died down, she waved a little paper umbrella. "It appears I lost the rum punch that went with this."

Archer appeared, balancing a silver tray. "Perhaps you would enjoy some conch chowder to go along with your rum punch. We have tables arranged on the patio and a dessert cart when you're finished. We also have suits available if any of you would care to swim."

Carly's boss took the arm that Nigel Brandon offered most gallantly. "Now I see why they call this place Paradise. Sunshine, water, and handsome men everywhere." She followed Archer toward the patio. "Conch chowder, anyone?"

Daphne and her father were the last to leave. Though the visit had lasted less than an hour and Carly had sat for most of it, it was still an effort to hide her discomfort.

"You're tired." The sun was slanting low over the trees as McKay leaned against the wooden rail of the veranda, watching Carly carefully.

"Why would I be tired? It's still early."

"Getting shot and losing blood make most people tired. There's no need to pretend. It's just the two of us here."

"I never pretend." But Carly closed her eyes in relief as she sank back onto a lounge chair covered with chintz pillows.

"Stubborn to the bone," McKay muttered. He held up the cup of chamomile tea Archer had delivered moments before. "Drink it."

"Why are you giving all the orders?"

A half-smile played across his mouth. "Because I can. You're going to be running below par for a week, Sullivan. I plan to take full advantage."

"To be arrogant and high-handed?"

"To goad, torment, and manipulate you into some semblance of a healthy lifestyle."

"I can barely contain my excitement." She cracked open one eye, sighing as she saw him holding up the tea cup. She drank the rich herbal brew and then sank back in the chaise. "Archer never forgets anything. If you take lime slices in your tea once, he'll still remember it twenty years later."

"He looks like a man who knows what kind of wine to serve with crème brûlée." McKay braced one shoulder against the edge of the veranda. "He also looks like someone you don't want to mess with. What happened to his nose?"

Carly chuckled. "He played cricket when he was a teenager. When his team went to London for a tournament, someone commented that he had a girlie face."

"Probably the last thing the poor fool managed to say before he got a broken jaw."

"And three missing teeth. Uncle Nigel happened to see the scuffle. He arranged for Archer to be released from jail, then asked him to become his personal assistant."

"And history was made."

Carly watched shadows race over the pool. "Archer has gotten Daphne and me out of some tight scrapes."

"I heard about your cliff climbs. What else did you and Daphne do for excitement?"

Carly shifted as her side began to ache. "I don't know you well enough to go into details."

"What else do you need to know? My favorite color is green, my favorite ride is a quarter horse, and my favorite beer is Foster's."

"How nice. That certainly fills in all the gaps."

Out to sea, a yacht cut cleanly along the horizon, its sails bloodred in the setting sun. "Looks like a fire ship," McKay murmured.

"What's that?"

"It's an old naval tactic. A ship was set aflame, then sent toward an enemy fleet. The fear value alone was devastating. Fire on a ship was every sailor's nightmare." He paused. "And still is."

"You know a lot about the sea," she mused.

"I was raised on Hemingway and C. S. Forester. Every boy should be." McKay frowned. "Every girl, too, come to think of it."

"Are we going to argue feminist theory now?"

"I'm feeling too relaxed to argue." He grinned. "Unless you want to take the ugly revisionist male point of view."

"Thanks, but I'll pass." Carly watched the yacht cut toward the east. "So you enjoyed all those freighters you took?"

"They had their moments."

"That's all you can say?" Carly rolled her eyes. "This feels like a bad rerun of *Remington Steele*."

"He was a liar. I'm just taciturn." McKay slanted her a smile. "There's a difference."

"None that I can see." Carly shifted again.

"Your side hurting?"

"I'll survive." But she didn't protest when McKay found a pillow and slid it under her arm. "You don't need to fuss over me."

"Someone has to. You won't take care of yourself."

Carly closed her eyes. "Why don't you go away so I can sleep?"

"I'll take you inside first."

Carly didn't want to think about having his arms around her. That long, sexy body holding her. For some reason, the image short-circuited all her good sense. "I'll stay right here, thanks."

"You agonize over angles of sunlight and the condensation on a champagne bottle. You remember batteries, light meters, and location details, but you forget to eat. Why?"

She couldn't resist a slight grin. "Because I can."

But the truth lay deeper.

Carly knew she worked at a fever pace because she had to. When the colors raced in her head and the pictures flowed, she couldn't see anything else. In those moments she and her camera became a perfect organic unit.

"Not true. Because I need to," she said quietly. "Just like my mother."

She stared at the bougainvillea petals floating in the pool, feeling all the old emotions churn to life.

Hating them. Hating herself for having them. "Let's pretend I didn't say that."

"I thought you didn't pretend."

Carly winced, moving again. "Let's pretend I didn't say *that,* either." She slid a hand over her eyes and thought she heard McKay laugh.

He shifted her pillow slightly, and again the pain receded. The man could be insidiously gentle when he wanted to be. If she didn't get away from him soon, she might find herself addicted to his attention.

She frowned as he put a box on the table beside her. "What's this?"

He opened the box and pushed aside the tissue. "A last-minute gift from Daphne. She asked me to give it to you when we're alone." He gave an approving whistle as he produced a delicate column of white lace with tiny satin straps. "Nice choice. As I recall, she also suggested that I help you change."

"I'll strangle her," Carly hissed. "I'll do it slowly and painfully."

"Why?" McKay studied the sweep of nearly transparent lace. "She's definitely onto something here."

Carly plucked the gown from his fingers, her face aflame. "Then let her wear it." She pushed stiffly to her feet, trying to ignore the instant burn along her side. "I'm going inside." She walked stiffly toward the house.

Relief warred with anger as McKay swept her up in his arms. "I can walk," she said through clenched teeth. In about two days she could.

"Congratulations. Next week we'll work on wind sprints."

"I could learn to hate you, McKay."

His hand settled briefly on her cheek. "You're afraid of me for some reason, but you don't hate me."

Carly closed her eyes as he carried her through the quiet house. "The great swami sees all, knows all."

"It doesn't take a swami to see that you're uneasy." There was a steely edge to his voice. "I won't cross the line, if that's what's worrying you."

Despite all her efforts, her head sank against his chest. "Why should I believe that?" she asked sleepily. "Why should I trust a stranger?"

"Because you can."

He carried her into a room with yellow walls and a white bed draped with white gauze curtains. She was too tired to ask or argue, too tired to keep her hands from circling his shoulders, burrowing closer against his warmth.

She was too tired to pretend she didn't hurt, didn't want a shoulder to lean on, just for a while.

"Go to sleep," he said, setting her gently on the bed. Through the open French doors came the distant crash of the surf and a breeze rich with citrus and roses.

"What about you?"

"I'll be nearby."

Carly looked up at him, touching his cheek. "Who are you, McKay? I don't know anything about you that counts."

"I'm the man who'll be watching over you while you sleep." A muscle moved at his jaw. "None of the rest matters."

Chapter 15

Paradise Cay was nice real estate, McKay decided, assuming you had a thing for extravagant multimillion-dollar homes. Since his lifestyle demanded a minimum of possessions and a maximum of mobility, he let his gaze skim past the English hunting prints and old Japanese porcelain, focusing instead on the house's interior security. He picked out infrared-beam motion detectors and pressure-sensitive mats. Doors and windows were wired to an internal alarm system.

Adequate, but hardly spectacular.

He made a mental note to check out the rest of the interior as soon as he reviewed the staff.

He found Archer in a garden at the side of the house, cutting roses that looked too perfect to be real. "I have some questions," he said.

Archer's big, powerful hands moved with skill, even tenderness, over the vines that clung to every inch of the east face of the house. "I'm happy to assist any way I can."

McKay watched the big, competent hands coax a blush-pink bud from gray-green leaves. "I expect you're responsible for a lot more than floral decorations in your work for Nigel Brandon, so I'll get to the point. I need to know the security layout here, including alarm systems, guards, and police patrol schedule. As you know, there was a problem, but it's not going to be repeated."

Archer pruned a stem expertly, nodding. "I'll see that you receive complete floor plans of the house and a layout of the estate, along with detailed staff schedules."

"I'll need names and photographs along with job descriptions."

"To be sure each person is where they should be when they should be?"

"That's the general idea."

Archer's brow rose. "Everyone on the staff was hand-picked by Patrick Brandon. Many of them have worked at Paradise Cay for two decades."

McKay crossed his arms. "Loyalty can be fickle."

"Your thoroughness is commendable, though disturbing. How else may I assist you?"

"What's your assessment of the situation?" McKay expected that a man like Archer wouldn't miss much. His impressions could be invaluable, especially since he was an insider.

"Santa Marina is a success story and everyone wants a part of that success."

McKay toyed with a crimson rose. "Criminals, too?"

"Sometimes. They talk, they make offers, and they threaten, but Mr. Brandon sees they are given no toehold on Santa Marina."

"What about Inspector St. John? Have you known him long?"

"At least three decades. We played cricket together. A good man."

McKay nodded. From what he had seen and read, Archer's assessments matched his own. "What about the grounds?"

"In addition to the domestic staff, there are three men here at all times for security."

"Armed?"

"Knives. There has never been a need for other weapons."

"There is now," McKay said grimly. "I was told that Inspector St. John has posted several of his men on the grounds, too. I'd like their names and photographs."

Archer trimmed a brown leaf from a perfect white rose. "I'll arrange it."

"What about beach access? I noticed a path leading from the swimming pool down through the woods."

"The beach is private, cut off by rocks at

both ends. The cove is too shallow for large ships, but smaller vessels pass nearby. Paradise Cay stands on its own headland, and at night the lights are visible for miles at sea."

McKay rubbed his jaw. "Any way to discourage visitors?"

"A heavy gate runs along the end of the steps, but it has never been closed in my years with the Brandon family."

"Close it," McKay said flatly. "It won't keep determined intruders away, but it could slow them down. And I want someone posted on the beach at all times."

"You're very careful," Archer mused. "For a rancher from Wyoming, I believe."

McKay gave a tight grin. "You should see me bring down a steer. It's a sight to behold. How about a tour of the house and grounds?"

"In that case, why don't you take these." Archer handed McKay a rainbow array of cut blooms, picked up his pruning shears and basket, then led the way into the house. "Have you known Ms. Carly long?"

"Four days. I saved her from getting backsided by a speeding volleyball."

"She must have been most appreciative."

"Not particularly. I misunderstood her business proposal for something more . . . personal. Women don't like being misunderstood."

"She appears to have recovered from her displeasure."

"If she has, I'd say that's her business," McKay said pleasantly.

"She is part of the family, and that makes her my business. You will not wish to cause her pain," Archer said. "Just as a note of information."

McKay shifted the roses to his other arm. "It sounded like a warning to me."

"I leave that to your powers of observation." Archer stopped beside a backlit portrait of a thin-faced Englishman in hunting pinks and an elaborate white wig. "She has always been a popular visitor on Santa Marina. She has never lacked for male companions since she turned sixteen."

McKay contemplated the aristocratic figure in the portrait. "Anyone serious?"

"Is that personal interest or a security question?"

"Both," McKay lied.

"Then ask her." Archer turned smoothly, opening a swinging door to a bright room with vaulted ceilings. Stainless steel ovens covered one wall, running perpendicular to a white marble counter that held a dozen small appliances. McKay noted a huge subzero freezer, a convection oven, and an indoor grill with an exhaust hood. "Patrick

Brandon must like to eat."

"He socializes a great deal as part of his work."

"Just a few small parties for him and three hundred close friends," McKay said dryly.

"Since Paradise Cay is an island show-place, much of his entertaining is done here." Archer's eyes held wry amusement. "An army still marches on its stomach, Mr. McKay, whether in war or in business."

McKay traced the side of a spotless copper pan big enough to hold a suckling pig. "Wellington knew exactly what he was talking about, which is probably why he blistered Napoleon in the end. Provisioning is everything. If a man can't eat, he can't fight."

"Something that every rancher from Wyoming would know," Archer said blandly. He interrupted McKay before he could frame a denial. "There's a vase in the freezer, if you wouldn't mind."

McKay was very conscious of Archer's scrutiny as he opened the massive walk-in freezer. Inside, meat was carefully sorted, packaged, and stacked on neat metal shelves. A neighboring wall held exotic chocolates and coffees in airtight canisters. "Those parties must be pretty spectacular." McKay carried the vase outside and watched the door close, sealing with a hiss.

There was even a gleaming temperature-controlled wine rack. "Everything the well-bred millionaire needs to enjoy the lifestyle to which he is accustomed."

Archer's face was impassive as he took the vase. "There is a much larger wine cellar below the house, of course. Some of the wines down there are a century old."

"Of course." McKay leaned against the polished countertop while the majordomo deftly arranged his roses. "Why the cold vase?"

"Roses last longer that way — the heat can be a problem here. Things bloom and die faster in the tropics."

"You're saying that beauty has its price?"

Archer didn't look up from his arrangement. "Or that speed has its price. Perhaps both."

McKay had a feeling that Archer was talking about more than flowers. They made a thorough circuit, crossing a library with floor-to-ceiling mahogany shelves and books that appeared to have been chosen for content, not decoration. Next came the ballroom, eerie and somber in the twilight.

Archer carefully straightened a fold in one of the damask curtains. "There used to be amazing parties here." He rattled off the names of two U.S. presidents, several members of the English royal family, and a well-known American starlet who had died tragically, all guests at one time.

"What about now?"

"Now most business is transacted discreetly on yachts or over cigars by the pool. Contracts are finalized during a quiet game of thousand-dollar-a-shot billiards in the conservatory."

"Nice job if you can get it."

Archer's eyes gleamed in the fading light. "Make no mistake, Mr. McKay. The Brandons all work hard, Ms. Daphne perhaps the hardest now that her heart is committed."

"I take it you mean to the Tradewind Foundation and not to the banker."

"Her fiancé?" Archer stood looking out at the swimming pool, lit by a dozen small metal lanterns amid the banks of bougainvillea. "He is most respectful and he dresses extremely well."

After a moment McKay smiled. "And you hate the hell out of him."

The man at the window neither agreed nor disagreed. "You still have the upstairs to see."

McKay watched Archer pad off down the corridor. If discretion had a human face, it would look just like Archer's, he decided.

The sky had gone dark by the time they finished checking the house. Next came the tennis courts and pool area, followed by a view over the cliffs to the narrow path that ran down to the cove.

"There's a man down there now?" McKay asked.

Archer nodded. "Inspector St. John arranged that this morning."

McKay rubbed the back of his neck. Paradise Cay was isolated, but isolation could be deceiving. The estate was far from impregnable, and he meant to follow up every security detail personally, starting with a list of problem areas to be discussed with Nigel Brandon the following morning.

He turned back toward the house. "We'd better go. I have several calls to make, and Carly might be awake by now."

Wind shook the bougainvilleas as they retraced their steps along the winding path. Lights shone in the library, and McKay heard a low scraping sound near the windows.

Every sense raced to full alert. He plunged through the doorway and found Carly at an ornate desk surrounded by sheets of crumpled paper. Her shoulders were hunched as she sketched with quick, restless movements, and whenever she moved, her chair leg scraped against the back of the window.

"Why am I not surprised?" McKay muttered. "If I gave her a fifty-pound camera, she'd probably try to bench-press it right now."

"She has always been very determined."

"Determined? Try stubborn, obdurate, intractable."

"Very literate. For a rancher from Wyoming," Archer added under his breath, watching McKay stride toward Carly.

"What are you doing?"

"Working. Go away."

"Dr. Harris had my promise to keep you quiet. If you refuse, I'll dump you right back in the hospital and see to it that you have no visitors."

"I feel great." As Carly gripped her sketch pad, McKay saw her face tighten. "Why don't you go hound Archer? I prefer to suffer in solitude."

"Suffering wasn't part of the doctor's prescription. Neither was solitude."

She twisted restlessly in her chair. "I can't relax until I've run through this location list."

"Keep this up," McKay said grimly, "and you won't be able to lift a camera to photograph anything."

Carly pulled out another sheet of paper.

"I've got to finish. Mel needs this list to finalize her budget."

"Mel gave you time off so you can recover." McKay swept up her sketch pad, scowling. "She's not hounding you; she doesn't have to. You're too busy hounding yourself, dammit."

Archer looked from one to the other, smiled faintly, and retreated down the hall. Neither McKay nor Carly noticed.

"You're going back to bed," McKay snapped.

"I'm not sleepy."

"Then you can stare at the ceiling or solve differential equations in your head, but you'll do it on your back."

"Touch this location list and you're toast, McKay."

"I'd be glad to tussle with you, but only after those sutures are out." Before Carly could react, her papers were jerked away and locked under his arm. "Why do you drive yourself this way?"

"None of your damned business." Carly stood angrily. "Stop interfering. Stop . . . distracting me." Her hands were white, gripping the back of her chair.

The pain was brutal, McKay knew. Not that she'd say a word. Stubborn right to the bone.

He cursed as her eyes filled with tears.

"I hate being sick. It makes me feel useless."

"You're going to be more than sick if you don't stop driving yourself." He picked her up and headed toward the stairs.

"I don't trust you, McKay. Just for the record, I'm not sure I even like you." Carly closed her eyes. "What I'm feeling is an inexplicable aberration. A hormonal surge, nothing personal." Her head sank onto his shoulder.

"Are you feeling this . . . surge right now?"

Carly sighed. "Definitely." Her eyes opened and she studied his face. "Daphne says I'm a complete idiot bent on self-destruction. What do you think?"

His mouth curved. "I'll take the fifth."

"She says I'm stressed out big time, but with the right man I'd turn to putty."

His body tightened at the thought of Carly turning to putty against him. "Daphne doesn't mince words."

"I think she's right. I should do something reckless for a change. Something dangerous."

McKay decided that the idea of Carly turning to putty with anyone but him was unthinkable.

"Want to give me some pointers?"

"Is that another offer? I wouldn't want to misunderstand you again."

"You mean me and you? Any idiot could see I'm way below *your* skill level. Why would you waste your time on me?"

"I can't imagine," he said dryly.

"I meant for you to tell me where to start, what qualities to look for in a man." She frowned. "Just hypothetically."

"Hypothetically," he repeated hoarsely. "Here's rule number one. If you can consider a man hypothetically, he's the wrong one."

"Why?"

"Because you don't take a hypothetical man to bed with you. You take a flesh-and-blood person with memories, needs, and an agenda." He laid her gently in the center of her bed and sat beside her, cursing the race of his pulse, cursing the heated trend of his thoughts. How had he gotten into this damned discussion?

Her tongue slid over her mouth, leaving her lips gleaming. "I'll keep that in mind. Anything else I should know?"

At the thought of her locked against a stranger, McKay's hands fisted.

"Something wrong?"

"Not a thing." Odd, but he couldn't drive away the awful image of Carly with another man. He opened his hand and rubbed his chest, dimly aware of a pain that wouldn't go away.

Satin pillows, linen sheets, and white gauze curtains framed her body as a soft breeze drifted in through the French doors, carrying the low whisper of the surf. He stared at her tumbled hair, her pale skin, her soft mouth, picking every word with care. "Here's rule number two. Choose a man with experience, so he will take the time to do things right. Roses on your pillow, champagne in the moonlight. Kisses that drive you both up for air."

Carly shrugged. "It's not going to happen. Everyone's too busy. Too self-absorbed and upwardly mobile," she said wistfully.

"The right man would make it happen." McKay found himself gripping the bedpost, mainly to keep from touching her. The tension moved, knotting at his groin. Suddenly he was far too aware of her breath, her skin, her perfume. "The right man would forget agendas and business and everything else while you turned each other inside out."

Her eyes darkened in the twilight. "Are we still being hypothetical here?"

His fingers tightened. He realized her robe had fallen from her shoulders. Beneath it she wore the lace gown Daphne had given her, its ivory fabric molding her breasts and making her skin gleam.

There was nothing remotely hypothetical about the sudden, hammering desire he felt when he looked at her. If he wasn't careful, he'd be shredding her gown and exploring all those ladylike curves.

"Sure we are," he said gruffly. "Absolutely." For a lie, it came out surprisingly well. Muttering a curse, he slid from the bed and tugged up the linen sheet. Even at that small movement, she winced, proving that what she needed most was a long rest.

And what he needed most was a long, cold shower.

McKay palmed the pain pills she was resolutely ignoring and shook out one tablet onto his hand. "Take it. I can see you're fighting the pain."

"I don't want to be groggy. Besides, I have to work. Work will take my mind off all the rest."

Without a word, McKay strode to the telephone.

"What are you doing?"

"Calling Dr. Harris."

"You wouldn't."

McKay began to dial.

"Fine, just fine. Give me the blasted pill."

With anger in every movement, Carly downed the medicine. "You still haven't told me anything about you."

"We'll talk about it later."

"No, we won't." She lay stiffly as he pulled a quilt over her and flicked off the light. "And I don't take orders." She yawned. "I *hate* taking orders."

Girding himself for another argument, McKay turned back to the bed.

She was already asleep, one hand beneath her pale cheek and her body curled beneath the quilt. Exasperation gave way to wry amusement as he stood in the darkness, watching the faint rise and fall of her chest while moonlight traced her cheeks.

He thought, not for the first time, how lucky they both were that she wasn't close to being his type.

In the darkness, in the silence, Nigel Brandon put down the telephone, replaying his last conversation, nuance by careful nuance.

Deception he understood. Greed equally well. Both were at work now.

He walked to the window, watching lights dart and shimmer in Bridgetown's busy harbor where yachts and trawlers, sloops and small rowboats rocked at anchor.

Free enterprise in all its rich diversity.

As he stared out, something continued to nag, to gnaw.

He walked back to the phone and dialed swiftly. "Inspector St. John, please," he said. "Immediately."

Two calls to make, he thought.

He hoped he hadn't waited too long for either.

Chapter 16

Carly opened her eyes, stretching gingerly in the channel of sunlight coming through the window. Then she froze.

McKay stood in the doorway.

Staring, just staring.

She sat up slowly. "What are you doing?"

"Watching you sleep." He wore jeans, low and snug at his lean hips. His chest was bare, still damp from a shower.

Carly swallowed a quivering knot of pure lust. "Adding voyeurism to your many character defects, McKay?"

His laugh surprised her, rich and relaxed. "I'm glad to see that you're feeling your old, nasty self. Care for breakfast? Archer's been busy this morning." He lifted a tray from the nearby table, not waiting for her answer.

Carly inhaled, then closed her eyes on a sigh. "If that's coffee you're carrying, you can name your price. Car, apartment, or bank account."

"In case you're unaware, bribery is illegal." He slid a steaming cup of cappuccino into her hands.

Carly savored a long, rich sip. "Archer is a genius. A dozen hotels have tried to steal him away, but he refuses to leave." She scanned the covered dishes on the tray. "Stay back. If Archer's famous avocado, mango, and bacon omelet is hiding under one of these silver covers, things might get messy."

"Bingo." McKay held out a warm plate with a steaming omelet accompanied by wafer-thin fried potatoes and papaya salsa. "I figure nothing can taste as good as this looks."

Carly took a bite. "Even better. The man hasn't lost his touch." She glanced up. "Why aren't you eating? If I know Archer, there's enough food for most of Barbados here."

"Already ate. Not all of us can sleep until eleven."

Startled, Carly looked at the bedside clock. "I never sleep past seven." She frowned, worrying her lip. "I need to start some sketches, then take a few test shots before —"

"Eat. Archer will be very unpleasant if any of that omelet remains. He told me that very clearly."

Carly began to eat, eyeing him warily. "You're being awfully nice. You must want something." Her fork froze in midair. "There isn't bad news, is there? If something's wrong with Daphne or Uncle Nigel —"

"They're fine."

Relief left her giddy, and she drank more of Archer's potent cappuccino to compensate. "Then let's have the bad news. Something's already wrong or it's about to be wrong, I can feel it along my shoulders."

"Nothing's wrong." McKay uncovered a plate with a goat-cheese crepe and fresh strawberries. He stole a bite before sliding it onto Carly's plate. "Just laying down the ground rules."

"I don't care for the sound of that."

"Relax. That's rule number one. Eating is rule number two. And if you have work to do or things to fetch, call me."

"Another rule?" she asked stiffly.

"Merely a suggestion. I can help you, so let me." He poured a cup of cappuccino and turned it slowly on a saucer. "I have some things in mind to fill your time."

Carly pushed away her empty plate. "No more of that fitness stuff. I've had my dose for the year."

He took her tray, then gestured toward the door. "Actually, this is something I think you'll enjoy."

Carly shrugged on a robe and followed him down the hall, reluctance in every step.

"I want to work."

"And you will. One half hour of work for every three hours of rest. That's rule number three."

She came to a quivering, furious halt. "I'm going to pretend I didn't hear that, McKay. You have no right, absolutely no right to —"

"Dr. Harris agrees with the me."

"Oh she does, does she? How long have you two been plotting and planning this?"

McKay studied his sleek black watch. "One hour and thirteen minutes. Approximately."

"I won't be — be *handled* this way."

"Nigel Brandon agrees, too."

"You called him?"

"He called me. He's dropping by later to see how you're doing. Meanwhile, if you want to work, you have to rest. Otherwise, you go back to the hospital."

Carly jammed her hands in her pockets. "And just how am I supposed to relax? With a mint julep and a sandalwood fan? By giving myself a pedicure?"

McKay took her arm, hiding a smile. "Anyone ever tell you you're beautiful when you're angry?"

"No, and don't start now." Her eyes widened as he opened a set of doors at the end of the second-floor hallway. "If this is some sort of spa thing, I'm out of here."

"See for yourself."

She stepped inside and all protests fled. Speechless, she ran a finger along velvet cushions and a gleaming lacquer projection table. "It's a screening room," she said with hushed awe. "One of the best I've ever seen." She struggled for composure. "Of course, the collection is probably limited. Quirky. You know, action thrillers and a few Fred Astaire."

McKay pressed a button and a lacquered cabinet door slid open to reveal floor-to-ceiling shelves with hundreds of neatly labeled videos. Another area held DVDs. Carly braced one hand on the back of a velvet chair. "Did the earth just move for you, too?"

There was a glint in McKay's eyes. "If it happens, I'll be sure to tell you." He ran a finger along the labeled rows. "So what will it be? We've got all the greats here."

Carly raised an eyebrow. "No, don't tell me. For you, that would be *Road Warrior* and *Pulp Fiction*." She crossed her arms smugly. "Right?"

McKay went to a shelf, pulled out a tape, and tossed it to Carly.

"*The Godfather*? Okay, it was decent work,

assuming you can forget the gory horse-head scene."

"Forget? That was American cinema at its finest."

"No way." Carly slid the tape back into its slot. "If you want classic, there's only one choice. Great plot, an amazing cast, and music that lingers." She moved along the alphabetized rows, selected a tape, and waved it at McKay. "The best of the best, as fresh today as it was in 1942. Won three Oscars. 'Here's looking at you, kid.' "

" 'We'll always have Paris,' " McKay countered. "Okay, Bogie works for me. Take a seat. Archer gave me full operating instructions. He even made us food."

When Carly was comfortable in the front center seat, he flicked a remote and sent the room into darkness. Without a word he handed her a bowl of popcorn drowning in decadent swirls of butter, then eased her back against his shoulder as stirring strains of music filled the room.

In minutes Carly was swept away to Rick's smoky café in war-torn Casablanca.

They were arguing even before the final credits began.

"No way. Bogart was good, but he was better in *To Have and Have Not*. And what about *The Maltese Falcon*?" Carly huffed.

"Competent, but I'll still take Brando or Pacino in *The Godfather* or John Wayne in *The Searchers*." McKay stood up and stretched. "I almost forgot Gary Cooper in *High Noon*."

"Yes, but —" Carly stopped as Archer appeared.

"Ms. Kirk is downstairs to speak with you. She looks quite upset."

"I'll be right there. There must be another schedule change." Carly looked down and realized she was still in her robe and nightgown. "I can't see her dressed like this."

"Why not? You're supposed to be having R and R."

Carly stood uncertainly in the doorway, then shrugged. "You've got a point. I'd better go."

"I'll be nearby if you need me."

Carly couldn't imagine why she'd need his help for a simple conversation with her boss. "Thanks. If a fight breaks out, I'll be sure to call you."

When she opened the door to the sunny study overlooking the pool, she was surprised to find Mel pacing nervously, her hands at her back. Hank was sitting in a chair near the window, a camera bag at his feet. "Mel, I'm glad you and Hank could come. But why —"

"No, don't say a word. I have to get this off my chest first. I haven't slept all night and I want you to understand that I fought them every step of the way."

"Fought who? What do you mean?"

Mel tugged at one earring. "Those slack-jawed fools in New York who can't see anything but balance sheets," she said viciously. She glanced toward the door. "Is McKay still here?"

"Yes, but —"

"Good. He should be here. Make him stay. You two take some time off, as much as you like. If money's a problem, I'll pay."

"Time off? But you said —"

"I know exactly what I said and what I planned, but I've been overruled by a bunch of tightwad accountants with liver spots for brains. Men who wouldn't understand energy and creativity if they bit them on their bony asses."

"What she means," Hank said tightly, "is that you've been replaced."

Carly's hands went to her stomach as pain burned deep. "I've been pulled?" She felt a tremor race through her. "Fired?"

Hank nodded, his experienced eyes filling with sympathy. "They started whining about the costs after the incident at the waterfall. They said they didn't want production delayed, but my guess is that they're really afraid of liability. Mel fought them tooth and nail, even offered to sign waivers. She assured them you'd be better and faster than anyone else they could find. Of course, this business with Griff in Martinique hasn't helped matters."

Carly wasn't aware of McKay behind her until he touched her shoulders. "Maybe you'd better sit down," he said gently. But as he studied Hank, his eyes were icy. "Maybe we should all sit down for the explanation."

Carly sank into a wing chair, feeling nothing but stabbing pain in her stomach. "What about Griff?"

"He gave a press conference, the little weasel." Hank toed the edge of his long camera case. "He and his girlfriend have been complaining to anyone who'll listen that you demanded money from them under the table. According to their story, when they wouldn't pay up, you arranged for someone else to fill in for the body shots. Now the media are on it and the client's furious at the bad publicity."

Carly ran shaky hands over her face. "I never asked Griff for a penny. Ask Daphne. Ask anyone."

Mel leaned close and gripped her hand. "I

know that and so does everyone else who's worked with you. You'd never compromise your vision for money." She smiled thinly. "We've argued over that particular issue often enough. Griff is just trying to recoup his losses and twist things so he comes out looking like a poor, misused victim. I had no idea he was such a barracuda, or I never would have hired him." Mel patted Carly's shoulder. "Don't give up hope. I'm flying back tonight to meet with the client and his bean counters to convince them these accusations are groundless. Daphne and Hank have helped me put together a new film clip from the old footage, and I plan to use it very effectively. If I have my way, you'll be back at work in a week."

Carly stared blindly at the floor, reeling from the unexpected blow. "Thanks for all you're doing, Mel." It was a struggle to speak, to think against the roar in her head.

"To hell with thanks. Just get yourself well, then plan some more fabulous footage. Once I have you reinstated, we'll have to move fast."

"If I'm reinstated." The words trailed off.

"You will be."

Carly heard McKay move behind her. "Here's another tidbit to toss in at your meeting," he said coldly. "If you want me involved, the job is Carly's. Otherwise I'm not interested."

Mel's smile was slow and feral. "I like how you think, McKay. Yes, I'd say that's going to help a great deal. The client's wife seemed very taken with you, and I doubt she'll want a replacement."

McKay's eyes narrowed. "That's the deal. If Carly's out, I'm out."

"You hear that, Hank?" Mel called to the smiling cameraman.

"Every word."

"Good. Now let's get going. I've got a nasty little war to plan." She tugged on her sleek, black jacket. "I'll send word as soon as I have something solid. Meanwhile, you stay put, and keep that fertile brain working."

"Of course," Carly said mechanically. Her fingers refused to stop twisting. Back and forth, back and forth. "I'll — see what I can come up with."

Mel exchanged a worried glance with McKay, then drew a breath. "There's one more thing. I don't like it, but it's standard procedure under the circumstances. I . . . I have to ask for your camera equipment and any film you shot as part of this assignment."

The words slashed deep, leaving Carly

shaken. "Film? My working camera and equipment . . ." She drove back the tears and hurt. "Of course. Since I'm fired."

"Temporarily," Mel said tightly. "As temporarily as I can make this. You can still work with your own camera."

"I didn't bring equipment of my own. I didn't expect to need any." Carly stared blankly out the window. "My case is downstairs. I'll go find it."

"Hank will help you. I don't like this, Carly. Actually, I hate it. But we'll have everything straightened out soon."

The words came in a blur. Carly felt McKay's hand on her shoulder in a hard grip. When he stood back and opened the door, she was surprised at the anger that burned in his eyes.

Not his fight. Not his problem. The man hated cameras. He should be relieved to be done with the whole business.

She shook her head, unable to think of anything beyond what she had to do next: packing up the gear that she'd babied and cherished to produce a dozen outstanding projects. She knew that when she closed the case and turned it over, the pain would be like losing her right hand.

"I'll get them back." Her fingers closed to quivering fists. "No mush-for-brains actor like Griffin Kelly is going to stop me from finishing this shoot."

"That's the idea. Fight back. The little weasel will fold as soon as he gets one good shove. I only wish I were there to deliver it personally."

Carly reached out blindly and squeezed his hand. "Thanks. In case things don't work out, I want to tell you you're the best I've ever worked with, Hank." Her throat was dry and tight. No matter how she struggled, tears threatened.

"Hell." The big man cleared his throat. "Let's go get this wrapped up. I'm flying back to New York with Mel, and there are a few heads I'm going to bash in as soon as I get there."

Upstairs in the quiet study, McKay watched Mel pace. Now that Carly had gone, she was considerably more agitated.

"Is it true?" he snapped. "Can you get her job back?"

"I'm going to give it my best shot, but reinstatement won't be easy. Griffin said some damaging things at a sensitive time."

"All lies."

"Of course they were. But they still cause damage." She strode to the door, then turned. "You'll stay on here?"

"As long as I can."

"Good. This goes beyond work with Carly, beyond mere dedication." She blew out an angry breath. "It's going to cut her off at the knees. Take care of her."

"Oh, I plan to."

She nodded. "I figured you would. Once it really hits, she'll need to talk, to cry."

"I'll be here," he said tightly. "You can count on that."

Mel smiled and for the first time all day there was a glimmer of pleasure in her eyes. "That's exactly what I hoped to hear you say."

Chapter 17

She stood at the window above the sea, her mind a blank.

It could have been hours before the stirring of the curtain against her cheek broke through her wall of pain.

As awareness returned, instinct made her check her watch before tackling the afternoon's work.

Except there was no work. Job, equipment, and deepest identity had been stripped away by the malicious lies of people with no talent and no scruples.

Carly pressed a shaky hand against her eyes. She *was* her work, and she measured nearly all the joy she knew in the quiet moments of planning or in the wild flood of creative power that swept over her when a shoot went well.

Now all that joy had been ripped from her.

She stared at her hands, clenched on the windowsill, sun dappled and tense. These hands had fussed and finessed, straining to claim a square of light or a curve of shadows against a world that never stood still. Her heart had sung to that chase, every skill awakened.

But not now.

Her fingers tightened. Word traveled fast in her small, competitive world. There would be a sprinkling of sympathy calls and even more calls from the curious or outright gleeful. Then the offers would dwindle and her fees would plummet.

Inside a week everyone in their business would know the story — true or not — and her career would be wrecked.

Fair or not.

The ocean stretched before her, savagely beautiful in the heat of midday. Its vast, azure sweep seemed to enchant even as it mocked, shrinking all her worries into insignificance. For Carly, only one photographer had ever caught the sea's fierce beauty and terrible allure. The framed photograph stood on a shelf behind her. There beneath towering skies rose the granite fingers of Ouessant, a fog-shrouded island in the Sea of Brittany.

Carly had no need to turn to see those deadly rocks banked high with sea spray. She carried the photo when she traveled, a reminder of the mother she had never understood, the mother who had been drawn inexorably by an island that claimed wrecks like a Siren claimed lovers. Carly whispered the ancient curse that every French seaman knew too well:

"Qui voit Ouessant voit son sang."
Who sees the rocks of Ouessant sees his own blood.

The photo was her mother's finest work, finished less than a month before her death.

Carly saw the rocks now, ancient and hungry, a place where wild winds carried the wail of desperate ghosts determined to drag the living down to share their restless graves. It was a place where dreams were shattered and life lost all meaning. To Carly, that would always be the heart of the sea, endlessly taking, endlessly consuming, permitting no master but itself. As it had taken and consumed her parents.

She heard those winds now, felt the angry slap of sea spray. She saw her own cold, granite Ouessant.

She turned away from the sea, turned away from the icy winds of memory. With the last of her will, she sank into a chair and studied the dark, brooding photograph sitting directly above the spot where her equipment had been.

Her tears were silent and bitter.

It hurt to watch her slide through the day. When he brought her food, she ate mechanically, her eyes on the window, focused on a place only she could see.

McKay was smart enough to know that all the usual platitudes would be useless. He'd been pulled off assignments often enough to know the pain of dismissal and how deeply it cut.

When she needed to talk, he'd be close. Until then, silence was his best gift.

After he made his hourly check of house and grounds, McKay found his way to the kitchen.

Archer looked up instantly. "How is she?"

"Just the same. She eats because I tell her to and says nothing. Then she just stares at a photograph of the sea."

Archer's mouth thinned. "Her mother's work, taken someplace in France. A terrible, depressing place. I've never liked the shot." He floured a mound of dough. "Mr. Brandon just phoned. He'll be arriving within the hour. He sounded furious."

"As he should be," McKay growled.

Archer passed him a cup of coffee, shaking his head. "Carly's work means everything to her. Any fool can see that. How could they take that away from her?"

"I'm sure they would say it was nothing personal." McKay stared out the window at the immaculate grounds. "Strictly business."

"Business be damned," Archer snapped.

"She has the best eye and the most skilled hands they'll ever find."

"I believe her boss was flying back to say exactly that. Carly won't go unrepresented."

Archer punched at the mound of dough meant for feather-light French brioche. "That she won't. Mr. Brandon has already set his lawyers to work and they're out for blood. They're pushing for breach of contract at the very least, and they've already slapped a libel suit on the viper-tongued actor who manufactured that story about her asking for bribes."

"Good. Let him take some heat. He's the sort who'll cave in as soon as the pressure mounts." McKay glanced at his watch, then stood up, his coffee untouched. "I'm going down to check the beach."

"There's an officer posted."

"I prefer to check things myself." He trusted no one, although McKay didn't mention that.

As soon as he left the house, he headed for the narrow steps that led through dense forest to the cliffs and wound from there down to the sea. Once he was out of sight of the house, McKay slid a small, secure radio from his pocket.

"Izzy, come in."

Static whispered. "Right here," Izzy said quietly. "I can see you."

"I can't see you, which is perfect. Any news about that silver Audi?"

"Registered to a couple of tourists from Iowa. It was reported stolen from their hotel last night. We're checking them out, but I think the story will hold. Meanwhile, the Barbados police have been notified to stop the car if it's seen." Izzy cleared his throat. "How is Carly holding up?"

"Not well. It's hard not to take a thing like this personally. Attached to her career as she is, being fired is devastating. I hope her boss can turn things around."

Izzy hissed. "Damn!"

"What's wrong?" McKay tensed, scanning the foliage.

"Stand down, McKay, just some badly placed thorns." Leaves rustled. "According to the business plan Comrade Vronski filed in Santa Marina, he had half a million in a local account. As soon as the contracts are signed, he's to wire in five million more."

"What's the catch?"

"He insists on having his own security force at the finished port facility. It's a non-negotiable point in all his ventures worldwide."

"I can't see Brandon accepting those

terms. Santa Marina is remarkably stable, and their crime rate is the lowest in the Caribbean."

"That could be changing. There have been a dozen armed robberies in the last week."

"Interesting they should happen right now."

"Isn't it? Vronski gets a nice bargaining chip in negotiating for his own security force. With crime on the rise . . ."

"Very neat. Vronski gets exactly what he wants, yet keeps his reputation clean. Very neat indeed. Brandon might need more help than he realizes," McKay said thoughtfully. "Keep me posted, Izzy. Right now I'm heading down to check the beach. Brandon is expected here within the hour, and I want to make a final sweep before that. Something tells me we'd better stay on our toes."

The sun was a ball of crimson against the horizon when Nigel Brandon strode up the steps to Paradise Cay.

McKay was glad to see two men escorting him. From their cool, alert posture he made them for plainclothes police.

"How is she?" Brandon demanded.

McKay shook his head. "She's trying, but it doesn't help. She wanders, then sits and stares out the window as if she isn't really here."

Brandon cursed, his eyes icy. "I couldn't get away any sooner. Business," he said, waving one hand irritably. "I need to speak with you after I've seen Carly."

"I'll be here."

Brandon looked out at Carly, sitting in a lounge chair near the pool. "She hasn't moved since I arrived."

"She hasn't moved for almost an hour," McKay said tightly. "And she's not asleep, because I checked her a few minutes ago."

"Hell." Beneath his expensive tweed jacket, Brandon's shoulders were set in a stiff line. "Someone is going to pay for this, believe me."

McKay watched him stalk outside, then halt at the steps, forcing a smile onto his patrician face.

Carly noticed none of it, staring at the waterfall artfully constructed of natural stones at one end of the swimming pool. She looked up as Brandon sat beside her, stroking her hair. McKay felt a sharp pressure when she buried her face against Brandon's chest.

Rejection was always raw, always personal, no matter how hard you tried to keep things objective. McKay suspected that for

Carly, because of her mother's success, being pulled from the shoot was especially painful.

He rubbed a knot at his neck, forcing his eyes away from the emotional scene on the patio.

Keep it loose, McKay. Keep it focused.

Most of all, keep it from turning personal, even though it's getting harder by the second.

"She didn't like it, but I'm going for blood." Brandon's face was shuttered as he rejoined McKay in the library. "I've got a team of lawyers who have instituted libel suits against both the agency and that fractious little actor. I won't allow them to harm Carly's career this way." He pulled at the cuffs of his suit jacket. "If she's not back on assignment by the close of business tomorrow, they'll all face hefty damages and a well-focused media campaign of my own, which is something I know exactly how to orchestrate — and the nastier the better." He took a last look out the window at Carly, then turned to McKay. "Meanwhile, there's something you should know. You recall that I mentioned the joint venture port project I am considering."

"With a man called Nikolai Vronski."

Brandon nodded. "I heard from him a few

hours ago. He's concerned about the recent robberies we've had in Santa Marina, so he's lowering his investment commitment from five million to two. In addition, he's pushing hard for a private security force at the finished port, something we would never consider under normal circumstances."

"But now circumstances have changed." McKay crossed his arms, smiling thinly. "Paradise just got a little less perfect."

"Something like that. There might be a connection, so I thought you should know."

"Glad for the tip. I presume you're digging deeper?"

"I'll have every detail of the man's background before the negotiations resume," Brandon said flatly. "I don't like being manipulated or played for a fool." He rose with a sigh. "Since I can't do anything more here, I'm returning to Bridgetown. Daphne and I are staying in a friend's town house there for the moment."

"Well guarded, I hope."

"You may be certain of that. Crime seems to be becoming a problem everywhere."

"Then round up the usual suspects," McKay suggested, recalling the worldly police chief in *Casablanca*. "If your normal criminal elements aren't involved, they might know who is."

Brandon's brow rose. "I'll relay the suggestion to Inspector St. John. He asked me to tell you that he is available if and when you need him." He slanted a last, anxious look at Carly. "Take care of her for me. Keep her safe." He met McKay's look frankly. "In whatever way will help her most."

McKay caught the meaning and the unvoiced request. Both would push him where he couldn't afford to go.

He stood up, rigid and controlled. "Personal isn't an option, sir. This is an official mission. I am under orders."

Brandon studied him from the doorway. "You're also a man. You've got a fine record, Commander McKay. Especially that last mission you led in Columbia."

McKay stiffened, aware of how many strings Brandon had pulled to access that bit of information, which was as black an op as they came.

"No denials?"

McKay shrugged. "Clearly, they would be useless. My compliments. You're very well connected, sir."

"Not well enough, it appears." A beeper chimed softly in Brandon's pocket. "Business again. Do you know what a famous

Chinese philosopher once said? Ruling a country is like frying very small fish. Delicacy. Speed. Preparation. All are key."

McKay cocked one hip against the mahogany desk. "Another Chinese genius said to keep your friends close and your enemies closer."

Brandon flashed a brief smile. "I will be sure to keep both points in mind, commander."

Chapter 18

McKay couldn't sleep.

Beyond his open window the sea crashed through air rich with jasmine and moonlight.

He gave up on the bed and moved to a sofa near the open door where a balcony wrapped around the elegant second floor. Carly's lights had gone out two hours ago, but every creak had him lurching to his feet to see if she was awake.

She hadn't moved once.

McKay crossed his arms behind his head and watched shadows flirt with moonlight on the floor.

Take care of her, Brandon had said. *In whatever way will help her most.*

McKay felt his body clench. The man was a bloody fool to ask for something so intimate.

And he was a bloody fool to consider it.

The creak of wood brought him to the door in a rush. He froze at the sight of Carly beside the balcony, her body rigid, gown traced by cold moonlight. If she was crying, she was doing it in utter silence.

Wind sent the gauze curtains dancing as

McKay moved through the darkness, searching for words to soothe her pain.

She turned her head, her face a pale oval in the moonlight. "I could ask you to leave."

"You could ask."

She drew a harsh breath. "I'm okay with this, McKay." She gripped the white rail of the balcony. "I have to be."

"No one's judging you here, Carly."

"I am."

He leaned back, moonlight falling over his shoulders. "Want to talk?"

"No."

He resisted the urge to skim her cheek. "Want to curse and throw something? I'll be happy to find a vase that will shatter deafeningly."

She didn't laugh the way he had hoped. "No, thanks." Her fingers moved restlessly, tracing invisible patterns against the railing.

"Why not? You're tough and resilient and you love what you do. You should be furious."

"Go away. Please, go away." A low whisper, it clutched at his heart.

"You can't get rid of me that easily." McKay stepped closer, itching to pull her against his chest. "They took your camera, so what? Screw them," he added savagely.

Carly stared out at the lawns, silver where

they ran to the dark forest. She didn't curse or snap back an angry answer. Her whole body shook.

"Get angry, Carly. That's what you need now."

He saw the misery in her eyes, pushed deep but impossible to hide. "I can't. I'm too frightened." Her tears slid free, glinting on her face in the moonlight. "What if Mel fails? What if they find someone else, someone who takes my ideas but makes them sharper, then produces faster? I'll be used up, finished." She pressed a hand over her stomach. "That's how I feel already. As if I'm nothing."

"You need to eat."

"I can't."

McKay cursed and slid an arm around her trembling shoulders. "It hurts to be slandered and betrayed."

She swiped at her cheeks. "It shouldn't. I'm not a girl anymore. It's not life-and-death. Dear God, none of this should make me think of —" Her body shook harder.

"To think of your mother," he finished. "To a grieving girl, death would be the greatest betrayal."

Carly straightened. "You see a lot, McKay."

"Enough to know how you're hurting,"

he said quietly. Enough to recognize how dangerously vulnerable her pain made her right now. "Take a few punches if that will make you feel better. Go on, I've got thick skin."

She shook her head tiredly. "I'd only feel guilty. None of this is your fault. I should have handled Griffin better. I should have seen what was coming —"

He held her face, cradling her wet cheeks. "No one could have seen this coming."

"I shouldn't care so much." She made a fist and slammed it against the railing. "I don't *want to* care."

He stroked a damp curl from her cheek. "It's not a crime, Carly. Caring is who you are."

She gave a half-laugh, her eyes huge in the moonlit pallor of her face. "Thanks, I needed that."

"No," he said hoarsely. "What you need is this."

The brush of his mouth was meant to soothe, but McKay felt heat, only heat. Where her fingers stole onto his shoulders, where her chest pressed against his, he felt only the reckless flash of desire.

It felt good to imagine how she would taste.

It felt even better to find out.

His lips were not quite gentle as they settled over hers, wanting and taking. Muscle by muscle, she relaxed, her mouth opening to his. With a groan he pulled her closer, sliding his hands down that sleek, elegant body to cup her hips through the thin barrier of lace while desire twisted, sinking to his groin.

Greedy, he found the shoulder of her gown.

Blind, he shoved it aside, filling his hands with the glorious weight of her breasts.

"What are we doing?" she whispered.

"Hell if I know. Just don't ask me to stop." He felt her shudder.

"I don't want you to stop."

The sweet thrust of her nipples undid him. He pulled down the lace, tormenting the dark crests with his fingers, then with his mouth.

Wanting more, he brought his hand to the shadowed softness between her legs. She whimpered, her fingers digging into his shoulders.

In a second more he would have shredded the lace, backed her against the wall in the moonlight, and pushed inside her, deeper and deeper . . .

"God."

He took a rigid step back, his breath

harsh. Her nightgown lay open, her body a mute seduction.

"No." His throat was dry. "Not like this."

She swallowed. "Like what?"

"This — or any other way."

She watched him rake a hand through his hair as he fought to clear his brain. "I didn't ask you to stop."

"You shouldn't have to."

She didn't blink, didn't move.

"Think it through, Carly. Incendiary sex is the last thing you need now."

"Incendiary sounds good to me."

Because he couldn't help himself, he traced the curve of her lips. "Now, yes. But not tomorrow, not in a month, when you've had time to think this through." Irritated, he pulled her gown up and smoothed the lace over her cool skin, watching his fingers tremble. "Trust me, I'm right."

She took a raw breath. "Right doesn't matter. I like touching you." She stared up at him. "With you I won't regret letting go or feeling you let go. If that's what you mean by incendiary sex, I want that, too." She stood tensely as he didn't move. "You're not making this easy for me."

"You're damned right I'm not." McKay closed his eyes, trying not to see the desire in her face.

Easy? He wanted her until the force of it clawed deep, drawing blood. Taking her would have been the easy way.

"You're not thinking straight right now. You're hurting, Carly. I'm not the man for you."

She touched his jaw gently. "My body says you are. I'm willing to take the risk." Brave and proud, she stared at him, her eyes as restless as the moonlight playing through the trees. "Are you?"

"It's not about risk. It can't be."

"Why?"

"Because." It was lame, and he was losing the argument fast, he realized. Maybe he wanted to.

He felt the weight of his holstered weapon beneath his arm and the high-tech pager in his pocket. Duty was a cold, iron weight, but a weight he was trained never to ignore.

"We're a universe apart," he said harshly. "In a week you'll be back in New York and I'll be —" He closed his hands to fists. "I'll be somewhere else." A place where he would be entirely out of contact and facing hostile fire. A place where he could likely die.

Even then, it took him a lifetime to step away from her.

"We're not rewriting the *Kama Sutra*,"

Carly snapped. "It's simple contact, McKay. Simple touch."

"Nothing's simple about it."

"What's complicated about one night?"

"You're not that kind of woman," he said tightly.

"So now I'm a candidate for sainthood. Perfect." She turned, glaring out over the balcony toward the ocean. "McKay one, Saint Carly zero."

He cursed. "I'm sorry." He raised a hand toward her shoulder, but she blocked the movement, stepping back.

"For a man who sees so much, you're blind." Anger flared in her eyes. "Enjoy your cold bed. Just remember that you could have been sharing it with me." Her voice broke, then steadied. "And it would have been amazing."

His body was telling him the same thing.

Somehow he forced himself not to listen. "Dammit, I've got nothing to offer you. Not time, not a future."

"I didn't ask for a future. Only for tonight."

"You're not listening, Carly."

"I'm tired of listening. I'm tired of taking the pictures, framing the action, while life passes me by."

She vanished inside with the curtains

drifting behind her, leaving an awful weight of silence to settle around him in the moonlight.

Carly awoke in a cold sweat. An hour before dawn, the darkness was oppressive and her body ached from fighting tangled sheets.

Her heart was pounding as she sat up. No wind or light filtered through the open balcony doors, and the house was quiet.

As a dream it was no worse than the others that had come with tormenting frequency over the years.

Pounding waves in angry seas. A hill of wildflowers withering beneath the sun. Worst of all, the woman with a camera, walking away, never turning back despite Carly's hoarse pleas.

This time the dream started with the gravestones on Tortola, high above the water that had claimed her parents. Then, in that odd way of dreams, Carly found herself at the edge of the sea she had every reason to hate. There in the scream of the wind she had watched sand flow beneath her feet, parting on a weathered piece of glass where she saw her own face.

First as a child, then as a woman.

And finally as nothing, an oval with no features and cold, dead holes instead of eyes.

Even now the image had her shaking, scrubbing at her clammy cheeks.

Just a dream.

She pushed stiffly to her feet and padded barefoot to the balcony. Mutely she stared out to where wave and wind met in a line of gray-black. Locking her hands across her stomach, she rocked rhythmically, grieving for the childhood lost too soon, for the innocence and trust never to be reclaimed.

For the mother she could never understand or persuade to stay.

When would she put the memories to rest?

Cool wind gusted through the curtains, brushing her damp cheeks, an answer to a prayer she couldn't remember making. Out near the horizon faintest streaks of light touched the sky as dawn stole closer.

She shoved down her regrets, shoved down her bitter memories, watching that tiny smudge of light grow, gray swirling to blue and pink.

No more regrets, she swore. She would find the colors and wrestle them onto film, reclaiming the job she deserved. By skill, occasional brilliance, and raw determination she would trap the restless images that danced before her even now.

Above her the clouds burned into pink

240

and red, making her yearn for her camera. Steadier now, she faced the first glow of day, welcoming anger like a friend.

Already she was framing her first new scenes.

Chapter 19

Carly was calm.

Deadly calm.

She had almost managed to blot the hurt of McKay's rejection. She'd offered and he'd refused, and that was that.

At midmorning she straightened the simple white sundress and smoothed her hair behind her ears. The tears were gone now. Even the dark circles from sleeplessness were hidden beneath a layer of careful makeup.

Pride demanded no less.

She squared her shoulders, refusing to show her pain. She had work to do, new scenes to plan. When Mel called with the news that she'd been rehired, Carly was determined to be ready to plunge back into action.

Clutching a dozen finished sketches under her arm, she headed downstairs, careful to keep her gaze away from McKay's room.

He was furious.

She'd taken his answers the night before and in seconds she had managed to twist them beyond recognition. But now he knew exactly what to do. He'd start by proving that short-term sex didn't suit her. It was time for action, not talk.

He strode down the long porch, every scrap of energy focused on the figure sitting beside the pool making sketches in a book. At least she was being creative again, working up storyboards or thumbnails or whatever the designs of her profession were called.

McKay stopped as he caught sight of her sketch of a sailboat and a man with one hand on the white canvas, his face turned as he stared far out to sea. He could almost hear the soft calypso music and the hammer of drums, followed by the low-whispered words *We have your dream.*

The power of her design shook him, but he pushed it aside, determined to make his point before she could twist his words again.

When she turned, her eyes were as cool as storms he'd watched fling hail over the Arctic Ocean. "Morning, McKay." She saw the direction of his gaze and closed the sketchbook with a snap. "I hope you slept well."

"Like a baby," he countered, as annoyed as she was cool. "We need to talk."

"Later. I'm working."

"Now." He moved in front of her,

243

blocking the sunlight. "Right now, dammit."

She clicked her tongue. "Angry, are we? Bad for the blood pressure, you know. Why don't you go run some laps on the treadmill to mellow out. I suggest twenty minutes, full incline, full stride." Her voice was icy.

"Exercise can wait. Right now I intend to clear the air. I'm accepting, Carly. Let's go." He gripped her hand. "Upstairs. My bedroom. Right now."

He was angry enough to enjoy the shock in her eyes as she stood up.

"Now? Upstairs?"

"Damned right. Don't make me the villain of this piece." He steered her toward the stairs, every muscle rigid. "I was wrong last night. I intend to make up for that now."

Right after he watched her fold, McKay thought.

She tugged at her scarf as they walked into the house. "I'm not sure the offer still stands," she said weakly.

"No?" He blocked her way, backing her slowly against the wall. "And why is that? Possibly because you agree with me? If so," he said smugly, "the subject is closed."

Color filled her cheeks. She shoved her fist against his chest. Her knuckles rose, grazing his jaw not quite playfully. "I think not. Your room or mine?"

"Whichever is closest."

"Yours, in that case." Smiling, she strode up the stairs in front of him, then pushed open his door and eyed the room with detached interest. "Bed or sofa?"

McKay didn't move. What was she doing? Much more and she'd have him on his knees.

But he swore he'd make his point first.

He tugged off his shirt, growing angrier by the second. "Why not both? I'm in the mood for quantity."

She ran her fingers over the neatly made bed. "So am I." She took off her scarf and tossed it onto the bed, then fingered the tiny buttons on her dress. "Well, what are we waiting for?"

For his witless brain to recharge.

He unbuckled his belt and snapped it free, determined to call her bluff. His eyes never left hers as he kicked the door shut and slid the lock into place.

He was certain he saw her swallow hard. "Did you say something?"

"N-no."

Hiding his triumph, he stalked closer, expecting at any moment to hear her launch into a breathless surrender.

Instead, she ran her hands along her body, stepped out of her short, lacy slip, and tossed it in his face. "Did you say something?" she purred.

McKay's vision clouded to pure lust-red. Enough was enough.

"Things may get rough," he growled. "It's been a while since I've had sex."

"I live for rough."

Swallowing his shock, he worked the button free at his waist and went for his zipper, pleased when her hand froze on her dress. "Any problems?" he asked coolly.

"Aren't you forgetting something?"

"You're not expecting me to get down on one knee and say a lot of nonsense, I hope. Neither of us believes in romance."

"How true. Let's skip the romance, by all means." She yanked her top button free. "You made it crystal clear last night that there was no place for emotion between us. Clearly, you were right."

Dammit, the woman was twisting things again. McKay hooked his thumbs into his pockets, tugging his jeans even lower. "Good. Now let's get this over with." He shoved an ottoman out of his way with one foot. "Can't you hurry up and get naked?"

Her eyes glittered. "Like this, you mean?"

She caught two fingers at the neck of her

dress and sent five buttons flying across the floor.

McKay fought an urge to grip the torn dress and shove it closed. "Shame to ruin a good dress," he said hoarsely.

"A bigger shame to waste valuable time." She pursed her lips, studying him from head to toe. "You're wearing too many clothes, McKay." With a small shrug she sent her dress pooling at her feet.

All she wore beneath were pink bikini panties with foolish red roses and a fresh white bandage. She was more beautiful than any woman had a right to be, all Grace Kelly curves and hellion eyes. The combination hit McKay with a one-two punch to the gut. Why did the woman have to have such a tiny waist and forever legs when a man was trying to make her see sense and stop behaving like a fool?

"How's that?" she murmured.

No drooling, McKay thought wildly. "Everything in the right place."

"There *is* one problem."

"The stitches?"

"No. They're just a mild annoyance as long as I avoid any acrobatics. I'm thinking of something else." Her eyes never left his face as she unclasped her pearl necklace and tossed it gracefully onto the bed. "I'm not protected. I was planning on business, not pleasure, this trip. I suppose you must have something handy."

Protection? McKay hadn't expected the scenario to progress half so far. He searched her eyes for any sign of a bluff but found only determination.

"Of course," he snapped, pulling open the top drawer of his bureau. "Right here. No problem. By the dozens." Drawer by drawer he searched, then pulled his canvas bag from beneath the bed, dug into a corner pocket, and held up a small packet.

Coolly, Carly pulled it from his fingers, trailed the foil along one shoulder, then down between her breasts.

McKay felt sweat break out on his forehead as she moved the square lower. He fought to keep his gaze away from those high, perfect breasts as her fingers feathered along the edge of her panties. She smiled at him lazily and slid the lace lower.

Drooling was a definite possibility, he realized.

He swallowed hard and accepted surrender, bitter though it was. As a soldier, he knew it was better to discuss terms while you were still coherent.

"Stop, damn it."

The snap in his voice made her tense and

the foil packet shot to the floor. Muttering, she went to knees and elbows in search of it, and the sight had McKay fighting a groan.

"Got it." She waved her prize smugly, lunging back to her feet.

Suddenly her eyes shifted into a blank stare. The color drained from her face. "Bad idea. I think I'm going to —"

She simply caved in at the knees. McKay shot forward, catching her only inches from the floor.

His heart pounded as he looked at her sheet-white face, lifting her gently. "Of all the baboon-stupid, pigheaded things to do, this takes the cake." He slid her onto his bed, trying to avoid touching any more of her than he had to, cursing when his hands took far too long to pull a blanket over her flushed skin.

"Carly, wake up."

There was no fresh blood on her bandage. That would have been encouraging if guilt hadn't already grabbed him by the neck.

"Okay, champ. Time to wake up. You're scaring me here."

He stroked her cool cheeks, feeling an odd pressure in his chest. She was still recovering from her wound. What kind of fool would goad her in her condition?

Him.

"Wake up," he repeated hoarsely. "Come on, honey, don't make me beg."

Her lashes fluttered.

She made something between a cough and a groan, then flung one arm over her head, smacking him soundly on the left temple.

She looked up at him dizzily. "Don't tell me I slept through all the good stuff."

McKay took a deep breath, fighting a need to kiss her, then shake her.

"Is that a yes or a no?" she asked weakly.

"You figure it out."

Carly tugged up the blanket, looked underneath, and frowned. "A no. I guess I didn't miss anything earthshaking. I think I'll get up and slink away now — before mortification sets in."

She tried to sit up, only to slip back with a little huff of pain. "Another bad idea. Apparently, I need more practice at this seduction stuff."

McKay brought her palm to his lips. "Try that on any other man, and I just might have to kill him."

She stared at him for an eternity, then shook her head. "What is it with you? You're high-handed, interfering, and secretive. I keep wondering why I like you." She yawned. "Maybe it's a virus."

"Virus?"

"You know, where you confound my normal defenses. Like white cells run amok." She yawned. "Or something."

"I like you, too," he said, his voice strained.

She smiled crookedly. "In that case, it would probably be a shame to go and spoil things by having incendiary sex. Good friends are hard to find." She linked her fingers through his, her eyes dropping closed. "Going to sleep now."

Her breathing slowed.

McKay stared at their linked fingers, aware of a roaring in his head. His jeans were stretched tighter than he had thought humanly possible for the male anatomy, and he was having a hard time breathing.

The reason came to him with devastating clarity.

It scared the living hell out of him.

He was in love with her. Stupidly, blindly, unforgivably.

Chapter 20

McKay was pouring himself a cup of Archer's amazing cappuccino when he spotted Daphne. She hit Paradise Cay like a whirlwind trailing a cloud of designer perfume. Today she wore three-inch heels, a white leather miniskirt, and a white T-shirt that stopped just short of looking sprayed on. The woman had great legs, McKay thought.

But his appreciation was entirely impersonal. It was another pair of legs that he couldn't scrape out of his memory, as much as he had tried.

Already familiar with the lay of the kitchen, he pulled down another cup and saucer. "Carly will be glad to see you when she gets up."

"You mean she's resting?" Daphne eyed him speculatively. "The woman never rests."

"She does now."

"You're busy working miracles, I see." She leaned closer. "Sorry to say it, but you look like hell, McKay. A long night?"

He hadn't slept, couldn't eat. He didn't want to think about why. He'd never felt so close to another human being, never sensed another person's moods so intensely. He found himself wanting to share all his waking moments with her, then slip off to sleep with his body wrapped around hers.

At odd moments he found himself thinking about buying land, breeding horses, building a house from scratch. All the while, need for her was shredding his focus, his calm, his sanity. He told himself it was the result of close proximity and a stressful mission, but he knew that was a lie.

This was something far deeper, far more complex. It wasn't every day a man discovered he'd fallen hard for a woman who showed every probability of destroying his career — along with his sanity.

Time for a another shot of caffeine, he decided. He filled Daphne's cup, then recharged his own. "I'll survive," he said. "Probably."

Daphne cradled the cup carefully. "If you want to talk, I'm a good listener."

"I'll keep it in mind." Like hell he would. Talking would only make things messier.

He pushed back his chair, then paced restlessly to the window, checking the staff near the woods.

Behind him stew simmered on the stove, filling the kitchen with the rich scent of garlic, basil, and vine-ripened tomatoes.

Loaves of bread cooled on a rack nearby.

All the comforts of home, McKay thought.

Up until now, having a home had never been a blip on his radar screen.

The thought only added to his irritation.

"Archer's cooking for an army, I see." Daphne toyed with her cup. "He does that when he's worried."

McKay didn't answer, aware they had entered dangerous waters. "How about some fresh dill bread?" he asked casually. "Archer just took it out of the oven a few minutes ago."

"No, thanks. With this skirt I can't even look at food." Her eyes hardened. "Besides, I didn't come to eat. Has there been any news from New York?"

McKay shook his head.

"Idiots. Is she throwing things yet?"

"She's working up to it." McKay smiled faintly. "If I keep provoking her, you might see a vase or two go flying."

"Good. An explosion would be therapeutic." Daphne's gaze flickered around the kitchen, then back to McKay. "You look jumpy."

"Trying times."

"True enough." Daphne sipped her coffee. "My father was on the phone until the wee hours. He's made sure his lawyers sink their teeth deep on this one. That no-talent weasel of an actor has finally issued a statement that his earlier charges were made in haste and might possibly have been misconstrued."

"Possibly?"

"Negotiation is all," Daphne said cynically. "He's holding out for extra compensation. He also wants guaranteed placement for two more jobs."

"Pushy bastard."

Daphne smiled. "But a nervous one. If his attack backfires, he'll be blacklisted in New York and everywhere else that counts."

McKay watched a bird fly low over the rose garden and thought about a new angle. Was Griffin Kelly capable of organizing the attack at the waterfall out of revenge?

No, McKay decided. From what he'd seen, the planning was beyond a lightweight like Kelly.

"Keep pounding him. He'll fold under pressure."

"Meanwhile Carly is left to dangle in the wind." Daphne pushed away her coffee. "It makes me livid."

McKay knew exactly how she felt.

Daphne stared down at her locked fingers. "Have you told Carly the truth yet?"

McKay wondered what secrets she had

managed to work out of her father. "You mean that I'm really Dennis Rodman with a lot of expensive surgery?"

"You'd look good with an earring."

"I'll pass on that — and the body tattoos."

"She should know why you're here."

"She already knows. I'm here to —"

"The truth," Daphne said tightly. "Not the slick story."

"Tell me the truth about what?" Carly stood in the doorway, her face soft from sleep. She looked anxious and vulnerable as she stared from one to the other. "Daphne, what did you mean?"

"Hell." Daphne sighed. "I'm worried about both of you. Apparently I'm better at worrying than I am at keeping my mouth shut. Maybe it's my imagination, but I'd say you two were involved. Or about to be involved." She waved a hand as McKay began a denial. "No, don't bother. It's not my business anyway. Just one piece of advice: Don't blow it. If there's anything I do know, it's that life's too short to be proud — or stupid." She moved past Carly and frowned. "Your buttons are crooked. Your scarf also happens to be twisted." She bent to pick something off the floor near Carly's foot. "Well, well, isn't this interesting?"

Carly swept the foil square from her fingers. "It's not what you think."

"I'd say it's exactly what I think."

Stiffly, Carly rebuttoned her dress. "Don't change the subject. Tell me what you meant about McKay telling me the truth."

Daphne crossed her arms. "Ask him. I've got to discuss a recipe with Archer. My father has some Japanese investors visiting tomorrow and I'm going to make them swoon over the conch fritters. After that, maybe some mango ice cream." She sauntered past Carly, headed toward the patio. "You two have a nice chat."

Carly rounded on McKay. "Tell me."

He rubbed his jaw. "I haven't got a clue what she meant." He reached for the foil packet. "Hand it over. You won't be needing it."

Carly's eyes glittered. "Maybe I'll just head into Bridgetown and drown my sorrows." She smiled icily. "So to speak."

"Think again." He'd kill the first man who looked at her, much less touched her.

Carly straightened her shoulders. "News flash from the Vatican: Saint Carly doesn't live here anymore."

"Nigel Brandon asked me to keep an eye on you. He thinks I can keep you from doing something reckless."

"Aren't you two chums all of a sudden. And by all means, let's not be reckless." Carly's voice rose angrily. "Let's just troop along nicely like good little campers."

Standing in the doorway, Archer looked thoughtfully from one to the other. "Your guests have arrived, Miss Carly."

"Guests? What guests?"

"Five members of your crew. Inspector St. John escorted them up from the main road." Archer glanced at McKay, who nodded.

"She'll be right out."

"She will?" Her face flushed with anger. "Camp just let out, McKay. You can stop trying to regiment my life." She shoved away his hand and headed for the foyer, her face mutinous.

"An old island expression comes to mind right now," Archer murmured.

"I don't want to hear it."

"I'd be glad to tell you," Archer continued mildly. "I believe it translates as 'some days suck.' "

"This is definitely one of them." McKay followed the laughter to the sunny porch above the rose garden, where Carly was surrounded by her crew. She studiously avoided him, all her attention focused on a painfully thin young man whose buzz-cut purple hair went very nicely with his purple earring.

"I put in my exposure meter with memory averaging and digital readouts. It does everything but takes the shot for you." His earring spun as he opened a padded aluminum case. "Here it is."

Recognizing the love-stricken expression in the staffer's eyes as he stared at Carly, McKay suppressed a twinge of sympathy.

"And here's my best tripod. One-touch opening and a top-of-the-line gear head. Just feel the movement on this pan wheel, smooth as butter. You'll grab some amazing shots with it."

Carly stared as a woman in ragged shorts and heavy hiking boots nudged the lighting tech aside and pulled something else out of the box. "Here are some light flags and a c-stand, my three favorite spots, and an amazing 3-D concave reflector. The translucent white gives you amazing softness along with clarity. The gaffer tape goes too."

"I can't take these. You know that." Carly took a ragged breath. "This is your personal equipment." Tears glistened in her eyes as she looked from one face to the next.

"Take it and put it to use." Expertly, Carly's lighting tech set up the camera tripod, then angled two light stands on either side of it. "Then send Mel some killer footage that will get us back here to finish the job."

"I can't tell you how much this means to me." Carly traced the tripod lovingly. "But I don't have a camera."

"Hank knew you'd say that." Daphne glanced pointedly at a box behind Carly's chair. "That's why he left you his new camcorder."

The lighting tech gave a low whistle. "That baby has 10x power zoom, a time-base corrector, and single-frame recording. Hank must like you big time — he won't even let me near it."

"I don't know what to say." Carly smiled shakily. "Thank you all so much, but I couldn't possibly borrow all this. It's out of the question."

"Hank expected you to say that, too." Daphne crossed her arms. "He said to tell you to stop making lame excuses and get back to work. He wants footage to look at tomorrow, when he finishes bashing heads in New York." She squeezed Carly's shoulder. "If people want to help you, let them."

McKay moved back into the shadows as Carly brushed at the tears streaming down her face. She had the loyalty of her crew, and McKay suspected she'd worked hard to earn it. He glanced across the porch as Inspector St. John climbed the steps from the garden and joined him.

"They're good friends. I'm glad they stood by her." St. John crossed his arms, studying McKay. "I've got some information for you. The men we're holding in custody know nothing. The attack at the waterfall was arranged entirely by phone, and the payment was handled anonymously, left inside a rental box at the airport. Someone was extremely careful."

"Have your people tracked down that silver Audi?"

"We found it two hours ago, abandoned near the airport."

"So they're smart as well as cautious." McKay didn't like the combination. "What about the Russian?"

"Vronski has tabled his negotiations. He told the governor he needed time to determine if Santa Marina was the best location for his investment." St. John frowned. "Under the circumstances."

"Shrewd move." McKay watched one of the estate security officers move unobtrusively through the trees at the far end of the garden. "Either that or it's a damned good bluff. Did Vronski mention the attack on Governor Brandon's family?"

St. John shook his head.

That could be equally shrewd, McKay decided. All news of the attack had been kept out of the local papers. If Vronski was involved, he'd hardly trumpet his knowledge of the event. "How about that crime wave you're battling on Santa Marina?"

"Quiet, for the moment."

McKay wasn't overly relieved by the news. He had a hunch there would be more pressure and more attacks. No one went to so much trouble without a substantial goal.

Laughter drifted through the courtyard. "Keep Daphne close," McKay said tightly. "It's not over."

St. John stiffened. "Why so certain?"

Sheer, gnawing instinct. The edgy feeling at the back of the neck that came from too many supposedly safe ops that went south from bad intel.

McKay shrugged. "Just a feeling."

"We could use your help, McKay. We're getting nowhere, and the governor is terrified that next time someone will break through security and harm his family or staff."

McKay didn't envy the governor. Being a target was one thing. Knowing that the people you loved were targets had to be the worst kind of torture.

"He doesn't need to worry about Carly." McKay ran his eyes over the rolling lawns and the dense woods beyond. "No one's getting in or out while I'm here. Even if they do, Carly will be right beside me."

St. John nodded, then motioned to his driver. "I'll be driving the crew members back to Bridgetown shortly. You've got enough on your hands without any extra distractions here." He smiled as Daphne swirled in a dramatic pose for Carly's new camera. "Miss Daphne will go with me. I've been trying to convince the governor to return to Santa Marina with her and his staff, but he won't leave while Miss Carly is here recovering. Nor will he give the impression that he's running scared."

"Running might be safer." But McKay sensed that whether the governor was on Barbados or another island, the threats would continue. There could be no letting down his guard.

"Be careful." St. John watched Daphne waltzing with Archer under a towering banyan tree while the crew fought laughter. "You're the final line of defense here."

McKay glanced across the road at the tree where Izzy was hunkered down, virtually invisible. "Count on it."

An hour later Daphne and the crew had left. McKay was nursing a cup of Archer's potent tea on a lounge chair near the man-made waterfall at the end of the pool. He was trying hard not to notice Carly, but his gaze kept snapping back like a pulled rubber band.

She was perched on the edge of the free-form pool, looking as if she were balanced on thin air with the Caribbean stretching away behind her. It was only an illusion, McKay knew, an image created by careful placement of the pool on a steep slope. The knowledge didn't keep him from itching to tug her out of danger.

Then there was the problem of her suit, two scraps of red spandex that had him itching in other, more primitive ways.

He managed to keep his expression cool and casual as he crossed the flagstone terrace. "I thought you'd still be trying out your new equipment."

Carly lifted her hand, shading her eyes against the sun. "I was tempted."

McKay dropped into a deck chair beside her. "Not blocked — or whatever you artists call it?"

"Not blocked. I meant what I said yesterday. I'm tired of framing the shots while life passes me by. I'm taking the rest of the day off."

"In spite of that lovely camera, just waiting for you?"

"That's right. I'm going to sit back, relax, and soak up some lovely sunlight."

"In that suit, you'll soak up a lot of sun."

"If you must know, I couldn't struggle into my one-piece suit without straining a few stitches."

McKay frowned. "Let me have a look."

"I'll be fine, McKay. Just stop me if I feel compelled to attempt the thousand-meter freestyle. Gaffer's tape was perfect to cover my bandage." She pointed at her side. "It's completely waterproof." She took a deep breath, dangling her feet in the crystal water. "It's also incredibly ugly, but since you've made it clear that you're not interested in my body, that hardly matters, does it?"

It would take more than a strip of gray tape to make her ugly. Especially in that siren-red suit she was almost wearing. But McKay was steering clear of that particular subject.

Concerned, he studied her fair skin. "Shouldn't you put on sunscreen?"

"Already done." Her lips quirked. "Don't tell me you're disappointed."

He was. Nothing would have felt better than running his hands over her smooth stomach and forever legs, if only to see her squirm the way he was squirming. "A little," he said mildly.

She propped one hand on the flagstones. "Why don't you change? The water's glorious."

He stood and stretched, at the same time scanning the hillside. "I'll pass for now." He was watching a boat steam beyond the cove when he heard Carly's low laugh, just before her heads hooked around his ankles. "I think it's time you got wet, McKay. That cool, competent way you study everything around you makes me nervous." Smiling, she tightened her grip.

McKay thought of the pistol holstered on his calf. "I don't want to swim."

"But I *absolutely* insist." Still smiling, she pushed off the edge of the pool, falling backward. McKay struggled to keep his balance, then plunged in after her. He twisted in midair to avoid falling on top of her, but grazed her shoulder, dunking her soundly.

Even at that she was laughing when he broke the surface, her eyes full of mischief. "You're all wet, McKay."

In retaliation, he shoved her underwater, then smiled when she came up sputtering.

"Looks like both of us are."

"At least I'm dressed for it." She shot water at his face, then dived for safety, surfacing at the far end of the pool.

She swam like a mermaid, he thought, all flashing limbs and smooth power. He remembered she'd spent every summer on Santa Marina, which had given her plenty of opportunity to practice.

He stroked to the edge of the pool, kicked out of his shoes and socks, then wedged his gun out of sight inside one shoe. After piling the clothes on the terrace, he circled slowly, tracking her across the deep end.

She avoided him, piking down and slipping through his fingers like liquid silver. For a moment he could only stare, struck by her restless energy as she shot past him and surfaced in an arc of bubbles.

"You're losing your touch, McKay."

"I'm losing more than my touch," he muttered, stripping off his shirt and tossing it with the rest of his discarded clothes.

Carly paddled sideways, careful to stay well out of reach. "If I'd known there would be a floor show, I'd have pushed you in sooner."

McKay slid underwater. As he'd expected, she followed, and he caught her ankle, pulling her farther down and capturing her face. Slowly he breathed against her parted lips while bubbles shimmered and danced around them.

He couldn't have said where the magic began or ended, whether in the touch of her lips or the restless brush of her body against his. Sunlight poured through the water, dusting her cheeks and hair, and there was a dazed look in her eyes as she pulled free and kicked to the surface, gasping for air.

McKay followed unhurriedly, well trained to stretch out one breath for minutes.

"Where did you learn to hold your breath that way?" Carly demanded.

"Taipei. Singapore. Fiji." He watched a frown line her forehead. "On my first freighter," he added.

"You're lying. I'm comfortable in the water, but you move as if water's your real home. Don't insult me with some lame story about being a champion surfer or I might have to drown you." Her frown deepened. "Except I couldn't drown you. I couldn't get away from you, either, if you were really trying to catch me." She stroked backward. "You're Navy, aren't you? One of those special forces people."

"Carly —"

"It was all arranged, wasn't it? All of it,

right from your arrival aboard the cruise ship. That's what Daphne meant." She shook her head, not waiting for an answer. "When were you going to let me in on your little secret?"

McKay lunged for her wrist, but she ducked sharply, kicking away from him. "Carly, stop."

"I trusted you, dammit."

He caught her at the ladder, his hands gripping her shoulders. "You can still trust me. Don't turn away. I'm not finished."

"Yes, you are." Her eyes snapped in fury. "It had to be Uncle Nigel's idea. I'll work the truth out of him. Until then, I have nothing to say to you." She stared pointedly at his hands. "Or is coercion part of your assignment, too?"

McKay let his hands drop. Considering that Brandon had maneuvered McKay into this fiasco of a mission, it was only right that Brandon choose how much to explain. Carly had a right to know the whole picture since she was one of the probable targets.

"What, no protests? No soulful assurances that I'm wrong?"

"You're not in the mood to believe anything I say."

Their bodies bumped gently, rocked by

the water, and Carly flinched. "Get out of my way."

McKay saw the pain in her eyes, glinting beneath the fury. She had trusted him, confided in him, and in return he had brought her more betrayal. The knowledge left an unpleasant taste in his mouth, though his orders had been crystal clear.

She glared at him, clinging to the ladder. "Don't bother with excuses, McKay. More lies are the last thing I need."

Water flying, she stormed up the ladder and was gone.

Chapter 21

Carly placed three tense calls to Nigel Brandon through the afternoon, only to learn that he was off island in back-to-back meetings. To her frustration, Daphne was also unavailable, courting potential sponsors for her foundation. On a hunch, Carly tried Inspector St. John, only to find that he was accompanying Daphne.

Carly sensed there was danger growing, and it infuriated her that no one respected her intelligence enough to discuss it with her openly and honestly. As soon as she snagged Daphne or Nigel, she meant to remedy that situation.

She spent the rest of her day in a blur of sketches, location planning, and general research on beach settings for future shoots. Narrowing the list of possible locations would help her plan visual themes.

Assuming that the whole project hadn't already been turned over to another creative team by then.

She drove the thought from her mind, working right through the afternoon, much to Archer's unhappiness. She managed to avoid McKay for a total of nearly four hours, though she heard his voice often enough to know he was never far away. In the late afternoon, Nigel Brandon's secretary phoned with his apologies, saying that he was still detained in meetings off island and would contact her as soon as he returned.

At sunset Archer knocked on her door and cast a disapproving eye over her open books, folded maps, and scattered paperwork. "Dinner will be served on the terrace in fifteen minutes."

"Thank you, Archer, but I'll just have some fruit here in my room."

"That you will *not* do. I will not have Mr. Brandon accusing me of negligence in my duties."

"But —"

"Seven-fifteen," the majordomo said imperiously. "Since your Mr. McKay has been equally recalcitrant, he was given the same ultimatum."

Carly wanted to snap that McKay wasn't *her* anything, but Archer had already gone back to the kitchen. Fuming, she closed her books and rummaged in her bags for well-worn blue jeans and an old tank top, refusing to primp before dinner. She ran a comb quickly through her hair, then strode outside, not bothering with shoes. By the time she reached the terrace, her nerves were raw and she was primed for a fight.

She came to an abrupt halt when she saw McKay's lean silhouette on the terrace, where he paced with equal aggravation. Tonight he wore nothing but black, his only ornament a narrow silver buckle at his belt.

Carly took a sharp breath and tried not to like what she saw. Even now she found it hard to resist the power of the man prowling at the edge of the candlelight. With a sigh, she straightened her shoulders and sauntered with cool arrogance over the flagstones.

The effect was spoiled when she slammed her bare foot against a wrought-iron candelabrum, staggered, then caught her heel with a shrill yelp.

He was at her side in an instant. "Where does it hurt? Your stitches? Your leg?"

"My foot," she rasped. "Just give me a minute here."

He held her steady while he checked her foot. "No blood. No cuts. What about your stitches?" he demanded. "Any problems there?"

Carly could only shake her head, intensely aware of his body against hers — though it was the last thing she wanted to think about.

The wind murmured though the trees,

cool against her flushed cheeks. McKay cleared his throat, then stepped away, thrusting his hands into his pockets. "It doesn't look serious."

He started to ask her a question but stopped when Archer arrived with a tray. Five magnificent courses followed, each served with Archer's impeccable style and Paradise Cay's finest silver, while the tension stretched out between them.

They said barely five words to each other for the rest of the evening.

"Everything all right?"

Carly looked up from a big, sweeping romance set in fifteenth-century Scotland. Her eyes narrowed on McKay, who wore a loose black nylon jacket. His collar was turned up and he looked as if he'd just come from a run on the beach.

"See for yourself," Carly said coolly. To her surprise, he did just that, checking the windows and bathroom. After that he closed and locked the French doors to her veranda.

She sat up straighter. "I like them open."

"You'll sleep better with them closed." Impassive, he held out a pill and a glass of water. "You're due for one of these. It will help you sleep."

"I'll sleep just fine, assuming you let me

274

get back to my book." She spoke curtly, unnerved by the thought that he was keeping track of her medication schedule.

His brow rose. "No more pain?"

"Nothing beyond an occasional tug. Dr. Harris must have magic hands."

After a moment, he nodded. "In that case, sleep well. If you need me, I'll be next door."

He'd be the last one she went to for help, Carly swore, attacking her pillow and fighting with her blankets. For two more hours she struggled to find the narrow corridor leading into sleep, only to throw off her quilt in frustration and pad to the window. Stars blazed in the immense velvet sky and the lights of fishing boats gleamed far out at sea.

Around her the house creaked softly.

Rubbing the small of her back, Carly went in search of a glass of milk, hoping the old remedy might actually work. Across the hall, she saw dim light filtering from the study. McKay's long body was sprawled in an armchair, a silver attaché case open on his right and a file folder spread out to his left. What appeared to be a faxed photograph lay on top of the folder.

Carly crept closer and studied the man in the fax, shocked that he seemed familiar.

She sank to one knee for a better look, trying to remember where she had seen those deep-set eyes. *Aboard the ship.*

Suddenly she was caught from behind, slammed forward, and pinned to the floor as powerful hands slashed out, trapping her wrists. A muscled forearm pressed at her throat, and she went absolutely still.

In the darkness, McKay's face was drawn and fierce above her. Carly waited, frozen by the sight of his eyes, cold and stony.

A killer's eyes.

"S-stop," she rasped, her throat burning under his forearm.

He stared, unblinking, his breath harsh and labored.

Then, as fast he had trapped her, he rolled away. "What the hell were you doing in here?"

Carly gasped for breath, wincing when she tried to speak.

"Don't talk." He pulled her against his chest and massaged her throat. "Give it some time."

She closed her eyes, swallowing hard. One of her questions had just been answered. Now she knew exactly what he was.

He was a trained killer who moved with icy will and lethal speed to dispatch his target. She had nearly been that target, thanks to her innocent blunder.

The realization should have left her frightened, but she felt only fury as she shoved away his hands.

"Stop."

"Stop, hell. I don't like your greeting style, McKay. A peck on the cheek generally works better than strangulation."

He reached out, but she slammed at his arm in blind panic.

"Fine. I won't touch you." He raised both hands, palms up. "Just relax."

She couldn't. The experience left her shuddering, unable to forget the marks of his fingers on her neck.

"I'm sorry I frightened you."

"Sorry, hell. It's what you do, what you are. You hurt things." She bit back a whimper of pain as she rose. "You kill people."

She stood unsteadily, waiting for him to deny it, praying he would say the words to prove she was wrong.

His silence came like a physical blow.

"Fine. End of scene. Wrap cameras." She turned clumsily, unable to think.

"We need to talk, Carly." His voice was low and strained.

"I prefer to talk with people who aren't trying to strangle me." She traced her throat unconsciously and shivered.

The gesture made him scowl, moving closer.

"Don't." Her voice shook. "I've got to think."

"Thinking won't help."

Wiping her cheeks, she shouldered past him, crossed the hall to her bedroom, then turned. "You're with the government, aren't you? Uncle Nigel arranged all this, didn't he?"

"I want to talk about us, not about Brandon."

"I saw that fax beside your feet. I recognized one of the faces."

McKay went still. "Which one?"

"The man with the deep-set eyes and the bad toupee. Who is he?"

"Where?" McKay asked tensely. "Try to remember exactly where you saw him."

She crossed her arms. "Probably on the dock in Bridgetown the day we arrived. On the ship, too, come to think of it. He was there by the pool the day I met you. Was that part of the plan? Did you play hard to get as part of the job?"

His shoulders rigid, he followed her across her room. "Stop twisting this."

She backed away. "Don't come near me."

"I won't leave. Not like this," he said harshly.

She took another unsteady step, then hit the bed and toppled back in midsentence, feeling a dull ache at her healing wound.

The ache in her heart cut far deeper.

He stared down at her, a slash of shadow at the edge of the bed. "Dammit, Carly, I need you to trust me."

"I can't. It's too late for that."

There was hunger in his eyes, driving out his icy detachment. She saw the pulse hammering at his throat.

"I would never harm you. I care too much, even though caring was never part of the plan." His hand opened on her lace gown. "I could prove it now." The words were fierce. "I could make you see." He cursed savagely, then took a step away from her. "I want you, Carly. That will never be a lie."

"If so, it's the only thing you've said to me that's true." She took a shuddering breath. "Go away. I'm afraid of the shadows in your eyes and the dead expression on your face. I'm afraid of how alert and careful you are. Come back when you can tell me the truth."

"You're making this harder than it has to be, dammit."

Her hand twisted against her chest. "Am I? Funny, I could have sworn I was saving us both from making a huge mistake."

Chapter 22

An hour before dawn, McKay glared at his face in the bathroom mirror. Carly hadn't slept well and neither had he.

Hardly surprising in her case since he'd nearly decked her, frightening her half to death. She'd put two and two together beautifully after that.

Answering her questions was Brandon's problem, but regaining her trust was his. Meanwhile, this damnable attraction he felt was going to be pushed deep and forgotten. Neither of them could afford that kind of complication now.

Beyond her door, he heard a whimper and the creak of the bed. He found her twisting, half pinioned by tangled sheets, her face pale with fear.

She was dreaming, he realized. Probably reliving the attack at the waterfall. Or maybe she was remembering the moment when she'd caught him by surprise.

Damn the mission, he thought grimly, sliding his hand gently over her hair.

She didn't wake and he stayed beside her until the shuddering stopped. By the time her breathing quieted and her hands stopped twisting on the quilt, his body was taut, knotted with need.

"Hell," he said as she rolled over and pulled him down, draping herself across him, boneless and utterly vulnerable in sleep. Her hand nestled in the hair at his chest and her mouth settled at his cheek.

In sleep, she trusted him. Awake, she would argue to her last angry breath, but asleep she held nothing back.

The thought amazed him.

He stayed where he was, careful not to wake her despite the need he was coming to recognize as an old friend. Only when the sun cleared the trees, signaling time for a security check with Archer, did he ease out of her bed, heading for a shower.

A very *cold* shower, he decided.

Carly awoke in a sprawl of tangled sheets. She sat up and squinted at the beamed ceiling, trying to remember where she was.

Too much sunlight. Not New York.

Paradise Cay.

She fell back with a pained sigh, remembering the attack and her move here to the estate.

Last night.

She dragged her pillow over her head, shivering at the memory of McKay's hair-trigger response when she'd come upon him sleeping in the study. In seconds she'd been pinned beneath him. In a few seconds more she could have been dead. She closed her eyes, trying to erase the memories.

Could she trust him? Could she be certain he would stop himself the next time she came upon him unaware?

There were no answers in the quiet room.

Only the cold fear remained as she pushed to her feet. She needed a shower, then food. After that, she intended to bury herself in work. And if she hadn't heard from Uncle Nigel by noon, she would go to Bridgetown and track him down personally.

When Carly finished her shower, McKay and Archer were on the terrace talking with two men in flowered shirts. She tossed on a jacket and jeans and headed for the kitchen, relieved to avoid McKay. In her pocket, she had a sketch book and a light meter so she could try some test shots outside after she ate.

Rummaging through the refrigerator, she found fresh fruit and juice, along with Archer's special peanut soup, which she ladled into a copper pot. The air was tinged with spices by the time she pulled the pot from the stove, broke off part of a fresh baguette, and went in search of butter.

No luck on any of the counters. No luck in the refrigerator.

The curtains moved at the open window, casting patterns on the long granite counters as Carly pulled open the door of the huge commercial freezer. She peered through a veil of cold air and waved her hands, looking for the butter canister. Seeing nothing but swirling air, she stepped in farther and was rewarded by the sight of three dairy containers next to a selection of pricy European sorbets.

Patrick Brandon definitely lived well, she thought, scanning a row of elaborate frozen pastries. He wouldn't miss one killer chocolate desert amid all this bounty.

Grinning, she scooped up a carton of butter along with an extravagant Italian chocolate truffle cake. After all, there was nothing like chocolate to soothe a wounded heart.

Hearing a sound behind her, she spun guiltily, purloined chocolate in hand. "Archer, is that you?"

The door was closing.

"McKay? Stop."

The door just kept moving.

Carly sprang forward, shoving her shoulder against the cold metal, but she was too late. The silver handle snapped shut with a hiss as she banged on the door, calling loudly and wrenching the handle up and down. Nothing budged. *Stuck tight.* Was the door locked from the outside?

She shivered, kicking at the refrigerator wall and calling hoarsely while icy air cut at her dry throat. As she rammed the door with her shoulder, the cold grew, wrapping itself around her legs and rising in billowing condensation whenever she breathed. She found an empty burlap bag on the floor and tied it around her shoulders over her thin cotton jacket.

The thermometer beside the door read fifteen degrees. How long could she hold out? Even when she was missed, who would think of looking for her inside the freezer?

Her face stung as crystals formed where her eyes had teared from the cold. Stubbornly she banged on the walls and door, her movements slower now, awkward, almost drunken. Finally she crouched on a crate of frozen produce and drew her legs to her chest to conserve heat while she tried desperately to think of a way out.

She pulled her jacket tighter, her sketch pad banging against her arm. Sliding her hands into her pockets, she glanced down at the long burlap sack beside her and the soup bone protruding through the open top.

But it wasn't a soup bone. It was a man's bent elbow emerging from the sack, which concealed the rest of his frozen body.

Carly's scream echoed hollowly off the icy metal walls as she realized she was locked inside the freezer with a corpse.

Chapter 23

Ford sprinted over the terrace toward Archer. "Where in the hell *is* she?"

"I believe she is still in her bedroom."

"Wrong. She was asleep when I checked five minutes ago, but now she's gone."

Archer set down a vase of blush-pink roses. "Gone where?"

"Hell if I know." McKay sniffed the air. "Someone's cooking. Maybe she's downstairs in the kitchen."

But the kitchen was empty. A pot sat near the stove, not quite cold, a cut baguette nearby.

"Did you heat this?"

Archer shook his head.

"She was here not long ago." McKay strode out to the terrace and scanned the rose garden. "Where did she go?"

"No one has left the grounds," Archer said tightly. "No one has come in since this delivery from Bridgetown." He pointed at the cartons of food stacked outside the pantry.

"What time was the delivery?"

Archer rubbed the bridge of his broken nose. "A little after seven. I signed for the food myself. The order was placed three days ago, and everything was as expected."

A uniformed officer opened the back door. "No one in the garden or on the beach. We've checked the road, too. She isn't there."

"Do it again," Archer ordered.

"But —"

"Do it," McKay growled. "I'm going to recheck the house. Maybe she was in the projection room and I missed her."

But she wasn't there or anywhere else. Searching the house took seven minutes, and Carly was nowhere to be found. Her clothes were still in the closet and there were no signs of a struggle. Her borrowed camera equipment lay on a table beside the bed.

"Call the company that delivered the food," McKay ordered. "Find out if the driver was a regular man or a fill-in. I'll need his address and current whereabouts."

As Archer picked up the phone in the upstairs hall, McKay scowled at the elegant grounds. The garden was filled with birdsong, and roses gleamed under the shelter of the high trees. McKay moved away from Archer and dialed his cell phone.

Izzy answered immediately. "What's all the activity?"

"Carly's missing."

"Impossible. She hasn't been outside. Only ones moving were the regular staff and a delivery van about seven."

"Keep watching." McKay cut the transmission. Where *was* she?

Archer put down the phone. "The driver was a regular man. He claims he saw nothing unusual on the drive. There was a school bus dropping off children and a telephone truck down near the beach road, but nothing else."

McKay sprinted back downstairs, gripped by the certainty that she was nearby. The grounds were being monitored and intruders would have been noticed. That left only the house. "Did you actually see the truck being unloaded?" he called.

"I'm afraid not. It didn't occur to me to watch." Archer turned at the low peal of a cellular phone. "That's coming from the office. I'll answer it."

McKay stayed behind, pacing the kitchen and staring at the cooling pot of soup. Carly had been here. What had made her leave? He checked the long pantry, then pulled open drawers and cupboards.

"No one there, just static." As Archer spoke from the doorway, the phone in the office rang again.

McKay raced down the hall and swept the

phone off a polished rosewood table. "What?"

There was only static.

"Who is this?" he snapped.

Out of the electronic hum came the low wheeze of labored breathing. "Here. Help . . ."

The words vanished into static.

McKay's hand tightened. "Who is this?"

"C-cold." The words were nearly drowned by a metallic whine. "Need you —"

"I can't hear you. Say again."

Suddenly, he knew.

With a curse, he turned, sprinted to the kitchen and saw what he hadn't seen before. Silver wire covered the freezer door handle, twisted tight to lock it securely.

McKay grabbed a cast-iron pan and slammed one side against the heavy, twisted wire. "Shears," he called to Archer, who thrust a pair into his hand. "I'm coming, Carly. Hang on," he shouted, tearing at the wire. "Get some blankets, Archer. Then run a bath. Not too hot."

Archer left, and McKay continued to hack at the wire. Finally, the metal strands tore free and he lunged into the freezer. Through swirling clouds he saw Carly sitting motionless with a burlap bag over her shoulders and her knees drawn up to her chest. A cell phone was clutched in her rigid fingers and he saw that she had stacked heavy cartons all around her in a vain effort to block the cold. Near her was a second burlap bag, a frozen elbow emerging from the ragged cloth.

Sinking beside her, McKay draped a blanket over her shoulders. Her skin felt unnatural and tight as he pulled her into his arms. "I'm here," he whispered. "Talk to me, Carly." His hands tensed when she didn't answer. "I'll cook if you want. I make a fair omelet. Just talk to me, dammit."

Her hand moved against his chest. "Hot. Something h-hot."

"I'll give you five-alarm hot," he said raggedly.

Archer had drawn a bath by the time they got upstairs. McKay stripped off Carly's jeans and jacket and carried her into the tub. She still hadn't opened her eyes and her breathing was labored.

Holding her tight, he sank into the warm water. "Can you look at me, Carly?"

"Hurts."

McKay raced through the basics of his first-aid training, knowing he had to do something about her eyes. Very gently he laid a wet washcloth over her face. "This should help."

He backed against the side of the huge Jacuzzi and pulled her closer, frowning as shudders raced through her rigid body.

She began to cry soundlessly, tears trickling down her cheeks where the washcloth had shifted. "Why?" she rasped, her fingers digging into his chest. "Why did they do this?"

"It doesn't matter. You're safe, and no one will get to you again." He stroked her damp hair. "I promise you that."

Her breath was shaky. "D-don't want to be here. I don't — know who I can trust. Take me somewhere else." She pulled away the washcloth and squeezed her eyes tight, as if she was afraid to open them.

"Look at me, Carly."

Her eyelids fluttered. She squinted up at him.

"Hey," he said softly. "Looking good."

"Looking like hell, and we both know it."

"Not to me." He eased a wet strand from her cheek. "Smart move, using the cell phone."

"I found it in the shirt. The man — the body," she said shakily. "The phone was in his pocket. If it hadn't been there —"

McKay's hands tightened. "Don't think about it now. Just tell me when you want to leave."

She drew a slow breath. "Now. I can't stay here."

"I know a place with people we can trust." Thank God for Izzy's plan B, he thought. There was clearly a breach in Inspector St. John's security, and from now on, no one but Izzy would know their location.

"Then let's go."

"You've got it."

McKay dried her off, then helped her dress and pack. He kept his arm securely around her as he guided her outside into the hall, where Archer was pacing anxiously.

"She'll be fine." McKay passed Archer, walking her carefully down the corridor.

"Thank God." Archer followed, frowning at Carly's packed bag. "You're leaving?"

"I'd say that's a stupid question, Archer."

The big man didn't speak for a long time. "I guess it was. She's not safe. Not even here, is she?"

McKay kept walking, his eyes wintry.

"It wasn't your fault." Turning, Carly put one hand on Archer's massive shoulder.

He only shook his head. "I should have noticed sooner. That makes it my fault. Take care of her," he said tightly to McKay.

"I'll have her checked out as soon as we get where we're going."

"You're not going to share your location?"

"Under the circumstances I doubt it would be safe. Meanwhile, you'd better phone Inspector St. John," McKay called from the door, his arm circling Carly's shoulders. "Tell him there's a body in your freezer. I have a feeling it's one of his men who got too close to some answers."

Chapter 24

McKay took no chances as they left Paradise Cay. He arranged for one of Inspector St. John's men to drive the Triumph out of the estate at dusk, while another man slumped low in the passenger seat. Ten minutes later, a dusty truck belonging to the gardener lumbered down the gravel drive and turned south onto the beach road toward Bridgetown.

Archer was at the wheel, delighted to make any contribution to Carly's safety. McKay and Carly sat hidden in back, with McKay checking the mirror constantly to see that they weren't followed. When he was finally satisfied that the ruse had worked, he motioned for Archer to stop.

Except for the drone of insects, the road was quiet in the darkness. "I'll take over from here." McKay opened the passenger door and jumped down. "It's less than a mile back to the fork. You can phone for a ride from the store there."

Archer watched McKay take his place at the wheel. When he was ready to close the door, Archer gripped his arm. "Keep her safe," he said stiffly.

Then he disappeared into the darkness.

McKay found the road on the third try.

The house belonged to an old friend of Izzy's, a man with a security background and unquestionable integrity. Most important, he was an outsider who would never be connected with Carly or McKay.

Following the narrow road, they climbed into the mountains along the center of the island. Ragged clouds veiled the horizon to the west, blocking the view out to sea. Izzy had said to make a sharp right at the baobab tree, and McKay did just that, passing beneath a huge tree with fantastic, intertwined trunks. Carly said very little, and he didn't bother her with questions, knowing she needed to work through the harrowing experience. She was too smart not to realize that somewhere in St. John's chain of command there was at least one traitor.

A big fieldstone house came into view, surrounded by crimson bougainvillea.

"These people are your friends?" It was the first time Carly had spoken since they'd left Paradise Cay.

"The owner is a friend of a friend. Don't worry, you can trust him without question."

"He isn't — someone from Santa Marina?"

The question cost her, and McKay was sorry for that. "No, he isn't. He doesn't even know the Brandons. He and his family settled here only a few years ago."

Carly nodded as two dogs exploded through the grass. A tall man walked behind them, improbably dressed in a dark kilt. He spoke calmly to the dogs, calling them to heel, then reached out to shake hands through the open window of the truck.

"You would be Ford McKay." He spoke in the soft burr of the Highlands. "Duncan Campbell. Welcome to Campbell's Hill."

"Glad to see you." McKay crossed around to the passenger door and helped Carly down. "This is Carly Sullivan."

"Welcome, Ms. Sullivan. Everything's ready for you. My wife and daughters are on a trip to St. Croix this week, but I've a stew and fresh bread prepared." He picked up Carly's bag and looked at McKay. "Any problems getting here?"

"All quiet."

The Scotsman nodded, tapping out his pipe on a granite seat at the edge of the drive. "The guest house is just beyond the garden. You'll have a view right down to the sea."

"We don't want to disturb you," Carly said uneasily.

The Scotsman studied her, one brow raised. "My dear girl, you are my guests, and all I have is yours." It was a simple statement, but said in a way that brooked no further discussion. "Why don't you go on ahead? Take your time and be comfortable."

McKay was fascinated by the race of emotions in Carly's eyes as they walked in silence toward the blue-shingled house. Her steps slowed as they neared the little fence marking the front lawn. "Duncan trained as a medic. I want him to check you out, then have a look at those stitches."

"Later." She ran a hand through her hair, then pushed open the wooden gate and stepped through. "It hits me when I don't expect it. First the cold, then the memory of that horrible body."

McKay saw the flash of fear in her eyes, the agonizing doubts about people she knew and loved. Right now one of those people could be trying to kill her. Down the slope the Scotsman ambled into view. Izzy's friend was still fairly young, newly retired from the SAS. He seemed content with his life as an island landowner, happy to turn his back on the shadow world of intelligence. But the habits were intact, McKay saw. As Campbell called his dogs to heel, he continually scanned the area, his body loose, yet well centered, ready for action.

As usual, Izzy had made a good choice.

Carly, too, watched their host as he calmed his golden retrievers and scanned the woods with the same quiet intensity she'd seen in McKay. They were from the same world, she realized. Both were dangerous men, well trained in deadly skills.

The thought did not repel her as it had only hours before. Carly knew those deadly skills might be the only things that could protect her.

She felt all her old rules and attitudes slip away like sand. Probably that was to be expected in the wake of a brush with death.

A red ceramic tortoise stood beside the door of the guest house, flanked by a bright blue rabbit. "Do you want to go in?" McKay asked.

She nodded. "I don't want to see other people. Not yet." Her voice was dull and flat.

"Take your time." He guided her into a room bright with batik pillows and painted rattan furniture. "Ready to eat?"

"Actually, I'd like to clean up and change." Maybe a shower would help erase the chill memories.

"The shower is this way." McKay pointed

beyond the kitchen to a small yard curtained by a high hedge of oleander.

"There?" Carly stared at the blue tiles set directly into the grass beneath an outdoor shower.

"It's completely private. No one will bother you here." He found a towel and draped it over her shoulders. "Not even me," he said gently.

"But —" She swallowed hard, aware of the pounding of her heart. It was time to face her fear, just as it was time to face her restless longing. Standing at the edge of the porch, she slid her hand into his. "It's everyone else I'm worried about, not you."

"You didn't trust me last night."

"How could I? Last night taught me how dangerous you can be," she said softly. "This morning taught me that I need that dangerous strength to stay alive."

His hand tightened on hers. "No one will find you here."

"How can you be so sure?"

"Trust me." He reached behind her to flip on the water. "You'll feel better after you shower. I'll take your suitcase to the bedroom."

Carly didn't move. "Don't go." She closed her eyes, feeling the weight of unspoken questions. "Talk to Duncan later."

"What do you mean?"

"I mean I don't want you to go." She tilted her head, smiling faintly as she tugged his shirt from his jeans. "Shocked?"

He took a hard breath. "Surprised. Why the change?"

Carly tugged open his shirt with trembling fingers. "This is the part where you stop talking, McKay. Then you close your eyes and let me drive you mindless with lust." His shirt opened and she ran her hands over his chest.

"You're sure?" he asked hoarsely.

"Sure enough to stake my life on it." Her hands trembled on his shoulders. "Don't go."

Gravely, he removed her jacket and sent it flying. Maybe they could work this out of their systems, and by tomorrow they'd be sane again, logical and back in control.

Fool, a voice whispered. She still had stitches.

But there were ways around that, especially if a man was experienced.

And McKay was definitely experienced. His hellion years had taught him the power of raw lust, and he sensed Carly needed that now to burn away her terror. With the right man she'd slide free, stripped of all fears and limitations.

The thought made him freeze. The right man?

He remembered the look on her face after he'd pinned her to the floor. He remembered, too, all the things he'd done in places he'd worked hard to forget. How could a man with no future, a man with blood on his conscience, be right for a lady like Carly?

"What about love?" he asked harshly.

"What about it?"

"You know what I mean. We're not talking about deathless vows of fidelity, Carly. That's got to be clear before things go any further." He growled the words, testing her resolve, lacerating his own.

"You mean no white picket fence and 2.5 children? No term life insurance? Are you telling me that I'm going to be a one-night stand, McKay?"

"I'm telling you there are rules," he said tightly. "One of mine is that things stay honest. I never make promises I can't keep, Carly." Only his control kept him from moving, from taking her quickly, blindly.

"Fine. No white picket fences." Her head tilted. "Anything else I should know? Blood type and medical history?"

His nerves were stretched too tight for

him to smile. "This isn't a game. Once we start, things will get hot and raw, probably out of control."

Her lips curved. "Is that a promise?"

"Dammit, Carly, this is serious. It's been a while since I've had sex." He spoke bluntly so that she would harbor no illusions. "That's what it will be. Sex. Not a relationship, not some heavenly melding of spiritual bliss."

"Spiritual bliss can be overrated." Her smile faded as she looked down at their entwined fingers. "Are you trying to shock me?"

"Damned right I am." His fingers clenched on hers. "Am I succeeding?"

She was too smart not to see the risks. Too proud not to consider them carefully. "Not a chance. I told you before that I was tired of watching the parade go by. Of course, I still have stitches."

"There are ways."

"I bet you know them all." Her voice was husky, almost wistful.

"Probably." *No illusions,* he reminded himself.

"You're a dangerous man, McKay."

"I can be." He didn't look away, didn't soften his tone.

The words hung between them until

Carly let out a ragged breath. "I'm not backing out."

"Because you think you owe me?" he asked harshly.

She stiffened, pulling free of his hands. "I don't pay debts with my body. If you think that, you're a fool."

"I don't," he said softly. "But I had to be sure."

"For a smart man, you can be awfully dumb, McKay."

"Then look at me," he said hoarsely. "Keep looking at me." The moment his mouth touched hers, he was lost. In an instant, rules faded and reason fled in a wave of need that drove him to claim and possess. She moved her head, changing the angle of their kiss. "You mean like this?"

He closed his eyes, fighting an urge to take her then and there, without patience or care. Speech beyond him, he simply nodded. No woman had ever stripped away his control so cleanly.

She touched his jaw. "You've got a scar beneath your eye. How did it happen?"

He couldn't remember. Something to do with a man with a knife. Choppy seas, noise, and fear.

The other man had died and McKay had pulled himself out of the water, then vomited up his guts until his ribs burned. It had been his first kill. "A swimming accident," he muttered.

She didn't answer, moving her hand to another scar at the side of his neck. "What about this one?"

McKay felt another kick of flashback. He'd been in a beachfront dive in a drug-rich South American hellhole with two killers rushing him in the darkness.

Only he had walked away.

"Deep-water dive. Current changed."

He withheld the gory details of the encounter. Honesty — within careful limits.

"The sea again."

He said nothing. His hands went still against her, though the effort cost him. "You want me to stop? Say the word and it will end here."

She drew a hard breath. "I don't want it to stop." His skin felt ready to ignite when she tugged his T-shirt from the waistband of his jeans. He caught her wrists, feeling her shudder as his hand skimmed her lace camisole, then slid beneath, closing around her breast. His lips followed, teasing and goading, stretching out the pleasure until she moaned restlessly.

"Your shirt," she rasped, yanking at the black cotton and sending it flying. Her breath caught as she struggled vainly with the buckle at his zipper. Cursing softly, he finished for her, grimly aware that this was supposed to be about turning her to putty, not him. Through a haze of desire, he felt her nails rake delicately over his back.

"Always a lady," he muttered, nuzzling his way up her throat. "Maybe we need to do something about that control." He claimed her mouth, dragging in the taste and heat of her while he shoved down her skirt.

She made a low sound when he stroked her thighs and drew away her last bit of lingerie, then parted the soft curls.

She sighed, gripping his shoulders as he found her tight, hidden center. With the water a glistening spray around them, he sank to the ground and took her with his mouth.

Her sudden stiffening told him she hadn't had this kind of pleasure before, and the discovery nearly undid the last remnant of his control. Her body shook as he savored her, drawing her moan of pleasure. Knowing that no other man had touched her this way, he took his time with his sultry exploration and drank in the sight and feel of her, his blood pounding. Slowly he snapped the pleasure tight and felt her shudder as another husky cry spilled free.

"I've wanted this, wanted you. Again and again." Rising, he backed her against the wall, needing to feel the pleasure race again, but she pushed away, tugging at his belt and cursing when the denim resisted.

"I may have to murder whoever invented jeans," she rasped.

"I'll help you." They finished the job together, their breath fast and straining. When it was done, she stared fiercely at him, her skin slick from the shower spray. And then her fingers closed around him, making him shudder when she grazed him delicately with her nails.

Honor, McKay thought, closing his eyes. *Distance and detachment.*

To hell with detachment, he decided. "Put your legs around me," he said, bracing his arm on the cottage wall. Cupping her hips, he rocked her against him beneath the hot, pounding water. "Okay? Your side —"

"Forget my side. Just let me have you now." She was wet and tight when she sank against him, taking him within her, inch by incredible inch.

So beautiful, he thought, bringing them together with deep, rocking strokes. But he cursed when he saw the tears dotting her cheeks. "I hurt you, dammit."

"No." She gripped his shoulders. "I want more. I want to feel your pulse deep inside me." Her legs locked as she drove against him urgently. "Do it now."

McKay fought a haze of need as her body clenched, each tremor dragging him to the very edge of control. Blindly, he drove upward while spray misted their joined bodies, and she cried out his name, rocked to a shuddering climax.

He realized he should have pulled free and found protection, but she continued to move against him, her nails raking his shoulders, and then all thought was beyond him. With the shower beating hot on his back, he held her, guiding her once again to a breathless climax. Only then did he close his eyes and cry out hoarsely, spilling himself inside her.

Chapter 25

"I'm falling."

He felt her fingers clutch at his arms. "Just let go," he said. "Slide your legs along me. I'll hold you."

She sighed as he left the haven of her body, and that sound of wordless wanting nearly brought him to his knees.

He knew that he had no right to touch her, just as he had no bright, glowing future to offer. He refused to make her promises he'd never be able to keep, though it tore at some deep part of him.

Silently he lowered her to her feet, keeping his mind cool and hard as he soaped her slowly, then did the same for himself.

None of it worked. He could no more wash away his need for her than he could forget her scent or the sleek tug of her climax.

Carly turned in his arms, studying their sodden clothes on the grass. "I should pick those up, but I forget how to use my hands. Any suggestions?"

"You're asking the wrong person," McKay said. "I'm barely able to stand up myself."

"Here I was counting on you for all the answers," she said huskily.

He managed to snag the towel off the grass. "If we can stagger inside, I could probably show you a few things."

Her eyes widened as she savored his wet, naked body. "Goody, show and tell."

McKay slid the towel around her shoulders, then picked her up in one smooth motion.

"Impressive, McKay, but what about our clothes?"

"We'll get them. In a decade or two."

She touched his jaw tenderly. "Does this mean you've got plans?"

His body was already stirring, need flaring back to life as he carried her up the steps to the cottage. "I'd say that's becoming obvious." He sank onto the poster bed and drew the towel along her flushed body. He had just taken her, but he already wanted her again.

Carly pushed to one elbow. "I thought there were biological parameters and endurance factors." Her gaze flicked lower, taking in his fully aroused body. She gave a soundless whistle. "Very impressive, McKay."

He grinned as he knelt beside her, pulling a foil square from his bag. "Glad you approve."

Carly smiled wryly as he smoothed the protection into place. "A little late for that, isn't it?"

"If there are consequences, I'm fully responsible," he said gravely. But even as he spoke, he fought down a sudden image of her body round with a child, knowing that a civilized, domesticated life was closed to him. Others of his profession had tried to live in that world, and most of them had failed. As far as McKay was concerned, they were fools to have tried.

He forced away his regrets and slid between her thighs, savoring the feel of her against his palm.

"How can you turn me inside out like this?"

He couldn't explain when his body was vised by the same need. All that mattered was sinking deep and hearing her small, broken cry as he filled her completely.

"Ready to stop?"

"Just try it," she muttered, closing her teeth around his earlobe.

He couldn't resist a grunt of triumph. "Good. This might take a while."

In moments he had them both panting, both straining breathlessly. He meant to take his time, but she convulsed against him, exhausted.

As he smoothed his hands down her shuddering body, she opened her eyes. "I can't."

"No?" Watching her face, he rocked deep, catching her cry of giddy delight with his lips. With his pulse hammering, he took and took until his orgasm tore free and he collapsed against her.

The sky was velvet and cloudless through the lead-paned windows. Somewhere a bird called in notes of pure, liquid wonder.

She knew where she was.

Vaguely, anyway.

Sighing, she decided it wasn't worth the effort to do anything but drift, sated and limp against the cool linen sheets.

A warm leg moved against hers and a hand covered her hip. With a supreme act of will she raised her head. "Are we still alive?"

"Just barely."

"Daphne said the right man would turn me to putty," she murmured. "I am now prepared to believe whatever she says."

"That could be dangerous." McKay traced a slow line over her hip.

"Probably. Next thing you know, I'll be wearing one of her leather miniskirts."

McKay gave her a lazy grin. "Leather's okay by me."

As moonlight poured around them, Carly

realized she'd never before felt so honest and easy with a man.

It was pure delight.

The trick, she decided, would be to keep everything simple and direct.

Starting now.

She feathered her fingers along his shoulder, studying his face in the flow of silver through the window, wincing a little when his arm brushed her side.

"Hell," he muttered. "Those stitches must be sore."

She put one finger to his lips. "Don't tell anyone, but I've found a great analgesic."

He didn't laugh. "I should have a look."

"Later," she whispered.

"No more gymnastics."

Her brow arched. She ran one bare toe along his thigh. "If you ask nice, I'll give you five minutes to recuperate."

"Like hell."

She pulled him down against her. "In that case shut up, McKay."

Suprisingly, he did.

The moon was gone. Through the window he saw the first hint of gray touch the sky. Turning, he felt a warm weight against his chest. At his waist and thighs, too, he discovered.

Carly was draped over him like a warm quilt, snoring very softly, both hands curved around his neck.

He smiled slowly. He'd known many women and shared nearly every kind of pleasure, but none of those steamy couplings had been half as intimate as lying motionless beneath Carly's warm body in the half-light before dawn.

How could something so chaste be so damnably arousing? he wondered. Even asleep, she was vibrant and utterly seductive.

Desire came in a heavy wave, and for long moments he savored the simple awareness of her skin against his. Then her leg shifted, cradling his hips, and she sprawled open to his full, heated erection. Even then she was completely oblivious.

He was sorely tempted to slip inside her while she slept and wake her in slow, breathless increments.

Cold logic prevailed.

She had to be sore, both from their lovemaking and from her wound, and he knew the situation called for restraint. Reluctantly, he slid from bed and tugged the quilt around her, marveling yet again at how completely she had given herself to him in the moonlight.

Shower, he thought. *Make it a cold one.*

McKay returned from his shower to find Carly awake and oddly tense. Despite her silence, he sat beside her, tracing the smooth line of her back.

She didn't look at him. "We need to talk."

"I thought that was supposed to be my line."

She sat up, gathering the sheet to her chest. "It's not a line. It's a request." She took a tight breath. "A seriously important request." She drew another breath. "To a man I care about deeply."

"Deeply," he repeated. "Why does that sound so ominous?"

"Because it is." She shivered as his fingers continued their smooth glide.

"Three. Four."

"What are you *doing?*"

"Counting your freckles. You've got two on your neck, another one above your shoulder blade. There's an amazing one just beneath your breast." He moved her arm and stroked the faint tan smudge with his tongue. "Who knew?"

"Stop." She shivered as he nuzzled his way expertly across her breast. "We've got to talk."

"I'm all ears." He trailed one finger along

her waist. "Eight. Nine."

"I can't concentrate when you do that."

"No?" The thought filled him with primitive pleasure as his hands moved lazily down her spine. "How about when I do this?"

"No," she said with a catch in her voice. "And stop repeating what I say."

"Repeating?" Gravely, he traced the line of her hip. "Twelve. That one is shaped like a flower."

She closed her eyes. "You're not listening."

"I'm memorizing every word."

"You should, because this is important." She stared at the tangled sheets. "I'm not good with relationships, McKay. Not with making them, not with keeping them. You need to know that."

"You've had a lot of relationships?"

"Enough." Carly pulled the sheet tighter. "It's part of the way I was brought up. My mother came and went. She loved me and she loved my father, but she couldn't stay. Not ever. The work was always there, pulling her away, tugging her off to immortalize some mountain in Chile or temple ruins in Burma."

He folded back the sheet, kissing her spine. "So?"

"So her work came first, that's what I'm

trying to say. So does mine," Carly whispered. "It's the way I am."

McKay's hand stilled. That really was supposed to be *his* line. "You want to leave? Is that what you're saying, Carly?" He felt weightless, as if the slightest wind blowing through the window would drive them apart.

She took a long breath. "Not yet. But I will. Something basic is wrong inside me. Something important is missing, maybe because of all those years of moving, always waiting for my mother to settle down. When it didn't happen, I gave up on believing and belonging." She turned away, staring tensely out the window at the sun-streaked sky. "Then everything fell into place. I'm just like her. I can't stay and I can't make a relationship work, but at least I know better than to drag other people into sharing my problem."

"So that's just the way you are, always a loner."

Carly nodded.

McKay wondered why he wasn't relieved. She had said the words first, sparing him the hard explanations and tearful questions.

Yes, he should have been relieved. For a professional, a soldier, it was the best possible situation.

But he wasn't relieved. He was confused and uneasy, rocked by regret.

So what? he told himself. She couldn't stay, but neither could he. He had never wanted to stay before, so why should he start now? "It's your call," he said. "I'm not holding you."

Tears were shining on her cheeks. "Thank you."

"You want to leave now?"

She shook her head.

"In an hour?"

"It's not a joke, McKay," she said stiffly.

"No, it isn't." He studied her face, pale in the golden dawn. "Nor is this." He pulled her down gently. Catching her wrists, he sank inside her before she could speak, before words or explanations could damage this recklessly beautiful thing that was happening to them again.

Panting, she rose against him, pulling him deeper, her eyes bottomless. "Just so you know," she whispered. "Just so we both know."

The words slid into his name, then caught on a moan as he drove them both over the edge, where words and questions were forgotten.

Chapter 26

Something was creaking.

Her head, Carly decided.

She opened her eyes carefully and found sunlight spilling through yellow curtains while a sea wind riffled her hair. She stretched lazily, remembering every second of the magic shared with her hard-eyed lover the night before. But she had always believed in guarding her privacy, keeping men at a distance because work always came first. Since she'd left Paradise Cay she hadn't even *thought* about working.

One more example of just how far her life had slid out of control since she'd met McKay. For Carly, the realization was terrifying.

She sat up slowly, the movement stirring muscles well used in the long hours of night.

A sound came from the doorway. Carly turned — and her heart lurched.

He stood with one arm braced on the door frame, dressed to kill in jeans riding low at his lean waist. "Morning, sunshine."

She felt a stab of pure lust at the sight of his chiseled abs. Having a body like that ought to be illegal, she decided.

"You look good in my sheets," he said huskily. "You're going to look even better out of them."

Heat flared into her face. With one short sentence, he had tangled her senses, turned her inside out. She looked away, fighting for calm.

"A problem?"

"No."

His voice fell, suddenly serious. "Feeling boxed in?"

"No." She dropped the sheet and shrugged into her robe.

"It doesn't take a genius to see that something's bothering you."

Carly studied his face, shadowed against the morning sun. She ached to know all the personal details hidden beneath his controlled mask.

The reason was all too clear: Despite her careful defenses, she was already halfway in love with him.

Terrified by the realization, she leaped to the offense. "What's bothering me is questions you refuse to answer. Like why you wear a gun. And what kind of threat is involved here?"

"For now you need to drop the questions, Carly."

"I can't. No sane woman would." She

jerked angrily at her belt, knowing the questions were simply an excuse to pull away from commitment.

"Put them on hold. I'll help you finish your photo shoot and I'll stay close. In return you're going to have to *trust* me."

His face was grave and she knew his request wasn't made lightly. She hesitated, hating her indecision. "At least tell me what you've got planned."

"We stay right here until the cruise ship returns. No one knows we're here — not Nigel Brandon, not Inspector St. John or any of his men."

It made good sense. Carly nodded slowly. "Then we'll take this one day at a time."

"That's the plan." He pulled her gently to her feet. "Why don't you go do whatever beautiful women do in the morning while I talk to Duncan and make breakfast." He slid a hibiscus bloom into her hair. "I'm one hell of a cook, you know. The trick is not to overmix the pancake batter, and to make sure the griddle is very hot."

"Show-off."

"Someone's got to make you eat. After that I want Duncan to look at your stitches." He crossed to his canvas duffel bag and pulled out a walkie-talkie. "Meanwhile, keep this within reach. If you need me, press this button and talk."

"But —"

He put the instrument into her hand, then leaned closer for a slow, searching kiss. "Or we could forget about breakfast entirely," he murmured.

Carly was determined to recover some measure of control, and she hoped a little distance would help. Clutching the walkie-talkie against her chest, she shrugged. "Go talk to Duncan while I shower. I'll meet you at the main house in an hour."

"I'm not sure I can wait an hour." His eyes were very dark.

"On the other hand, delay makes the final event more . . . potent."

McKay kissed her cheek. "If my event becomes any more potent," he said, "I won't be able to walk."

"Are you expecting visitors?" Standing near the front windows of the main house, McKay watched a truck lumber up the gravel drive. "Someone in a big gray delivery van, for example."

Frowning, the Scotsman moved to the doorway. "No one scheduled. I'll see who it is."

McKay fingered a switch on his walkie-talkie. "Carly, are you there?"

"I'm here," she answered. "Is something wrong?"

There was a sudden edge of fear in her voice, but McKay knew fear could be good if it kept a person from being reckless. "There's a delivery truck outside on the drive. Can you see it?"

He heard the faint rustle of fabric. "I do now. The shower was running and I didn't hear him drive up."

"No problem. Just stay out of sight until he leaves."

He heard her swallow. "Of course. But . . . will you keep the line open until then?"

Just in case. The phrase drifted, unsaid.

"Will do. And don't worry, I'm right over at the main house."

Duncan returned a few minutes later, pocketing his cell phone. "He's gone. It was a clay delivery for my wife's pottery company. I checked with the store in town, and they confirmed the driver was theirs. He's gone now." Outside they heard the distant backfire of a truck.

"Coast is clear, Carly. I'll come get you."

"Not yet. I need to primp a little. I want to surprise you. Daphne loaned me some clothes."

McKay had a sudden image of Carly in a

skintight miniskirt. "White leather, by any chance?"

"You're getting warm, McKay."

"You have no idea how warm."

"Give me twenty minutes."

He was still staring down the hill when he broke the connection. "One more down."

Duncan looked up from the kettle he was filling with water. "Anything you can talk about?"

"Afraid not."

"I expected that was the case. You're welcome to stay as long as you like, since my wife and daughters are away. For their safety, I couldn't have gotten involved otherwise."

"Neither Izzy nor I would have expected it. He remembered that your wife buys supplies off island this time of year."

"Luckily, what she doesn't know won't hurt her." Duncan grinned conspiratorially. "Meanwhile, it's invigorating to have a hand in again."

McKay studied his host, who was wearing a white shirt and crisp khaki trousers today. "You were SAS, weren't you?"

Duncan reached for two cups, nodding. "Professional to the core. I never planned to leave, believe me. In fact, I broke off with Risa after several months, certain a relationship couldn't survive when I was constantly out of the country on one mission or another. Risa accepted that. She never wanted to make me choose between her and the job, and she didn't believe me when I told her I'd left the service. It took the deed to this property to convince her I was serious."

"You never looked back?"

"Not often." Duncan poured two cups of tea, a wry smile on his face. "I have no question I made the right choice, if that's what you're asking. What about you? Thinking of retiring?"

"A month ago I'd have laughed at the idea."

"And now?"

McKay glanced down toward the guest cottage. "Right now all I can think about is keeping her safe."

"What about when the job is over?"

"Then there'll be another one somewhere else. I don't deal in long-term commitments. They don't fit with my line of work."

"Priorities change." Duncan found his pipe and filled it thoughtfully. "Maybe you should consider that."

"Carly's not the sort to settle down. I gather her mother set some sort of pattern about that."

Smoke drifted from Campbell's pipe.

"I've seen her mother's work. Pure magic, it was. Children caught dancing in a summer rain, and a white horse racing along a field of wildflowers at sunset. The images took your breath away." He drew gently on his pipe. "That kind of skill is a rare thing."

"Carly says she never stayed. She was too busy chasing down the perfect composition and camera angle."

The Scotsman watched smoke twist up in lazy spirals. "A difficult thing, one our society doesn't look kindly on, especially when children are involved. So what are you two going to do next?"

McKay rubbed his neck. "Enjoy the time we have together."

The Scotsman pursed his lips. "And when that time is over?"

"We'll go our separate ways. We both know the rules."

"Ah, rules. Not breaking them usually turns out to be the hard part, especially where the heart is involved."

Wraiths of smoke trailed up in the sunlight while wind chimes echoed on the porch.

"Hell." McKay jammed his hands into his pockets. "Who am I kidding? I'm halfway gone already. When she looks at me and that slow smile starts growing in her eyes . . ." He shook his head. "I shouldn't have let this happen. I'm supposed to be the experienced one."

"A man can't always be perfect."

"But he'd damned well better try," McKay said grimly. "In my line of work, not trying will get you killed."

"Unpleasant, but true." Duncan stared out the window. "Any way I can help?"

"You can stop painting such a picture of marital bliss."

His host chuckled. "Afraid I can't help you. I love Risa more today than when I met her. A man can ask for nothing more."

McKay fought back images of a lifetime spent with Carly in a noisy house full of intrepid children. Irritated at his daydreaming, he pulled the secure cell phone from his pocket.

"You're calling Izzy, I presume."

"Someone else."

"But you will call Izzy. When you do, give him my regards and tell him I haven't forgotten a long-ago night in a crowded alley in Bangkok. While you make your calls, I'll take a walk and make certain we haven't received any more unexpected guests."

Chapter 27

"St. John, it's McKay. I want an update."

"McKay?" A chair creaked sharply. "Where in the hell are you?"

"No need for you to know that."

"Governor Brandon will need your location in case —"

"The governor-general doesn't need to know either," McKay snapped. "Whoever locked Carly in the freezer had to have contacts inside your organization. No one else had access to the house."

"Are you accusing me of trying to kill Carly?"

"I'm simply stating what we both know is true. Someone got past all our security. I'm not risking Carly's life on another leak."

St. John sighed. "How is she?"

"Holding up."

"I'm glad to hear it. A hell of a thing, being locked in a damned freezer. If not for that cell phone . . ." St. John cleared his throat. "As of now I've assigned every available man and woman to this case. Meanwhile, the driver of that food van didn't arrive at his next call, and we've tracked him to St. Thomas."

"I want facts, not an itinerary, St. John. He almost killed Carly."

"You'll get your facts just as soon as I have them. You were right, by the way. One of my men is dead. They shoved him inside a bag and saw to it he was frozen solid." The officer's words snapped out in a hard staccato. "He had two bullets in the head."

"He knew something," McKay said flatly. "Find out exactly who he was working with, and maybe you'll find out what he knew."

"I'm questioning each of my officers personally, but it's going to take a while."

Silence.

"I'm glad you got her out in time."

"If she hadn't found that cell phone, I might not have."

St. John's chair creaked again. "You should call Governor Brandon. He's very worried."

"Tell him to concentrate on doing what he has to do. I'll do the same."

"You'll be reboarding the ship together, I take it. I'll escort you to the dock and see you safely on board."

McKay watched bright wings flash over a wall of hollyhocks. "I'd rather you didn't. The less attention paid us, the better."

"So you don't trust me either."

"Right now I don't trust anyone but myself."

Papers rustled. "Maybe that's best. If I were you I'd be skeptical too. Bon voyage, McKay. Don't let her out of your sight."

Forty-eight hours later he still hadn't let her out of his sight.

She was the picture of contentment lounging in a chaise, idly twirling a hibiscus blossom. It had been a whole day since she'd asked for her sketch pad or camera.

And only three hours since they had raced across the bed, desperate to tear off each other's clothes.

Unfortunately, their peace was at an end. Mel had finally called with the news that Carly was reinstated and the project was back on line. In two hours they would board the cruise ship for its homeward jaunt to Miami.

McKay had anticipated the security concerns and discussed them with Izzy. Both knew that protection would be easier on the ship, especially since the man Carly had recognized from Izzy's fax, an Austrian national with an arrest record that crisscrossed four continents, was now being detained for questioning in Barbados.

Another one down, McKay thought grimly.

Carly glanced up and studied his face. "Problems?"

"A few thousand. Nothing important, though."

She twirled her hibiscus wistfully. "I wish we could stay. I'm not sure I want to be civilized again. I like walking barefoot and being clothing optional."

"It had to happen sooner or later. Besides, you've got a shoot to finish. Griffin Kelly bit the dust even sooner than I expected."

"He's a weasel." She lifted a fallen red petal. "Do you think he was involved?"

That possibility was currently being considered, McKay knew, though he wasn't at liberty to tell her that. "It seems unlikely. He's malicious, but I doubt he'd try murder to boost his career."

Her eyes met his. "Will the ship be any safer?"

"I guarantee it, because you won't be out of my sight."

"Not ever?"

"We can negotiate terms."

Her lips curved. "What if I want to go shopping?"

"Fine by me, as long as you make a stop for lingerie. Of course, you'll have to model it for me."

Her eyes were thoughtful as she slipped her hand into his. "What are we waiting for?"

They were watched as they turned onto the main road heading south. They were watched as they wove along the small coves bordering the sea. At the edge of Bridgetown, a man at a roadside fruit stall noted their progress and radioed ahead.

By then, four men were already waiting at the dock.

Chapter 28

Mayhem ruled at the dock.

Laughter and complaints mingled with the sound of the ship's powerful engines, the raucous call of sea birds, and shoving tourists eager to make their way aboard.

McKay circled slowly, and by the time he had parked and helped Carly out of the car, the last passengers were boarding the launch for the ship.

He moved in front of her as she started for the line of embarkation. "Not that way. We're taking the crew boat."

"For security, I take it, not simple convenience?"

"Both." He guided her to the end of the dock, where another launch was waiting, full of crew members with assorted booty from their shore excursions. McKay spoke with a uniformed security guard, showed his and Carly's passports, then led her aboard.

The wind was high as they cruised out toward the liner. Once on board, McKay guided her toward a set of elevators at the far end of the corridor. "How can you remember the ship's layout so well?" Carly asked.

"I studied a diagram." The elevator chimed and McKay pulled her inside, glanced at the buttons, and selected one. "It's a little walk to our quarters. We need to go up three decks, then jog to port." He guided her off the elevator, then set off briskly.

Carly watched him as they climbed a spiral staircase and passed a string quartet playing Vivaldi. "Not studied, memorized."

McKay shrugged. "Call it a hobby. Come on, I'll buy you a drink before we go to our cabins."

Carly had more questions to ask, but she found herself in a quiet corner with a perfectly salted margarita, and as she listened to a strolling mariachi band she let her questions drift.

She raised her glass. "Here's to adventure."

"Be careful what you wish for."

She took another sip of her margarita. "We have four days left until we dock in Miami and I intend to enjoy them." She stared at him over the salted rim of her glass. "Care to join me?"

"The offer is irresistible."

"Good. First things first. I need to unpack. Then you promised to take me shopping."

"Did I really say that?"

"Good try, big guy, but a deal is a deal."

He raised his hands in a gesture of surrender. "Just ignore me if I whimper now and then."

"Real men don't whimper."

"They do if they have to take a woman shopping for shoes."

"Shoes? You jest. That's only the start."

"Maybe I can convince you to pick up a few frivolous, overpriced undergarments while you're at it. I'll have to see everything up close, of course, so I can advise you."

"I might be persuaded." Listening to the music, Carly watched the ocean shimmer beyond the lounge windows.

Magic, she thought. There was a rich, expectant mood to the day that left her smiling. For once in her life, she was going to live in that magical flow and stop questioning all the details.

As they stood to leave, McKay took her arm and she saw two women follow him speculatively with their eyes. It didn't take much imagination to guess they were wondering about him — and hating her for being with him.

Four days. Her questions could wait that long, until they docked in Miami.

She was startled when they turned down

an unfamiliar corridor. "Why here?"

"Your luggage has been moved to the suite adjoining mine. There's a connecting door between us for convenience." His voice fell. "I can't take care of you with a deck separating us."

Not for convenience, but safety. Because she was still a target.

Carly toyed with her watch uneasily, then nodded.

"Stand to my left, away from the door," McKay said softly.

The corridor was silent as he slid a card into the door, then swung inside and scanned the interior. With a start, Carly realized he had drawn his gun, which was now pointed at a man sitting inside the suite.

The room steward, she realized. But there was no fear or wariness in his expression. He smiled faintly, as if amused by the whole scene.

Releasing his breath, McKay holstered his gun beneath his jacket, then pulled her inside and shut the door. "Glad to see you, Izzy."

"Same goes."

Carly studied the big man in the crisp white jacket. "You're partners, aren't you?"

The steward sauntered closer, hand extended.

McKay found a quarter from his pocket and slapped it into his hand. "Yeah, we're partners. And if he doesn't stop asking for tips, I'm going to deck him."

With a snort, the steward pocketed the coin, gave Carly a wink, and left, his broad shoulders nearly filling the doorway.

McKay said nothing as he checked the bathroom, the closet, and finally the veranda.

"I'm sure your friend has already done that," Carly said. "He doesn't look like the type to miss much."

"I prefer to do my own checking. Call it habit."

"Are you going to tell me who you really work for?"

He opened the connecting door and stepped inside her cabin, subjecting it to the same silent scrutiny. Carly followed, certain he was stalling to avoid her question. "Well?"

He caught her by the elbows before she plowed into him, pulling her into his arms. "Who I work for isn't important."

"It is to me," she said stubbornly.

He angled her head for a long, openmouthed kiss that left her pulse zinging. "Adjoining cabins is definitely the right idea."

Carly ignored his innuendo. "I need to check in with my crew, then call Mel in New York."

"Fine. Just keep the chain on. Don't open your door for anyone but me or Izzy."

"How will I know it's you?"

He whistled the theme from *Close Encounters of the Third Kind.*

"You're kidding. A secret whistle? Gee, do I get a secret decoder ring, too?"

McKay didn't hide his smile. "Simple is usually better. When you're ready to leave, call me on the phone in your suite." His smile faded. "Remember, don't unchain the door for anyone else."

Carly realized he was deadly serious.

It took two hours to check in with Mel, then track down all her crew. Hank was back from New York, sporting new camera equipment. While she checked out his high-tech camera, they ran through half a dozen ideas for the next set of shots.

It seemed that her career was back on course, despite Griffin Kelly's malicious ploy, and Hank assured her there would be no more sniping from New York. All she had to do now was deliver fantastic footage in record time.

A knock brought her to the door. "Name, rank, and serial number," she whispered. Satisfied by the distinctive five-note whistle, she pulled back the chain and swung open the door.

McKay studied her face. "You look tired, Sullivan."

"Busy morning. Everything's set for tomorrow. We begin shooting at seven."

He hid a grimace. "Then today you're going to have fun. That's an order." He moved to the teak bar and poured her a glass of sherry. "Relax."

"I've heard that word somewhere."

"Not the way I define it. Tonight I'll show you in detail. Unless you want to start now," he said huskily.

Carly turned her glass in her hands and surrendered to a hot, explicit image of the two of them ripping off each other's clothes in a frantic race to the bed. She cleared her throat. "No way. You promised me a shopping trip, remember? I want to impress you tonight."

"I was impressed from the first moment I saw you and Daphne by the swimming pool, checking out my thighs."

"We were *not*. It was your chest we were checking out, and for professional reasons only. We needed the best man for the job."

He tilted her head up to his and traced her flushed cheek. "Then you're lucky, sunshine. You definitely found him."

Chapter 29

McKay was starting to understand the primal frustration that drove fur-clad Neanderthals out of the cave into sweaty, hand-to-hand combat with saber-toothed tigers.

In the last hour and a half, he had watched Carly acquire swimsuits, sandals, a hammered silver choker, a quarter ounce of jasmine perfume with matching bath salts, and a slinky black evening gown with a beaded bodice.

Grappling with a saber-toothed tiger would have been more pleasant.

"Well, that was fun," Carly said, shifting a bag from her right hand to her left as she surveyed another row of shops.

McKay worked hard not to groan.

The cruise ship's promenade was not as large as Rhode Island, but it looked like it was. Mirrored elevators reflected a bustling four-story village of shops, bars, and restaurants surrounded by stained glass and false skylights.

Carly took his arm, smiling serenely as she headed for a boutique advertising crystal perfume bottles. "Anytime you want to go into a corner and whimper, just let me know."

"Aren't you about ready to take a break?" He managed to keep his voice calm, though whimpering was a real possibility.

"Maybe in a few more minutes." Carly gnawed at her lip, studying a shop that displayed a replica of a red British phone box.

McKay managed not to remind her that she had said the same thing three times in the last hour.

"Aphrodite's Secret. I can't wait."

He could, about a century or so. But a promise was a promise, and his patience was rewarded when he saw the frothy lace negligees draped over a pink satin chair in the window. "Now you're showing good judgment."

"You think you get to watch?"

"You'd better believe it. I have serious consumer input to give. If you're nice, I won't even charge you." As he spoke, McKay glanced around the boutique.

No thugs were crouched behind the Louis XIV armchairs. No assassins were taking aim beside the plush velvet banquettes.

He decided he could finally relax just a little. He liked watching Carly enjoy herself, and he was certain it wasn't something she got around to often in her fast-track life.

The mirrored boutique was full of brisk saleswomen and their polished, high-maintenance customers. A smiling floor attendant sailed past with iced champagne in a silver bucket.

"Stay close," Carly said. "I may suffer credit card burn unless I'm restrained."

"I'll be right beside ya, little lady," he said in his best John Wayne voice. "A man's gotta do what a man's gotta do."

"I'm so glad to hear it." Carly headed straight for a lace corselet and matching gown.

"If this is a dream, don't wake me," McKay said hoarsely. Just imagining the lace ensemble draped on her elegant body left him decidedly aroused. He was looking for a chair nearby when he heard Carly's delighted laughter. Between the displays he picked out Daphne, her arms full of lingerie, obviously intent on serious shopping of her own.

He peered at Daphne over the display. "Nice to see you again."

Daphne's eyes twinkled. "Same here. I'd like you both to meet my fiancé."

"David's here?" Carly looked flabbergasted.

"In the flesh. No more faxes or transatlantic phone calls. He flew in yesterday." She looked over Carly's shoulder. "He was here a minute ago, but he had to arrange for a fax to Switzerland." She waved to a tall man with a heavy jaw who was crossing the crowded boutique. His navy double-breasted blazer was Armani, his tie Hermès, and his teeth were perfectly white as he smiled at Daphne, a sheaf of papers beneath one arm.

"Out of champagne already, or did you want my opinion on a purchase?"

"You've been back and forth to send faxes three times — I could be buying baggy sweats and you wouldn't notice," Daphne huffed.

"Not true. I follow every detail." He touched her cheek with one knuckle. "As a matter of fact, I can tell you exactly what you've purchased and how much it cost to the penny," he added. "It just so happens that I can work at the same time."

Daphne's eyes clouded. "No business. Not today, David. You promised."

"Forgive me. The rest of the day is yours." He slid his papers into an ostrich-skin briefcase and snapped it shut with a flourish. "Where do we begin?"

"With an introduction. I know you re-member Carly. And this is Ford McKay, who's been helping out with Carly's project for the cruise line."

David turned, rubbing his hands in de-light. "Carly, it's been too long." He enveloped her in a hug, kissing each cheek with European flair. Then he turned to McKay. "You must be the man who handled that problem in Barbados."

The man was the perfect fiancé for the daughter of a head of state. He oozed charm and affability, and his clothes were immaculate.

But to McKay his eyes seemed restless, maybe even calculating. The combination of the pricy suit, the perfect haircut, and the orthodontically enhanced teeth seemed too deliberate, suggesting that David Halloran had not been "born to the purple" but worked hard to convince people otherwise.

When Halloran looked at Daphne, his eyes softened and he smiled with real warmth. There was also a hint of possessiveness, as if Daphne were a prized and fragile piece of art.

"Glad I was around to help," McKay murmured.

"I'd like to show my gratitude. In fact I insist." The banker gestured to an attendant across the aisle. "Another bottle of Cristal and two more glasses. Carly, feel free to choose something extravagant. We'll make it my gift."

Carly shifted uncomfortably. "I don't think . . ."

Daphne linked arms with her fiancé, shaking her head. "There's no arguing with him, I warn you. You'll just have to accept that you're about to be showered with gifts. David's generosity is one of his failings."

David glanced at Daphne in surprise. "That disturbs you, my dear?"

"You can be a little overwhelming at times." Daphne patted his arm. "You spend too much time with cold numbers and stock certificates. A gift means so much more if you choose and present it yourself. Perhaps a bottle of perfume."

"Only fair, since you overwhelmed *me* the instant I set eyes on you. In a room with a thousand women, there was only you," Halloran said gravely. "And you claimed my heart."

McKay was glad to be saved from further lyricism by the arrival of the champagne. Halloran nodded to the attendant, who eased the cork free and filled two more glasses.

"A drink to new friendships." It was a polite order. Glasses clinked, but McKay remained silent as the others echoed the sentiment.

As soon as possible he moved aside, his voice falling as he spoke to Carly. "Why don't you take a look at that lace outfit? Let me know if you need any help with the buttons."

A saleswoman appeared, attuned to the prospect of more sales, and Carly cleared her throat. "I'd like to see the pink lace set."

Daphne's fiancé studied the frothy items appreciatively. "Admirable taste."

Carly's taste is none of your damned business, McKay thought. The man's manners could use some work.

Daphne pulled Carly toward the dressing room. "While you try it on, you can fill me in on the shoot."

Halloran watched the two women vanish into the dressing area. "So, McKay, have you known Carly long?"

"We met on the cruise."

"Very romantic." He swirled his champagne carefully. "It's important for Daphne to have a friend with her now."

"I don't follow."

"She's worried about her foundation and about the plans for our wedding. Unfortunately, my business keeps me in Europe a great deal, and this bothers her, too." Halloran watched bubbles burst in his glass. "She also broods about her father."

"He seemed fine when I met him in Bridgetown."

"Daphne thinks otherwise." The banker

shot one immaculate cuff. "Some problem with the local government in Santa Marina. The political alliances can be unpredictable there." He smiled as Daphne's laughter spilled from the dressing room, and then he turned, refilling McKay's glass. "You're from Wyoming, Daphne tells me. A big spread?"

"We run about five hundred head of cattle along with some quarter horses. The land's been in the family for five generations."

"Impressive. Of course in Europe, five generations is a mere instant. But dreaming of the past can be a curse." He shook his head, then stood up as Daphne emerged, her dress crowned by a purple feather boa and matching mules.

"How do I look?"

"Lovely, as always. Why don't you add them to the other things?" He put down his glass and consulted his watch. "I'm afraid we have a spa appointment at four o'clock, followed by a waltz class at six-fifteen," he reminded her.

Carly emerged the dressing room, lace in hand. "Did someone mention waltz lessons?"

"Bankers can't be bothered to learn how to dance unless a woman threatens them with bodily harm." Daphne draped the boa over her arm and slid out of the mules. "You, meanwhile, are under direct orders to go forth and shop," she said to Carly. "Buy one in every color or I'll never forgive you. And we'll see you for drinks in the Crystal Club. Why don't we say seven o'clock?"

With the time set, David beckoned to a saleswoman carrying at least a dozen boxes, and the three set off for the front counter.

"I'm exhausted just watching them." Carly studied McKay. "You don't like him, do you?"

"I don't have to. I'm not marrying him." He lifted the lace from her fingers. "How did it fit?"

"Let's just say we might need to keep fire extinguishers handy," she purred.

"In that case, this one is my gift."

"But —"

"Don't even think about arguing," he said gruffly. "I'm going to enjoy seeing you wear this almost as much as I'm going to enjoy taking it off you."

"Is that a promise, McKay?"

"Count on it."

Chapter 30

Carly was nearing a sensory overload when she reached the door to her cabin. She dropped her shopping bags and dug out her room key. "Same procedure as before, I take it?"

Ford held his finger to his mouth, waited for two passengers to move past, then nodded. He inserted the door key and scanned the room from beside the door, then circled to check the rest of the cabin, moving like the cops she'd seen on TV.

To her shock, Carly was getting used to the procedure.

She frowned as McKay glanced at his watch. "Going somewhere already?"

"Speaking for myself, the two major food groups sound appealing."

Carly raised one eyebrow.

"Steak rare and whiskey neat," he explained.

"Oh, those food groups."

"Only ones that count. Why don't I come back in ten minutes?"

Carly laughed. "Getting ready for tonight is going to take me at least an hour." She waved her bags with a flourish. "I have to do my hair, try on a few purchases, then linger in a hedonistic bath."

"I could help you with the hedonistic part."

"Get lost, McKay. Getting gorgeous is serious work." She pulled a lace camisole out of one bag and let it slide through her fingers, capturing his complete attention. "Especially since Daphne will be sleek, polished, and loaded down with diamonds."

"You'll look better."

"Have you had your eyes tested lately? She was a cover model, in case you hadn't noticed."

"I noticed. Daphne's nice, but her smile isn't in the same league with yours." His gaze roamed over Carly's body. "And I can personally testify that you have the most amazingly beautiful pair of —" He broke off, exploring one of her bags.

She yanked it away. "Go on."

"Eyes. And a few other things."

"Very smooth, McKay."

"Trust me, all my smooth moves will come later."

Carly knew that if she didn't show some control, they'd never get to dinner. She wasn't about to be rushed with a night of glamour and seduction before her. She meant to stretch out the pleasure and make McKay sweat just a little.

Maybe more than a little.

Meanwhile, one thing continued to bother her. "What did you really think of Daphne's fiancé?"

"That he knows what he wants and exactly how to get it."

"You really don't like him."

"He's not my type. Whether he's Daphne type is the question."

"Before this she was always involved with creative types. Painters, musicians, and poets. David is so . . ."

"Rich?"

"Not just that. He's so *competent*. In a few minutes he seems to take over a room, and yet . . . sometimes he seems to try too hard. Of course, he probably wants to make a good impression on Daphne's friends."

A good impression and then some, McKay thought. Why would an international banker and jet-setter try so hard? Either the man had a deep need to prove himself or he was trying to cover something up. McKay still hadn't figured out which.

"I don't care if he's rich or not. I simply want Daphne to be happy." Carly glanced at the clock and gasped. "Go. I'll never be ready on time."

"Just tap on the connecting door. No need to worry if you're not completely dressed. I'll be delighted to help out with stockings, straps, or lingerie problems." He gazed appreciatively at the tangle of lace and silk on Carly's bed. "Scout's honor."

With a low laugh, Carly nudged him outside. "There are no merit badges for what you're thinking about, McKay."

Izzy was waiting when McKay unlocked his cabin, and he looked glad to be working indoors again.

"I take it you checked everything here? No bugs or unwanted electronics?"

"I was just finishing up when you arrived. No sweat, the place is squeaky clean. Carly's quarters, too." Izzy scratched at his shoulder. "At least there aren't any flying nasties to deal with here. I'd forgotten how much I hated field work." Izzy paced the room slowly. "It appears that Vronski is putting extra men on that new yacht of his. He could be planning to make his move."

"Or he might simply be enjoying the glorious Caribbean sun," McKay countered.

"He left Brandon hanging on the investment project, and now Brandon's enemies are sniping that he doesn't have the clout to close a major deal like this."

"I knew there was a reason I hated politics," McKay said. "Any intel on Vronski's hidden agenda?"

"Nothing certain. I'll pass through any information as soon as it's available. I've got full electronics set up in my cabin, so I'm I touch with D.C. twenty-four/seven. Just remember, you may not have the luxury of choosing when it's time to pull out."

"Tell me something I don't already know." McKay looked down at the shopping bag he'd tossed on the bed, a gift from Carly. "It wasn't supposed to happen this way, dammit. None of this was supposed to get personal."

Izzy whistled as a pair of men's paisley satin pajamas spilled out of the bag's colorful tissue paper.

"Don't say a word." McKay scowled. "Not a single word."

Izzy gave a mock salute. "Aye, aye, sir. Maintaining radio silence."

At six-twenty, the black marble bar in the Crystal Club was packed. The only danger appeared to be the deafening music from the dance floor, along with the glares of Carly's former model and his girlfriend, who were drinking steadily at a nearby table.

Since their cruise was already paid for, they appeared to be determined to enjoy its full benefits, despite their failed campaign against Carly. McKay planned to keep an eye on the pair. His resolution was reinforced when he saw the girlfriend aim a furious glance at Carly's back.

And what a back it was.

Her gown was simplicity itself, smooth silver fabric that clung to every curve. The back dipped several inches below her waist and swayed with every step she took.

McKay wasn't sure he'd make it through the evening.

As Carly sipped an exotic concoction with lime wedges and a paper umbrella, he worked on a Dos Equis, which was his quota for the night.

Leaning back against the bar, he allowed himself a long, thorough look at her. "That's quite a dress. You can't be wearing too much underneath, given that back and neckline."

Carly's smile was glittering.

"What *are* you wearing underneath?"

"Chanel No. 5, here and there."

McKay was sorry he had asked.

"No sign of Daphne." Carly surveyed the crowded dance floor. "She's usually so punctual."

"Maybe the waltz lessons ran over," he

said dryly. He wasn't particularly worried since he'd excused himself, called Izzy, and verified that the lovebirds were still in their cabin, safe and sound. Meanwhile, Izzy was staying close to them and had observed the two security people Daphne's father had placed in the rooms adjoining Daphne's.

"Is something wrong?"

"Not a thing. Dance with me and I'll prove it."

Halfway to the dance floor, they found their way blocked by Griffin Kelly. Red-faced and furious, his girlfriend confronted Carly. "You think you know everything, but you wouldn't recognize a good photo angle if you tripped on it." She swayed as she spoke, sloshing liquor from her glass over the nearby table. "But it's not over yet, understand?"

McKay was ready to intervene, but Carly was smiling, so he knew she wanted to handle this herself.

"Let Griffin do his own dirty work next time, Aimee. Now if you'll excuse us, I believe our dance is beginning." Carly put her hand on McKay's arm and they started toward the dance floor.

"I'm not finished with you yet. We've got business to discuss." The woman tottered toward Carly.

"I think we're finished."

"No way. I'm going to give you a piece of my mind." Her breath had to be a hundred proof, McKay noted.

Enraged, Aimee gripped her drink. "I'm talking lawyers. I'm talking court orders. I'm talking lit . . . liti—"

"Litigation?" McKay suggested.

She paid no attention to him. "Neither you nor your sleazy, overpaid boy-toy can stop us."

"I take exception to being called overpaid," McKay said under his breath.

Carly chuckled. "Point noted."

"You've been warned," the inebriated girlfriend continued. "Both of you." She staggered into McKay, righted herself, then lurched away on stiletto heels.

Carly took a deep breath, her hands trembling.

"You okay?"

"Fine. I'm not letting a no-talent shark in five-inch heels ruin my evening."

"Good for you," McKay said, guiding her onto the dance floor and pulling her into his arms. "Let's get back to the part where you tell me what's under your dress. Or what's *not*." He twirled her expertly, then eased her into a low dip.

"You aren't kidding. You really can dance."

As she eased in close, he had to force himself to concentrate on the dance rhythm. "Will Aimee be a problem for you?"

"Not really." Carly sighed. "Only a nuisance. Griffin took his best shot and lost. The rest is pure bluster. She knows she hasn't got a leg to stand on."

"Literally. They'll carry her away dead drunk any minute." He pulled her closer. "Now about your dress."

"Curious?"

"Every time I look at it, I think about that one silver clasp at the waist and how easy it would be to open. Of course, then the whole dress would slide off. Actually, my imagination is getting downright painful."

Carly patted his cheek. "That's the general idea."

McKay cleared his throat. "Let's eat." At least eating would occupy his hands and keep him from tearing off her dress.

Carly glanced around the bar area. "Since Daphne isn't here, we might as well go."

"I planned for us to —"

She covered his mouth with one finger. "Surprise me." He started to speak, but she shook her head. "Don't argue, McKay. Tonight I win all arguments. Surprise me first, then find me a patch of moonlight and waltz with me. What we do after that is up to you."

"Do you have any idea what you do to me?" he said huskily, as they left the pulsing music of the bar for a quiet corridor lit by mock gaslight. "In a minute I won't be able to walk."

She guided his hands to her breasts. "This is what you do to me." Through the sheer silk of her dress he felt the press of her nipples against his palms.

Need hit him like a gut punch. "You say that, then expect me to walk you into a crowded restaurant and eat a meal?"

"Absolutely." Her lips were a soft curve in the flickering light. "We're both going to enjoy the suspense, even when it's killing us. And we have so little time left before —"

She looked away, shaking her head.

McKay understood why she had cut off any reference to the future. It was smart of her, careful of her, but suddenly he wished they weren't so smart and life wasn't so damned complicated.

He enjoyed her look of surprise when they stopped outside an intimate restaurant decorated like a Russian hunting lodge. Samovars gleamed on lacquered tables, and strolling musicians in flowing white peasant shirts sang passionately to the hum of balalaikas. Izzy had suggested the restaurant, and judging by Carly's dreamy smile it was the perfect choice.

Their conversation was laced with laughter as their legs brushed, their hands lingered. Tension hummed, nearly feverish by the time their dinner was finished. He had arranged for the maître d' to present her with a single perfect rose the color of finest Baltic amber at the end of the meal, and she held it now, turning the soft petals against her cheek.

"How are you going to top this?"

"Wait and see." They made their way to the empty, windswept deck, fingers linked, bodies expectant. The wind ruffled Carly's hair into a soft cloud at her shoulders as he offered her the sleek leather box he'd carried in his pocket since the afternoon.

The single strand of antique gold coins and graduated amber beads left her speechless for long minutes. "You saw me coveting this today, didn't you?"

"You've got no secrets, I warn you."

"I don't want any secrets from you. Maybe that's why I'm feeling reckless tonight, as if the whole world is mine." She angled her head and bit his jaw gently. "What are you thinking? Now, right now."

His eyes were hard with shadows. "How many seconds it will take to get from here to your cabin. And then to the bed."

"Too fast, McKay. I haven't made you sweat yet."

"You like making me suffer, don't you?"

"Making us both suffer," she corrected, turning in his arms and sliding her hands beneath his jacket, then lower, where she found hard proof of his arousal.

He tried to keep his breathing steady as her fingers moved with wicked skill. "I'm almost afraid to ask what you're thinking."

"About how I'll model this necklace for you. I'm trying to decide what *else* I'll wear."

"I was thinking Chanel No. 5." His hand drifted over her hair. "But that happens to be a personal fantasy of mine."

"You might just get lucky," she whispered.

He pulled her closer. "I have big plans for that rose later, and they may take a long, long time."

She drew a husky breath. "Your dacha or mine, comrade?"

"Call me greedy." McKay slid the amber necklace into place. "I want you in both."

They made the jaunt to her cabin in record time, both breathless and fevered when they reached their corridor.

McKay stood listening at the door, then

took a step backward, pulling her against the wall. "Don't move," he whispered.

"Why?"

"Because someone's in there."

Chapter 31

Carly edged closer. "Maybe it's the hall maid turning down the bed. Or your partner."

"Or maybe not."

In a smooth, practiced movement McKay reached for the gun beneath his jacket, then motioned her back out of sight and inserted her key. Sweeping open the door, he entered the room with weapon leveled, making quarter turns while studying the shadows.

Something rustled near the curtains. Perfume drifted on the air.

"Carly, is that you?"

McKay recognized the voice. "It's Daphne." With his gun still level, he flipped on the light and frowned at the sight of Daphne curled on the sofa, her face white and drawn. Quickly, he finished checking the room and the adjoining bathroom, then holstered his weapon. "You can come in now, Carly. All clear."

She charged in after him and sank down beside Daphne, who looked confused. "Does he always enter a cabin with his weapon drawn?"

McKay smiled broadly. "Only on a quiet

day. Sometimes I carry grenades."

Daphne gave a chuckle, but the sound was shaky. "I know I shouldn't bother you." Her shoulders fell and she seemed to turn in on herself. "It's . . . David. We were going to have the whole cruise together and I was all set to tell him about the baby, but there was no time. He didn't even stay one night. He's already on his way back to Switzerland."

"He's *what?*" Carly hissed.

"Gone. Via helicopter, two hours ago. He said there was an emergency in Geneva, but I should stay and enjoy the cruise. As if I could."

"And you didn't tell him you're pregnant?"

Daphne drew a ragged breath. "In the middle of waltz lessons didn't seem the right time to announce it. After that there were always people around — his assistant, who came with the helicopter, and then someone from the ship's crew." She swept a hand over her damp cheeks. "Maybe I won't tell him. Maybe the wedding is off. If he's this way now, what kind of husband and father will he be?"

"First things first," Carly said briskly. Daphne responded best to challenges, not commiseration. There was also her health to be considered. "Have you eaten anything?"

Daphne shrugged. "A shrimp cocktail this afternoon. Some caviar later."

"Nothing like hitting the important food groups. First you're going to eat a proper meal. Then you're going to rest."

Daphne straightened her shoulders. "I shouldn't be here bothering you. I'm sure you had better things planned for tonight than playing nursemaid to a maudlin female."

"You're not maudlin," Carly said firmly. "I'll call room service while you wash up."

Daphne looked at McKay. "Does she order *you* around like this?"

"Sometimes I get to order her around. She's beautiful when she's angry."

Daphne gave a shaky laugh. "Do you happen to have any brothers?"

"Two of them, but I'm afraid neither one is the marrying kind. They never have settled down and probably never will."

"There's a lot of that going around," Daphne muttered. "But David's got a surprise in store. I'm not going to mope about a man who considers faxed notes to be quality social interaction."

"Hard to hold hands in the moonlight via fax," McKay agreed.

Daphne vanished into the bathroom, and Carly rang the floor steward to order a meal to be sent to Daphne's cabin. After she hung up, she stared out the windows at the darkness of endless water, lit only by the ship's lights. "Why would a man do something like that? Doesn't he know the pain he's causing?"

"Hard to say why people do anything."

"But why would he arrange this whole trip, then leave five hours into the voyage?"

"Maybe he was telling the truth about his business."

Carly cut off a sharp answer as Daphne reappeared, pale but smiling. "I promise I'll be out of your way in a few minutes."

"No rush." McKay opened the door, checked the corridor discreetly, then stepped outside.

Daphne watched him intently. "Did my father set this all up?"

"Afraid so. But he was right to get involved. There have been too many problems."

"I can't tell you how distraught we were about what happened at Paradise Cay."

Carly shivered. "I didn't think I'd ever feel warm again. And that horrible body." She linked arms with Daphne, frowning. "Let's talk about something more pleasant."

"Good idea." Daphne slanted a glance at

Ford in his tailored tuxedo. "All I can say is, that man has one prime, sexy butt. In the unbiased assessment of a simple observer," she added.

"There has never been anything simple about you," Carly said as McKay motioned them across the hall into Daphne's cabin. "And kindly keep your assessment of his body's parts to yourself."

"Anytime you want to share details, I'll be happy to listen."

"Dream on."

Daphne actually laughed as they walked into her cabin. Due to the magic of a flawlessly trained kitchen staff, her meal arrived only seconds after they did. McKay stood back as Izzy guided in the service cart with a flourish.

"You were supposed to be watching her," he murmured.

"I was. I let her into Carly's suite," he whispered while Carly took Daphne into the bedroom to change. "When I saw how upset she was, I thought she'd better wait there for you two."

"It worked, I guess." McKay watched Izzy clear off the elegant teakwood side table, shift a huge vase of white roses to a nightstand, then deftly spread a linen tablecloth. "You've been practicing, I see."

"Got to do something while you live the high life."

McKay raised a domed cover and pretended to examine a plate of perfectly cooked fettucini with pesto sauce and pine nuts. "Any news about the galloping financier?"

"All I know is, money was flowing like water on deck today. It's not cheap to get choppered out of this floating pleasure palace."

"Money doesn't appear to be Halloran's problem," McKay said dryly. "See what you can find out," he added. "Something about him bothers me."

"No kidding." Izzy turned. "Is everything satisfactory, ma'am?" he asked smoothly as Daphne and Carly returned.

Daphne gave him a dazzling smile. "It looks lovely. I can't wait to eat."

"By the way, someone named Thompson has been looking for you," Izzy said quietly as McKay followed him to the door. "For Carly, too. I haven't found out why, but I know he's with the captain's staff."

"I'll keep it in mind." McKay closed the door, only to find Carly right behind him. "How is she doing?"

"She's eating, at least. I could murder the man."

"She's got hard decisions to make. With a baby involved, things get complicated." McKay frowned. "But Halloran should know so he can be involved."

"*His* idea of being involved would be to send congratulations via the Internet."

"He has the right to know," Ford said firmly. "Any man does."

"That's up to Daphne. She'll have the stretch marks and the midnight feedings."

"Takes two to make a child, last time I checked."

"What are you two arguing about?" Daphne called.

"Nothing important. You've got to eat more than that." Carly crossed her arms. "Otherwise I'm not leaving."

McKay braced one shoulder against the veranda door. "Carly's right. You should eat more."

Daphne picked at some salad, took another bite of pasta, then pushed away her plate. "That's it. You two get going now. I'm going to settle in with a good book, and tomorrow I'll decide what I'm going to do about David." She squeezed Carly's hand. "Go away and dance till dawn."

Carly hesitated. "You'll be okay?"

Daphne stood up, smiling wistfully. "I'll manage. Meanwhile, there's a moonlit deck somewhere just waiting for you. Go find it."

"Nice lady," Ford said as he walked Carly to her suite. "Tough decisions."

"She'll do the right thing."

McKay toyed with the silver clasp at Carly's breast. "Am I finally going to see how this thing works?"

"Right here in the hallway? That must break some ship rule."

"I'm in the mood to break a few rules." His fingers combed through her hair and he felt her tremble, responsive to even that light caress.

Suddenly her mood changed and she tugged him to a halt outside her door. "I have one favor."

"Only one?"

"I'm serious, McKay." She stared at his shirt, her body stiff. "When the time comes to leave, don't say goodbye. Don't say anything, just go."

He tilted her face up to his, surprised. "Why?"

"Just because."

"You're asking me to walk out without a word or a backward glance?"

"It's the only way," she whispered. "After my mother . . . I hate goodbyes."

Her answer made sense, even though he

didn't like the idea, but before he could question her further, low footsteps down the corridor made him turn swiftly and pull her behind him.

A balding man in a gray uniform swept around the corner and bore down on them. "Mr. McKay?" He studied Carly as if checking her face against a photograph. "And you are Carolina Sullivan?"

McKay interrupted Carly's answer. "Why? Is there some problem?"

The man's mouth thinned. "I'd call it a problem. I've got a dead body upstairs. I'm afraid I have to ask you some questions."

Chapter 32

Carly gripped McKay's shoulder. "Dead?" she whispered.

"That's right, Ms. Sullivan."

"Are you Thompson?" McKay demanded.

"That's right. Ship security. The deceased was a woman named Aimee Joy Fiorento. I believe she was a friend of yours."

Carly just stared. "Aimee is dead? She was involved with the model we hired for the onboard shoot."

"You have some ID?" McKay asked curtly.

"Of course." The officer produced a badge with a recent photo, which Ford glanced at and then returned. "Let's go inside," he said, closing the door and ushering Carly to a chair. "When did it happen?"

"I'll ask the questions, Mr. McKay." Thompson eyed the spacious suite as if looking for clues. "First, I need to know where you two were between the hours of five and nine tonight."

"What the hell for?" McKay snapped.

"Because the victim's body showed signs of contusions and severe bruising along the neck. Neither suggests a simple accident."

"You think we were involved?" McKay snarled.

"A number of people reported seeing Ms. Fiorento and Ms. Sullivan arguing tonight in the Crystal Club." Thompson cleared his throat. "As I understand it, there was some dispute over a broken contract."

"Check again. Aimee was the only one arguing tonight." Carly sat tensely, her face far too pale. McKay had an urge to deck the security officer and cut off any more questions.

He allowed himself to enjoy the fantasy as he poured Carly a glass of champagne. "You're out of line, Thompson. You'd better get your facts straight."

"That's exactly why I'm here, Mr. McKay." The officer flipped open a small notebook. "Why were you two arguing?" he asked Carly.

"*She* was the one arguing. Her boyfriend had recently been replaced on this project for professional reasons, which was within the terms of our contract. I might also point out that the two retained their free cruise, along with half of his booking price, as reparation."

Thompson tapped his pencil on his notebook, and McKay had the impression that the man knew he was in over his head. He probably didn't have that many people buying the farm on a luxury cruise, McKay thought. "What happened to her?"

"Drowned. Her body was floating in the pool on the promenade deck when the attendant went to secure the net covers for the night. That was less than forty minutes after she spoke to Ms. Sullivan in the Crystal Club."

"If you know that, you also know she was staggering drunk when we saw her. Is there anyone aboard to do a forensic exam?"

Thompson shook his head. "It's not something we often require. The cruise physician is making an initial report, but the autopsy will have to wait until we fly the body to Miami. Now, to return to my question — where were you between five and eight tonight?"

"Together," McKay said curtly. "We left for the Crystal Club a little after six and arrived about six-twenty. We had dinner reservations at La Russie at seven-fifteen and returned here a little before nine. Ms. Sullivan was with me the whole time."

Thompson's pencil flew back and forth. "Anyone see you come back here?"

"Another passenger."

"I'll need the name," Thompson said.

"Daphne Brandon. She's upset right now because her fiancé had to leave the ship unexpectedly, so I suggest you talk to her in the morning. We've just spent the last half hour trying to calm her down."

Thompson took more notes.

"The hall steward will verify that," McKay added. "He made a meal delivery to her suite while we were there."

"Did Ms. Brandon know the deceased?"

McKay answered before Carly could reply. "If you check, you'll see that Daphne Brandon is the daughter of the governor-general of Santa Marina. I doubt she would know the deceased."

"Beyond their connection with the shoot, you mean." Thompson looked up from his notebook. "Anything more you'd like to tell me?"

"Have you spoken to Griffin Kelly yet?" Carly asked. "He is — was — Aimee's boyfriend."

Thompson nodded. "He wasn't much help. He'd been drinking heavily and he wasn't making any sense after he heard the news. I'll take his formal statement tomorrow."

"You can verify the information I gave

you by picking up the phone," McKay said. "The restaurant must keep a record of their reservations."

"I'll do my work, and you do yours, Mr. McKay." The officer scanned the cabin again. "You took Griffin Kelly's place in the shoot, is that correct?"

"He wasn't happy about it. He'd filed a suit for damages against Ms. Sullivan, then dropped it when his charges were shown to be groundless. That should be in your notes too."

Thompson neither agreed nor disagreed. "All the information will be checked. Meanwhile, I require that you both be available for further questioning."

"It's a big ship, but it's not that big," McKay said tightly. "Are you finished now? It's been a long night and Ms. Sullivan is too polite to tell you she's exhausted."

Thompson looked as if he wanted to ask more questions but didn't know where to start. "Do not attempt to leave the ship," he said soberly, walking to the door.

"Guess I'll scrap my plan to jump overboard," McKay muttered. The man probably relished every hint of power his job gave him, and having a corpse on board gave him more power than he'd had for a long time. "If Ms. Sullivan has a midnight urge to dive from the veranda, I'll be sure to restrain her, too." He held open the door, waiting pointedly. "Good night, Mr. Thompson."

"Very well, but I'll leave my card. If you have anything to add, I suggest you phone my office."

McKay placed the card on the table. "We won't."

Carly didn't move as the door closed behind the security officer. "He was only doing his job."

"He didn't have to like it so much. Besides, you're beat."

"Thanks, McKay. Do I look like such a hag?"

"You look beautiful," he said gently. "Beautiful and completely beat. Hand over your rose and I'll put it in water. At least we can salvage that."

Carly took a deep breath. "I can't believe this happened. Why would anyone want to hurt Griffin's girlfriend?"

"She wasn't exactly Miss Congeniality." He slid Carly's rose into a small vase. "There's still no evidence it wasn't an accident. She probably tripped on the edge of the pool, hit her head, and was unconscious by the time she hit the water. The way she was drinking, I doubt she felt anything."

"Whether she felt it or not, she's still dead." Carly rubbed her forehead as if it hurt. "It just doesn't seem possible. I never thought I could feel any sympathy for Griffin, but after this . . ."

"No, it's not pretty. No one deserves to die like that. But they're not your problem." He carried Carly's rose into the bathroom and filled the vase with water. Clicking off the light, he carried the glass outside, resolving that seduction was no longer on the agenda. "Why don't we —"

He stopped when he saw Carly curled up on the bed. She had one shoe on and one shoe off, and she was clutching a pillow to her chest.

Sound asleep in two minutes, he thought wryly. If that wasn't beat, he didn't know what was.

"I guess the midnight tryst is off," he murmured, setting the vase down beside the window.

With a pang of regret, he scooped her up into his arms. She was still clutching the pillow when he removed her gown and tucked her chastely beneath the covers.

She was right. There had been nothing but Chanel No. 5 under her dress.

So much for his evening of high-seas romance.

He stroked her hair and heard her say something about moving the gel filters on the key light before she pulled the pillow down over her head.

Chapter 33

"Busy night," Izzy remarked. It had taken him all of three minutes to appear after McKay had called for room service, ordering a dessert he didn't want and a brandy he wouldn't drink.

"Looks that way. Carly's out for the count." He glanced next door, where she was sound asleep. "Being involved in a murder investigation isn't part of her usual agenda." He closed the adjoining door carefully. "Thompson's trying to pin it on us."

Izzy muttered one word that showed what he thought of that idea. "Thompson wouldn't know an exit wound from a dinner buffet." He rocked back on his heels. "I have an update on Daphne Brandon's fiancé. The man's got holdings in oil, wireless technology, and about a hundred genetic-engineering patents."

"Where does he run this far-flung empire?"

"He's got an office in Geneva and another one in London, but I haven't been able to maneuver past his firewalls to get specifics. His electronic security is airtight, and that bothers me."

"Hurts your professional pride?" Izzy's handsome features tightened on a scowl. "Hell, yes. The man's gone to a lot of time and expense to be more secure than most small governments. What does he have to hide?"

"Maybe he's practicing the corporate equivalent of safe sex."

"If I were your ordinary hacker, I might agree. But as we both know, I am not your ordinary hacker. I can be inside secure Pentagon systems in under two minutes. No, there's something going on with David Halloran." Izzy shook his head slowly. "The man shouldn't be this good. There's another thing you should know: I ran a background check, and I can't find anything on him earlier than seven years ago."

"That's strange, isn't it?"

"You're damned straight it is. I can give you name, birth date, data on deceased parents, then *nada*."

McKay jammed his hands through his hair. "What the hell does it mean?"

Izzy tapped his long fingers on the window. "In the U.S., it means Witness Protection Program and a manufactured identity. I keep telling people they need to create a complete file, not just for the last few years, but no one ever listens."

McKay gave a low whistle. "But if this guy is in Witness Protection, wouldn't you be able to find some record of it?"

"If he's one of ours, he's so high that the strings are invisible except at the very highest levels. Of course, there's another possibility. His identity could have been manufactured by someone else. Someone with all the right moves." Izzy looked over his shoulder. "Someone who's not a friendly."

"Find out which it is," McKay snapped. "Meanwhile, what happened with the woman in the swimming pool? Thompson seems convinced that we were involved."

Izzy shrugged. "Thompson's due to retire next year with twenty years of service, and he doesn't want any black marks on his record when he goes out. What I've heard is that she was having problems with her boyfriend, and she was coming on to the bar staff earlier today, bragging how she was going to be a very rich woman. But here's the kicker. She was running up quite a tab, and she paid it off early tonight." Izzy paused. "In cash. Hundred-dollar bills. I managed to snag several and I'm having them checked right now."

"Maybe she's one of the leaks," McKay mused. "She could have pinpointed the shooting schedule and location. Probably a whole lot more." He stared at the connecting door to Carly's cabin. "I can't shake the feeling that we're being played here. The attack at the waterfall and Carly being locked in the freezer were meant to pressure Brandon, but they were also meant to keep us jumping at shadows while someone launched the real mission. This murder is too timely to be unrelated."

"More pressure on Carly, and maybe getting you tied up in a criminal investigation, you mean. But if it's Vronski, he still hasn't made a move that we can tag him for." Izzy frowned and pulled what looked like a large pager from his jacket pocket. He shook his head as he studied the screen. "Well, I'll be damned. Brandon just withdrew his request for assistance. That ties our hands in the worst way."

"He goes from desperate to the cold shoulder," McKay said. "Maybe Vronski gave him an ultimatum."

"Or maybe he decided he can't trust his own security force," Izzy suggested. He glanced at his watch with a grimace. "Gotta go send a reply. I'll keep you posted." He rolled his service cart smartly to the door. "One thing for sure, I'll be glad to get off this floating pleasure palace. It's too tempting to break a few rules."

"Tell me about it."

"One reminder." Izzy looked thoughtfully at McKay. "The first rule I learned was never mix business and pleasure. Somebody always gets hurt."

Dishes rattling, he left McKay to ponder his warning.

Chapter 34

Ford awoke in Carly's bed the next morning with her hair against his shoulder and her body draped over him like a quilt. He lay still, savoring her gentle breathing and the soft hint of her perfume.

He smiled as she shifted, nuzzling his neck, one arm skimming his chest.

He drew one finger along her shoulder and delighted in her instant, shivering response. Already he wanted her badly.

Because that need threatened his self control, he made his body freeze. Control had always been basic to him, as automatic as breathing, and no woman had ever come close to shattering that will.

Until now. The thought left him irritated and confused.

With a silent oath he slid out from beneath her, amazed at how tempting it was to forget all his discipline and training.

Exercise, he thought.

Maybe a few thousand push-ups would clear his addled brain.

Something cool touched her cheek.

Carly raised a hand, expecting to feel

McKay's hard body beneath her, as it had been all night. But when she opened her eyes, the other side of the bed was empty.

A muffled sound drew her to her feet. She saw that the adjoining door was open.

The rustling came again.

Carly slid a sheet around her and moved closer. McKay was stretched out on the floor with his fingertips turned inward as he did a strange, intricate push-up. Sweat beaded his back and shoulders as his body rose and fell with sleek power.

He was muttering. Carly realized he'd just said "three hundred."

So that's what gave him the chiseled abs and perfect thighs.

The heat came as a surprise, as did the blind wanting. She had never been keen on voyeurism, but watching his body tighten and flex left her light-headed and punchy with desire.

The man was dangerous, she thought, and that body of his should have been illegal. Which made all the more reason not to let it go to waste.

Holding the sheet, she stood in the doorway and whistled their prearranged five-note signal.

At the first note, he rolled to his side, his eyes going hard.

Carly raised open hands. "Just me, McKay. I'm unarmed, I assure you." She smiled as the sheet began to slip down her body. "Oops. Now you've made me drop my sheet."

The white cotton shifted, parting over her breasts. McKay's body had relaxed, but his gaze was locked on the falling sheet.

"I . . . didn't want to wake you," he said hoarsely.

"Very noble. Do you always exercise like that in the morning?"

He wiped a line of sweat off his chest, looking distracted. "Usually."

"Very impressive." The sheet continued its downward drift, pooling at her waist. "May I put my hands down now?"

He rose in one smooth movement. "I don't think so. Anything might happen. I'll need to investigate thoroughly."

Carly took a step back, measuring the heat in his eyes. As she did, the sheet slid down to her thighs. "Tricky thing, sheets." Her voice was breathy.

"Damn, Carly."

"You shouldn't have gone away." *Not when we have so few hours left.*

"I thought you needed your rest." He ran a finger along the edge of the fallen sheet, his eyes very dark.

"I needed you more."

He made a hard sound of frustration, pulled her against him, and crushed his lips to her mouth.

Glorious, she thought.

His hands rose to her breasts. "I'm delighted to see you're still wearing my necklace."

"Along with Chanel No. 5."

"An excellent combination. Wear it often."

"I intend to," she said, pulling him down for a hungry kiss that left them both panting.

"Carly, I'm sweaty. I need to shower."

"Mmm." She walked backward, pulling him with her, the sheet sliding farther with every step.

When it fell away, he stared at her body, taking in the flushed skin and the clear signs of her arousal. His gaze tightened as he pushed her back onto her bed and pinned her beneath him. "I'm losing my mind," he said hoarsely, driving his fingers into her hair and savaging her mouth.

"I'm delighted to hear it." Glorying in the instant tension of his wonderful body, she hooked one toe beneath the band of his track shorts and slowly pushed them down, sighing with pleasure as the rest of him slipped into view. Reckless now, she raked him with her nails, then nuzzled his torso and drew him into her mouth.

He was iron hard.

His eyes closed on an oath as she savored him slowly, drawing her teeth along every inch. When she bit delicately, desire hazed his eyes and he toppled her backward, shoving apart her legs.

And then he feasted, exploring her thoroughly until she twisted and rocked against him, arms sprawling as desire slammed her up into a hot, glorious wave of release.

She sank back and took a shuddering breath. "No fair, McKay," she rasped. "You cheated."

"I always cheat." He slid his hands high, dragging her wrists above her head. A drop of sweat fell from his chest onto her waist. "And I think I'm going to cheat again."

He kneed apart her legs, entering her slowly, then driving up the pleasure with powerful strokes that left her breathless and straining.

"More," Carly said, shoving urgently against him.

Only then did she see his face, masked in his effort at control as he held the rose salvaged from the night before. As he pulled away from her, the soft petals teased her softer skin. The flower turned, circling her heat, driving her to an exquisite fever of need until she shattered beneath his hands.

Limp, breathless, she collapsed against the covers, her body misted with sweat. There couldn't be more, she thought dimly. She didn't have the strength.

The hot slide of his body inside her proved she was wrong. Trembling, she rose against him, shocked at how much she wanted him again, shocked at how effortlessly he twisted her inside out.

"Hold me," he ordered, braced above her.

She wrapped her legs around him, her nails raking his back.

Blindly, he plunged deep until a wall of darkness tore away the world around them.

Carly was dressed when McKay emerged from the shower. Papers were lined up on the coffee table and her face looked strained.

"Mel just arrived," she said flatly. "She says we need to speed up the shooting schedule."

He stifled a groan. "First they fire you, then they expect you to make wine out of water."

"Welcome to show business."

"How much time do you have?"

"Not enough. She wants all the body shots finished today."

"Is that possible?"

"I'll have to make it possible," she said tightly.

"Hell." McKay had a nasty vision of more oil being slathered on his bare chest.

"It should only take seven or eight hours."

"Only?"

"Very funny." She gave him a pretend right hook. "I'm not exactly thrilled about this. I'd prefer to bolt the door and spend the rest of the day right here."

"You've got my vote." He nuzzled her shoulder. "Let's go back to bed."

She stepped out of reach. "We can't. Mel needs this footage finished today, and I made a promise that she'd have it."

There was a knock on the door. "Carly, the crew is set up." It was Hank, her cameraman, sounding very harried. "Mel is waiting and we're ready to roll."

"Be right out." Carly gathered her papers quickly. "We have to hurry. Hank is getting panicky. I can hear it in his voice."

With a sigh, McKay tugged on a shirt. "We'll finish on time. But if I see any more baby oil within a foot of me, I might have to deck a few of your crew," he said darkly.

"Hank, we need to go diffuse with that fill light. Remember, we're doing a slow dissolve from the sparkling bubbles in the champagne glass to the sparkling diamonds by the roses."

As the cameraman nodded, Carly checked her light meter one more time.

Across the deck, McKay stood motionless on his taped cue mark, one elbow braced on the rail. His endurance and concentration were amazing. He had run the same scene again and again, each time managing to look calm and unruffled. She wondered yet again about his background and whether staying silent and motionless on cue was part of his training.

"We've got a shadow on that champagne bottle," she called to Hank, who nodded and rearranged the main key light. "And we're getting too much shine off the label again."

Hank waved a can of dulling spray and went to work. With this schedule, every shot had to count, and they both knew it.

To make matters worse, at the last moment Mel had flown in to oversee the new shooting. Having her nervous boss underfoot definitely hadn't helped Carly's state of mind.

"The man is a dream," Mel said, sotto voce. "Are you sure he isn't a professional? Maybe he's worked in Europe and that's why we don't know him."

Carly knew McKay was a professional at something, but it definitely wasn't modeling. "I doubt he's worked in Europe, Mel." *Not as an actor, at least.*

Carly's boss sniffed. "If the man's not in the business, he ought to be. I'm going to have a talk with him when we wrap. I could have him fully booked within a week."

Over his dead body, Carly thought.

Hank did a slow pan, then zoomed in on McKay's face.

"That should do it for this scene. Only two more to go." Mel rubbed her neck. "I need a cigarette."

She was searching her pockets when the ship's security officer appeared, headed doggedly toward them. "Do I know that man?" Mel asked.

"Thompson is the security officer investigating Aimee Fiorento's death," Carly explained.

"I can't imagine what he wants with us," Mel snapped. "We paid that snake ten times what we should have, and he still wanted to gouge us for more."

"Ms. Kirk, I need to ask you a few questions." The notebook was already out, pen readied.

"You know everything there is to know about our contract with Griffin Kelly and Aimee Fiorento," Mel said irritably. "And if you recall, we're *trying* to finish a project for your employer right now."

Thompson frowned, momentarily put off. Then the dogged look returned. "This will only take a moment." He held out a grainy image that appeared to be taken from a passport photo. "Do either of you recognize this man?"

Bland eyes in a bland face. Groomed hair and a sober gray suit. There was nothing distinctive about the man.

"Never seen him. What about you, Carly?"

Had he been standing behind Aimee Joy at the bar? Carly tried to re-create the crowded scene, certain she had seen the man very recently. Maybe at the dock?

"I'm not sure," she said, her voice firm. "I may have passed him somewhere on the ship, but I've never spoken with him."

Thompson held out the photo a moment longer. "You're certain?"

Carly nodded.

"I'll note your answers. Now I need to speak with Mr. McKay."

"He's busy," Mel said impatiently. "We're trying to shoot a commercial here, and I resent your intrusion."

"Your comment will be duly noted." Thompson pocketed the photo along with his notebook, then headed toward McKay.

"Unpleasant man." Mel sniffed. "As if one of us tossed that woman into the pool." She smoothed her Armani jacket. "Although I might have been tempted once or twice." She pursed her lips. "Be a dear and finish up here, Carly. I want to check this morning's footage. And come down as soon as you wrap. Daphne is getting everything ready, and I'd like to discuss some ideas I had for the sound track." She strode away without a backward look, not waiting for Carly's answer.

It wasn't rudeness, Carly knew. It was simple obsession. To Mel, the job was everything — sun, moon, and stars.

Carly was well on her way to that same obsession. Only now for some reason she found herself wondering if she wanted to continue knocking out fourteen-hour days, with family, friendships, and all hope of a personal life sacrificed in the process.

It was the price of a career in the fast

track, she thought.

Why had it never bothered her before?

Across the deck, Thompson was showing the photograph to McKay, who shook his head, then reached into his pocket, looking annoyed and distracted as he studied the high-tech pager he always carried.

It appeared to be more bad news, and Carly had had her fill of bad news.

To the east trade-wind clouds ran across the horizon. The scene was done, and she had more than enough footage to call for a wrap, but she couldn't seem to move. Some part of her wanted to continue like this forever, cruising turquoise waters with the sun on her shoulders and the protection of a man she barely knew.

As the wind gusted in great waves across the deck, and seabirds wheeled overhead, Carly realized that she couldn't face the goodbyes that were only days away. The man was lethal in bed and his body left her giddy, but that was only the start of what she felt for him. Love was the middle and end.

She nearly buckled at the realization. She had planned to be so careful, guarding her heart from any thought of happily ever after. But somewhere the script had changed and things had gone terribly wrong.

She stood in the wind, hands locked

across her chest, watching Ford at the rail, watching her crew. Watching herself and knowing she was not the same woman as the one who had boarded this ship, ambition and camera case firmly in hand. She would never be that woman again.

Now she wanted the happily ever afters and was naïve enough to believe she deserved them. She was snagged tight, head over heels in love with a man who had made it clear there could be no tomorrows for them.

Carly was walking away before she knew it. Her shoulders stiff, she made a quick gesture to Hank, knowing he'd see to the wrap.

She refused to let her eyes fill with tears.

Carly Sullivan did not cry over the way sunlight skimmed the ocean and dusted a man's cheek. She did not dream about a big wedding or how to trim her workload so she could be home in time for wine and a quiet dinner. No strings, no commitment. That stipulation had been hers.

Behind her, footsteps echoed over the deck. She knew it was McKay following her. But when the danger was gone, he would be gone too.

She heard him call her name but she didn't stop walking, her senses in turmoil. She had never planned on more than a pleasant, sweaty bout of shipboard romance. There were no white picket fences for her. She was her mother's daughter, and she had seen too well the pain that false expectations could inflict. The ones you loved never stayed.

No white picket fences and no goodbyes.

Yes, Carly had stipulated the terms herself. They guaranteed her safety and her sanity.

She continued to walk blindly, bumping into strollers, joggers, and happy couples wandering hand in hand through the warm afternoon sunlight. She wasn't going to love Ford McKay or any other man.

She swore that again and again as she brushed away her tears.

Chapter 35

What was wrong with her? What had happened to change her expression from cool professional scrutiny to unfocused sadness?

McKay's first instinct had been to pull her to a halt and demand to know exactly what was going on inside her head. Then discretion intervened. There was no sign of threat or physical harm. She was smart and stubborn and doggedly independent. If she needed him, she would have let him know.

But he couldn't forget the raw panic in her eyes — as if her world had shattered.

Carly finally took stock of her surroundings, frowned, and made her way to Mel's cabin. McKay was nowhere in sight when the door swung open to the thunder of rock music.

"I was just going to call to see where you were." Grabbing Carly's arm, Mel pulled her into a room that looked like postapocalyptic chaos. Books, magazines, and shoes were piled on the bed and couch, and computer equipment took up all the remaining space.

"Well, what do you think?" Mel demanded.

Carly managed to smile. "I like the beaded negligee, but the purple sneakers have to go."

Mel shot her an imperious look. "The sneakers were purchased in a moment of temporary insanity. I was asking about the film." Impatient, she gestured to the huge flat-screen monitor where a man stared into a fiery sunset with a glass of champagne raised to the horizon. He looked even more amazing on film than she remembered, his face burnished by sunlight and his eyes dark with secrets.

Secrets she would never know.

Carly's heart lurched painfully. "It's got punch."

"It's got more than punch, my dear. That shot is going to make the cruise line millions — and it's going to make us flat-out famous, to say nothing of drumming up a flood of new projects."

Carly summoned a tone of enthusiasm. "Let's hope you're right."

Mel's brow rose. "Hope has nothing to do with it. They've shown the edited footage in New York, and the client is over the moon. Do you know what that means?"

"No retakes?"

"You jest at a time like this. What it

means," Mel said with a dramatic flourish, "is that our budget just got doubled again, and no questions asked. It means prime-time ad placements and maximum exposure for the agency. It means a celebration because lots more work will be coming your way, which is exactly what you wanted."

"Of course it is." Carly wondered why her words sounded so hollow.

"In that case, listen up. The cruise reps want us to work up different story lines for each of their ships. We're talking twelve different itineraries, my dear, and you're going to be traveling on every one over the next six months as part of your preparation. Is that heaven or what?"

Carly tried to focus, tried to remember that this project was the culmination of years of struggle and dedication. "Wow. Six months . . ."

"After we dock in Miami, we head right into meetings. Two members of the marketing team will meet us in port so we can set up a preliminary schedule. After that we'll tackle a budget." Mel frowned. "Are you listening to all this? You look spacey."

"Of course." Carly swallowed. "It's just a little hard to take in, considering the size of the project."

Mel pursed her lips. "This is no time for

second thoughts. We'll be working twenty-hour days to get this project wrapped in time for fall scheduling. If you've got a problem with your commitment, I need to know now."

"No problems." Carly told herself it was true. Having a personal life wasn't half as important as an opportunity like this. "When do we start?"

Mel flipped off the monitor. "Tomorrow we strategize. Tonight we celebrate. You've earned it. And bring Ford along. I intend to convince him that he needs a major career change."

Carly turned away, wrestling her emotions back into some semblance of control. "I'll let him know. Is there anything else you wanted to discuss?"

"No, that's it." Mel's gaze tightened. "Are you certain you're okay with this? I get the feeling you're on autopilot, and that's not like you."

"I'm fine." Carly felt the first stab of a headache. "I need to take care of a few loose ends and then I'll talk to Ford."

"Dress up," her boss ordered. "Slinky and glittery. I want everyone in the mood to celebrate. This is going to be a major campaign, and I plan to launch phase two with full pomp."

Feeling oddly empty, Carly went back to her cabin. She told herself there would be plenty of time for relationships after the campaign was finished. If McKay was interested in staying in touch, he could arrange it. Six months wasn't so long to wait.

Yeah, right.

She hesitated at her cabin door, remembering all of his security precautions. Taking a deep breath, she unlocked the door and shoved it open with one foot, feeling like a fool.

No shots were fired.

Always a good sign, she thought tiredly.

A quick look told her the room was empty. The bathroom and veranda were also empty. As she kicked off her shoes, she noticed a vellum envelope angled against her pillow.

Cruise-line stationery. The expensive kind.

She tore it and read the message, then read it again, feeling her body go numb. There were three handwritten lines:

Have to go. Can't explain now.
Izzy will come by today, and you can trust him completely.
He'll be right behind you until you dock.

— M

The words ran at a slant, as if written in haste. Carly blinked sharply as they started to blur.

So this was it. No soft vows, no romantic declarations. Not a goodbye or a hint of an explanation.

That was exactly what she'd told him she wanted, wasn't it?

She tossed the note onto her desk and stared at the silent room. Who was he to discard her like an old shoe without making any attempt to explain in person? It wasn't that easy to leave a cruise ship in the middle of the ocean.

Maybe something had happened on Santa Marina.

She swept up the phone to call Daphne, then put it back down slowly. Daphne would have told her if there were problems, which killed that possibility. Meanwhile, Carly realized she couldn't even reach McKay without calling every ranch in Wyoming — assuming his story of owning a family ranch was true. The thought made her crumple his letter and toss it angrily into the wastebasket by her bed.

The bed where they'd ripped off each other's clothes and nearly killed each other.

There was a soft tap at the door. Carly froze, willing the visitor to go away.

As she waited tensely, the tapping came again. "Carly, are you in there? It's Izzy. I need to speak with you."

She opened the door, then stood back as he moved inside and put a pile of neatly folded towels on her table, all the time watching her face carefully. "You got his note?"

She nodded.

"He had to go."

"Why?"

Izzy ran a hand across his jaw. "I can't tell you that."

"Where did he go?" Carly fought to keep her voice steady.

"I can't tell you that either."

"Then tell me how I can reach him."

"You can't," Izzy said quietly. "I'll be your contact now. If you have a problem, call me at this number." He held out a slip of paper with ten digits. "Use it anytime, day or night, and I'll answer."

"You mean while we're on the ship?"

"I mean anywhere in the world. That number will reach me in three rings max."

Carly stared at the numbers. "Does McKay have a phone number like this?"

Izzy ran a hand over the folded towels, his expression guarded. "Just memorize that number," he said softly.

Carly looked down, committing the string to memory. "I've got it."

"Good." He took the paper, crumpled it in one hand, and went into the bathroom.

Carly heard the rumble of plumbing. "What if I need to talk to him?"

He emerged with his usual quiet, confident gait, but he looked different now, she realized. Expectant, even excited.

"Talk to me instead. Is there anything I can do for you?"

"Tell me where he is."

"I can't do that."

"At least tell me if he's in danger." She heard her voice crack slightly.

He stared at her for long moments. "You want the truth or something to make you feel better?"

"The truth."

"Then here it is. I think you already know that if he isn't in danger now, he will be soon. It's what he does," Izzy said gently. "No one does it better. Tight spots happen to be McKay's specialty."

"That's all you can tell me? Not where he is, or why? If something happens, I won't even know." She turned away, struggling against raw fear.

"Worrying won't help." Izzy gestured to the digital camera equipment on Carly's desk. "Right now you've got your own work to handle. Why don't you focus on that?"

As if she could. As if she wouldn't be wondering every second where he was. If he was bleeding, or even dead.

Dead.

She squeezed down hard, trapping all the panic, fighting a wave of dizziness.

Izzy continued to study her face. "Remember the number?"

Carly rattled off the string.

"Good. Use it if you need to. Meanwhile I'll be close. Try not to worry."

"Sure. I'll try," she said hollowly.

The door had barely closed behind him when the phone rang. Carly picked up the receiver, feeling a wild burst of hope. "McKay?"

"No, it's Mel. Everyone's waiting for you. What's wrong?"

"Nothing." *Everything.*

Carly swallowed hard. "It's t-taking longer to get ready than I thought."

Tinny calypso music echoed from the other end of the line, mingled with the sounds of loud laughter.

"Well, get into gear, love. The wrap party is about to start, and it's your baby. Come and take credit for your success. I warn you, if you don't, I will."

Carly looked around the room. The rose was still in its vase beside her bed. The amber necklace he'd given her gleamed on the desk, and night was falling. Through the windows, sea and sky ran together in a blur of restless silver.

It was time to focus, she told herself. This project was hers, and she had carried it off well. It was time to file McKay under past history and move on.

If he isn't in danger now, he will be soon.

Tears were running down Carly's cheeks as she saw the crumpled note in the garbage. Blindly, she retrieved it, smoothing it open on her lap. "I'll be there," she whispered. "In a little while."

"Carly, I can barely hear you. Is everything okay?"

Watching the endless expanse of water shimmer beyond the windows, Carly thought of a man who had made no false promises, a man who faced danger without blinking. "Everything is exactly the way I wanted, Mel."

Her hands were shaking now, so she put the receiver down very gently, feeling as if something deep inside her had torn free and lay bleeding.

Chapter 36

It was raining when McKay hit the tarmac at Little Creek, Virginia. It had rained for six hours straight since he'd left Miami, and there was still no sign of a letup.

So much for sun and fun in paradise, he thought grimly. He'd been summoned back to HQ abruptly, so he knew something serious was in the works, and it wasn't taking place on any cruise ship.

The attacks had been a diversion — or maybe designed to put extra pressure on Brandon. Now that Brandon had caved in, Vronski's focus would shift to the main event — whatever that was. Meanwhile, Carly would be all right, he told himself harshly. Izzy was under orders to watch out for her, and Izzy's moves were good.

His instincts were on full alert as he shouldered his duffel bag and trotted to the waiting Jeep. The driver, a fairly new arrival from Georgia, saluted smartly, with excitement in his eyes.

Something big was definitely going on, judging by the charged atmosphere on base. Everywhere, personnel moved with silent competence as they readied for an unknown mission, their adrenaline spiking with the knowledge that drop orders were imminent. There was no time for fear and no room for second thoughts. Fighting was what SEALs did best, and McKay knew that better than anyone because his team was the best of the best.

Train hard and fight harder. McKay made damned sure it was a principle they lived by. Now it looked like training time was over.

Grimly, he pushed a final thought of Carly out of his mind as the Jeep fishtailed over the wet runway into the darkness.

He barely had time to stow his bag, wash his face, and make sure there was no sign of *GQ* polish left before he headed off to be briefed. No one he passed made any comment, but McKay was experienced enough not to expect any.

The mission briefing room was full when he arrived, and he snagged a seat against the wall, instantly hit by the hum of expectation that meant an active mission on the boards. Turning his head, he glanced around in search of his team, frowning at their absence. Where the hell were they?

The door closed. Everyone in the room sat up straight as a lean, gray-haired man strode to the front podium.

His eyes scanned the room. "Gentlemen, I'm afraid we have a situation in the Caribbean."

The muscles tightened at the back of McKay's neck. It had to be Santa Marina.

The dock in Miami was hot and noisy as Carly wrestled her bag of camera equipment onto her shoulder, caught in a stream of sweaty, milling tourists.

By sheer force of will, she had endured the rest of the cruise with her emotions locked down tight, though pain continued to throb just below the surface. If Daphne and the crew had noticed her strain, they had been wise enough not to mention it. Only Mel had sent her an occasional questioning look, which Carly had resolutely ignored.

She plunged toward the taxi line, all too aware that she would be late for her two o'clock meeting at the hotel. After that, she and Mel would join representatives of the cruise line for drinks and a discussion of themes for the new ads.

Work, she told herself fiercely. She had to forget about the man with the shadows in his eyes. If there was any honesty in what they had felt for each other, he'd find her when his mission was over.

Assuming he was still alive.

She swallowed hard, clutching her camera bag. In the process she brushed against a man in a dark suit. "Sorry," she mumbled, lurching around him.

It took her a full minute to realize that there was another man in a dark suit walking just in front of her and a third man off to her left. They seemed to be keeping pace without trying, despite the human flood around them.

Carly glanced around uneasily and saw she was near the edge of the taxi stand, with the two suits holding steady on either side of her.

She sped up.

So did the suits.

A dark Ford sedan cut out of the line on the opposite side of the street and pulled up in front of her.

She spun and charged back the way she'd come. As she did, the suits moved in close, flanking her. Two of them took her arms.

"Let go!" she cried, the sound all but drowned out by the shouting and laughter around her.

"You have nothing to be alarmed about, Ms. Sullivan." The tall man to her right spoke flatly, his eyes hidden behind sunglasses. "We simply need to ask you some questions."

"What kind of questions?" Carly tried to twist free. "Who are you?"

"It will make things easier if you come with us quietly," the tall man said.

"Maybe I don't want to make things easy," she snapped. "And I'm not going anywhere with you."

"You have no choice," the man on her left said flatly as he opened the rear door of the sedan. They hustled her inside, one in front with the driver and the other two beside her. The door closed, and Carly struggled to reach the handle, only to find it was locked.

"Stop the car or I'll start screaming."

If the men were disturbed by the possibility, they didn't show it.

"I mean it. This is kidnapping," she hissed, seriously alarmed now.

"In point of fact, it's not." The tall man turned to study her and she saw that his sideburns were touched with gray. "In a case like this, different laws apply."

"In a case like what?"

She received no answer. Her throat was dry and her heart was pounding. Were these the men McKay had been protecting her from? If so, what would he want her to do

411

now? Thinking furiously, she clutched her camera bag to her chest as panic churned through her. She couldn't be sick now.

Or maybe she should be exactly that.

With a strangled sound, she pitched forward, clutching her knees.

"Hell, you're not going to be sick, are you?" Sideburns edged away with a sound of disgust.

Carly kept her head down and summoned more unpleasant rumbling sounds from deep in her throat.

"Damn, she is sick. Stop the car, Willis. I don't want to clean up a mess in here."

The sedan immediately veered into the right lane, and Carly saw they were still near the terminal at the dock. There was a rest room to her right, half hidden by a row of tour buses. "The cruise," she said breathlessly. "Must be something I ate."

Muttering, Sideburns gestured to his companion. "Go with her."

Carly lunged from the car, bag in hand. At the restroom door, the tall man took her arm firmly. "You have five minutes. Then I'll come in after you."

She charged past him, her mind racing as she found an empty stall, tossed down her bag, and fished out a change of clothing.

Old jeans and a black sweater.

Sunglasses, too.

Working fast, she changed, then stuffed her other clothes back into the shoulder bag and checked it in a locker near the door.

Now, for a diversion.

Most of the stalls were occupied when she struck a match and carefully set fire to the crumpled paper towels in the garbage bin. Smoke drifted, then billowed as the damp paper finally caught. Within minutes, the area was a haze of acrid gray smoke.

Women began to scream as the sprinkler system kicked in and water jetted down from the ceiling. Carly grabbed a newspaper from a chair and spread it over her head to shield her face, then pushed into the middle of the human stampede racing for the exit.

Her handler was pacing outside, anxiously monitoring the distraught women pouring out of the rest room.

"What the hell is going on?"

"Fire! Police! Call 911!" A woman in red beads and a Miami Dolphins T-shirt pushed him out of the way. In the chaos, Carly skittered past and walked calmly in the opposite direction.

A shuttle bus was loading only a few feet away, and she flew up the steps, the sodden newspaper still clutched over her head.

"Miami airport?" the attendant asked politely, eyeing her strange headgear.

"Absolutely," she said breathlessly. "The sooner the better."

Chapter 37

McKay sat stiffly, every sense focused on the man with the gray hair.

William Grace was sixty-five, but he moved with the bristling energy of a man half his age. Retired from Air Force intelligence, he was currently on assignment with the NSA. McKay had worked with him before on highly sensitive missions, and he knew the man was sharp but low-key, with no shouting and no lip twitching.

The lights dimmed and a map flashed on the wall at the front of the briefing room. McKay made out Barbados, the Caymans, and then a zoom shot of Santa Marina.

No surprises there.

A photograph appeared beside the map.

"Some of you may recognize this man. His name is Nikolai Vronski, an ex-Soviet general with a background in satellite technology. He was something of a rising star in the 1960s, a man who evoked blind loyalty from his troops. With the 1980s came the Soviet decline, and Vronski eased into the free market, selling weapons, technology, and state secrets to anyone with a modem and hard currency."

Grace tapped his pointer against his wrist. "For a few years he sold us military intelligence, but our people eventually found him to be a loose cannon and severed relations with him four years ago. Since then Vronski has dabbled in international joint ventures in countries known for their political instability."

A new slide clicked into place, showing the tanned and aquiline features of Nigel Brandon.

"This is the governor-general of the Caribbean commonwealth of Santa Marina." Grace pursed his lips. "We have reason to believe that upon the return of the governor's daughter from a recent cruise, he and his family were taken hostage by Vronski and his men. Our intelligence indicates Vronski intends to set up a power base on Santa Marina, possibly for a high-tech counterfeiting operation involving U.S. currency."

A ripple went through the room.

"Sir, have demands been presented?" McKay asked.

Grace studied the map. "None so far. Frankly, I don't expect any. Vronski doesn't want ransom; he wants Santa Marina as his playground. In any event, gentlemen, our government does not intend to let the situation progress to demands or barter of any sort." His gaze traveled to every person in the room, settling finally on McKay. "Is that understood? Our job is to neutralize Vronski's operation *and retrieve all hostages.* There will be no barters, no trades, and no negotiation. Not under any circumstances. The official position is absolute on this point."

Thanks to her ruse, Carly had finally managed to ditch the team of suits at the cruise terminal. She still had no idea what they wanted, but she doubted it was to set up a fourth for bridge.

With only a book of matches and a damp newspaper, she had outsmarted them. Score one for modern woman.

Hot and tired, she charged into the Miami Hilton, scanning the crowded lobby. When she was certain that no one was paying any attention to her, she relaxed her shoulders and pocketed her plastic key card. Heading to the elevators, she passed a pair of professional women and an overweight man in a safari jacket with a shabby umbrella.

She considered calling the number Izzy had given her, certain that if someone was trailing her, McKay's partner could help. At the very least, he ought to be told about the situation, which would be the first thing she did when she got to her room.

Actually the second. She winced down at her new sandals, which were killing her. *They* would be the first thing she dealt with.

The elevator doors opened and Carly stepped in. The man in the safari jacket was still reading his newspaper when the doors closed. Carly was turning to press the button for her floor when the elevator chimed and the doors opened again.

Smiling, Sideburns got on right in front of her, along with his two friends. How had they found her so fast?

She tried to push past, but Sideburns hit the button and the doors closed.

"You can't do this," she hissed.

"Looks like we just did." The man to her left smiled thinly, sunglasses still in place. "Nice trick at the dock. Don't try it again."

The elevator whined past the public floors down to the basement levels, where Sideburns produced a key that directed the elevator down to a restricted floor.

"What do you want with me?" Carly rasped, trying to stay calm.

"Later, Ms. Sullivan." Sideburns fingered a cellular phone and spoke quickly. "We're here. West side near the service elevator. We've got her."

"Later, what?" she demanded.

The elevator doors whooshed open. "You'll find that out soon enough." Without another word, Sideburns and his stocky companion caught her arms and dragged her, fighting and kicking, to a dusty black sedan idling at the curb.

Carly decided there was no point in further struggle. "Where are you taking me?"

No one answered.

"This is *kidnapping*."

"Why don't you relax and enjoy the ride, Ms. Sullivan? We don't have far to go." Sideburns spoke, just as before, and Carly decided he was the one in charge.

"I don't want to relax and I don't want to go anywhere. This is a *crime*."

Sighing, he sat back in the front seat as the car sped along gleaming canals facing palatial white homes. "Suit yourself." With a shrug, he crossed his arms and appeared to go to sleep.

Carly was fuming and frightened, but most of all she was confused. Had something happened to McKay? Had there been more problems on Santa Marina? If so, were Daphne and her father in danger?

She stared out at the bright, burning sky, battling panic and endless questions. Her hands were shaking and she took a hard breath, forcing herself to relax.

They had said it wouldn't be far. She swore that at their final destination, she would find someone who would give her answers.

Two hours later, the sedan pulled off onto a gravel road bordering what appeared to be an abandoned airstrip. Old Quonset huts rose like rusting skeletons beneath the baking sun as the big car purred past. The driver stopped at a fence that looked surprisingly new, and a man in uniform, bearing insignia Carly didn't recognize, emerged from a gatepost up the hill, waving them forward.

"Is this the place?" She sat up straighter as the driver stopped before a cluster of one-story prefab buildings.

Sideburns stretched and sat up. "What place?"

"The place you take everyone you kidnap."

He shook his head. "You've been one royal pain in the butt, Ms. Sullivan. I'll be glad as hell to get rid of you."

"My thoughts exactly," Carly snapped. "So where is the Gestapo?"

The driver turned around. "You've got the wrong country, the wrong century."

"No, I haven't. Not if men like you are in

charge." She crossed her arms angrily. "Not that it matters. I won't say a word to anyone. Your little kidnapping effort has been pointless."

"We'll see." The driver moved around to open her door, then took her elbow when she resisted, depositing her roughly on the sidewalk in front of the largest of the buildings.

No windows, she noticed, her heart hammering. No cars and no other people. She glanced around and saw nothing but the road disappearing into a dense forest. The air was heavy with humidity and she felt sweat trickle between her shoulder blades. "I'm not going inside."

Sideburns smiled thinly. "Of course you are. Kidnapped people do exactly what they're told."

She gasped as she was shoved forward, propelled relentlessly toward a heavy, windowless door.

She drew a ragged breath, light-headed with fear. Who were these men? What could they possibly want from her?

She realized she should have been more insistent with her questions to McKay, but the regret came too late. Now he and Izzy were long gone, despite all their promises of protection.

Obviously, the danger hadn't disappeared with the end of the cruise. They should have known that, instead of vanishing like smoke.

Carly was still struggling when the metal door in the main building opened and an older man in a gray turtleneck and an expensive tweed jacket sauntered out.

He was carrying a pipe and shaking his head. "No, no, not like this. Let her go."

The driver took a step back, as did Sideburns.

"Good to see you, Ms. Sullivan. I hope you enjoyed your trip."

"Enjoyed?" Carly stood stiff with anger. "Being kidnapped, forced into a car and dragged to the middle of nowhere? *That's* enjoyable?"

The man waved his pipe at Sideburns. "Didn't you tell her she wouldn't be harmed?"

"Of course." His lips flattened in irritation. "It didn't make any difference. She was hell-bent on making us the bad guys."

The man in the tweeds shook his head again. "I take it you made their job difficult, Ms. Sullivan."

"I did my damnedest," she said flatly. Apparently, they didn't mean to tell their boss how she had given them the slip at the dock, or that it had taken all of them to get her into the car both times.

"Did these men harm you in any way?"

After a moment Carly shook her head.

"There, you see." He was beaming, avuncular. "It's all an unfortunate misunderstanding. Why don't you come in and have some tea while we chat."

Carly glared at him. "I'll come inside because there's nowhere else to go, but I won't talk to any of you, no matter who you say you are." Faking the courage she didn't have, she marched into the building.

She was alone, held at some sort of guarded installation where anything could happen, with no idea who had ordered her brought here or why.

They wanted information. What would they do to her to get it?

McKay had told her not to trust anyone except Izzy, and logic told her if she talked, they would have no further reason to keep her alive.

So she wouldn't talk.

Nor did she.

Not a single phrase or detail.

For what felt like hours she kept to her grim resolve, sitting motionlessly on a rough wooden desk chair and ignoring the questions of five unsmiling men who entered in turn. They refused to answer any of her questions, so Carly refused to answer theirs, but with every minute that passed her fear grew.

Their questions became more urgent, their voices sharper, and still Carly told them only her name, her address, and that she was a United States citizen and wanted to speak to a lawyer.

Finally, the man in tweed began to show his impatience. He shifted the box of doughnuts that lay open on the table in front of Carly, untouched.

"We need to know about Santa Marina," he repeated. Sideburns had been the bad cop, and Tweed was playing the good one. "Tell us about the Brandons. They are your friends, aren't they?"

Carly ignored him.

"What if I told you they were in danger?"

Her panic spiked. This was the the first bit of information they had offered her, but she couldn't give in. The Brandons might be in danger from the very man now facing her.

She turned away, afraid to reveal any anxiety. No answers, she thought fiercely — not until she knew exactly whom she could trust.

"Still nothing to say?" Tweed tapped his

pipe against his wrist, frowning. "Hell," he muttered. "Time is running out. Why didn't anyone tell me you'd be this way?" He nodded at the man beside the door, who left immediately.

Carly gave no sign that she had noticed. Instead, she pulled an emery board from her pocket and began to file her nails with pointed indifference.

Anything for distraction so that the panic wouldn't show on her face.

"You're making this far harder than it needs to be, Ms. Sullivan."

She just kept filing her nails, her face aching with the effort required to stay expressionless. She couldn't hold out forever, but she could damned well try.

"Have a doughnut and be reasonable."

A hysterical laugh built at his words. Have a doughnut and be reasonable? Where were the handcuffs and the Pentothal? If this was the worst they could do, maybe she really could hold out forever.

With a sigh her interrogator pushed back his chair and stalked outside, leaving Carly alone with one guard.

She glared at him.

He touched his sunglasses and stared back impassively.

Moments later the door banged open and

bounced off the wall.

A man stood in the threshold, silhouetted by the sun. Carly couldn't see his face against the light, but he was tall, muscular, and physically intimidating in a way none of the others had been.

She sat up straight, shoving down her fear. "Goody," she drawled. "Another doughnut delivery."

Chapter 38

The man didn't answer.

Carly's heart pounded as she stared at the doorway. She finally made out his uniform as he stepped inside. Camouflage. Navy insignia. An officer.

The door swung closed behind him, and the dimmed light gave her a sudden glimpse of a chiseled face and wintry eyes.

"McKay," she whispered, her whole body sagging in relief.

"Out," he snapped at the man in sunglasses, his gaze never leaving Carly.

The guard hurried outside.

"You're not hurt," Carly whispered. "Thank God. I was so afraid."

Emotions raced across his face but were quickly suppressed. "No, I'm healthy enough, though I've had my tail chewed by my commanding officer, who then ordered me to make a certain female informant be more helpful to the current investigation."

"Me," Carly whispered.

"Yeah. You."

She swallowed, stunned by her physical response to seeing him again. Her pulse was ragged, but she didn't move. Too many questions hung unspoken between them.

"Why didn't you tell me you were leaving?"

"I couldn't," he shot back. "Didn't Izzy explain?"

"He didn't tell me anything that mattered."

"Dammit, Carly, there are some things you have to take on faith. That's the way it's got to be."

She stood up and slammed her palms on the table. "I took *everything* on faith, and what happened? I was nabbed at the dock, tracked down like a criminal, and dragged here by force. No one has bothered to tell me a thing since I was brought here. They've been asking about Santa Marina and the Brandons, but how was I supposed to know they're the good guys? When Izzy disappeared, I assumed that he'd been hurt or you had been sent somewhere together."

"Izzy's fine," McKay said gently. "He knew that our men would take care of you."

"It would have been nice if *someone* had shared that information with me, the kidnappee." Carly's voice was shaky. "When was someone going to fill *me* in? Santa Marina is the closest thing to home I've got and the Brandons are my only family."

"You should realize that certain things have to remain classified."

"I understand that official business takes priority." She studied his face. "Seeing you like this, I realize you were under orders every minute. But those men who kidnapped me at the dock —"

"Goons," McKay said. "Someone should whack them around a little to teach them some manners." He took her hands and turned them over, his thumbs caressing her palms. "They didn't use force, did they?"

"Threats more than anything else." One touch and her pulse was racing. In a minute, she'd be trying to unbutton that nifty camouflage shirt he was wearing.

She pulled away before he realized his instant effect on her. "They wouldn't say who'd sent them, and you told me to be careful who I spoke to."

"So you refused to answer." McKay smiled crookedly and shook his head. "Lady, you sure do know how to stir up a hornet's nest. Men from three different agencies have failed to make you talk." He cleared his throat. "No doubt you would have held them off even longer, too."

Carly stiffened. "Are you making fun of me?"

"Hell, no. You're probably the toughest

case these intel geeks have seen in months. I'm damned impressed." He frowned and began to pace the room.

She'd missed that long stride, that deceptively loose way he held his body as he prowled a room. In his uniform, he looked bigger and more dangerous than ever. He also looked every inch the soldier. How could she have been such a fool not to notice sooner?

"Tell me what's going on."

"Nothing good. It looks like Daphne and her father may be hostages. We have satellite reconnaissance photos that show them being taken from their home to their yacht, in the company of an ex-Soviet general turned international smuggler. The consensus here is that a counterfeiting operation is in the works, and Brandon got in the way because he refused to go along with the program."

Carly felt the blood leave her face. "What will happen to them?"

"Nothing, assuming I get my team in place and pay an unexpected visit to Santa Marina before things get out of hand."

"Team?"

"U.S. Navy SEALs."

"Oh." What else could she say? She'd trusted him nearly from the start because she'd believed that he could never be on the wrong side. It made perfect sense that he was a member of the best of the best, a brotherhood of unsung heroes.

She placed her hands on the table. "What do you need to know?"

"Everything. Staff habits, floor plans of the estate on Santa Marina, and the layout of the Brandon yacht. You stayed on the yacht six months ago, didn't you?"

Carly nodded. "I have some film I made during the trip, but it's back in New York."

"We'll send someone to pick that up immediately. We'll need as many details as possible to plan our operation. Do you have films of the estate, too?"

She leaned forward eagerly. "I took a whole videotape last year at Daphne's birthday. Once a filmmaker, always a filmmaker. They'll have more detail than your satellite photos, too."

McKay took her arm and escorted her to the door. "Lady, this news is going to make a lot of people here damned happy. Let's get to work, shall we?"

Carly's heart slammed at the contact with his hard body, even as questions raced through her head.

She held them back.

They would come later.

Now was for Daphne and her father.

"That's everything I can think of." Carly stared at her cup of cold coffee with disgust. She had been cooped up in a windowless room for eight hours straight, dredging up information on the Brandons' staff, their estate on Santa Marina, and their yacht.

A courier had brought her films from New York and she had run through each one a dozen times as part of formal briefings. Her suited escorts from the dock looked peeved, but the tables had been turned. Now the questions came from McKay and two other Navy officers, along with a gray-haired man in civilian clothes.

Carly finished the truly awful cup of coffee, feeling the zing of caffeine overload. "How will this information help you?"

"We need every possible detail for training purposes," McKay said.

"What kind of training?" Carly desperately wanted to do more to help than sit passively answering questions, but to do that she needed to know more about the operation.

McKay glanced at his superior officer, who nodded. "We already have a scale model of Brandon's yacht under construction, based on design plans from the builder and augmented by your films. In an hour I'll start putting my team through live-fire hostage recovery drills to get them in the mood."

"Live fire?"

"We're going in hard, Carly. Every second of training has to count. Live fire reinforces the message."

"Someone may be hurt."

"Not on my team." From another man the words would have sounded arrogant, but from McKay they came out as simple, God's-honest truth.

Carly shivered, remembering what Izzy had said about tight spots being McKay's specialty. "What if Daphne isn't on the yacht by the time you reach Santa Marina?"

"We're also running drills for the Brandon estate. Constructing those models for CQB will take longer, but they're already in the works."

"CQB?"

"Close Quarters Battle."

Carly studied her clenched hands, paling at the thought of a firefight around Daphne and her uncle. "I want to go with you. I know everyone on the staff, and none of them would question my paying an unexpected visit. You can put some kind of radio or microphone on me and relay the feed.

That way you and your men won't be going in cold."

"Out of the question," McKay said tightly. "You'd be walking right into fire. This is a military mission, and you're a civilian."

"But I'm *volunteering*."

"And it is very honorable of you," the gray-haired man named Grace interrupted. "But it's impossible. It's Carnival time down there and things are going to be damned tricky."

"Have you managed to get any current information from the Brandons' compound?"

Neither Ford nor his superiors answered.

Carly glared across the table. "So you're going in by satellite photos and my eight-month-old films. That's not good enough."

"Not entirely. We have some recent ground intel," McKay replied. "For the moment no one is going in or out of the Brandon estate, and the yacht is now under constant surveillance."

"Let me go. I can help you."

William Grace stood up and held out a hand. "I'll be very clear, Ms. Sullivan. You've been an enormous help, but now you'll have to leave the details to us. Commander McKay and his SEAL team are equipped to handle missions like this, trust me on that. Now I'll have someone take you to your quarters and you can rest while our people get on with their business."

McKay's face was carefully guarded. Carly knew that he agreed completely.

At any moment she expected the two men to pat her on the head and give her another doughnut.

They needed her badly enough to shanghai her there and detain her for hours before telling her the truth. Now that they had what they wanted, they planned to brush her off like some kind of dimwit?

She hid a smile, a plan forming in her mind. If they wanted a retiring female who knew her place, that's exactly what they would get.

"Of course," she said quietly. "That's probably the best idea." She smiled demurely.

But not too demurely. McKay was no fool. "It's been a long day, what with being kidnapped and all," she added.

"Excellent." Grace looked relieved. "You enjoy your rest tonight and we'll talk again tomorrow. Meanwhile, leave it to us to decide what's best for your friends in Santa Marina."

Carly didn't consider resting, not for a

second. By eight the next morning she was strapped into the passenger seat of a private plane flying over the Caribbean with Santa Marina dead ahead.

"Excellent visibility, Ms. Sullivan." The pilot pointed to the speck of land growing on the horizon. "You want me to set you down at the main dock?"

"No." Carly scanned the horizon with a pair of binoculars lifted from the base before she'd slipped out. "I'm looking for a yacht called *Daphne's Choice*. It's usually moored just off Sunrise Point. You can set me down in the water about a half mile out to sea, and I'll take the inflatable boat in from there."

"But —"

"Don't worry. I know these waters, and the weather's perfect. No storms are expected." *Except the storm that hits when I arrive.*

She couldn't let McKay and his team go in without updated information, and no one was more familiar with Sunrise Point than she was. As an old friend, she could pay an unannounced visit to the Brandon yacht without raising the slightest suspicion. If she found nothing amiss, she would notify McKay, then head for the Brandon estate.

The plane banked and she watched the white granite walls of Santa Marina's government house glow in the sun, all the while reviewing her plan one more time.

"What do you mean, she's gone?" McKay towered over a crestfallen MP. "When did you last check?"

"Five minutes ago, sir," the officer explained in a thick Georgia accent. "I was told to get the lady some breakfast from the mess. I wasn't gone long, sir. When I returned, she didn't answer the door, so I went inside and —"

"And she was gone," McKay said in disgust. "Did anyone actually see her go into her room at the barracks last night?"

"Yes, sir. Took her in myself, sir."

"And have you seen her since?" he demanded.

The soldier flinched, yet remained at attention. "Sir, no sir. She said she was tired and was going straight to bed. I believed her, sir. We never expected that she would —"

"When I want excuses, I'll ask for them, soldier." McKay picked up the telephone on the worn desk. "Get me the gatehouse," he said gruffly. "This is Commander McKay."

The line clicked, then was answered by a deep bass voice. "Sergeant Riley here. How can I help you, sir?"

"I'm looking for Ms. Sullivan. Have you seen her?"

"Affirmative, sir. I called her a taxi myself at 0500 hours." Papers ruffled. "She said she had to go to Miami for some photos and tapes you required for today's briefing."

"I don't suppose anyone considered phoning me for verification," McKay said as he rubbed his forehead.

"No, sir. Ms. Sullivan was not on my 'detain' list. I checked just to be sure."

No, of course she wasn't, McKay thought sourly. No one had expected her to sneak off right under their dumb, unsuspecting noses. The lady had done a number on all of them, him most of all. She'd had no intention of staying behind while her friends were in danger, and by now she was probably halfway to Santa Marina.

The thought chilled him to the bone.

"We'll discuss operating procedures later, Sergeant," McKay grumbled. He hung up, then dialed the CO, already working out an alternate plan. With Carly in the field headed toward a hostile force, they would have to push the drop schedule forward. If she wasn't careful, she could tip off Vronski that an action was imminent. Meanwhile, there was no way in hell he would allow the irritating woman to get herself hurt.

They were going in.

Chapter 39

The sea was blessedly calm when the pilot launched an inflatable boat from the sea plane and Carly wriggled inside. He had given her water, a compass, and careful directions on how to start the outboard.

Now he watched anxiously while she yanked the motor cord. On her third try the engine growled to life, and Carly waved, checked her compass, then sliced through the water toward the Brandon yacht, moored a half mile due west.

Her costume, as she thought of it, was artful yet simple. A scanty string bikini hugged her beneath a gauze shirt, which she would dump when she got close to the yacht. Her small, glittery bag held sunscreen, a bottle of designer water, a miniature camera, and a cell phone.

At her feet lay a bottle of excellent Russian vodka to be used as a prop, should she require it.

As she bumped along through the water, Carly fought down her anxiety. Panic was out of the question or she'd fall on her face.

With the white bow of *Daphne's Choice* rising before her, she pulled on a floppy hat and surveyed the deck discreetly. Two men with crew cuts and huge arms were standing near the stern. They were dressed casually in loose, flowing shirts.

No one Carly recognized, and she knew all of the Brandon staff.

Which meant that *these* were the bad guys.

One of the men turned. Carly saw him point toward her while his companion raised a set of binoculars. Quickly she slipped off her gauze shirt, then began to wave wildly.

Keep it light, she told herself. She was a woman on vacation traveling in search of an old friend, no more. Nothing to raise suspicion. By sheer determination she kept a big smile in place as she pulled up beside the gleaming yacht. One of the big men sprinted along the railing above her.

Her heart pitched when she saw his gun leveled at her face.

McKay was making a final predeparture check of satellite photos of the Caribbean when his second glanced up.

"Sir, I think you'd better take this call. It might be Ms. Sullivan. She sounds funny —"

McKay snatched up an extension before the man had finished speaking. "Who is this?" he demanded.

The connection was tinny, broken by occasional bursts of static. A cell phone, McKay thought, or maybe a marine connection.

"This is Carly calling for Ford. That's you, isn't it, dearheart?"

Dearheart?

"This is McKay. Is something wrong?"

Her laugh echoed over the line, but there was something forced about it. "Oh, everything's fine down here in Santa Marina, dear. Sun and fun and lots of lovely things to drink."

Ford heard the clink of ice cubes and then a brittle laugh from Carly. "Oops. I just spilled another drink. Maybe I've had one too many."

Her giggles sounded as if she were halfway to Margaritaville.

"Carly, what the hell —"

"I'm here on *Daphne's Choice* and I miss you terribly. It wasn't at all nice of you to choose your job over a week of partying on the yacht. There are at least fifteen men here that I don't know. Doesn't that make you jealous?"

McKay's nerves snapped to full alert. "Fifteen men," he repeated, understanding that Carly was feeding him clues. "Russians?"

"Mad and bad ones, I'd say. They are all so . . . big and masterful."

"They're heavily armed?"

"Mmm. There are two of them right here, and I just know they think I'm a crazy red-head."

"You're crazy, all right," McKay muttered, a shaft of ice slicing deep into his chest at the thought of Carly surrounded by Vronski's thugs.

"I'm lonely without you, too, dearheart. Now hush and listen to me. I have to watch the minutes here." She gave a loud, dramatic sigh. "I think you should bring your work down here right now. You've had enough time to look at old videos and relax. Round up some of your friends and bring them along, too. I'll make you real glad you came. Know what I mean?" She gave another drunken giggle, which he knew was forced. Carly seldom drank — and never giggled.

He tried to match her light tone. "Better watch that drinking, honey lips. Whiskey goes right to your head, remember."

There was a pause, and then Carly chuckled. "That's me, old honey lips." She made a string of loud kissing sounds. "Better hurry up because it's getting pretty wild here with Carnival. Lots of noisy strangers." Her voice tightened. "Even some big truck thingies with turrets in the streets."

"I hear you," McKay said curtly.

"You want to talk to Daphne?" Once again ice cubes clinked near the receiver, as if Carly was waving a glass. "I don't know where she went. Daphne!" she called, her words slurred. "Where did you go? Uncle Nigel? Too bad. I guess someone took them away in that big silver boat with all the radar. And things were just starting to get fun. Hey —"

McKay heard a man's voice and rustling, as if there was a struggle going on. The cry of seabirds rose in counterpoint to a man's voice speaking Russian. Furious Russian.

"No way, I'm not done yet," Carly said breathlessly. "I want to say goodbye to my friend. Why, you big —"

There was another burst of angry Russian, then the line went dead.

McKay gripped the phone, his jaw clenched. Carly was in deadly trouble. Evidently her guards thought she was making a frivolous call to her boyfriend, thanks to her clever performance, but she'd been caught. The two men would be shark bait for allowing her to make any kind of communication. Whoever the new arrival was, he hadn't bought her story and he wouldn't let her out of sight again.

McKay stood rigidly in the center of the briefing room and stared at a fixed point, marshaling his panic and summoning up the cold professionalism on which his life and the lives of others depended.

Carly's life, too.

He couldn't afford to make any mistakes in a reckless rush to find her.

Review the message, he told himself. *Assess. Plan.*

Implement.

Get Carly the hell out of there.

Then he would lock her up to keep her from ever pulling a crazy stunt like this again. But first he swore he'd kiss her senseless for being so damned smart and providing him with such excellent intel, at the risk of her life.

He'd read her message loud and clear: There were strangers, probably hostile, everywhere on the island, and fifteen men positioned on the yacht, where Carly was currently being held. She'd also managed to warn him that Daphne and her father had been taken from the yacht to a vessel equipped with lots of radar, and that there were "truck thingies with turrets in the streets." Tanks?

All in all, it was excellent intel. McKay and his team would act on it immediately, once he relayed the information along the chain of command.

Striding from the room to alert his team, he barked out an order to his second. "Get me a printout of that call immediately, then run it for translation. Someone was speaking Russian and I want to know exactly what he said, even if he's only ordering another case of cold Stoli from the galley."

But McKay knew the Russian was issuing far more serious orders. He prayed desperately that they didn't include harming Carly.

Chapter 40

She was going to throw up, Carly thought.

She was curled on a dirty cement floor, her hands and feet bound by heavy industrial wire that cut into her skin every time she moved. Her stitches ached and her forehead throbbed from the blow she'd taken from one of the goons aboard the yacht.

After that, everything slid into a blur.

She had awakened in darkness with a shattering pain at her temple and imminent nausea. Through the wall she heard the low rumble of machinery and an occasional burst of voices, but no one had come to check on her.

Fear left a cold, metallic taste in her mouth as she sat up, fresh pain spearing through her stitches. She hadn't seen Daphne or her father since several of the thugs had pulled them from the yacht at gunpoint. Two other boats had been rocking nearby, both bearing the logo of the Santa Marina police, but with the Brandons held captive at gunpoint, she doubted that Inspector St. John and his officers would attempt an armed rescue.

Carly fought back tears at the memory of

Daphne's white, frightened face as their captors pushed her flat on the seat and thundered away. She prayed that her information to McKay had been helpful and his team would reach Santa Marina in time to avoid disaster.

A door creaked to her right. A square of light opened against the darkness and footsteps clicked closer. Carly sucked in a breath as something slammed into her side and a string of low curses jolted her from pain to full awareness.

"Daphne?" she whispered.

"Thank God." Daphne gasped as she felt the metal biting into Carly's wrists. "The bloody swine. Are you hurt? Did they —"

"No. Other than a bang on the head, I'm fine. Where's your father?"

"They took him off the yacht. I don't know where or why." Her voice broke. "Ransom, maybe. Or for political leverage. I never thought this could happen here in Santa Marina. My father is well respected and he never took security for granted. Why, Carly? Who are these people?"

"I don't know. Russians, I think." She chose her words carefully. "Have they made any ransom demands yet?"

"Not that I know about. I was taken to the estate for several hours, then blindfolded and brought here — wherever here is."

"Were they rough?" Carly had a sudden, terrifying thought. "What about the baby?"

"So far so good. But we have to get out of here." More footsteps rang outside the room. A door banged shut nearby, and angry voices echoed beyond the wall.

Carly frowned, hearing something familiar about the voices.

The door swung open. Light cut through dancing dust motes and cobwebs, where a man stood silhouetted. A moment later Daphne gave a ragged cry of surprise and hurled herself against the shadowed figure.

"David — why are you here?"

"Later," he said gruffly, holding her close. "You're safe now."

Daphne sank tighter against his chest. "You came."

"As soon as I could." Her fiancé's voice broke. "By God, they didn't hurt you, did they?"

"Just a few bruises. They didn't even bind my wrists like they did to Carly. But we have to go now, before those goons return."

"Of course," he said soothingly, pushing a strand of hair from her face. "You're certain they didn't harm you?"

"I'm fine." Daphne's hand slid to her waist. "But I'm afraid they could. David, I meant to tell you before." Her breath caught. "I'm pregnant."

"A baby?" Breathing harshly, he laid his hand over hers. "My baby," he whispered. "I never thought —"

"Ours," Daphne said.

He cursed under his breath. "There's no time. St. John is right outside." He spoke slowly, as if he couldn't focus. "I'll talk to him and see that he helps us."

"Inspector St. John?" Carly tried to ignore the uneasiness in the back of her mind. Inspector St. John was a close family friend, and his presence changed everything. For the first time since she'd been hauled aboard the Brandon yacht, she felt the odds shifting in their favor.

Grimly, Halloran produced a pocketknife and cut Carly's knotted wire bonds at her feet. She sighed as the metal sprang free, then pushed clumsily to her feet and held out her hands, painfully aware of every passing second.

Daphne's fiancé looked up as St. John appeared in the doorway with a lethal-looking weapon cradled in one arm. "Get the car and bring it around," Halloran snapped. "Daphne's pregnant, and we have to get her away from here immediately. She never should have been brought here in the first place."

"Pregnant?" The tall policeman sucked in a breath. "A damned fine time to discover that. Still, it's no problem. I'll take care of her."

"No. It's too late for that." It was a low, anguished hiss. "Get the car. That's an order, St. John."

Carly stared numbly from one man to the other, her horror growing as St. John leveled his weapon with silent purpose.

Furious, Halloran stepped in front of Daphne. "I said get the car."

St. John didn't move. "I'm not pulling out now," he said tensely. "Not with two million dollars at stake. Not even for a baby."

Carly choked back a wave of nausea. Halloran had found them only because he was one of the kidnappers, as was the man whom Nigel Brandon had trusted and worked with for more than three decades.

Cold-blooded traitors, both of them.

Daphne went rigid in her fiancé's arms. "I don't believe this." She stared in horror. "You're involved?"

Halloran studied her distractedly. "Not now, Daphne. Nothing matters but getting you out." He pulled her toward the door, cursing as the inspector stepped in front of them. "Don't try to stop us, St. John."

"We'll play this out exactly as planned and no one will be hurt."

"You'll get your money, St. John. I gave you my word. Now put down the gun and move away."

"I'm afraid your word isn't adequate." St. John inched sideways, his face grim and determined. "A man's entitled to have something to show for thirty years of service, but all I have is debts and promises." He gestured with the rifle. "Give me the money now or move back against the wall."

Halloran bent to reach into his pocket, and as he did, he covertly pressed a knife into Carly's hand.

"Stop moving around," St. John ordered.

"You're a fool," Halloran hissed. "He'll kill you first. Your only chance is with me. He'll —"

St. John was pitched sideways against the wall. A stocky man kicked St. John's weapon across the floor, then barked a sentence in what sounded like Russian. His eyes blazed as he stared at Halloran.

"Go on. His only chance is what?" he rumbled, his voice heavily accented.

No one moved.

"I asked a question."

St. John struggled up onto one knee. "I wouldn't let them leave. I kept to the terms,

451

the way we agreed. I even arranged for the woman to be trapped in the freezer, as you wanted, but you said no one would be hurt, Vronski."

"Did I really?" the Russian said slowly. "My memory is not always reliable, I'm afraid."

"You killed one of my men."

"A casualty of war."

"This isn't war, dammit." St. John struggled to rise. "You lied to me. I made certain that your distribution system was set, and you promised —"

A hail of bullets slammed St. John down onto his back. Carly bit back a cry and turned away from the explosive burst of blood.

"Promises are for old women and fools," the Russian spat. "Did you think I would trust a man who betrayed his oldest friend?"

Daphne shrank back as the Russian turned and studied her coldly.

"No," Halloran snapped.

"You question me?"

"No one was to be hurt, or have you forgotten in your greed?"

"Remember who you speak to. Remember what is before you." The Russian spoke in cold fury. "And all of what is behind you."

"You mean the money? I have enough of that to last a lifetime." Halloran pushed Daphne protectively behind him. "It was never about money for me. It was always about proving myself and making you proud of me."

"There can never be enough money, you fool." The man called Vronski tossed a videocassette bearing the logo of Daphne's foundation at St. John's lifeless body. "Soon we will swim in money. Hundreds more like this one have been packed and are ready to begin shipping tomorrow — as soon as Brandon is brought to heel." The Russian nudged the plastic case with the toe of his shoe. "Otherwise, he will be crushed. There will be more money than you can imagine, and you will help me build an empire here on Santa Marina."

"No one was to be hurt," Halloran repeated shakily.

"Are you so weak to care? Your woman has served her purpose. Her father is very close to full agreement."

"It should never have come to this." Halloran's designer suit was rumpled and dusty, but he stood straight and tall. "Daphne will not be touched."

"Imbecile." Vronski's face filled with ugly color. "Have you forgotten what I gave up to make you all that you are? I cut you from my life and erased your name from my lips. I gave up all the years we could have had together as father and son so you would be free, unquestioned, a man of power with the perfect education, the perfect clothes, and the perfect friends."

Daphne gave a sob of shock and tried to move, but Halloran pushed her back. "She is worth more than all you gave me." He gripped Daphne's arm, breathing hard. "You will not harm her or the child she carries."

"David, no." Daphne's voice was a tortured whisper.

"Silence," Vronski said coldly. "I eat with jackals and walk with traitors." His eyes glinted, and Carly thought they carried the unfocused sheen of madness. Careful to draw no attention to herself, she eased Halloran's knife into the pocket of the loose cotton pants the Russians had insisted she change into.

Vronski turned to a uniformed man in the doorway. "Take the two women back to the yacht," he barked. "You know what to do there."

"I ask you to stop now. I ask as your son, the son you loved enough to sacrifice everything for." David spoke firmly, though his hands were shaking. "I can't allow you to do this."

A vein beat madly on Vronski's forehead. "No?" he whispered. "And how will my only son stop me? You know nothing of threats, Dimitri."

"David. That's who I am. The rest is a bad dream."

Vronski seemed to stagger. "All because of this woman? This weak, shiny creature and her silly friend?"

"Yes. Because of her. Because I love her."

Vronski turned slowly, almost wearily. "Because of a beautiful face you can forget your father and a lifetime of plans written in his tears?"

His son nodded stiffly. "Yes. Keep the money. Just let us go."

"Very well." Vronski's shoulders slumped. "Then it is done. The money is forgotten, just as you are." Before Carly's stunned gaze, he drew a gun and leveled it at his son's chest.

In a blur of movement he fired, his eyes hard, every inch of his body held rigid in a soldier's stance.

Chapter 41

"Get me an update," McKay snapped. "If things are falling apart on that damned island, I want to know it now, before we hit the drop zone."

Two hours, he thought, watching the ocean glint outside the windows of the noisy C-130 transport plane, glad for the headset that allowed communication over the unholy din of the engines.

The call from Carly had come only two hours before. They had immediately moved forward their departure, and now the plane was nearly within sight of Santa Marina.

"Eight minutes to drop zone," the jump-master said, cutting into the conversation.

"We have updated records as of twenty minutes ago, Commander McKay. These faxes of satellite photos just came through." The intelligence liaison officer was ruddy and built like a fire hydrant, with a Maine accent that could score granite. He pointed to two spots on the grainy photographs and adjusted his headset slightly. "Our best assessment is that Brandon is still being held at the family estate near the southern tip of the island. Only one car has left the area, and it was carrying a woman our spotter identified as Daphne Brandon. She was accompanied by one of Vronski's top men."

Then where in hell is Carly?

McKay didn't voice the question, knowing that the intelligence officer would first present all the details concerning the governor, since his rescue from a hostage situation held top mission priority.

"The car was tracked?"

"Affirmative. She was taken to a building near the docks. We have two spotters on site now, and they've identified the location as one of the warehouses used by her foundation." The officer cleared his throat, looking uncomfortable. "We still have no information on the whereabouts of Ms. Sullivan."

McKay's hands clenched and sweat trickled along his Kevlar vest, which he wore beneath a load-bearing harness carrying fifty pounds of equipment and ammo.

Damn, damn, damn. Where was she?

He forced himself to stay calm. "Tell them to keep searching. I don't want her stumbling into the crossfire."

His headset clicked. "Five minutes to drop zone, commander."

Ford nodded at the jumpmaster, then turned to his men. Seasoned professionals, they were completing a final check on each other's equipment. One team would carry out a high-altitude, low-opening jump one mile out to sea. A second team would drop to the waters south of the island and swim to Vronski's yacht, which they would board and search, neutralizing any opposition in the process. Absolute precision and silence were crucial to mission success. If news of their landing reached Vronski in advance, hostages might be lost.

McKay looked at his second, who nodded his readiness. Glancing down at his watch, McKay ran through variables and contingency plans should they meet heavy resistance. His breathing was steady, and he forced his body to remain relaxed as the plane began to bank slowly to the south.

"Three minutes to drop point, commander."

The two SEAL teams lined up, their faces intent and their eyes hungry for action.

They were the best, McKay knew. He'd cursed and sweated alongside them in swamps, jungles, and stormy seas. He knew there were no better fighters anywhere on God's green earth.

"One minute to drop zone." The warning thundered over the intercom. McKay closed off all personal thoughts, all worry and indecision as the jumpmaster moved into place near the C-130's scuffed loading ramp.

The jumpmaster signaled sharply as the green light flashed. McKay's mind was clear and deadly focused as he stepped out into the screaming air thirty thousand feet above the ocean and felt the icy wind grab him.

Daphne screamed as her fiancé jerked beneath three fast bullets, then toppled to the cold floor only inches from the inspector.

Carly knew he was dead.

Only fury and outrage pulled her out of her shock. She caught Daphne, preventing her from dropping to her knees next to Halloran's fallen body. Vronski was beyond reason now, shattered by his son's betrayal, and if she and Daphne didn't stay calm, they would die just like the two men on the cold cement floor.

At least Halloran had cut the wires at her hands and slipped her his knife. Later, she would grieve for him and wonder about a father who valued his son less than scraps of elaborately printed paper.

But right now she had to think.

She inched toward Daphne and pulled her closer as Vronski barked out a torrent of orders in Russian.

"The animal. David —" Daphne shuddered, her eyes wide and unfocused.

Carly pressed a hand to her mouth and shook her head, afraid to draw Vronski's attention. "Think of the baby. David would want that," she whispered.

Daphne nodded, one hand pressed against her stomach. After one last, agonizing look at her fiancé's body, she forced her gaze to the door.

Outside, a line of men were carrying boxes along the corridor, their feet shuffling on the bare cement. Vronski gestured to his aide, then pointed to his son's body, his eyes full of weariness. Turning back, he stared at Carly and Daphne, then gave an order in Russian.

The two women were shoved toward the door.

"He was your son," Daphne said sharply, fighting her captor. "How could you kill him?"

Vronski turned the black videocassette over in his hands, seeming to shrink inward, lost in a world no one else could see.

"I have no son," he said tightly. "Perhaps I never did." He did not look up as the two women were pushed past him into the dusty corridor.

They were herded into the back of a truck filled with boxes, then locked in with a muscular blond guard whose gaze never wavered as the truck wound through the crowded streets of Santa Marina.

When the truck bumped to a halt, the big guard pushed them into a metal cargo case. Neither woman was foolish enough to argue while he held an ugly assault rifle inches from their faces. Carly wrapped her arms around Daphne, cushioning her body as the cargo case was hauled over what felt like a dozen steep steps.

Finally they stopped and the lid swung open.

The blond guard motioned for them to get out. Carly and Daphne obeyed in silence as they were pushed into the galley of the Brandon yacht, bound back-to-back with heavy electrical tape.

The guard glanced at his watch, then strode to the door. A bolt clicked, and his heavy footsteps echoed up the companionway.

Carly released a slow, painful breath. "We've got to get out."

Daphne nodded, white faced, still struggling with the horror of what she had just witnessed. "We've served our purpose," she said flatly. "Just like David and Inspector St. John." She pressed her lips together hard. "What about our hands?"

"Move closer." Carly searched until she could touch the knife hidden in her pocket. After long, agonizing minutes, she worked the blade out and hacked away the tape, then ran to the door.

It was locked, as she had feared.

No windows. No other exits.

"There's an air vent above the stove," Daphne said as Carly went to work on her bound hands. "Father had it put in last year after we had a grease fire down here. We might be able to crawl through to the upper deck." When Carly freed her hands, she rubbed her wrists, frowning. "It won't be pleasant, I warn you."

"Who needs pleasant?"

Footsteps hammered somewhere over their heads. An outboard motor roared to life.

Carly pulled away the aluminum grating over the vent, then climbed onto the closest counter. "It's going to be close," she said, peering inside.

Daphne nodded, following Carly on hands and knees into the darkness. Overhead, the deck was silent. The roar of the outboard motor had faded and Carly suddenly had the sense that they were alone on the yacht.

You know what to do there.

462

Remembering the Russian's cold instructions, she climbed quickly, urging Daphne to do the same. The guard had left them alone, and Carly didn't want to hang around to find out why.

She tried not to think of an explosive charge ticking beneath her as she crawled through the rough metal duct, with Daphne close behind her. Her knees were scraped raw when she finally saw a square of light six feet ahead, blocked by a heavy grate. She froze and listened intently, but heard only the angry cry of a seabird against the wind.

She looked back at Daphne and together they shoved at the grating. One side shook, then swung free. When there was no shout or sound of alarm, they attacked the other side.

It seemed like an eternity before the heavy aluminum plate pulled free and plunged out of sight, landing in a splash somewhere below them. Her knees burning, Carly crawled to the four-foot opening and saw that they were about twenty feet above the water. The jump would be uncomfortable but not dangerous, though she was worried about Daphne.

She gripped Daphne's hand. "We jump from here. It's only a few feet down. When we're in the water, we'll check our location and swim ashore. If they haven't moved the yacht, we should be only a quarter mile out."

Daphne nodded weakly.

"Hey, you okay?"

"Scared. What if my father won't give them what they want?" Daphne had been schooled since childhood in security precautions and knew exactly what danger her father faced. She also knew his stubbornness and absolute refusal to deal with criminals.

"McKay and his men are on the way," Carly whispered. "Let them handle Vronski." She inched toward the vent. "I'll be waiting for you below. Be careful. The opening is sharp."

She listened for the drone of the circling boat, but heard only the slap of water against the yacht's hull. With a deep breath, she rocked forward, executing a crisp dive that plunged her deep into the crystal water.

Daphne was waiting when Carly broke the surface. Closing her eyes, she followed.

A quick assessment showed that they had no more than a twenty-minute swim before them. Their only company was a motorboat cruising at the far side of the cove.

Two men stood in the stern. Carly saw

the flash of metal as one of them pointed toward the yacht.

Some sharp instinct made her grab Daphne's hand. "Swim. We've got to get away from here."

She set off toward the beach, keeping Daphne in sight, glad for all the summers they had spent exploring the broad, shimmering cove.

Out of the corner of her eye, Carly saw the man on the boat gesture, calling to his companion. She shouted for Daphne to dive, then jackknifed and headed deep. Water churned and sea seemed to growl and claw at her as a wall of water slapped her up into the air like a huge, angry fist.

Then there was only darkness.

Metal fragments and burning timbers raked Carly's back. Opening her eyes, she fought her way toward the glimmer of light high above her, veiled by swirling debris.

She had no idea how much time had passed since the explosion that had tossed her up, then sucked her down again. Turbid water churned around her as she hit the surface with a deep, wheezing gasp, fighting desperately for air. Her throat was too raw to speak, so she treaded water in a circle, searching every shattered piece of teak and metal that swept past. Clutching at a passing wood fragment, she finally spotted Daphne afloat on a piece of deck. There was no sign of the two men who had been cruising the far side of the cove.

Carly closed her eyes with a prayer of thanks, then pushed off into the shifting debris.

Something brushed her foot. Not wood or metal, but smooth and pulsing. *Probably a fish,* she thought.

Another powerful movement brushed along her leg.

A *big* fish.

Blocking an immediate image of a shark, she forced herself to stay still, presenting less of an attraction to a hungry predator.

This time something shook the water and bumped her side.

Carly shrieked as spray churned and a dozen grotesque forms rose from the debris-filled sea around her.

Chapter 42

Not grotesque.

Not a shark, Carly realized as rubber-gloved hands gripped her waist. *A man.*

Behind him more soldiers floated on the water wearing wet suits equipped with high-tech goggles and sleek breathing equipment.

Carly gasped wildly as muscular arms caught her close and crushed her against a hard body.

The goggles and mouthpiece slid away.

"McKay," she whispered.

Glinting amber eyes bored into hers as he searched her face. "Honey lips and dearheart," he muttered, lifting her onto a shattered plank from the ruined yacht. "You're a damned hard woman to find, Sullivan. If you ever sneak off on me like that again, I'm going to tan your sweet behind from here to St. Thomas and back."

"Nice to see you too, McKay." Carly heard her teeth chattering. She clung to both the rocking piece of wood and McKay's shoulder, crushingly weak now that the danger had passed. "Impeccable timing. But where's Daphne?" she croaked in panic.

"She's in good hands. My medic is checking her out now." McKay nodded toward the wooden plank where Daphne clung with the aid of one of the SEALs, her head nodding or shaking in reply to his questions. Somehow the medic was also managing to take her pulse and check her pupils.

"Think of everything, don't you?" Carly managed a lopsided smile, feeling the first letdown after the mother of all adrenaline rushes.

"I try." For a moment, emotion burned in his eyes. Then his face turned impassive. "We've got a Zodiac nearby."

"A what?"

"Inflatable boat. We'll get you two aboard and out of harm's way. Izzy will keep an eye on you from there."

"What about you?" Carly whispered.

"Brandon's being held somewhere on the estate. We're going in to spring him."

It was exactly the answer Carly had expected — and also feared, knowing the terrible danger involved. "How will you get past the guards? Every inch of the fence will be watched." Despite her weakness, she was thinking fast, dredging up every scrap of information that might help him.

"We'll wait until dark, if possible. If

things start falling apart sooner —"

Carly shook her head, cutting him off. "Things already have. Vronski is unstable. He — he killed Inspector St. John when the two argued."

McKay's face hardened. "So St. John *was* the leak."

"There's more," she said grimly. "David Halloran is — was — Vronski's son." Carly closed her eyes. "Vronski shot him, too."

McKay cursed softly. "If he's losing control, we can't take a chance on waiting until dark. We'll have to go in through the drainage pipes from the beach, near the back of the compound." He gestured sharply to one of his team, then issued several terse commands into a small black radio. "Izzy should be here in the next ten minutes." He studied Carly's face, the deep creases on his forehead betraying his worry. "Can you hold on here until then?"

"Go. I'll take care of Daphne if you'll give me a push over to her."

McKay gave her a smile of encouragement and one slow brush of his lips. "Vronski's men are all at the estate. The two who set the bomb on the yacht put to shore as soon as the boat blew. You'll be safe here. Sit tight and wait for Izzy."

Carly nodded as McKay gestured to the

other SEALs floating amid the wreckage. Then he slid his mask back into place and the group vanished beneath the churning surface of the sea as silently as they had come.

A low rumble echoed over the water.

Daphne and Carly were clinging to their fragment of deck when they heard the approaching growl of an outboard motor.

Izzy's face appeared over the passing bulk of a shattered deck chair, looking cool and professional in a headset with a small microphone. He was speaking rapidly as he approached.

"Made it . . . I'll get them aboard ASAP. Give the bad guys a whack or two for me." He leaned down and extended his arm. "Welcome aboard, ladies. Who goes first?"

Since Daphne was closer, she gripped his hand and squirmed over the side of the black rubber boat. Within seconds, Izzy had them both settled aboard, wrapped in warm blankets. He handed them each a thermos.

"Enjoy the soup. We'll rendezvous a half mile out and get you ladies into something warm and dry as soon as possible. Then you can tell me how you managed to escape from that yacht."

Despite his casual expression, Carly saw

his gaze rake the distant beach and the red tile roofs of the Brandon estate. She wondered if he was worried about the mission, but there was no way to tell. Like McKay, his face revealed nothing.

After a last glance at the island, he brought the Zodiac around sharply and set a choppy course due south, out to sea.

Wind whipped at Carly's face as she paced the deck of the liaison ship, waiting for news from the estate. Daphne had finally gone below to rest, but only after making Carly promise to call her at the first hint of news about her father.

As Carly studied the estate with high-powered binoculars, Izzy slipped a jacket around her shoulders. "The wind's picking up. It will be colder now that the sun is down."

Carly shrugged on the jacket, dwarfed in its folds but glad for the warmth. "Any news yet?"

"We know that Brandon is being held in the storeroom beneath the main house. So far, there's no sign of unusual activity there."

"Vronski?"

"He's expected from Bridgetown within the hour," Izzy said grimly. "If there weren't hostages involved, the team would hit his car en route, but now that's not an option."

Carly forced down a knot of fear as she remembered the flicker of madness in Vronski's eyes before he killed his son. "He kept talking about money and all the things it could do. He seemed obsessed by the idea."

"That he is," Izzy said, watching the harbor. "Money and power." With the darkness complete, he exchanged his binoculars for a low-light scope.

Suddenly, his hands tightened. "There's movement at the front gate. Looks like a truck and two sedans. Could be Vronski."

Across the water, the lights at the house flickered, then died.

"That would be McKay. Their first objective was to cut all the inside power." Izzy frowned as static burst from his headset. "Team one is inside. They're going after Brandon," he said tensely. "Team two will target Vronski. Let's hope he's in one of those sedans that just arrived."

"You mean they might only be a decoy?"

"It's been done before."

Automatic-weapon fire erupted and shouts drifted over the water.

Carly opened and closed her trembling hands. "When will we know?"

Light filled the sky, followed by the crack

of explosives. "They have Brandon out safely. Team one is pulling back with Daphne's father, but they're taking heavy fire," Izzy murmured, one hand on his headset. "McKay and his men should be hitting Vronski any second now."

Carly could barely hear over the thunder of her heart. As she continued to watch the compound, another explosion rocked the night, followed by more gunfire.

Izzy's headset crackled with a torrent of voices. His eyes hardened.

"What's happened?" Carly demanded.

More muffled shouting drifted from the headset. A helicopter thundered over their heads, moving low and fast toward the island. Izzy's gaze fixed on the helicopter as if willing it to move faster.

Why? Carly thought. The explosions were fading, and the gunfire had slowed to scattered bursts.

Surely they had spirited Nigel Brandon out safely. Otherwise Izzy would have heard. She thought she should go below and tell Daphne, but Izzy's expression, rigidly intent on the path of the helicopter, held her still.

She caught her breath, willing him to explain, yet afraid to hear the rest. "Tell me."

"They took out Vronski and most of his

men. Unfortunately, he'd already booby-trapped the house with C-4."

"I don't understand."

"Plastic explosive. He remote detonated just as the team was closing in on him." As he spoke, the helicopter descended, vanishing in the darkness above the estate.

Carly felt a dizzying burst of intuition. "He's hurt?" she whispered as the wind burned, making her eyes tear.

Izzy made a sharp, frustrated gesture with one hand. "He was caught in the blast when the last of the C-4 blew. His team called in the chopper to fly him out."

"How bad?" she demanded, steeling herself to hear the worst. She knew how dangerous Vronski was. She'd twice witnessed his cruelty, indiscriminate and almost inhuman.

"Pretty bad," Izzy said. "They don't know if . . ."

Carly clutched at the rail. Her cheeks were stinging with tears as lights flashed overhead. In a burst of noise the helicopter roared above them, then banked and thundered away into the night.

Chapter 43

She waited and prayed and hoped. She paced and worked and cursed. But no letter came and no calls were put through.

All Carly knew was that Ford was alive and mending.

Days passed, slipping into weeks, then months. Carly finished her cruise project, sublet her apartment in New York, and moved to Santa Marina to be with Daphne.

Her friend's face was paler than it had been. There were new lines at her mouth, and a new hardness snapped in her eyes. But four months had passed since the kidnapping in Santa Marina and life went on.

Daphne's stomach was a lovely curve of growing life beneath her neat white linen sundress. With the efficiency born of loyalty, workers had restored the house to all its beauty after the explosive destruction of one wing. Now hibiscus petals dotted the flagstone patio and floated in the large, freeform swimming pool. Fortunately, the blast had been on the opposite side of the house from the garden, and Archer's roses had been nursed back to their full glory.

Santa Marina would survive, and so

would they, Carly thought. But with each day of waiting for word from Ford, each day of silence as no message came, her hope began to fade.

She shoved away Archer's artful fruit salad, untouched, and studied the shimmering water in the pool instead, absently noting the hibiscus blossoms with a photographer's sharp eye. It might make an interesting project to capture the play of light and shadow over iridescent blue water and drifting red petals.

But the water made her think of sunlight on a man's strong shoulders and shadows playing across a chiseled face, and her heart broke again, just as it had every day for the last four months.

No commitments, she had insisted. Stubborn and blind, she hadn't seen that she was not the cold perfectionist her mother had been. She had learned the value of close friendships and camaraderie.

Now she also knew the bittersweet desperation of love.

Apparently, McKay didn't.

"Hell." She pushed away the photographs, trying to block out the rest of her memories.

Three of Vronski's men had been recovered alive from the maelstrom at the

Brandon estate, and under intense questioning they had revealed the full scope of Vronski's international counterfeiting plan. Aimee Fiorento had run afoul of that plan when she demanded more money for the information she was providing Vronski's contact. As a result, she had been drowned in the ship's pool.

A chair creaked. "Did you say something, Carly?"

"No."

"Finished with your work?"

As finished as she'd ever be. "Just about."

"Then take a break and come over here. I need some help."

Carly turned, instantly worried. "Is something wrong?"

Daphne's face was composed, but she looked tired, and Carly doubted that she had slept well. David's betrayal and his death had taken their toll. His attempt to protect Daphne before his death had only left her feeling more miserable and somehow responsible. Carly had been up enough nights pacing until dawn to notice that the light was usually on beneath Daphne's door.

Damn men, anyway.

She stood beside Daphne's comfortable lounge chair. "Is it the baby? Are you having early contractions?"

"Heavens, I've got a full three months yet. No, I want your opinion on this maternity dress." She tapped the page of a glossy magazine. "Will it make me look like an emerging nation or simply a very rounded mother-to-be?"

"A stunning mother-to-be," Carly corrected, dying a little more as she looked at the radiant model and harbored her own anxious thoughts about the child she carried inside her, a miracle she had never expected.

Daphne's fingers slid into hers and tightened. "You're going to have to tell him," she said. "He needs to know."

Carly frowned and pulled away. "I've tried to reach him. I've asked every contact I know, along with most of Uncle Nigel's." She took an angry breath. "He's alive, we know that much. If he doesn't answer my messages, it must mean he doesn't want to be found. Not by *me*, at least."

"You don't know that for certain."

"I don't know anything for certain," Carly shot back. Then her face softened. "Correction. I know that I want this baby. Absolutely and without reservations."

"Then eating would be a good idea," Daphne said sternly as Archer appeared with two plates of exquisite seafood salad. "Starting right now."

"I'll have something later." Carly brushed the slightly convex curve of her stomach. "Things are still churning inside, I'm afraid."

"It will pass." Daphne spoke with the solid conviction of someone who had just been through the same ordeal. "Drink some juice and sit in the rocker and relax for once."

Archer frowned down at Carly's untouched plate. "Miss Daphne's right. You sit and finish this orange juice."

Carly smiled, unable to withstand the gentle tyranny of people so dear to her.

Archer nodded in satisfaction when she was finished. "Now then, I've brought the small television out to the table. There's to be a news story on the Tradewind Foundation."

After a short introduction, Daphne's beautiful, composed face appeared on the screen as she detailed new plans for a shipboard medical center that would cruise around Santa Marina and its neighboring islands.

"Lord, I do look like a blimp," Daphne muttered, rolling her eyes.

"Nonsense, you look happy and vital and

very lovely," Archer said briskly, well used to her complaints. "Hush, so we can listen."

After a round of questions about the foundation, the reporter asked Daphne about her father, who was working on corporate support for upgrading elementary-schools on Santa Marina. The interview ended with a beautifully executed shot of Santa Marina's busy harbor area.

Before anyone could move, a different image filled the screen.

Carly watched, frozen, as a man's face appeared, silhouetted against a tropical sunset as he raised a crystal champagne glass. His dark hair was ruffled by the wind and his muscular shoulders were guaranteed to stir a woman's dreams.

Just as she had been dreaming for four long months.

Archer sprang forward and changed the channel, but tears were already burning in Carly's eyes. She rose to her feet as a low, overdubbed voice whispered, "We have your dream."

She swallowed a knot of pain and brushed past the table, sending a stack of photos to the flagstones as she walked blindly to her room.

Knowing that even there she would see his face.

"There must be something we can do," Archer said, watching Carly walk away.

"You're damned right there is." Without a qualm at invading her friend's privacy, Daphne dug angrily through Carly's briefcase and pulled out a folded sheet of paper, her expression determined as she picked up the phone.

"I need to speak to McKay," she snapped as Izzy answered the private number he'd given Carly months before. "That's right, McKay," she continued ruthlessly. "Commander McKay, U.S. Navy SEAL, and don't give me any more of your lame excuses."

"I already told you he's alive and well," Izzy said guardedly.

"And not a damned thing beyond. Where is he?"

"I can't answer that."

"Then tell me why he hasn't phoned Carly yet."

Izzy drew an audible breath but said nothing.

"She needs him," Daphne said. "She's too proud to tell you that, but I'm not. Tell him to call her."

"I'm afraid I can't do that. It's his choice, not mine."

"Tell that to the woman who loves him. And tell that to his *child*." Daphne slammed down the phone, only to hear it ring a moment later. "Yeah, that's exactly what I said. A child. Ford's child. Carly is pregnant."

"What could possibly be taking so long?" Carly paced restlessly, her hands in the pockets of the loose linen tunic she wore over black leggings. Daphne had been experiencing some unusual pains and her doctor in Santa Marina had referred her to a specialist in Florida for a full array of tests, just to be certain nothing was overlooked.

Carly and Nigel Brandon had been waiting in the crowded hospital for two hours when a door swung open and Daphne appeared, smiling and radiant.

"What did they say?" Carly demanded.

"It will be a few hours yet." Daphne exchanged a quick glance with her father. "While we're waiting for the results, let's go for a walk." She took Carly's arm. "I could do with something to drink."

"There's no need for you to go," Carly said immediately. "I'll get it."

"The doctor said moderate exercise was the best thing for me, so stop trying to turn me into some kind of pathetic invalid." She started down the corridor. "See you in a few minutes," she called to her father, who smiled broadly as soon as they turned a corner.

Near the end of the hall, Daphne stopped abruptly.

"What's wrong? More pain?"

"No, this is about you." Daphne opened the door to a waiting room and gently pushed Carly forward. "In you go."

"Me? What do you mean?"

"Since you were going to be here anyway, I made an appointment for you to have an ultrasound. The technician is waiting for you."

"But —"

A technician approached, clipboard in hand, rattling off questions before Carly could protest further, and Daphne took advantage of the distraction to slip back outside. She was joined a few moments later by Izzy, who looked devastatingly handsome in a gray polo shirt and jeans.

Daphne raised one hand. "High five," she murmured. After a resounding slap, she checked her watch. "Should be anytime now."

Izzy spoke quietly into a walkie-talkie he took from his pocket. "Situation report?"

Static crackled, then a voice responded. "Target in sight, sir. ETA 1140 hours."

"Roger," Izzy said, thumbing off his receiver. "Time to disappear." He guided Daphne out of sight into a storage room across the hall.

Even as the door closed behind her, McKay appeared in the corridor, balanced on a cast from foot to lower thigh. A scar ran across his jaw and disappeared beneath the collar of his white naval uniform.

Izzy saw the strain in his eyes and remembered his first sight of McKay after the C-4 had sent him flying. A lung had been punctured and more than a few bones had shattered as he'd been flung into the air and slammed back to earth. He'd had a torturous crawl back to health, and only Izzy knew how much pain still haunted him. SEAL to the end, he had defied the odds against a full recovery and rejected the potent pain medications after three weeks, claiming that the pain helped him concentrate on all the places he had to nurse back to health.

His face was thinner, almost stark, Izzy noted as McKay maneuvered along with fierce concentration. He'd grappled with more than physical pain in the last four months. His extensive wounds meant that his days of combat field assignments were over, and he had been recommended for a desk job at a primary SEAL base in Virginia, overseeing operations. Vronski's final act of destruction had yanked Ford out of the life he had carefully planned and the career he had single-mindedly pursued for over a decade.

Izzy knew he worried about how much mobility he would regain in his right knee and whether he could make the transition to being a desk jockey.

Or if he even wanted to.

Now he was about to confront another change — whether he liked it or not.

If he refused to marry the woman carrying his child, then Carolina Sullivan had a right to hear that from the horse's mouth and not over the telephone.

Horse's ass was more like it. But Izzy was betting on the lady to cut through McKay's intractable wall of pride.

"You're late, Commander," Izzy drawled. "But then what should I expect from a man who refused to show up for the nice funeral Vronski had planned for him? How's the knee?"

"I've already signed us up for a week of black diamond snowboarding in Vail," McKay shot back. "I'm going to whip you good." Only the set of his jaw betrayed his concentration as he made his way past a cart loaded with meals and cutlery.

"Dream on." Izzy resisted an urge to

move the cart out of McKay's way. He knew the gesture would meet with a silent glare. As stubborn as he was proud, the SEAL refused any special treatment.

"Where's the party taking place?"

Izzy ran his tongue across his teeth. "Right down the hall."

It had required an intricate web of deception to summon McKay from the naval hospital in central Florida, but Izzy had felt no compunction in fabricating a story about a mutual friend who had been badly hurt in a training exercise in Puerto Rico.

McKay stared at the door down the hall. "Hamilton's in there? Are they doing some kind of test?"

"He should be done any minute. Why don't you go in and surprise him?" Izzy opened the door, all innocence as he watched McKay shuffle inside to the reception desk, where he was guided to a smaller examining room, just as Izzy and Daphne had arranged beforehand. Slowly, he approached the door in question and peered through the glass.

McKay's lips tightened. He seemed to be having trouble breathing.

He rubbed his eyes hard.

Then his hand opened, pressed tightly to the glass.

Chapter 44

Carly lay restlessly on a gray examining table, her linen tunic hiked up above her stomach. A smiling technician was sliding goo over Carly's skin while keeping up an unbroken string of comments about the Caribbean cruise she planned for the following week. Without a pause, the woman placed a small scanner on Carly's stomach and began moving it slowly.

"Look at the screen on the wall. Let's see what we have here."

Dry-mouthed and breathless, Carly watched the incredible evidence of the life growing within her. Would she see delicate feet? A tiny face?

The nurse moved the probe sideways, expertly working the controls of the ultrasound scanner.

Carly had asked not to be told the gender. Technology was wonderful, but she preferred that secret to remain until the actual delivery.

Fuzzy black-and-white images shifted and spun on the monitor. The tech stopped the probe and grinned broadly. "There's a foot, right at three o'clock. One hand at eleven-thirty."

Carly squinted hard, trying to see if the white outlines were blotches or tiny fingers.

"Let's take a closer look," the tech said. "Especially over here to the left. I want to get some measurements."

As the door opened, Carly turned her head and looked up, expecting to see Daphne.

Her heart plunged into free fall. She blinked, half convinced this was another full-color daydream like the others that had plagued her over the last four months.

A man in a dazzling white uniform stood staring back at her, his mouth set, his gaze fixed on her face.

"McKay?" Her voice shook. She couldn't seem to breathe.

"Right here," he rasped, looking fairly shaken himself. He was paler now, his face more angular, and Carly saw that he had lost weight.

He stared at the technician, then up at the monitor with a look of awe. "A baby," he whispered, a universe of shock and wonder in the word.

"Is that why you're here?" Carly asked, her hand rising toward his face, then dropping back to the table. She wanted desperately to touch him but knew that her control was too fragile to risk it.

McKay didn't seem to notice as he watched the screen raptly. "Here?" he repeated, distracted. "Izzy told me an old SEAL buddy had been hurt in a training exercise. That's why I came." He laughed tightly. "I'm going to have to murder that man."

Right after I finish murdering Daphne, Carly vowed. "This isn't right," she whispered. "They shouldn't have brought you here like this, because of a trick." She was awash in conflicting emotions, and the worst of them was pain.

He hadn't come to explain himself. It was strictly a cold case of deception that had brought him to her side.

Her heart ached. Carly wasn't about to bring the child into this, at least not until he'd come up with some reason for his callous indifference to her over the last four months.

"No, they shouldn't have used a trick," he agreed, his gaze skimming her stomach, then fixing on her face. "The hard fact is, they shouldn't have needed a trick to get me here. But I can't say I'm not grateful. Maybe I needed a good swift kick in the behind." He nodded toward the screen. "I think this qualifies."

The technician watched McKay curiously. "Shall I go on, Ms. Sullivan?"

"No."

"Yes," McKay countered flatly. "Is that the head? Is he up or down? Is he normal?"

"He or she," the woman answered. "Ms. Sullivan has requested that the gender remain undisclosed. And at a first reading things appear to be normal. Of course, we don't always see —"

McKay didn't wait for her to finish. "Sweet Holy heaven, a baby," he whispered. "How old?" he asked Carly.

"A little over four months."

"I didn't know."

"Of course you didn't know. You didn't return my calls. You didn't give any sign of interest or concern."

McKay's body tensed. "I was damned well concerned. I knew you had called." He shook his head and glanced down at the cast, the crutches. "I couldn't call at first. After that I didn't know if I should."

Carly refused to let her anger melt in a wave of tenderness at his obvious injuries. The future had to be discussed, and she had to stay hard and focused to do that. "You're not a man given to indecision, McKay," she said in a monotone. "I can't believe the only problem was your wounds. After all, people can still punch in a phone number in spite of a leg cast."

Behind them the technician cleared her throat uneasily. "Perhaps I should come back later," she said.

Neither McKay nor Carly paid the slightest attention as she shook her head, glanced at the monitor, then slipped out of the room.

"There are — were — reasons," McKay said. "Damned good reasons."

"Name one."

"This," he said, tracing the jagged scar above his collar. "There's another across my back."

"So? You think all I wanted was a pretty face?" Carly's hand opened and closed on her tunic. "No commitments, McKay. We agreed, and I can accept that. But you had a right to know about the baby and I had a right to know that you were safe. If you wanted to move on, you should have told me. Dammit, it was wrong to make me wait and worry." *To make me bleed inside day after day.*

"You don't get it, do you?" McKay raked his fingers through his hair. "I've got a plate in my head and two new joints, Carly. I've got a knee that may never work right again." He spoke in a rapidfire burst, as if the knowledge cut him to the quick even now.

491

"I was there, remember? I saw the explosion and the helicopter going in to airlift you out. My imagination conjured up a lot worse than a few new joints." She pulled the gown down over her stomach and struggled to rise. She didn't like the idea of settling her entire future while lying flat on her back. She certainly wasn't going to cede any psychological advantage to this man who already wielded too much power over her future.

His hand shot out, helping her to sit up, then preventing her from leaving the table. "You think I don't want you?" His gaze fixed on the wall, as if he couldn't bear to look at her. "I wanted you. I want you now, dammit. The memory of your face brought me awake every morning and followed me down into sleep every night. Thinking of you always helped me find a way through the pain." He frowned. "But wanting isn't enough. I had to know what kind of future I could offer you. I wanted my answers to be cut and dried, with no maybes or complications when I finally saw you again." He gave a mirthless laugh as he glanced at the monitor. "But this definitely qualifies as a complication. Now I don't have the luxury of time to make it up to you as I'd planned."

"What are you saying?" She clamped

down on her urge to touch his hand.

She wouldn't give in yet. The stubborn man would have to spell it all out, for better or worse.

McKay closed his eyes. "I'm saying I couldn't allow myself to want you, not with this banged-up body and a career that was over just when it was getting interesting."

"You think I care about a few scars or a limp?"

"No, you wouldn't care, but I would. At least I thought I did." He gave her that irreverent grin she had been so drawn to from the first. "Call it a 'man thing.' " Abruptly his hand closed on her shoulder, his expression grave. "I was a damned fool, but I had to know there was something I could offer you. Both of you," he added hoarsely.

"I won't let this baby become a bargaining chip." Carly took an angry breath. "I'm not pulling emotional strings here."

Fury roiled over his face. "You think I could leave now, knowing you're carrying my child? You think you could make me leave? There's not a chance in hell." His hands were shaking hard as he tilted her head back, his eyes blazing. "I told you once that I'd be responsible and I meant it. It's my fault that we —"

"I was there too, remember? The fault belongs to *both* of us, and it's a consequence I will never regret, whether you're in my life or not." Carly pushed his hand off her shoulder. "You know that I'm perfectly capable of taking care of myself and my child. You can walk out that door right now if you still have any questions about that. I won't say a single word to stop you."

His hand slid along her tear-streaked face. Funny, she hadn't even realized she was crying.

"Dear God, don't cry, sunshine. I can't take seeing you cry and knowing my stupidity caused it. I should have called you." He paused. "Every day I walked to the phone and had to fight not to dial your number. But I told myself I was doing what was right, what was best, even though every thought of you drew blood."

Her breath caught at the sound of his admission. She wasn't above hoping he was as miserable as she'd been over the last few months.

He smoothed her wet face with his strong hand. "Good sweet God, don't cry or you'll have me crying, too."

"Is that another thing SEALs don't do?"

"SEALs don't do a lot of things, including make good husbands. You don't think that's been on my mind?" McKay pressed his fingers to his eyes. "But that's no longer an issue. I'll be manning a desk at headquarters, coordinating operations in Virginia. I still don't know if I can handle that, but seeing you — *you,* sunshine, not the image on that screen — makes me think I've got a decent shot of succeeding. I'll enjoy the hell out of being able to come home every night. I'll like knowing that someone will be missing me. I won't even regret not having to pack up and pull out at a moment's notice."

"Of course you will," Carly said with a tight laugh, not quite ready to believe what he was saying.

"Yeah, I'll miss it," he conceded with a grin. "Maybe for an hour here or there. But it will be nothing beside how much I'd miss you. Now I have one more thing to get off my chest." Stiffly, he slid a small box from his pocket.

Carly watched, dazed, as he took out a ring with a diamond surrounded by a dozen tiny sapphires.

"I've been carrying this around for eight weeks now, telling myself I was the worst kind of idiot. I guess I knew I'd give in to reason eventually, and I wanted to be prepared when I did." Tenderly he slid the ring onto Carly's finger. "Live with me. Share my life. I thought I was a strong man, but you taught me that a strong woman makes a man even stronger."

Carly stared at the ring on her finger.

"I can't hear you. Is that a yes?" He raised his brows, favoring her with that commanding look he used so well. "It had damned well better be a yes."

She couldn't speak, staring at the glittering stones.

Remembering a champagne bottle at sunset and a diamond bracelet. Remembering a man who had brought light into her life.

McKay hadn't known about the baby when he'd bought the ring, yet he'd opened his future to the child without a single stumbling word. Only terrible wounds had made him wait, determined to do the right thing.

Foolish, stubborn man.

She kept her face calm. "It's a maybe."

Emotions swirled across his face and Carly thought he wavered on his crutches. The enormity of her love terrified her at that moment, and she knew she could delay her answer no longer.

"Make that a yes. A definite yes."

A shudder went through him. He braced his forehead on hers and brought her hand slowly to his lips. "I should never have made us wait."

"No, you shouldn't have."

"If I do something that stupid again, I'm counting on you to give me another boot in the butt."

"Glad to oblige, commander."

She sank against him, her hand on his shoulder, feeling safe beyond words with his arms wrapped around her.

"You've been healthy?" he demanded suddenly. "You've been eating properly?"

"I'm fine, McKay. I'm just here because Daphne needed some tests."

He slid a finger beneath the top button of her tunic and studied the lush swell of her breasts. "You're different." He traced a faint blue vein. "Because of the baby?"

Carly shivered as his thumb brushed her nipple. "Everything is sensitive right now." Her breath caught as McKay traced her other breast with exquisite tenderness. "Don't take it personally."

"Oh, I intend to take it very personally, you can count on that. I'll start tonight. I've got some leave coming, and I've got the perfect idea how to spend it."

"Can I bring some baby oil for your chest?" Carly murmured wickedly.

His answer was lost in the slow, delicious

madness of their kiss.

Outside in the hall, Izzy stood guarding the door and grinning broadly at the members of Ford's team who had appeared with all the stealth and instinct of Navy SEALs.

"Told you she'd bag him. The man's been walking wounded since the first moment he set eyes on her."

"Gotta be a boy." This smug announcement came from Ford's second, a tall, wiry man with a broken nose and a million freckles. "Give you odds on that."

Izzy shook his head. "No way, Brew," he said confidently. "It's going to be a girl. Someone guaranteed to drive men wild and make her father stark raving mad. I'll lay a cool fifty on it."

"Deal." The two men shook.

"Make it a hundred," another one of the team countered.

Daphne and her father watched the big men trade good-natured insults while Izzy presided over the betting as proudly as if the child were his.

All heads turned to the door as it opened. McKay emerged, his arm anchored around Carly's waist and a large lipstick mark branding his cheek, to which he was entirely oblivious.

"Well, sailor," he said to his freckled second. "What are you looking at? Stop grinning like a drunken hound and come meet the woman who's just promised to become my wife."

Daphne rushed to hug Carly, and Ford's team members broke out in catcalls and cheers.

The noise almost drowned out the sound of the door opening a second time.

"Ms. Sullivan?" The technician raised her voice to be heard over the din. "Mr. McKay?"

As Carly and McKay turned, she held out a grainy black-and-white image freshly printed from her equipment. "You didn't give me time to finish inside."

McKay bent close to Carly. Together they looked at the paper.

The tech tapped one corner, where a white form nudged the edge of the image. "That's one, already a good size."

"One?" McKay croaked.

She smiled as she pointed out another shape. "Here's number two. Quite an active little thing, judging by the movements I picked up."

McKay swallowed hard. "You mean —"

"Actually, I mean triplets," she said, pointing out a shape near the bottom of the image. "This is three."

Ford's face went sheet white. "You mean there are *three* of them in there?"

Carly traced the images on the paper, counting them for herself, feeling joy bubble wildly inside her. Three babies. Three amazing destinies that would be entwined with McKay's and hers.

"Give the man a cigar," Izzy announced, initiating another wild round of cheering that had doctors, nurses, and curious patients peering out of neighboring rooms. "Better make that three cigars!"

"I just might be dying here," McKay muttered, unable to look away from the black-and-white picture in his hand. He took a rough breath. "Did she actually say three?"

"Today, basic math; tomorrow, advanced physics," Carly said, then pulled her dazed husband-to-be down for a long and very satisfying kiss that raised another round of rowdy cheering.

Chapter 45

Western Puerto Rico
Seven months later

Moonlight glinted coldly.

A lone figure jogged over the deserted beach. Straightening his headset, he listened tensely.

"Message received, Panda. Tracking target now." Sweat dotted his brow as he kicked up his pace, sprinting across a stretch of mud, vaulting a cement wall, all the while scanning the underbrush through the pale green glare of night-vision goggles.

Forty feet ahead of him a figure crouched at the edge of a sheer cliff. Sweating heavily now, the runner plunged down the trail and dropped beside his target. "Get on the radio and bring him out," he ordered. "Do it now."

"No can do." The figure at the cliff shrugged without turning. "The mission has begun. No one goes in or out until completion."

"Yeah? Just watch me." The runner jumped, caught the rope dangling above the pitted rock face, and pulled himself up, hand over hand. By the time he reached the cliff top, his face was streaked with sweat beneath his headset and his arms were burning. He sprinted across a rocky slope where a broad-shouldered man stood motionless in the moonlight, his night-scope binoculars trained on a small runway beyond the trees. The officer in black didn't glance up as the runner moved in beside him.

"Sir." The new arrival saluted smartly.

"I left orders for no interruptions. We have two minutes to secure that perimeter and retrieve our hostage before he's dog meat."

The runner cleared his throat. "Yes, sir. Sorry to intrude, commander."

"You'd damned well better be sorry." The binoculars tilted sharply. "That's real ammo they're firing out there, in case you weren't listening."

Three bursts of yellow-white light rocked the landing strip, followed by a shrill blast of sound. The binoculars froze. "Good placement on those flash-bangs," the officer in black said. "Now blow that hatch or the hostage is gone."

The air filled with smoke and cordite. Automatic weapons hammered from the runway as a black-clad force stormed the main cabin stairs and blew the forward hatches.

In fifteen seconds the team was in, the cabin under their control.

Only when the news was relayed did Ford McKay relax his tense stance and survey his team with pride. "Not bad," he said, aware that it was a sweeping understatement. "Next time we'll do it even faster."

Beside him, the runner cleared his throat. "Sir."

"Fine. Now you can tell me what was so damned important that you had to interrupt my training mission," McKay said curtly.

"We've got a chopper waiting for you down at the beach, sir."

"What for?" McKay rubbed his shoulders. "Not another ambassador nabbed in Afghanistan, I hope."

"No, sir. Operation Blue Panda," the runner explained tensely.

The SEAL commander took a sharp breath. "My wife's not due for another month," he said hoarsely. "Something must be wrong. Let's have the rest of it."

The young soldier tried to keep his voice emotionless but failed. "Sir, I'm afraid . . . there were complications. The delivery wasn't going smoothly."

McKay turned and ran toward the beach,

his face a grim mask.

Dear God, let her live.
McKay hunched forward, his head bowed, blind to the jungle rushing past the chopper's window.

Pull her through this and I swear you can take me anytime you want.

Just don't take Carly. Please . . .
But there was so answer in the night, no break in the rushing darkness below.

When McKay burst through the double doors of the hospital's delivery wing, he found Nigel Brandon pacing in the corridor.

"Where is she?" McKay snapped.

"Inside with Daphne."

"How bad is it?"

The governor-general looked gaunt. "There was a problem with the fetal heartbeat. Abnormal basal rate, they called it." Brandon ran a hand across his forehead. "On top of that, the labor's not progressing."

"Nigel, you're scaring me."

"I'm scared too. Carly looks so tired." Brandon's jaw worked hard. "I can't bear the thought that she might not —"

"We'll bring her through this, and that's

504

final." McKay clamped a hand on Brandon's shoulder. "I need to see her right away."

"Wait." Brandon summoned a wisp of a smile as he tossed McKay an elegant linen handkerchief. "Lose the black camouflage paint. Otherwise you'll *scare* her into hard labor."

McKay told himself he was ready for anything. He kept telling himself that as he pushed through the doors to the delivery room. His face was scrubbed clean and he wore a blue hospital gown along with a confident grin, which wavered when he saw Carly's strained face.

He exchanged a quick look with Daphne, then sat down beside Carly. "Looking good, sunshine," he said huskily.

Carly gripped his hand hard, her body straining beneath another contraction. "I look like h-hell," she said between panting breaths. "Something's wrong."

McKay cradled her cheeks. "Nothing's wrong. All you have to do is breathe, okay? Now let's get to work." He made the short, puffing breaths that they'd learned together in prenatal classes. Fully briefed on what to expect, he spoke calmly and slowly, though his stomach was tied in knots. "First this nurse is going to give you some oxygen. Then the doctor will help you move into a better position." He spoke gently, holding her gaze and letting her feel his unshakable confidence. "After that, we're going to welcome our new family into the world."

Tears ran down Carly's face. He kissed her softly, then moved back as the nurse slid an oxygen mask into place. At that moment, with machinery beeping and humming around them, McKay remembered dozens of high-altitude jumps and missions gone south and knew his toughest assignment was right here. For Carly's sake, he couldn't lose his cool.

He took her hand, squeezed hard, then leaned close, kissing her ashen forehead. "Okay, let's get this show on the road, sunshine. I'll count, you breathe."

In the waiting room, Izzy drained his sixth cup of stomach-scouring coffee and glared at the closed doors of the delivery room. "What's taking so long? This never happens in the movies."

"It's her first delivery, and they don't go fast. Daphne took ten hours." Nigel Brandon rolled his stiff shoulders. "At least McKay's here. Now she can relax, and things should speed up."

Izzy began to pace. "Are you telling me that because you believe it or because you *want* to believe it?"

Brandon paced right beside him. "Don't ask."

The door swung open and Daphne emerged, her hospital gown flapping over the strapless silver evening gown she had been wearing at her first Tradewind Foundation charity event when Carly's contractions began.

"How's she doing?" Izzy and her father spoke in unison.

"Better, thank heavens. You should have seen her face when Ford walked in. She lit up the room. It won't take long now," she predicted confidently.

"But what about the fetal heartbeat?" her father demanded.

"They're taking precautions. Carly's been given oxygen, and the doctor's prepared for a C-section if necessary. He's going to give her ten more minutes, then he'll decide."

Carly's ragged cry of pain echoed from the delivery room. Nigel Brandon sank white-faced into his chair. "Heaven spare me, I can't take this. I'm an old man. Please, no more babies, any of you."

Daphne patted his shoulder. "She's nearly there."

The door opened again. A gowned and masked obstetrics nurse pushing an EKG machine bustled from the delivery room. McKay's low, calm voice drifted through the doors as he counted with Carly, helping her focus her breathing as the contractions came faster.

"That's the way," Brandon said. "You can do it, Carly. Just breathe."

Izzy wiped his forehead and sat down beside Brandon. "I hate feeling helpless like this. When will something happen?"

A muffled wail wafted from beyond the double doors, and another nurse rushed inside.

Daphne looked at the big doors. "What was that?"

"What was what?" her father asked.

"Shhh." Daphne cocked her head. "Listen."

Over the murmur of voices came another quivering wail. Seconds later it was followed by a full-out howl.

"Two of them." Brandon closed his eyes. "One more to go. Sweet God, I'm too weak for this. I just hope McKay is holding up in there."

"He'll do whatever he has to do," Izzy assured him. "Even if his stomach is jelly, he'll look like steel. Carly won't know."

"She needs him to be strong now," Daphne whispered. "Delivering the last baby won't be easy."

An uneasy silence fell, broken only by the low hum of the monitoring equipment and McKay's muted words of encouragement to Carly.

"Did he say something about a secret decoder ring?" Izzy looked confused. "What was *that* all about?"

"I haven't got a clue." Daphne pulled her hospital gown closer, shivering. "This is taking too long, and she was already weak. Maybe they couldn't rotate the last baby. Maybe they'll have to do a C-section after all." Her hands tightened. "Or maybe the third baby —"

Her father took her hand and locked down hard. Izzy clutched her other hand. "No way. *No damned way.* That's not going to happen," Izzy said gruffly.

Beyond the doors came the swift tap of feet and a ripple of laughter. In the silence that followed, the delivery wing echoed with a new squeal — angry, vital, and completely healthy.

Daphne hugged her exhausted father. They both began to cry.

McKay staggered out of the delivery room ten minutes later, looking exhausted and absolutely ecstatic. "I'm a father. I've got girls." He shook his head. "Three beautiful, amazing girls."

"So we heard." Izzy smiled broadly. "How does it feel?"

"Like hell. I'm wasted." McKay sank into the chair beside Daphne. "Carly was incredible. She never wavered, never complained. I didn't know a person could be so brave. I didn't want her to know that I was a wreck." He drew a deep breath. "A father. I'm — a father," he repeated softly.

"Make that a father times three," Izzy corrected proudly.

"I'm not sure I'm cut out for this kind of work. Bullets, sure. Underwater explosives, fine." McKay shook his head. "But babies . . . diapers." He swallowed hard. "Dating. College. One day they'll leave home and get married."

"You'll be just fine, Pop." Izzy gave him a thumbs-up. "You're going to get a truckload of practice." He glanced at Daphne and Nigel. "You'll also have plenty of help from your friends, me included. After all, someone has to teach these little ladies how to set up firewalls and hack into secured facilities," he said. "What else is a godfather for?"

Daphne rolled her eyes. "Why am I suddenly seeing *Charlie's Angels* here?"

"Hey, you never know," Izzy said, his expression thoughtful. Then he patted his pocket and grinned broadly. "Cigars, anyone?"

Epilogue

The wind sang, clean and cool as it crossed the warm sand.

Down the slope, Ford McKay sat back, tanned and relaxed, his two baby daughters staring at him from their blanket. The third gazed up unblinking from the carrier on his chest.

"Okay, troops, listen up." McKay tickled his closest charmer, then nuzzled the two on the blanket. "Today we cover a few ground rules. Good intel comes first, and the best intel is what you gather yourself. Remember, never take secondhand information uncritically, because the techno-geeks reading high-res satellite photos can mess up big time. And frequently do."

Three sets of eyes glinted up at him in adoration, oblivious to the azure sky and the ocean waves licking at the beach.

"Okay, team, next comes unit integrity. You can have the best intel and prep in the world, but without unit integrity you're dead in the water."

512

Sunny — or was it Olivia? — made a cooing noise, and the doting SEAL gave her a loud, sloppy kiss, much to her sisters' delight. "Rule one: the team always stays together. No one is *ever* left behind."

McKay settled back on one elbow, with his spellbound girls secure against his broad chest. "That means the unit eats together, trains together, moves together."

Six keen blue eyes stared at the big, tanned officer. Olivia — or was it Sunny? — wiggled her toes and giggled.

"No back talk in the ranks," McKay said with mock severity, swooping low for a noisy kiss on smooth, scented cheeks. "Only your mother is allowed to countermand the superior officer, although something tells me you three are going to turn strong men into putty in seconds." He moved the umbrella carefully, screening them from the tropical sun. "Okay, now for specific terrain issues. Going to be near quicksand? Always carry a pole. If you feel yourself going down, that's your best escape option."

McKay's lips curved in a rugged grin. "How? I thought you'd never ask. First you toss the pole down and then you lie across it, which keeps you from sinking as long as you don't panic and start struggling. Then work the pole beneath your hips and inch your way back onto solid ground. Got that, team?"

Olivia slid her thumb into her mouth with a happy pop, while her sisters yawned.

McKay gave a low, five-note whistle that brought all three of his girls to giggling attention. "Remember that whistle," he said, suddenly grave. "Someday you may need it. If you ever get into trouble, signal once, and I'll be there. That's a SEAL promise."

On the other side of the slope, Carly stood motionless. Through a haze of emotions, she fought to concentrate and hold her camera level. She focused carefully, framing her husband's tender smile as Sunny and Olivia crawled off the blanket onto his chest. Her next shot caught the squirming triplets as McKay rolled sharply, making his tiny girls scream with delight.

At that instant, Carly clicked off another shot, and her heart seemed to stop midbeat, engulfed by currents of love so rich and full she felt giddy. As she stood unseen, a wave of memories surged inside her.

The pain and exhaustion of labor.

Her delirious joy as she cradled her tiny, red-faced daughters for the first time. After that came other firsts: Olivia's first smile; Cleo's first laugh; Ford changing Sunny's wet diaper, then staring in disbelief as she repeated the process with vigor.

Sweet, so sweet, every memory. Each one as close as yesterday.

Carly's rugged SEAL had been beside her every free moment, besotted with his girls, enchanted with this uncharted adventure they were sharing. With time he had even begun to relish his new teaching role, which put him more often on the training field than in the middle of a firefight.

To her amusement, Carly had discovered that commitment held no more terrors. Her heart was claimed, given once and forever to her three red-cheeked imps and their roguish father. In the process, her bitter-sweet memories of losing her mother and father had finally been laid to rest.

Cradling her camera, Carly studied the scene. On her blanket, Cleo kicked her feet in noisy abandon. Tucked against Ford's chest, Sunny sucked her fingers, and Olivia smiled radiantly.

Carly looked up from her camera, then back at the beach. There were a dozen more shots she yearned to catch while the light was good. She knew all of them would be unforgettable.

But in that moment Carly also knew, with stunning clarity, that across the slope was where she wanted to be, not standing to one side with her camera. There would be other shots, other times, long, happy decades of adventure and discovery to be shared.

Yes, her camera could wait. Now she needed to touch and be touched, to feel her husband's strong hands as he pulled her gently down beside him. It seemed a miracle that she had lost her heart and gained a future, no longer content to be a spectator in the crazy, wonderful parade of life.

Ford's eyes were dark and intent when she settled beside him. He took her camera and set it gently on the blanket. "Working again?"

"Just a few quick shots. Nothing important."

"How do you feel?"

Carly stretched luxuriously. "Like I could eat midtown Manhattan."

"Not that." He kissed her cheek. "Are you . . . sore?"

"Boasting again?" She smiled slowly. "One time wouldn't leave me sore, tough guy."

"It wasn't once. It was three times, but who's counting."

"Certainly not me." Carly settled her head against Ford's shoulder and drew Olivia close against her chest. "As a matter of fact, it was four," she admitted with a silky laugh.

"You're a dangerous woman, Mrs. McKay."

"Where you're concerned, I intend to be nothing less, commander. You can count on lots more of the same." She tilted her head. "I'd say sixty or seventy years' worth, at least."

McKay's fingers linked with hers. "Sounds damned fine to me."

There in the thick, golden sunlight, Carly's world stretched out, perfect and complete. Wounds that she hadn't even felt were healed, old circles closed.

Home.

She took a long breath and let the knowledge slide deep.

Home at last, she thought. Where she was wanted, needed, the way she could never have imagined in all her wild dreams.

Best of all, she knew home would always and ever be as simple and as close as this. Home would be anywhere she stood within the sound of a baby's laugh or the careful reach of her husband's strong arms.

"So, Mrs. McKay. What do you think of married life so far?" Ford murmured.

"Marriage? With you?"

"Yeah. With me."

Carly gave a slow, five-note whistle that had her girls giggling and her husband grinning as he drew her down against his chest for a long, brain-numbing kiss.

Author's Note

Have you been practicing your secret five-note whistle?

Something tells me that Ford will be busy keeping his three headstrong daughters out of trouble for many years to come. On the other hand, with the kind of tactical training he's providing, they might just save *him* from a tight situation one day!

If you enjoyed your visit to Barbados and want to read more, you'll find a nice taste of the island's rich heritage in *Barbados: A World Apart*, by Roger LaBrucherie.

Interested in the SEALs? There are dozens of books on this hot subject, each with a different slant on the elite group of fighters. Try *Inside the US Navy SEALs* by Gary Stubblefield for a basic introduction. For more of an historical overview, look for *SEALs in Action*, by Kevin Dockery, which includes information on BUD/S (Navy training course, Basic Underwater Demolition/SEAL) and the rigors of Hell Week.

In case you find the stories of Brittany intriguing, just as Carly's mother did, look for *Pierre Deux's Brittany*, by Linda Dannenberg, Pierre Levec, and Pierre Moulin. This lavish book will sweep you away to the rugged outpost of northwest France, making you smell the sea wind, glimpse the flash of bright blue fishing boats, and feel the fury of slashing waves on the jagged rocks of Ouessant.

If Izzy seems familiar, he should be! The first time he charmed his way onto the page was in my 1999 book, *The Perfect Gift*, and I have a strong suspicion this is one computer genius who will be back for another visit.

In the meantime, I would love to hear from you. If you'd like a signed bookmark and a copy of my next newsletter with information about past characters, upcoming books, and details about my books set at hauntingly beautiful Draycott Abbey, please send a stamped, self-addressed envelope (the longer-size envelope works best) to me at:

P.O. Box 25145
Scottsdale, Arizona 85255

And don't forget to visit me online at: *www.christinaskye.com*.
The fire is always burning and the tea is always hot. You can sit for a while and enjoy my favorite recipes, as well as contests and

writing tips. You can also drop me an e-mail at:

talktochristina@christinaskye.com.

My next book?

Let's just say you'll find what happens when a tough, cynical man stumbles on a little piece of paradise and discovers that the right woman can bring him to his knees — and then make him whole again.

Stay tuned to my website for more details!

With warmest regards,
Christina Skye